THE ROYAL LACEMAKER

Seventeen years old, Lily Rose scratches out a meagre living making lace, responsible for her siblings following the death of their parents. Hundreds of miles away, in London, Queen Victoria is preparing for her wedding. She will wear the most exquisite dress, bearing the famous Honiton lace. Lily is selected as one of the few to work on this top-secret commission, quickly making an impression, working day and night. But there are those who want to see Lily fall, including Squire Clinsden who issues her with a terrible ultimatum – work for him, and be subject to his unwanted advances, or put loved ones at risk.

I dedicate this book to Pern
for his faith, encouragement and
endless cups of tea

THE ROYAL LACEMAKER

by

Linda Finlay

Magna Large Print Books
Long Preston, North Yorkshire,
BD23 4ND, England.

British Library Cataloguing in Publication Data.

Finlay, Linda
　　The royal lacemaker.

　　A catalogue record of this book is
　　available from the British Library

　　ISBN　978-0-7505-4175-6

First published in Great Britain by Penguin Books 2014

Cover illustration © Gordon Crabb by arrangement with
Alison Eldred

The moral right of the author has been asserted

Published in Large Print 2015 by arrangement with
Penguin Books Ltd.

Magna Large Print is an imprint of Library Magna Books Ltd.

Printed and bound in Great Britain by
T.J. (International) Ltd., Cornwall, PL28 8RW

Chapter 1

Peasants can't be pickers.

Lily could hear her father's voice as if he were in the room beside her, and with it the vision of the lavish breakfast she'd served at the manor house faded. Sighing, she stirred their customary pot of porridge and wondered what it would be like to start the day with chops, black pudding, bacon and sausage. All that meat for one meal seemed astonishing.

The back door clattered open, shattering her reverie and sending a cloud of acrid smoke from the fire billowing around the room. Wiping her smarting eyes, she opened her mouth ready to take her brother to task, but the angry words died on her lips when she saw the worried look on his face.

'Agent Pike's sent word you're to see him straight away,' said Rob, hobbling into the room and collapsing onto the chair beside the fire.

Lily's stomach churned. 'Did he say why?'

'It's about that lace the journeyman collected from you yesterday. You're a skilled worker, Lily, so I'm sure there's nothing wrong, but you'd best not keep him waiting.' Although he spoke gently, she could see by the look in his eyes that he was anxious. At nineteen, her older brother was still very protective of her and she appreciated his concern. Instinctively, she glanced towards the next room. 'Go on, Lily. I'll see to Mother and Beth.'

Nodding gratefully, she jumped up and headed for the door, passing the table where her pillow and bobbins lay ready for the day's work. She had quite enough to do without making the four-mile trek to the next hamlet, Bransbeer, but an order from Agent Pike couldn't be ignored if she wanted to continue getting work. Throwing her shawl around her shoulders, she hurried outside.

Despite it being early May, the morning air was thin, and Lily pulled her cap down further over her ears. Surely there hadn't been anything wrong with the lace? She'd thought it quite her best work yet, and had been careful not to waste any yarn so she knew the finished weight would have been correct. True, she hadn't been paid much but, as her father had always said, peasants couldn't be pickers, and they needed every penny she could bring in.

Since the farming accident two months ago that had killed him instantly and badly injured her brother, her mother had taken to her bed and hardly knew what day it was. Robert, now virtually a cripple, wasn't able to earn a living or do much around the cottage. The responsibility of bread winner had fallen heavily upon Lily's slender shoulders.

She hurried along the rutted track, her thoughts racing as fast as her feet, so that she hardly felt the sharp stones digging their way through the holes in her worn hobnailed boots. The arduous journey up over the cliffs would take her the best part of an hour and that was time she could ill afford to be away from the cottage. If she didn't fulfil the order she'd been given, there were others who would. Already the demand for pillow lace was waning now some of the larger towns had moved on to producing lace by machine.

The uphill climb was steep but finally, as the first rays of the sun were bathing the limestone cliffs a soft pink blush, she reached the crest and paused to catch her breath. Far below, like miniature toys, the fishing boats were returning to harbour laden with their night's catch. Lily spotted her betrothed's red-sailed lugger, with its distinctive white painted spars, already pulled up on the beach, and her heart leaped. With Tom fishing the deep waters off Lyme Bay or gathering winkles on the shore when bad weather prevented him from putting out to sea, and she trying to eke a living from making lace as well as caring for things at the cottage, their time together was precious. Still, the tide should be right for him to be ashore after she'd seen Agent Pike.

Reminded of her mission, she began the long descent eastwards towards the thatched roofs of Bransbeer, where plumes of wood smoke spiralled from the chimneys then drifted up the valley on the gentle morning breeze. Entering the village, she noticed that despite the early hour, people were already going about their business. Some called out in greeting, others eyed her curiously as she sped by, lifting her skirts to dodge the worst of the mud.

On reaching the agent's premises, a large brick and flint building linked by a maze of corridors to a row of cottages and outbuildings, she hurried through to the collection room. As usual, Mr Pike was sitting behind his desk in his long black coat and, as was his wont, he made her wait before looking up and staring at her over his half-moon glasses.

'Ah, Lily Rose, you're here at last.'

'I came as soon as I got word, sir.'

'Mrs Bodney's waiting to see you.'

Her eyes widened in amazement. 'Mrs Bodney wants to see me?'

'Yes, Lily, she does, so stop parroting what I say and tidy yourself up. Come along, follow me.'

Hastily smoothing the creases from her dress and pushing strands of dark hair back under her cap, she hurried along a narrow passage after him. Eager to keep up, she followed so close on his heels that when he stopped suddenly, she went careering into him. He turned to glare at her, then rapped smartly on the door and ushered her inside.

'Miss Lily Rose, ma'am,' he announced to the seemingly empty room.

Puzzled, Lily peered around, taking in the huge table covered with bolts of material in sapphire blue, emerald green and ruby red, spools of matching threads laid out alongside them. She had never seen anything like it and stood studying them in fascination. Suddenly a smartly dressed woman bobbed up from behind the piles of material, making Lily jump, and two dark beady eyes stared directly into hers.

'Is this your work?' the woman asked brusquely, holding up a sprig of lace.

Lily recognized it immediately. 'Yes, Mrs Bodney. Is something wrong with it?' she asked anxiously.

'No, as it happens, it's some of the finest work I've seen.'

Lily let out a sigh of relief, then became aware the other woman was still speaking.

'I've asked you here to offer you six months' work.'

Lily felt her heart flutter like a fledgeling bird. Six months' work! How wonderful. No more worrying where the next job was coming from; she could feed the family, buy things for her betrothal drawer for when she and Tom were married; why, she could...

'Are you listening to me, Lily Rose?' Mrs Bodney's sharp voice snapped her back to the present and she flushed. What a time to be caught woolgathering, she thought.

'Yes, of course, ma'am.'

'My business has won an important order. A most prestigious order, in fact. However, before you can know more, I must ask if you are prepared to take an ability test and I warn you, it's a stringent one.'

Lily nodded and the other woman, as if anticipating her answer, produced a pillow, pattern and bobbins, explained what she had to do and then bustled out of the room.

Gently Lily pricked out the pattern, then wound the bobbins with thread. Fearful of making a mistake, she worked slowly at first but before long she was absorbed in her task and the bobbins became an extension of her fingers as they flew back and forth across the pillow. Methodically she enclosed her pin after each completed row, checking the tension. After a while, though, even her experienced fingers became stiff and sore, but she didn't dare stop. By the time Mrs Bodney returned, the sample she'd requested was finished.

Carefully lifting the sprig from the pillow, Lily handed it to the older lady, who walked over to the window and held it up to the light. Silence hung in the air as Lily watched her inspect the lace. She tried not to fidget but she could hardly contain her impatience. Finally, when Lily thought she could not stand it a moment longer, the woman looked up and smiled.

'Well, Lily, congratulations. You may present yourself at my cottage at daybreak tomorrow. Now take yourself back to Pike and he'll tell you my rates and conditions.'

Delighted, Lily almost floated out of the room. Then, when she found out what she'd be earning, she was all but speechless, and it didn't matter a sprat she'd be working from dawn till dusk. She had been chosen! Picking up her skirts, she raced down the street to the harbour, willing Tom to be there, for if she didn't share her good news soon, she would burst.

As if she'd conjured him up, there he was: broad-shouldered in his blue serge jacket, brown cap perched jauntily on the back of his fair hair, striding up the pebbled beach towards her.

'Tom,' she cried.

'Well, if it isn't the prettiest girl in Devonshire, her eyes shining brighter than the stars in the heavens because she's bumped into her beloved,' he grinned.

'Oh, Tom, stop teasing and listen,' she retorted, tugging at his lapels to gain his attention. 'You'll never believe what's happened. It's the best thing ever, other than you asking me to be your wife, of course. It's for six months and I'll be earning regular pay and it's more than you'd imagine and...'

'Slow down, Lily my love. Let's sit while you tell me about this wonderful news,' he said, helping her up onto the wall adjoining the brook, then pulling himself up beside her. She was so excited she hardly noticed the smell of fish that clung to the rough material of his shirt.

'Oh, Tom, she loved my lace work. Said it was some of the finest she'd seen.'

'Who, my sweet?' he asked, gently pushing back the strands of hair that had again escaped her braid.

'Mrs Bodney.'

'Phew,' he whistled. 'Now that woman takes some pleasing, so I've heard.'

Wriggling along the wall, she added: 'I had to sit this test, but I passed, and she wants me to work on a special commission but, Tom...' her blue eyes clouded as she turned to face him, '...I'm sworn to secrecy as to what it is. I know we shouldn't have secrets when we're to be married but she wouldn't take me on until I'd promised not to tell a soul.'

He shook his finger at her. 'If it involves any dark, handsome strangers then I insist you tell me right now.'

'Of course it doesn't, silly,' she said, laughing. 'I'll have to work long hours at her cottage here in Bransbeer, and I'll only have the Sabbath off, but the wage is more than I'd ever make working from the cottage.'

Tom frowned. 'Lily love, that's nigh on an eight-mile round trip each day. You can't possibly walk that and work six long days at a stretch. Who would look after your family and the cottage? It's you who's kept everything going this past couple of months.'

Lily looked down at her worn boots and groaned. In all the excitement, she'd quite forgotten the responsibility she had for her family. Making lace at home meant she could keep an eye on her mother and young Beth, whilst Rob went about the chores he was able to manage. Everything took him so much longer now that he could only hobble around. They also shared the cooking and, on the rare days her mother felt like eating, she insisted it was Lily who fed her. How would they manage if she was away all day?

'Oh, Tom, what am I to do?' Lily wailed.

'Don't worry, we'll think of something,' he said, patting her hand. Then, he turned towards her and grinned. 'Why, I have the very answer. You can share my room here in the village.'

She glared at him. 'Tom Westlake, you should be ashamed of yourself. This might be 1839 but folk would still make me an outcast. Besides, I'm not a strumpet, as well you know.' She jumped down from the wall and went stomping back up Sea Hill.

'Wait, Lily!' Tom shouted, running after her and catching her by the arm. 'I'm sorry. That was a stupid thing to suggest. It's just I'm that impatient for us to be together.'

Pulling away from him, she continued up the hill. How dare he spoil her happy news with such an outrageous proposal?

Cursing himself for upsetting her, Tom hastily plucked a handful of pink sea thrift from the side of the cliff, and again hurried after her.

'I'm sorry, Lily,' he said. 'Please accept these sea roses by way of apology.'

Ready to give him a piece of her mind, she whirled round to face him but when she saw him meekly holding out the flowers, looking more like a naughty schoolboy than the grown man she'd vowed to marry, her anger evaporated like a summer mist.

'Tom Westlake, I'd thank you to take this seriously,' she admonished.

'Yes, miss,' he said, giving her a mock salute, but her thoughts were racing again as they continued their way up the hill together.

'There's nothing for it, I'll just have to tell Mrs Bodney I can't take the position.'

'Now don't be hasty; Lily. Think it all through before you make a decision,' Tom advised, before stopping and peering at the horizon. 'That's a fair old mackerel sky and we've had the dry: you'd best be getting home. Wind's freshening; there'll be rain before dark.'

'You're right. I've been away since daybreak and Rob will be wondering what's happened to me.'

'Wait,' Tom said, and she watched as he ran down to the beach. He returned moments later holding out a parcel.

'Here, some fish for your tea,' he puffed. 'I'll wager you've not eaten since first thing.'

As if on cue, Lily's stomach rumbled. How well he knew her. Smiling gratefully, she turned and walked back up the cliff path. Gingerly, she picked her way through the furze that edged the track. The fulmars, perching on the cliffs with their young, spat in warning as she passed. She quickened her pace, keeping as far from them as she could, for the oil they projected not only stank but was hard to remove from clothing. When she was safely past their nesting sites she turned to wave, but Tom was already preparing to sail out on the evening tide.

'Godspeed and bring you home safely, my love,' she whispered before continuing on her way.

Chapter 2

Already the sky was darkening with heavy clouds lowering to the west ahead of her, and the tang of salt carried on the wind stung her lips. As waves pounded the shore below, so Lily's thoughts pounded her brain. She really wanted this job and, goodness only knows, they needed the money, but if she worked in Bransbeer, who would look after her family in Coombe? The light was fading completely by the time she reached the straggling hamlet. As she headed past the thatched inn opposite the rickety old forge, her own cottage came into view and, just as Tom had predicted, the heavens opened.

Pulling her shawl tighter against the biting wind and driving rain, she stifled a yawn. It had been a long day and all she wanted to do was go straight to bed, but Rob and Beth would be waiting for their dinner. Since the accident, her elder brother could manage only the lighter tasks like tending the chickens. Of course he did a good job of looking after their four-year-old sister, enabling Lily to concentrate on her lace making, but that did not ease her household burden. With her thoughts a jumble, she let herself inside.

'I'm home,' she called, throwing her wet shawl onto its nail by the door. Going through the tiny scullery to the living room, she saw Robert sitting by the fire, cradling Beth on his knee. That's strange, Lily thought usually her little sister ran to meet her. Then she noticed they were both looking subdued and she heard raised voices coming from the adjoining bedroom. Before she could ask what was going on, a figure appeared in the doorway.

'Lily dear, you're home at last.'

'Aunt Elizabeth,' she gasped in surprise. 'What are you doing here?'

'The children I've been caring for are being sent to school and my services are no longer required. Having time to spare, I decided to pay a visit, and not a moment too soon from what I can see.'

'Is Mother all right?' Lily asked, noticing her aunt's flushed cheeks. 'I'll let her know I'm home,' she said, turning towards the door.

Aunt Elizabeth pursed her thin lips. 'She seems, well, distracted, is the only way I can describe it, so I'd let her be, Lily. When I arrived back from Exeter and heard about the dreadful accident, I was that upset I came straight over on the donkey-cart. Really, your mother should have let me know.'

Lily put her hand to her head, wishing she could wipe away the memory of that terrible time. Nightmares of the heavy roof limbers and cob wall crashing down on her poor father's body as the byre collapsed had haunted her ever since.

'Why, child, you look fair worn out,' Aunt Elizabeth said, patting her arm. 'Sit down and warm yourself by the fire. I'll go and see if there's anything to rustle up for supper.'

'Tom gave me these fish.' Lily handed over the parcel, then sank thankfully down on the floor beside the blaze. Beth came over and snuggled against her. Smiling, Lily put her arms around her and pulled her close.

'All right, little one?' she asked, kissing the top of her silky, fair hair.

'Sing me a song, Lily,' Beth whispered. Although she was exhausted, Lily could tell her little sister was unsettled and so softly she began to croon the lullaby that usually sent her to sleep. Sure enough, it wasn't long before she felt her sister's body growing heavy, her breathing deeper.

Still cradling her in her arms, Lily leaned back against the chair. The crackle of the logs and warmth of the room relaxed her and soon she felt her own eyes growing heavy.

Waking with a start, she peered round the darkened room and saw her kindly aunt sitting watching her.

'Where are Rob and Beth?'

'Beth's in her bed, bless her. She didn't even stir when I took her from you. Robert's checking on the chooks. Poor fellow; that accident has left

16

him weak as a worm, hasn't it?'

Lily nodded. 'It's certainly taken its toll on him. He gets frustrated not being able to do the things he did before.'

'Well, your insides must be gnawing, my dear. Here, I've kept your supper warm. Eat up and then you must tell me what's been going on.'

Gratefully, Lily took the plate of dabs, their appetizing smell reminding her just how long it had been since she'd last eaten. She ate hungrily and then, hands cradling her mug of hot milk, spoke about the terrible accident and the struggle they'd had to keep the cottage going. Unable to help herself, she gave a yawn.

'Poor child, you're drowsy as a dormouse. I'm guessing your mother's been no help?'

'She's been out of her mind, Aunt Elizabeth. The shock of losing my father brought on the nervous prostration and she took to her bed. She's seldom left it since.'

Her aunt pursed her lips as she glanced around the sparsely furnished room. 'Judging from this mess of a muddle, I'm guessing not much cleaning's been done either.'

Following her gaze, Lily's eyes widened in horror as she took in the mud on the stone floor and the string of cobwebs festooning the low beams and fireplace. A thick layer of dust had settled on the dresser, which housed their few bits of crockery, and the old blankets covering their two rickety chairs needed washing. She also saw that the cover over Rob's straw mattress on the other side of the room needed repairing. Only the table in the corner on which she kept her bobbins and thread

17

was free from dust; she wouldn't be able to sell her work if it wasn't spotless. She hung her head in embarrassment. Before the accident, her mother had taken pride in keeping their modest home clean and tidy.

'I've been too busy with my orders for lace to do much around the cottage. Rob does his best but some days his legs pain him so bad he can hardly move. But he's good with Beth and keeps her amused whilst I'm working.'

The other woman put her head on one side, quizzically. 'I'm sure you do your best. Forgive me for asking, Lily, but do you have any other money coming in?'

'We're managing,' Lily retorted, her chin rising defensively. 'Working from home means I can care for the family well enough, but I have to confess that jobbing pay is paltry and orders for pillow lace are dwindling.'

'Rob said you'd been summoned to see Agent Pike?'

'Yes, Mrs Bodney has offered me a position for six months but it will mean working from her cottage in Bransbeer along with the other lace makers. I'd have to be away from here all day, and with the family and cottage needing looking after that's not possible. The money she offered is more than you'd believe, but we will only be paid at the end of each month. So you see, Aunt Elizabeth, with the family to feed, I can't afford to take it anyway,' Lily said, shaking her head.

'Now let's not be impulsive, Lily my dear,' her aunt said quickly. 'Mrs Bodney is a reputable businesswoman as well as an accomplished lace

18

maker, so I'm guessing her order is for someone of renown. Am I right?'

'Yes, it is. But you've been living in Exeter so how do you know about Mrs Bodney?' Lily asked.

'You're forgetting that I too was brought up here in Coombe, where everybody knows everybody. It seems like only yesterday,' her aunt said. 'Your mother and I used to have such fun. She might have been the elder by a couple of years, but the japes she used to get into...'

'Really?' Lily asked, eyes widening at the thought of her staid, thirty-six-year-old mother misbehaving.

'Oh, yes, I was always having to cover up for her. Of course, the tables were turned in the end...' Her aunt's voice petered out and she stared into the flames, seemingly lost in thought.

'It sounds as if you were really close, Aunt Elizabeth, so why did you move away?' Lily asked, her curiosity getting the better of her. Her aunt looked at her sharply. 'Sorry, Aunt Elizabeth, I had no right to pry,' she added gently.

'No, dear, that's all right, and when we have more time I will explain. It was always my wish to have more of a presence in your life. I kept in touch as much as I was able and, as you know, returned for visits when my duties permitted. Your mother was good at keeping me informed about family news so I was right puzzled when her communication ceased. Now, of course, I know it was because of the accident.'

Lily nodded, remembering the excitement Aunt Elizabeth's occasional visits had caused, and letters that came periodically by the stagecoach.

Then her thoughts returned to the present and her own news. Despite her predicament, she felt excitement bubbling up inside.

'Mrs Bodney said the work has to be done to a strict timetable and we need to work sunrise to sunset to have it completed in time.'

As if tuning into her thoughts, her aunt brought the subject back to the present.

'Regular work's not easy to come by around here, is it?' she asked.

'No, and Tom says I won't be able to walk the eight-mile round trip six days a week as well as look after everything at home.'

Her aunt glanced down at Lily's boots sitting beside the hearth with their scuffed toecaps and worn soles.

'Your Tom sounds a caring man, Lily, but how you've walked anywhere in those boots is beyond me. Things have been difficult for you these past months and I'd like to help. Seeing as I'm between situations, I'm free to suit myself, so why don't you let me take care of things here while you work at Mrs Bodney's cottage?'

'You'd do that for us?' Lily stared at her aunt in amazement. 'Why?'

'Because we're family and, as I see it, a family's like that lace you make. A single thread by itself is not very strong but when worked together with others it gathers strength. You won't be able to manage everything by yourself but if we work together...'

Lily's heart almost skipped a beat. 'What can I say? It's such a kind offer and I really don't know how to thank you, Aunt Elizabeth,' she said and then frowned. 'But if I take the job we don't have enough put by to last until I get paid at the end of the month.'

'Well, not having to pay out for my board over the past years means I have eggs nested,' her aunt said. Lily looked puzzled for a moment, then realized what she meant.

'But you can't use those to pay our bills; you hardly know us,' she spluttered. Her aunt looked at her sadly for a moment, then shrugged.

'I can't think of a better way to spend them than on helping my family.' Then, as Lily began to protest, she held up her hand. 'Call it a lend until you get paid.'

'But where would you sleep, Auntie? Mother, Beth and I share the bedroom and, as you can see, Rob has his bed in here.' Lily nodded towards the mattress.

'My, my, Lily Rose. All you see is problems. As it happens, I visited my friend Grace Goode before I came here, and she kindly offered me a bed. If I'm going to stay in Coombe for any length of time, I'll sort out something sounder.'

'Thank you, Aunt Elizabeth,' Lily cried, jumping up and throwing her arms around the other woman. Her aunt returned her embrace then, looking flustered, became brisk again.

'Now, we really have to do something about those boots or your feet will be shredded. I left Doris in the back paddock; you can hitch her to the donkey-cart and ride to Bransbeer tomorrow. That'll start you off on the right foot. Put her in the stable behind the hostelry, and if old Ned's still there, tell him he's to look after her whilst

21

you're at work.'

Lily was hardly able to believe her luck. Only an hour ago her hopeful future had been threatened. Now, thanks to her visitor, her dilemma was solved.

Smiling, her aunt Elizabeth gave her a quick hug. 'Now, my dear, off you go to the land of nod I'll tidy up here and tell Rob what's happening when he comes in.'

Next morning, as the first streaks of grey were lighting the sky, Lily carefully steered the donkey-cart down the lane from Coombe, turning eastwards onto the sunken cliff track with its canopy of wind-bent ancient oaks. Seeing the splashes of mauve dotting the verges, she felt her heart lift. Wild violets were her mother's favourite flowers. She would stop and pick her some on the way home. They'd be sure to cheer her up, she thought, as the donkey-cart began its descent down the cliff path towards Bransbeer.

As she guided the cart into the yard behind the hostelry, old Ned, the stable hand, shuffled over and took the reins.

'Aunt Elizabeth said to leave Doris here for the day while I'm working at Mrs Bodney's,' Lily said, smiling nervously as she climbed down from the cart.

'Ah, come back, has she?' he asked curiously, taking the reins and leading donkey and cart towards the stables.

With excitement bubbling up inside her again, Lily clutched her lace pillow to her chest and made her way down the lane towards Mrs Bodney's cottage, which stood close to Agent Pike's house. Her thoughts raced as fast as her footsteps as she finally allowed herself to think about the job she'd been offered and the secret she'd managed to keep since the previous day. Who would believe that she, Lily Rose, was going to make lace for Queen Victoria's wedding dress?

Chapter 3

Suddenly Lily stopped in her tracks. Supposing her work wasn't good enough? She stood in the lane dithering, her excitement replaced by doubts.

Peasants are plucky people. Remember, you can do anything you set your mind to, our Lily.

Hearing her father's whispered words, her heart leaped and for one magical moment she thought he was standing right beside her. Of course he wasn't, but she remembered he'd always encouraged her to believe in herself and, certain she could feel his presence spurring her on, she continued her journey. An old lady stopped and waved as Lily walked between the terraces of cob and thatch cottages, and she smiled happily back.

On reaching Mrs Bodney's property, she noticed it was larger than its neighbours and set well back from the others. As she carefully skirted the brook to reach it, her stomach began to churn once more. Clutching her pillow tighter and reminding herself this was the chance of a lifetime, she stepped through the gate. Never had she seen a cottage as grand as this before, she thought, marvelling at the red and blue patterned brickwork. Resisting the urge to peer through the leaded windows, she lifted the little brass knocker.

The maid who answered seemed younger than Lily and was impeccably dressed in the customary black cotton dress, but her snowy white cap and apron were edged with lace. As she was shown through to the large, open workroom, Lily looked down at her own brown woollen homespun skirt and coarse linen apron, and felt decidedly drab. With money being tighter than ever these past few months, new material had been the last thing on her mind. When she got paid, she'd visit the draper in Sidmouth. She was pondering the colour she'd buy – and the look on Tom's face as he walked her along the promenade in her new finery – when a voice as sharp as a butcher's blade sliced through her thoughts.

'Don't stand there cluttering the doorway, girl. Since you've decided to grace us with your presence at last, be seated and we can commence the day's work.'

Embarrassed, Lily snapped back to the present to find Mrs Bodney, lips pursed in a tight line, staring at her with those all-seeing conker-bright eyes. Glancing around the room, she deduced she was the last to arrive and hastily sank onto the only vacant stool beside her eight or nine fellow workers. Across the table, a woman of middle years with silver streaking her tawny hair shot her a sympathetic smile, but before she could respond Mrs Bodney's strident voice was addressing the room.

'Ladies, welcome to this, my most important

24

venture yet. I say welcome and you are, provided you heed the following instructions. We are working together in my cottage because this commission is confidential. Before we proceed, I must remind you not to reveal a word to anyone about what is being made here. Do I make myself clear?' She paused and they nodded.

'There will be some people intent on finding out what you are making. They may even offer you a bribe to reveal the secret, and anyone doing so must be reported to me immediately. You all know for whom we are undertaking this work and you can believe me when I tell you that, in months to come, the eyes of the highest gentry in the country will be upon our handicraft. You are the finest lace makers in Devonshire; however, do not flatter yourselves that you are indispensable.' Mrs Bodney stared at each of them in turn. 'If necessary, you can, and will, be replaced.'

There was silence as she studied them again, and Lily held her breath in case she was already found wanting.

'However,' Mrs Bodney continued, 'I expect you to work diligently. In return you will receive the wage already mentioned, which is above the going rate.' She afforded them a rare smile before continuing.

'Usually you receive your wages in credit, which you have to use to purchase goods at exorbitant rates from your employers' huckster shops, do you not?'

The women groaned their agreement, for the trucking system had long been a sore subject with them.

'Well, ladies, good news. As you know, your money for this commission will be paid at the end of each month.' A collective groan sounded around the room but then their employer smiled. 'You will, however, receive it all in cash.'

Lily's heart soared as a cheer went up. Conditions here were better than she could ever have dreamed and her impression of this straight-backed, dignified woman rose ever higher.

'Use the money wisely, ladies, and, better still, maybe put some by for the hard times,' Mrs Bodney continued, looking so serious Lily forced herself to concentrate. 'In return, I expect total loyalty and will have no hesitation in dismissing anyone who breaches my trust. Before I hand out the cotton thread, please ensure your hands are scrupulously clean. If they are even slightly grubby, go outside and wash them at the pump in the yard.'

The ladies glanced at each other but their employer was continuing with her speech.

'Our Queen has decided to break with tradition and wear a white satin wedding gown, which is being made at Spitalfields as we speak. Our job is to produce the lace for the flounce, veil and collar along with other embellishments. As the flounce alone is to measure 25½ inches deep by 4 yards in circumference, you can see the challenge that our time restraint poses. All the lace must be ready to be sewn up by the beginning of November.'

'Surely we won't be able to manage all that work in six months,' exclaimed the tawny-haired woman.

Mrs Bodney smiled. 'You leave the details to me, Mary. Now, ladies, are you ready to begin making the finest lace ever?'

As a wave of agreement rippled around the room, Mrs Bodney's eyes twinkled, her features softening for a second before she resumed her strict composure. Well, I'll be, thought Lily, her lips twitching. The old girl's got a heart after all. She spoke too soon.

'Would you care to share your secret joke, Lily?' Mrs Bodney asked, giving her such a penetrating stare Lily was sure the other woman could see into her heart.

'Oh, no, Mrs Bodney, I don't have any secret to share,' she stammered, feeling her cheeks grow hot.

'Good. The only secret I want here is that which is made in this room. Now let us begin our day's work.'

As Lily began pricking out the pattern, she risked a glance around the room. The other ladies, all working industriously at their pillows, seemed older than she. Quickly she looked down at her own lace, determined to be as conscientious as they.

The morning passed swiftly as they all followed Mrs Bodney's instructions. She was a stickler for perfection. Just as Lily felt she had mastered the pattern, their employer picked up a little brass bell and shook it vigorously.

'Ladies, time for you to take a break. Due to the delicate nature of our work no refreshments are permitted in this room. However, you may partake of your nuncheon in the back yard. The fresh air will invigorate you, ready for a productive afternoon's work.'

Eagerly, the women picked up their noon pieces and filed outside. Lily perched on the low stone wall enclosing the little yard, enjoying the warmth of the midday sun as it eased the stiffness from her shoulders. Being hunched over her pillow for hours on end was agony on the back. Looking around, she took in the pump with its stone trough and the privy in the corner. Biting into the bread her aunt had baked the previous afternoon, she thought how good it was to have someone else looking after her family at the cottage. The other women were chattering like magpies as they compared their morning's progress and Lily smiled, happy to be amongst them. Then, Mrs Bodney appeared, ringing her little brass bell and reminding them to wash their hands before starting work again.

'It's like being back in Sunday school,' whispered Mary, the woman with the silver streaks in her tawny hair, as they rinsed their hands at the pump.

'Lord help us if she expects us to say grace,' copper-haired Nell shrieked, quickly turning it into a cough when Mrs Bodney glanced their way.

'Where is your cap, Nell? Please see that you are properly attired before you return to the workroom,' their employer instructed as they filed past her.

'Can't stand wearing the blooming thing,' Nell muttered to her friend Cora, but Lily noticed the girl quickly did as she'd been told.

Under her employer's watchful eye, work resumed and the room was heavy with concentration as they carefully followed the new pattern. Finally, the sun began to sink behind the cottage and just when Lily thought she couldn't concentrate a moment longer, there was a knock on the door. The maid stood there bearing a silver tray and Mrs Bodney snatched up the calling card.

'Right, ladies,' she said, turning back to them. 'As this is your first day, you may leave early. From tomorrow, expect to be working on for another hour at least. Now I'll bid you all a very good evening and expect to see you at sunrise. Please cover your work with the sheeting on the shelves behind you and leave by the back gate. Tilda will bolt the door behind you.' Skirts rustling, she swept out of the room.

Quickly, the lace makers placed their bobbins tidily on their pillows, then duly covered their work. Relieved to be finished for the day, they clattered through the back gate, chattering away like excited children so that they didn't notice the carriage that had pulled up alongside the cottage.

'Goodbye,' called Lily to the others.

'Aren't you staying to chat?' Cora asked, looking surprised.

'Not tonight, Cora. I've someone to see,' she said, smiling.

'Well, get you, Lily Rose,' Cora sniffed, green eyes glittering. Lily shivered, wondering why the woman had taken umbrage.

Glad to be out in the fresh air, and knowing the tide meant Tom would be ashore, Lily hurried down to the harbour. Her heart flipped as she spotted his boat pulled up on the beach, only to sink when she could find no sign of him. She'd been longing to tell him about her first day in her new job.

Disappointed, she trudged back up Sea Hill and made her way to the stables. But a group of haulers and handlers were congregated outside the alehouse opposite, shouting and swearing. These men, who helped unload the fish and drag the boats up the steep shingle beach, were renowned for sinking copious amounts of beer. Remembering her father's warning about men's unpredictability when under the influence of intoxicating liquor, she made to give them a wide berth. As she hurried on her way a hand suddenly grabbed her arm and she cried out in fright.

Chapter 4

'Well, if it isn't my own sweet Lily.'

'Tom Westlake, you fair made me jump,' Lily cried. 'Whatever are you doing here?' She stared apprehensively at the rowdy group.

'I was hoping to see you, of course. Why don't I buy you a drink and you can tell me about your day?' Ignoring the whistles and catcalls, he took her arm and led her towards the more salubrious surroundings of the hostelry.

Settling her at a bench overlooking the bay, he asked, 'What do you fancy, my lovely?'

'Barley water would be good. I'm dry as dust,' she said, pulling her shawl tighter round her against the freshening breeze. Gazing out over the harbour, she saw the sun was dipping its orangey-red fingers into the sea and decided not to dally too long. She didn't wish to impose upon her aunt any more than she had to.

'Here you are then,' said Tom, returning with two jugs and settling himself beside her. 'Have I told you I can't wait till we're wed, Lily my love?'

'Oh, you might have mentioned it,' she said, glancing down at the third finger of her left hand, imagining a gold band gleaming there one day. Tom, following her gaze, frowned.

'We must see about getting you a betrothal ring, Lily. I'd love to buy you one with a stone the colour of flames, to match that fiery nature of yours, but I'm afraid you'll have to wait until my boat comes in, as they say.'

Knowing he didn't have money to spend on fripperies, she patted his hand. 'I'll be content to wear your wedding band, Tom Westlake. Now, aren't you going to ask me about my day?' she asked, grinning at him.

'Well, let me see,' he said, studying her face. 'You're looking mighty happy so I'm thinking it must be because you've met up with me.'

'Of course,' she said, laughing, 'and it has nothing to do with the fact I started working for Mrs Bodney today.'

'I was wondering about that,' Tom said, furrowing his brow.

'That's the strange thing, Tom. When I arrived home yesterday, Aunt Elizabeth was there. It seems the children she's been looking after are going away to school and her services are no longer needed. She decided to pay us a visit, and has offered to stay on and help. Isn't that amazing?' she told him, her eyes shining.

'That explains it then,' Tom said, smiling. 'Anyway, seeing as you're bursting with excitement you can tell me more about your day.'

'Mrs Bodney told us everything we'll be making over the next few months and the lace makers seem friendly. It's nice to have the company of others, but best of all, Tom, we'll be getting all of our wages in cash.'

He raised an eyebrow. 'My, that will make a big difference, won't it, Lily? You won't have to worry about paying the bills.'

'Yes, but we will only receive it at the end of each month,' she explained.

'Monthly?' He was frowning again. 'How will you manage till then?'

'Aunt Elizabeth said she has savings put by and is happy to help us until I get paid.'

'It's all a bit strange maybe, isn't it?' he asked.

'What do you mean?'

'Well, from what you've told me, you don't really know her.'

'Tom, you're such a worrier,' Lily said, punching him lightly on the arm.

'That's as maybe, but it's only because I care about you, Lily,' he protested.

'It's kind of you to be concerned, Tom, but she is my mother's sister and wants to help. She's even lent me her donkey-cart until I can get my boots mended.'

'Get you, our Lily. Riding into town like a lady, eh? You'll be considering yourself too high and mighty to walk out with the likes of a mere fisherman soon,' he said, grinning.

'Oh, don't be daft. Anyway, it's only a donkey-cart. But I'd best be on my way. I mustn't take advantage of my aunt's kindness.' Draining her jug, she rose reluctantly to her feet.

'Allow me to walk you to your carriage, my lady,' Tom said, jumping up, affecting a bow and then holding out his arm.

'Why, thank you, my good man,' she giggled. Linking her arm through his they made their way through the cobbled yard to the stable.

'Up you go then, my lovely,' he said, helping her into the cart. 'Keep safe and, God willing, I'll see you at the same time tomorrow.'

'Oh, I'll be an hour later, Tom,' she said, frowning down at him. 'Mrs Bodney let us off early as it was our first day.'

'Doesn't sound like Mrs Bodney to me; that one's business through and through, so I've heard. More like she had something or someone to see to, I'll be thinking,' he added, patting the donkey's withers.

Raising her eyebrows, Lily turned the cart for home. She was so busy reflecting on her first day at work that she passed by the clumps of violets without noticing them.

The days passed and Lily settled into her new job with enthusiasm.

Then to her surprise, on arriving back at the cottage a week after she'd started in Bransbeer, her mother was dressed and sitting by the fire. Rushing over, Lily bent to give her a kiss, but her joy quickly turned to concern when she saw the tears rolling down her cheeks.

'Mother, whatever's wrong?' she asked, putting her arms around the woman's shoulders. But her mother just stared at her with vacant eyes and Lily felt a shiver prickle her spine. It was almost as if she didn't recognize her, she thought.

Just then, Aunt Elizabeth came into the room with Beth.

'I've been to play with Harriet,' the little girl said, running over to Lily and throwing her arms around her legs.

'That's nice, and what did you play?' Lily asked, smiling down at her. Then, she looked back at her mother, her brow creasing again.

'You go outside and wash your hands, Beth,' their aunt said, intercepting the look. 'You can tell Lily about your day over supper.' As Beth hurried out to the pump, Aunt Elizabeth turned to Lily.

'Your mother had a visit from Squire Clinsden earlier and I'm afraid what he had to say saddened her something sorry. She's been sitting like that since he left an hour ago,' she said, shaking her head.

'What did he say that upset her so much, Auntie?' Lily asked.

'He was here to serve us an eviction notice,' growled Robert, hobbling into the room with an armful of logs. Angrily he threw them down by the fire.

'What?' Lily gasped. 'That can't be right. We're not behind with the rent; I made sure it was paid on the last quarter-day.'

'Yes, but the cottage went with your father's work as a labourer. Knowing the state of your mother's health, the squire's been kind enough to let you stay on these past few weeks. Now he's had to take on someone new to work the farm.

Goes by the name of Stanton, apparently. Any-how, his lordship visited today. He could have just sent his land agent but had the decency to come himself,' her aunt said.

'But he can't just evict us, surely?' Lily asked, her eyes wide with shock.

Her aunt looked at her and sighed. 'I'm afraid he can, Lily dear. As I said, this is a coupled cottage and Stanton's moving in on the next quarter-day. However, the squire has generously said you can stay till then.'

'But that's no time at all. It's May already. Where does he expect us to go?' Lily asked, her voice rising in panic. Beth, who'd crept back into the room unnoticed, gave a whimper and Aunt Elizabeth scooped her up into her arms.

'Now calm yourself, Lily. You're frightening Beth. I suggest we have our broth. Things always look better when you've a full stomach.'

Lily nodded absent-mindedly as she went over to her mother, who hadn't yet stirred.

'Don't worry, Mother, we'll sort it out,' she promised, patting the woman's thin shoulders. But her mother didn't answer. She just sat there staring blankly ahead of her.

Her aunt, meanwhile, was filling mugs with broth from the pot over the fire. Despite the savoury aroma, they had little appetite and it was only Beth who ate. Gloomily they sat there, lost in thought as they pondered the future. A sudden tug at her skirt brought Lily back to the present.

'Will you tell me a story, Lily?' Beth asked, clambering onto her lap. Forcing a smile, Lily nodded and put down her mug.

'Rob, you clear away and I'll see to your mother,' Aunt Elizabeth said. 'I'll give her some valerian root to calm her, then settle her in bed.'

Lily looked over at her mother and, seeing she was still in a trancelike state, her heart sank. Will she ever recover from Father's death? she wondered. And how will she cope with having to leave the home she's lived in since she was married?

'Come along, Sarah,' Aunt Elizabeth said, gently leading her sister from the room.

Later, with her mother and Beth asleep, Lily crouched on the floor beside the fire while her aunt and Robert settled themselves in the chairs.

'So I guess we'd better talk about where we're going to live,' she said, wondering how her aunt could seem so calm about it.

'The squire said he was disappointed you weren't here when he called as he was worried about your wellbeing.'

Lily snorted and her aunt frowned. 'I told him you were working for Mrs Bodney. He's a nice, caring man to take such an interest in you, Lily.'

'So interested, he still intends making us homeless,' she retorted.

'Well, he did have a solution.' Rob leaned forward in his seat. 'He said to tell you there's a job for you up at the manor house.'

'Go into service for him? Never,' she spat.

'But, Lily, I don't understand. Squire Clinsden owns the whole of the Coombe and Dean Valleys and he's offering you a respectable position,' said her aunt, looking bewildered.

'Respectable?' Lily retorted, her voice rising.

'Yes, respectable, Lily. You'd get a roof over your

head up in that fine house, as well as a living wage. Why, he even offered to help you move. And he said there's a gamekeeper's hut in the grounds that could house your mother, Robert and Beth. Now, it seems to me that would solve all of your problems.'

'But it wouldn't,' Lily said, shaking her head.

'Why wouldn't it?' Aunt Elizabeth asked, looking at her sharply.

Lily felt her insides wrench. If only she could tell her aunt the truth.

'I like working for Mrs Bodney,' she muttered, looking at Robert for support. However, the desperate appeal in his eyes made her heart sink. Obviously, he wanted her to take the job, but there was no way she could or would work for the squire.

'I can't pretend to understand you, Lily. You've been handed the answer to your problems so why won't you take it?'

Not trusting herself to answer, Lily, looked at the ground.

'Well, perhaps you'd prefer to discuss it by yourselves. I'll take myself back down to Grace's,' said their aunt, getting to her feet. 'Grace and I have had such a good time reminiscing, she offered me a bed for as long as I want. While she's busy with young Harriet and her lace making during the day, she gets lonely in the evenings now her husband's gone. As her cottage is only a couple of minutes away it's the obvious solution. I can continue to come up here first thing and be away when you get home. Now, I'll bid you good night, but think hard, Lily. Make the right decision, you get a job and the family get somewhere to live.'

Lily watched her aunt go and then turned to Rob.

'I have my reasons for not wanting to work for the squire, you do realize that, don't you?' she asked.

He shook his head. 'All I know is that we've been served our eviction notice and the squire's offered us a roof over our heads. The solution seems simple to me. But, of course, if this lace making job is more important to you than your family, then there's nothing more to be said,' he growled, getting up and hobbling from the room.

All night Lily tossed and turned, unwelcome dreams invading her sleep as lusting hazel eyes burned through her clothes and pudgy fingers slithered like slugs over the contours of her body. *I want you and I shall have you,* his voice echoed over and over, taunting her; haunting her.

Chapter 5

When Lily woke, she was trembling and drenched in perspiration. Clambering wearily out of bed, she dressed quietly, so as not to wake her mother and sister and then tiptoed out to the yard.

Quickly she splashed her face with water from the pail, hoping it would cool her fevered thoughts as well as her skin. Hurrying past the linney to the barn, she grabbed a handful of straw to quieten Doris whilst she hitched up the cart. Then, anxious to be away before anyone woke, she snatched up the reins and urged the reluctant donkey out into the cool air and onto the rutted track.

Although her conscience was troubling her, she needed to think things through before facing Aunt Elizabeth and Robert. She knew they expected her to put family duty before her own wishes. But then, like most of the county, they believed Squire Clinsden to be an honourable man. And he could be charming when he got his own way, which he usually did as few people dared to cross him for fear of losing their livelihoods and the homes that went with them.

Preoccupied with her thoughts, she'd just reached the narrowest part of the track, when a chestnut stallion came galloping straight towards her. Tugging on the leather straps to avoid a collision, she glared at the rider as he thundered by. But just as she opened her mouth to shout after him, he reined in his horse and trotted back towards her. As soon as she saw those hazel eyes glinting, her stomach dipped to her toes and the words died on her lips. It was as if her dream had conjured him up.

'Well, what a surprise. If it isn't young Lily,' the squire said, tipping his hand to his hat in salute, while his mocking smile sent shivers of revulsion sliding down her spine.

'Squire Clinsden,' she acknowledged, gathering up the reins ready to urge the donkey on.

'How opportune, Lily. I take it your mother has told you of my generous offer?' he asked pleasantly, but she saw the hard set of his jaw and wasn't fooled for one moment.

'My mother's in no fit state to deal with any-thing, let alone the shock of learning she's to lose her home,' Lily retorted. 'Now, if you'll excuse me, I'll be late for work if I don't hurry.'

'Ah, yes. That'll be for Mrs Bodney,' he stated. She stared at him in surprise. Then, remem-bering her aunt had told him about her job, she realized this was no accidental meeting at all.

To her dismay, he dismounted and moved closer until she could feel the heat emanating from his body. He smelled of sweat and stale liquor, and she shivered as he put one hand on the cart, preventing her from moving on.

'Of course, your work there is only temporary whereas the position I'm offering could be per-manent,' he said, raising a wiry eyebrow suggest-ively. As his eyes dropped to her chest, her throat tightened like a wound bobbin. Hastily, she re-adjusted her shawl, which had slipped from her shoulders when she'd yanked the reins. 'I've been impressed by the conscientious way you've cared for your family since the sad demise of your father.'

'Sad demise?' She heard her voice rising and took a deep breath. 'Father never stood a chance. That building was on your land and had needed seeing to for years. He told your agent every time he called for the rent. It was an accident waiting to happen, everyone knows that.'

Ignoring her remark, the squire continued, 'You're a dutiful young woman, so I'm sure you'll wish to ensure your family continue to have a roof over their heads. As I explained to them, the accommodation I'm offering is much better than the cottage they have at present.' He paused, smirking at her with the air of a lion playing with its prey. But she was no mouse and had no intention of rising to his bait.

Forcing a smile, she said, 'The wellbeing of my family is my main concern, sir, you can be sure of that. Now, if you'll excuse me, I really must be on my way. Mrs Bodney will be waiting.' Ignoring the podgy hand resting on the cart, she urged the donkey onwards. The squire's caustic laugh followed her, but she didn't look back.

'Be sure we'll meet again soon, young Lily, for there's nothing I love better than breaking in a spirited filly. Remember I always get what I want, one way or another,' he shouted after her.

Dear God, he was loathsome. How she'd like people to know his true worth. But he was deemed a pillar of the community, always seeming to be helping people when really he was furthering his own needs. Of course, people spoke well of him – they couldn't afford not to when he was the largest employer for miles around. She shuddered, remembering his improper behaviour at the manor. Just the thought of his lecherous leers and furtive fumbling made her feel sick. She cringed, knowing that the finger of suspicion would be pointed in her direction if she spoke up, for people would say there was no spark without fire.

'Lily, wait for me.'

Roused from her reverie, she looked up to see Mary hurrying towards her. Lost in her thoughts, Lily hadn't realized she'd already arrived in Bransbeer.

'You're late this morning,' the other woman

gasped, stooping to catch her breath.

'I know, Mary. I started out in good time but Squire Clinsden waylaid me.'

'Oh, he's such a charming man and kind with it. Only the other day he gave my Jimmy a penny for returning his horse,' the older woman gushed.

A whole penny for returning his thoroughbred; how generous, Lily thought. And as she looked at the woman's beaming face, she knew she'd have great difficulty persuading people the squire was anything but a gentleman.

The morning passed in a blur. Luckily, Lily had mastered the pattern, for her thoughts were whirling as fast as her bobbins as she desperately tried to think of a solution to her domestic problem. She could never work for the squire. Yet, the family were relying on her and if she didn't agree to go into service at the manor, they would be left without a roof over their heads. More than ever, she wished she'd confided in Tom but she hadn't dare risk him confronting the squire; for they'd have been out of their cottage as fast as a fox snatching a chicken. Yet wasn't that the situation they found themselves in now?

'Well, Lily, you appear to be making good progress this morning, despite being in a trancelike state these past few hours.'

Looking up guiltily, she found her employer's all-seeing eyes staring shrewdly at her.

'Thank you, ma'am. I admit this pattern does take some concentrating on,' Lily said, but the woman had already moved on.

'No, no, that will not do at all, Abigail,' Mrs Bodney berated, making the girl jump so that her slender fingers caught one of the pins.

Lily watched in horror as berry-red blood dripped onto the virginal white of the lace. Silence hung heavy in the air as the lace makers all waited to see what would happen. Mrs Bodney, her face as stiff as a starched napkin, ushered the sobbing Abigail from the room and the remaining women glanced at each other in dismay. Then, anxious not to be the next person to incur their employer's wrath, they bent their heads over their pillows in fierce concentration. They didn't even dare to look up when, a short while later, Mrs Bodney reappeared with a woman they'd never seen before and began showing her the pattern to be pricked out.

'Heavens, that was quick,' Nell whispered to Cora as she quickly straightened her cap. But for once even the quick-tongued Cora didn't reply.

Lily shivered. Obviously, Mrs Bodney didn't take any prisoners and, true to her word, had replacements ready and waiting if any of them were found wanting. Not wishing to risk her job, Lily made a determined effort to push her domestic problems to the back of her mind, and bent her head over her pillow.

Their nuncheon break was a subdued affair with none of them feeling inclined to talk. The realization that one mistake could see them instantly out of work had sobered their mood. Lily leaned back against the stone wall, wishing the sun would appear and warm her numbed body. The workroom as well as the atmosphere had been decidedly chilly. She was also hungry, for in her haste to leave the cottage, not only had she skipped breaking her fast, she'd forgotten to bring her noon piece.

She wondered how things were at the cottage and if her mother was feeling any better today. No doubt Aunt Elizabeth and Rob would be discussing the squire's proposition.

'Where's your nuncheon, Lily?' Mary asked, breaking into her thoughts.

'I was in such a hurry this morning, I forgot to bring it,' she answered, shrugging as if it wasn't really important.

Mary broke her bread in half. 'Here, have this. I've plenty,' she said, handing a piece to Lily.

'Oh, I couldn't, Mary' she protested, for the other woman was a bag of bones and looked as if she needed all the nourishment she could get.

'Go on, Lily, it's been a bad morning already without you starving yourself,' Mary insisted and, smiling her thanks, Lily took the proffered bread and bit into it hungrily.

The solemn atmosphere continued throughout the afternoon and, although Lily concentrated on the lace growing on her pillow, time dragged like the legs on a lame horse. She wondered how Beth and Rob were. It was surprising how much she missed them, but a relief to know her mother was being looked after as well, for, if Lily were honest, she had to admit she'd been finding it difficult to cope with her.

Finally, when the shadows had grown long and they were all bleary-eyed from staring at the white thread, Mrs Bodney rang her bell to signal the end of work. Relieved to have made it through the day without making any mistakes,

Lily quickly covered her work, called goodbye to the others and hurried outside.

Her head was throbbing and her eyes burned from the continual concentration. Although it was a short walk up to the stables, she was bone weary and couldn't wait to climb into the cart and let Doris take her home. But to her horror, the door was hanging open and the stall was empty. Frantically, she stared round the yard but there was no sign of Doris at all. Nor was Ned there to help her.

Fighting back tears of frustration, and feeling sad she'd have no time to meet Tom now, she put her head down against the rising wind, and began the long trek up the cliff towards Coombe. As her feet trudged the path, her boots throwing up red mud in her wake, her thoughts were in turmoil. She was certain she'd tethered Doris securely so how could she have got free? Could someone have taken her?

Gaining the brow of the hill, she paused to catch her breath. Surely she could hear the sound of hoofs? Squinting into the distance, she could just make out the outline of a donkey with someone seated on its back, coming towards her. She watched as they drew steadily closer. Then the rider waved and her heart flipped. It was Tom.

Tiredness forgotten, she tore down the hill towards him. As she reached him, he sprang from the animal's back, landing so close she could smell the salt on his skin. Then a soft, velvety muzzle nuzzled its way between them and they burst out laughing.

'Where did you find her?' she asked, stroking

the donkey's ear.

'I happened by on my way back to Bransbeer to meet you, and there she was cropping the grass,' Tom replied. 'Thinking you must have come home early, I knocked on the door. Your aunt was in a right old lather when she realized you weren't there so I offered to come and find you. What's going on, Lily? What's happened?' His blue eyes, serious for once, studied her intently.

'I went to collect Doris after work, but the stall was empty. It gave me a real fright, I can tell you.'

'Didn't you ask Ned where she was?' he asked, looking concerned.

'He wasn't around so I had no choice but, to walk back.'

'You look exhausted, poor thing. It seems right strange that old Doris here would set out to walk all the way back by herself. Your aunt reckoned she's a lazy beast and never goes any further than she has to.' Tom scratched his head, trying to fathom it out.

'I can't think what happened,' Lily said, but then she remembered the squire's words and a germ of suspicion flickered. 'Anyway, what were you doing passing by the cottage?' she asked, eager to change the subject. 'And why are your hands caked in soil?' To her surprise, his cheeks flushed and he didn't meet her gaze.

'Oh, I had something that needed seeing to,' he said, winking. 'Anyhow, you'd best be getting home. Your aunt was that worried she was flapping around like a broody hen. I'll wait outside Mrs Bodney's tomorrow and we'll take a walk. It'll do you good to get some fresh air after being cooped

46

up indoors all day.' Then tipping his hand to his forehead in salute, he continued along the path to Bransbeer.

Watching him go, Lily couldn't help thinking that if they could be wed, many of her problems would be solved. But etiquette decreed she must wait six months since her father's passing. Thank goodness she didn't have to walk the rest of the way home, she thought, wearily climbing onto the donkey's back.

Back at the cottage, she found her aunt hovering anxiously on the step.

'There you are, my dear. I was that worried when Doris came back without you. You'll have to make sure she's securely tethered in future. I suppose old Ned was too busy supping down at the alehouse to notice she'd gone.'

'Yes, Aunt Elizabeth,' Lily replied, deciding to keep her suspicions to herself for the time being. 'How's Mother?'

Her aunt clucked her tongue and shook her head. 'She's gone into decline. The shock of losing her home, on top of everything else, is plaguing her something dreadful.'

'I'll go straight in and see her,' Lily said, shrugging off her shawl.

'No, don't disturb her. I've given her some more valerian root to make her sleep. Beth's woolly to the world too. Now sit yourself down and tell me what you've decided to do about the squire's proposition?'

Lily smiled wryly. If only her aunt knew how close to the truth her words were.

'I've thought of little else. In fact I'm surprised

I've been able to work at all.'

'Well, that's probably your conscience pricking you. Poor Robert's been fretting all day. He feels bad he can't take over here as your dear father intended, God rest his soul. Of course, if your brother Timmy had lived, then things might have been different,' her aunt said with a sigh.

Lily thought of the little brother she'd loved and then of the twins who'd been born sleeping two years later. And now her father was buried in the churchyard alongside... Realizing her aunt was still speaking, she forced herself back to the present.

'Still, I told Robert you'd have the right answer for the squire when he returns in a couple of days, what with you being such a sensible lass,' her aunt said, patting her hand.

'Look, Aunt Elizabeth, you might as well know that I have no intention of going into service for the squire,' Lily said.

'I know you like working for Mrs Bodney, but your family need a home and working for the squire would provide the perfect solution.'

'I said no, Aunt Elizabeth, and I meant it,' Lily shouted.

'There's no need to get uppity, Lily. Sometimes we have to think of others in this life. Out of the goodness of his heart, the squire is offering you a respectable position.'

'Respectable?' Lily shrieked, shaking, her head so violently, her aunt looked momentarily shocked, but then reached out and patted her arm gently.

'Well, if you're that insistent, where do you propose living?'

Lily looked down at the ground, for the truth was, although she'd thought until her head hurt, she hadn't been able to find a solution.

'There's the old cottage Pa Perkins had before he died. Perhaps the squire would let you rent that,' her aunt suggested.

'I hardly think so,' Lily spluttered, hating the thought of even asking.

'Well, you'll have to think of something soon, my girl. Sometimes we have to put up with things not being exactly as we want them to be in this life. Surely working for the squire is preferable to being out on the streets?'

'Never! You do know he preys on innocent girls up at that fine manor of his? Why, he–'

'Tut, tut!' Aunt Elizabeth cut in. 'And he's tried it on with you, I suppose? You should be careful what you insinuate, Lily. There are smuts where there's smoke, and smuts stick, believe you me.'

'And you'd know about such things, I suppose,' Lily said, narrowing her eyes. For a moment she thought she'd gone too far.

Then: 'Just be careful, that's all I say,' her aunt muttered, looking away quickly. In the heavy silence that followed, Lily felt as if the walls were closing in on her. Unable to bear the tense atmosphere any longer, she fled back outside.

A stiff breeze was blowing in from the sea, and she shivered, wishing she'd grabbed her shawl. Hearing the sound of waves pounding the base of the cliffs made her think of Tom. How she wished she could talk things over with him. Still, it was obvious her aunt didn't believe her so why would he?

Doris ambled over and nuzzled her pocket.

With a sob, Lily buried her head in the animal's fur. What was she to do? Despite what her aunt thought, she knew that if she agreed to work for the squire, he'd take it as a signal she was willing to accept his advances. If she didn't they'd have nowhere to live and it would be her fault.

Chapter 6

Although it was barely light when the lace makers filed into the workroom next morning, Mrs Bodney was pacing the room, impatient to address them. Seeing the stern expression on her face, their friendly chatter turned to silence. Lily hurriedly took her seat, determined to push her domestic worries to the back of her mind.

'Ladies, I want you to listen carefully to what I have to say,' their employer said, pausing to make sure she had their attention. 'Whilst you've been learning the pattern and making a start on the sprigs for the flounce, I've let you work at your own pace. Yesterday evening, I inspected your work and whilst the quality is acceptable, the quantity is not. In order to meet the deadline, it is imperative your output increases substantially.' Again she paused, her bright eyes surveying the room to make sure they were paying attention. Lily bit her lip, wondering if they were going to have any money deducted from their wages.

'You've all mastered the design now, haven't you?' Mrs Bodney asked. Anxious to please their employer, they nodded. 'Good. Then I'm sure your speed will pick up and this won't pose any problem. Now I'll leave you to get on.'

On that note, she swept from the room, leaving the lace makers feeling stunned. Lily and Mary exchanged worried looks. The intricate pattern took great concentration and hurrying would only increase the chances of making mistakes. As if she didn't have enough on her pillow, Lily thought.

'Slave driver,' Cora muttered.

Well, even if I agree, I'm not saying anything. I need the money to feed my kiddies till my old man sees fit to find a job,' Anna said.

'I've still a good mind to tell her what she can do with her job,' Cora snorted, narrowing her green eyes.

'Hush, Cora, Mrs Bodney might hear you,' Lily whispered, bending her head over her work.

'*Hush, Cora, Mrs Bodney might hear you,*' Cora repeated, imitating Lily's voice. 'You're such a Goody Two-Shoes it makes me sick,' she spat.

Lily stared at her, wondering why she seemed to have taken exception to her, but before she could respond, Mary hissed, 'For heaven's sake get some lace made before we all find ourselves out on the street.'

Obediently, they picked up their bobbins and the room fell silent. As she worked, Lily couldn't help thinking back to the conversation she'd had with her aunt the night before. She was hurt the other woman didn't take her seriously about the squire and resolved to have it out with her as soon as she got home. If there was one thing she wasn't, it was a liar. It wasn't like her aunt to act

51

like that so perhaps, she was in awe of the squire's social position. So intent was she on sorting things out in her own mind, she almost put a pin up in the wrong place. Cursing under her breath, she pushed the thoughts of her aunt to the back of her mind and focused on her work.

All morning, she willed her fingers to move quicker, concentrating so hard her head began to throb, for although she'd memorized the pattern, she knew it would take longer to rectify any mistakes than it did to make them. As she worked, though, she couldn't help dreaming of Tom and the lace she'd be making for her own wedding dress.

Lost in thought, Lily jumped when Mrs Bodney reappeared and rang the bell for their noon break. Mindful of the woman's earlier words and determined to increase her output, she didn't look up from her work. As usual, though, the other woman's keen eyes missed nothing.

'Come along, Lily Rose, stop your work and join the others in the yard. The sun's shining and it's rather pleasant outside.' Lily looked up, surprised to see Mrs Bodney giving her a rare smile.

'I'll just complete this first, Mrs Bodney,' she answered.

Instantly, her employer's smile vanished. 'No, Lily, I must insist you go outside now.'

Lily stared at her in surprise. 'But if I carry on I'll get more done.'

'You won't, Lily. Your body needs sustenance and your mind time to clear, or you won't be productive at all this afternoon.'

Hearing the firmness in the other woman's

voice, Lily picked up her piece from her bag and took it outside. The warmth of the sun was a welcome tonic after the gloom of the workroom and as she tucked into her bread and cheese, she found herself relaxing.

'Hobnobbing with the boss lady now, are yer?' Spinning round, Lily saw a plump figure glaring at her from the side path.

'Seems to me yer makes a habit of sucking up to them what's higher than yer, Lily Rose.'

'I don't know what you mean,' Lily gasped in surprise. The figure sneered; her lips almost vanishing into a mean slit.

'No, course not. Thinks yer better than us and can use yer slim figure and long hair to—'

'Molly Baker, you're paid to deliver victuals, not slander, so take your gossiping tongue off my premises before I set the goose on you.' Mrs Bodney might have been half the size of the rotund Molly but, as she stood there, hands on hips, eyes icy as a morning frost, it would have been a formidable person who dared argue with her.

As Molly slunk away muttering curses under her breath, Lily shivered. Two years older than she, Molly had been at the charity school with Tom and had taken offence to what she saw as his rejection, when he'd started walking out with Lily. Knowing Molly would do anything to make her look bad in his eyes, she sighed.

Looking up, she saw her employer eyeing her speculatively before ringing her bell to signal the end of their break.

'I never knew Mrs Bodney had a goose,' whispered Nell as they rinsed their hands together at

53

the pump.

'She hasn't, silly, you're the goose,' answered Mary, and as they dissolved into giggles Lily felt her spirits lift.

Back in the workroom, they resumed their lace making, working as quickly as their fingers would allow. Once again; the room fell silent apart from the rhythmic clicking of bobbins, for they had no time to waste on idle chatter, and the afternoon passed in a haze of concentration. None of them could afford to be dismissed for not meeting their quota.

Although Lily was working diligently, she couldn't help glancing up when a shadow clouded the window. A tall, dapper gentleman with a shock of dark hair, wearing a fine black coat, was alighting from a carriage that had pulled up outside. When he saw her, he gave a broad smile. Mortified she'd been caught staring, she quickly bent her head back over her pillow, but as she weaved the threads back and forth she couldn't help speculating about the handsome stranger. Who was he and why was he visiting Mrs Bodney?

Her musing was interrupted by a plaintive wail. Looking up, she saw Mary shaking her head from side to side, tears coursing down her cheeks.

'Whatever's the matter, Mary?' Lily asked, fearing the older woman was ill.

'I've gone wrong and I can't see where. I tried to work faster and now I've made a mess. Dear God in heaven, what can I do? Mrs Bodney will dismiss me, I know she will,' she cried.

'Hush now,' Lily soothed, jumping to her feet. 'Here, let me take a look.'

54

'Oh, would you?' Mary asked, looking at her hopefully. What about your own work? You can't afford to get behind too.'

'Don't worry, Mary,' she said, bending over the other woman's pillow and immediately spotting where she'd gone wrong. 'Look, here's the problem.' She pointed to the twist some rows back. 'You've put the pin up in the wrong place, there see?'

Mary groaned. 'That'll take me ages to put right. I gets in a right muddle working the bobbins back again.'

Lily sympathized, knowing the older woman had struggled to get to grips with the intricate pattern in the first place.

'You carry on working my pillow and I'll sort things out here.'

'You'd let me work your pillow?' Mary gasped in disbelief.

'Quick; swap places,' Lily whispered. 'The sooner we start, the sooner it'll be done.'

Ignoring the curious looks from the others, Mary went and sat on the stool Lily had vacated.

'Blimey, you're taking a chance,' Nell gasped, shaking her head so vigorously that her cap fell sideways and her copper curls cascaded onto her shoulders.

'I know,' Lily whispered. 'But I really must help Mary. I'm sure it won't take long.'

'Rather you than me,' Nell muttered, impatiently scooping her hair back under her cap and picking up her bobbins again.

'Don't expect us to support you if you get found out,' snorted Cora.

'Oh, don't be so mean, Cora. We'll be working together for the next few months so it makes sense to help each other if we can,' Anna said, smiling at Lily.

Lily smiled back gratefully then settled to her task. It took her longer to correct the work than she'd thought it would and, whilst outwardly she appeared calm, her insides were churning like butter in the dairy. She just hoped Mrs Bodney's visitor would keep her entertained until she was back in her own place, for her hawk-like eyes missed nothing and to swap pillows was an unforgivable sin. She also prayed Mary wasn't making a mess of her sprig otherwise they'd both be sent packing.

'There, Mary, that's fine now,' she whispered, a while later.

'Oh, Lily, I can't thank you enough.' The older woman's eyes shone with gratitude as they swapped back to their own pillows, but Lily barely had time to check her own work was in order before Mrs Bodney swept into the room, the full skirts of her long black dress swishing around her ankles.

'Right, ladies, time to call it a day,' she announced and there, was a collective sigh of relief and much scraping of stools as they reached for the sheeting to cover their work. As Lily hurried to the door with the others, Mrs Bodney called her back.

'Lily, I'd like a word before you go, please.' Although her employer spoke mildly, Lily's heart flopped.

'She's found you out,' Cora smirked, her eyes sparkling, as she strutted outside.

Slowly, Lily retraced her steps and Mary,

looking worried, came to stand by her.

However, Mrs Bodney waved her away, saying, 'No, you can go home, Mary. It's Lily I wish to see.'

Mary glanced at Lily. 'Better do as she says,' she whispered, but as the woman scuttled away, Lily's heart was beating furiously. Cora was right. Somehow her employer must have found out she'd swapped pillows with Mary.

'Right, Lily,' Mrs Bodney said, firmly shutting the door. 'Tell me how this afternoon's lace making has progressed, if you please.'

'Everyone worked hard, Mrs Bodney,' she said, striving to keep the tremor from her voice.

'There have been no problems then?' The other woman shot her a penetrating look. Lily shook her head and Mrs Bodney arched an eyebrow.

'Well, in that case, let's see what has been achieved,' she said, walking over to the first pillow and lifting the cloth. As she went around the room inspecting all their work, Lily held her breath. By the time she reached Mary's pillow, Lily's heart was thumping so loudly she was sure her employer must hear it.

'Hmm,' Mrs Bodney said, before moving on to Lily's pillow. A few moments later, she turned to Lily, frowning. 'Whilst you were having your noon break I checked your lace and was impressed with the progress you'd made. I have to confess, I'm surprised you haven't produced more this afternoon.' Mrs Bodney's eyes bored into hers and Lily almost wilted under the woman's scrutiny. 'Of course, had you been helping somebody else, that would explain why your own work has suffered,' she said, looking at Lily knowingly.

'I might have done,' she stammered

'Well, whoever corrected Mary's mistake has done a fine job. It's not discernible, even to my expert eye.'

Lily's eyes widened; was the woman a witch?

As if guessing her thoughts, Mrs Bodney smiled. 'No, I'm not clairvoyant, Lily, merely observant. I spotted Mary's mistake at lunchtime.'

'Well, if you did, why…?' her voice trailed off. She didn't wish to appear impertinent.

'Why didn't I point it out? I wanted to see how long it was before she noticed and what would happen when she did. I must confess to keeping my ear to the wall, so to speak. I suppose Mary panicked and thought I'd send her packing? No, don't answer,' she said holding up her hand as Lily opened her mouth to protest. 'I can see you're trying to be loyal to your friend and I respect that.'

Lily really couldn't see where this conversation was leading. If Mrs Bodney was going to dismiss her why was she smiling?

'Sit down, Lily, and I'll come to the point,' her employer said.

Thankfully, Lily sank onto her stool for the suspense was making her feel quite sick.

'I've been watching you closely these past few days and have been impressed with what I've seen. You are a highly skilled lace maker and conscientious too. If this afternoon is anything to go by, you are also proficient at correcting mistakes, which regrettably can and do occur. Now, if you remember, I mentioned earlier that output needs to increase?' She paused and Lily nodded.

'I have realized that if we are to meet the deadline, I will need someone to watch over the lace makers here whilst I attend to my other team.'

Lily frowned. 'I didn't know there was another one.'

'Let me explain, Lily. Not only is this commission highly confidential, the Queen has specifically requested that nobody except me should have knowledge of the design detail. For this reason, I have kept the various lace patterns separate, with a different set of lace makers working on each. Time is of the essence, and in order to minimize any mistakes I now need to ensure both teams are supervised, as I no longer have the time to do that. Therefore, I propose working up at High House and want you to see to the ladies here.'

Lily shook her head, trying to take in what she'd been told. Bemused, she stared at her employer.

'High House?'

'I have rented High House at the top of the village and that is where the other team are working. You do realize I'm offering you the job of overseer here?' Mrs Bodney said impatiently.

'Me? But I'm the youngest,' Lily said, shaking her head in surprise.

Mrs Bodney waved her hand dismissively, in the way Lily had come to recognize. 'You might be the youngest, Lily, but you are also the most capable and the loyalty you've already shown is commendable. Now, the job entails extra work but will merit a substantial increase in your wage.' Then, as she went on to mention a figure that made Lily gasp, there was a knock and Tilda put her head around the door.

'Sorry to interrupt, ma'am, but Mr Mountsford would like a word before he leaves.'

'Tell him I'll be with him directly,' Mrs Bodney said, but a man with dark hair was already entering the room. Lily's eyes widened in surprise, for it was the stranger she'd seen earlier and he was so tall he had to stoop low to avoid banging his head on the lintel above the door.

'Forgive the intrusion, Mrs Bodney. I can see you are busy but I merely wish to bid you farewell and give you this,' he said, holding up a small package. Then to Lily's surprise, his piercing blue gaze was aimed in her direction. 'That's quite all right, Mr Mountsford, and thank you,' her employer said, taking the package and quickly pocketing it. 'Before you go, I'd like to introduce you to Lily Rose, my new overseer.'

Lily jumped to her feet.

'Delighted to make your acquaintance, Miss Rose; Rupert Mountsford at your service,' he said, smiling at her warmly. She bobbed a curtsy, which for some reason seemed to amuse him.

'Mr Mountsford is one of my best merchants, Lily, and pays us regular visits,' Mrs Bodney said, by way of explanation.

'Then, you being Mrs Bodney's new overseer, we shall surely be seeing more of each other, Miss Rose?'

Lily glanced at Mrs Bodney.

'Indeed, you will, Mr Mountsford, and I can see from your expression that it won't pose any hardship, to you,' her employer said smiling.

'It will be my pleasure,' he answered, turning the full force of his smile on Lily. Then, bowing briefly, he left the room. She stared after him, wondering why her insides were fluttering like a butterfly.

'Well, young Lily, I think you've made quite an impression there,' Mrs Bodney said, breaking into her thoughts.

Immediately, she felt heat flushing her cheeks and cursed that, despite having recently attained her seventeenth birthday, she still had the childish tendency to blush.

'Right, run along now. I've kept you long enough. First thing tomorrow, I shall explain your new position to the others and then be away to High House. Now I'll bid you good evening and pleasant dreams,' she said, her eyes twinkling.

Letting herself out into the lane, Lily saw the sun was already setting, the pink sky turning to deep mauve. There was no sign of Tom and her heart sank. Obviously he'd got tired of waiting. For some reason, her need to see him was greater than usual. Fighting down her disappointment, she made her way to the stables. At least Doris was there this evening. As she hitched up the cart and climbed in, she couldn't help wondering if her suspicions about the donkey's disappearance the previous day were founded.

As usual, thoughts of the squire unsettled her. Determinedly, she brushed them aside, then spent the rest of the journey plucking up the courage to confront her aunt. First, she'd make it clear she was no liar and point out that she felt hurt her aunt should think she was. Then she was going to tell her she would be continuing her job with Mrs Bodney, and that she'd now been promoted to overseer. This was too good an opportunity, to turn down, and for once she intended putting her own future first.

As excitement bubbled up inside her, Lily couldn't help smiling. With the extra money she'd be earning, they'd be able to afford to rent somewhere in Bransbeer.

Chapter 7

However, when Lily reached the cottage, her good mood vanished for it was neither her aunt nor her brother who came out to greet her, but the bulky figure of Parson Peddicombe. He was looking so grave she was immediately anxious as she jumped down from the cart.

'Lily, my dear, you need to be brave for I'm afraid I have very sad news.'

Lily felt her stomach churn.

'What is it?' she asked.

'I'm sorry to have to tell you your mother passed away earlier this afternoon,' he said, patting her shoulder. She stared at the parson for a long moment, trying to take in what he'd said. Then she gave a cry of dismay and rushed into the cottage.

'Tell me it isn't true, Aunt Elizabeth?' she cried, dashing at the tears that were coursing down her cheeks.

Her aunt put her arm around her shoulders and sighed. 'I'm afraid it is, my dear,' she said, wretchedly. 'I took her in the beef tea I'd made specially and there she was, gone in her sleep, just like that.' She snapped her fingers. 'She looked just like a little doll lying there so peaceful.'

'But, she wasn't even ill. Not really,' Lily cried, shaking her head in bewilderment.

'Not in the true sense, perhaps. But, since your father died, she was only existing, wasn't she?'

Lily nodded, realizing that what her aunt said was true.

'Now, mop those tears and I'll take you in to see her.'

Lily shuddered, then wiped her eyes with the back of her hand.

'She's all laid out. It looks just like she's sleeping so come and say goodbye to her,' her aunt said, gently taking Lily's arm and leading her into the room she shared with her mother.

Lily looked down at the figure on the bed. It was her mother lying there and yet somehow it wasn't. Aunt Elizabeth was right, though, she did look at peace. In fact, she looked more like the woman she remembered her mother being before the accident.

'Goodbye, Mother,' she whispered. 'Sleep in peace.' At least she could say farewell this time. It had been different when her father had died for his body had been flattened by the falling building and nobody had been allowed to see him.

'Now then, Lily,' Aunt Elizabeth said gently, breaking into her thoughts as she handed her two shiny pennies, 'you place these over her eyes.'

Blankly, Lily stared at her aunt. 'Why, will they open otherwise?' she asked.

'No, silly, it's to pay for her safe passage to the

afterlife. Now, while you do that I'll open the window to let her soul fly free.' With trembling hands, Lily did as her aunt directed. Then, as the tears began to flow again, her aunt put her arm around her shoulders and led her from the room.

'You've had a nasty shock, Lily. I've banked up the grate, so you have a warm while I make us a hot drink.' Aunt Elizabeth said, nudging her towards the chair by the fireplace. Feeling her legs giving way, she sank thankfully into it then leaned towards the crackling logs, trying to coax some warmth back into her ice-filled body. She'd only just stopped shivering when Robert burst into the room.

'I hate you, Lily Rose. It's your fault Mother's dead,' he spat.

Eyes wide, she stared at him in horror.

'Now then, Robert, enough of talk like that,' Aunt Elizabeth rebuked, coming into the room, a steaming mug in each hand.

'Well, it's true. Miss High-and-Mighty here refused to work for the squire and Mother knew we'd be out on the street. It was the shock that killed her. I wish it was you that was dead, Lily Rose,' he shouted.

'I said that's enough, young man. Pull yourself together and show some respect for your poor mother lying in the next room.'

Robert glared at them and then hobbled from the room, banging the door behind him. Lily rose to go after him but her aunt stopped her. 'Let him be. It's the shock talking. He didn't mean it and will see reason when he's calmed down. You sup your drink, dear, you look as if you've seen a

64

ghost, not that I meant...'

'But it is my fault Mother's dead,' Lily muttered, oblivious to her aunt's blunder.

'Of, course, it's not. It's nobody's fault, she just lost the will to live. Besides, she never knew you weren't taking the position the squire offered. It was the shock of having to leave the home she'd shared with your father that was too much for her. You said yourself, she never recovered from his death so you've nothing to blame yourself for, my dear,' her aunt said, cuddling her close. 'It's you that's kept the family going these past couple of months. If anything, you should be proud of yourself.'

Remembering her aunt's accusations from the previous day, Lily opened her mouth to say something, then realized this was not the time.

'Where's Beth?' she asked instead. She hadn't seen her little sister since she'd come in.

'Don't look so worried. Grace came and collected her while the parson was giving your mother the last rites. There's no point in the little lamb having to know before she needs. She'll be better off staying with Harriet whilst we sort things out here, and happen you need a bit of looking after yourself, after the shock you've had...' Her voice tailed off when she saw that Lily wasn't listening.

'I can see that Beth can't sleep in the same room as ... oh, Aunt Elizabeth, it's all so horrible, and to think I was planning to tell Mother my good news...'

Her aunt leaned forward and patted her hand. 'What good news was that, Lily?'

'Mrs Bodney's made me up to overseer,' she cried. 'She increased my wages by quite a lot and I was planning to move us all to Bransbeer.' She looked sadly towards the next room. 'What happens now, Auntie?'

Aunt Elizabeth patted her shoulder. 'The parson said he could do the funeral next Wednesday. Would you like me to see to the arrangements?'

Woeful Wednesday, how appropriate, Lily thought.

'Yes, please. I really wouldn't know where to begin.'

'Perhaps you'd like to choose a couple of her favourite hymns?' her aunt suggested and Lily nodded, relieved there was something she could do.

'Why don't you go down to the church and look in the hymnal? Then you can tell the parson.'

As Lily got up to leave, she glanced towards the next room. 'What about–'

'Your mother will be quite all right, my dear. I should imagine she's with your father by now, God rest her soul,' her aunt said, sighing and making the sign of the cross.

Glad to be out of the cottage, Lily ran down the shadowy lane towards the church, almost colliding with Tom, who was hurrying up the lane towards her.

'Oh, Tom, something dreadful has happened,' she cried.

'I know,' he said, taking her hand. 'Parson Peddicombe told me. I came as fast as I could. Ran all the way,' he gasped, pausing to catch his breath. 'I'm that sorry about your mother, Lily, but I likes to think she's at peace now.'

'She is, Tom. I'm sure of it. She was lying on the bed just like she was asleep, but she looked – oh I don't know – it was as if all the sadness had drained out of her.'

'She never recovered from losing your father. Happen they're together again now.'

'That's just what Aunt Elizabeth said. She's sent me to the church to choose some hymns for the funeral. It's next Wednesday. You will come, won't you? Please?'

'Of course, I will.' He sighed. 'I waited for you earlier, Lily.'

'Mrs Bodney asked me to stay on. She had something important to discuss...'

'Sorry, Lily, I have to go. I wish I could stay, but we're sailing at first light. I just had to come and make sure you're all right,' he murmured, squeezing her hand. 'Look, Lily, leave the hymns until tomorrow. There's talk the owlers will be busy transporting their goods this night, so I'd feel better knowing you was indoors.' She shuddered and Tom patted her shoulder. 'I wish I could walk you back but there's no time. Promise me you'll go home now?' he asked. Reluctantly, she nodded and then watched as he ran back down the track.

'Godspeed and bring you safely home, my love,' she whispered. A hoot nearby made her jump, sending her scuttling back to the cottage. Whether it was an owl or owler she wasn't waiting to find out. She'd heard that the menacing hoodlums who moved their wool under the cover of darkness made short work of anyone they encountered and she wasn't going to risk bumping into them.

Besides, she knew her mother's favourite hymns had been 'Love divine, all loves excelling' and 'Rock of ages'. She'd taught Lily all the words and they'd often sung them as they worked side by side at their pillows. Her heart tugged at the memory, and she dashed away the tears as she ran back down the lane.

Glad to be safely home, she hurried indoors, eager for some company. However, her aunt had already left and Rob was nowhere to be seen. He was probably consoling himself with his beloved chickens, she thought.

Unable to contemplate sleeping in the same room where her mother was laid out, Lily dragged her mattress out and placed it in front of the fire. Then, covering herself with the blankets, she tried to sleep but her thoughts kept going over the events of the day. She was still awake when her brother hobbled into the room.

'Rob,' she said, but he didn't answer. Instead he climbed onto his mattress and made a show of pulling the covers up over his head. Oh, blow him, Lily thought, turning over and falling into a fitful sleep.

After a restless night, Lily was roused by the cockerel raucously heralding the dawn. Stiffly she rose from her makeshift bed. She could hear her brother's gentle snoring and, not wishing to wake him, hurried outside to the barn. Climbing into the donkey-cart, she thought about calling in to see Beth, then chided herself. Her sister would probably still be asleep and Lily would not be popular if she woke the household.

Urging Doris onwards, she relaxed in her seat

and let her thoughts drift back to happier times: how thrilled she'd been when her father let her help him in the orchard, claiming he would never be able to pick all the apples by himself; sitting beside her mother learning to make lace, and how excited she'd been when she'd finished her first sprig; paddling in the stream with Rob, catching tiddlers and having water fights; cradling young Beth in her arms just after she'd been born and declaring her to be wrinkled as a prune, much to her mother's dismay.

When she arrived at the cottage, she found Mrs Bodney waiting for her.

'I was sorry to hear about your mother, Lily. I know it will have come as a great shock to you. Are you quite sure you feel up to starting your new position today?'

'Thank you, Mrs Bodney. I'll be fine.'

The other woman patted her arm and Lily couldn't help but notice how relieved she looked.

'It's better to keep busy, my father always said.'

'Quite. As overseer, it is your responsibility to ensure only the lace ladies enter the workroom. Tilda has been given strict instructions to that effect. Now, come with me,' Mrs Bodney instructed, leading the way upstairs and into what appeared to be her own bedroom. 'You need to look the part of overseer, for it will be your duty to receive merchants and tradespeople in my absence.' She pointed to the bed where a fine black cotton dress, white linen bonnet and apron were laid out. Then Lily noticed the corset and grimaced. The other woman smiled.

'The female figure is enhanced when it is contained and your dress will hang in a better fashion. It is a good discipline to adopt and, I can assure you from personal experience, it will correct your posture and guarantee you move in a ladylike manner. Now hurry and change so you're ready when the others arrive. After I've explained your new position to them, I shall go and see to the ladies at High House. However, I will endeavour to be back before you leave this evening to find out how you've managed,' she said.

There was so much to take in, Lily's head was spinning. Then, seeing her employer was waiting for an answer, she nodded. Seeming satisfied, Mrs Bodney bustled from the room.

Looking down at her new outfit laid out on the bed, she felt a tingle of excitement, but when she tried to wriggle into the corset she felt like the contortionist she'd seen at the Cuckoo Fair in April. Then, when she did finally manage to get the wretched thing on, she could hardly breathe. It was so tight she was sure she'd faint. She struggled into the white cotton petticoat and then the dark dress, marvelling at the softness of the material. It was far superior to anything she'd ever worn before and to her delight the full skirts swished about her ankles when she moved. It was a good job it was black, she thought with a pang, for now she was in mourning for her mother.

Hearing the chattering of voices coming up the path, she hastily donned her apron, wondering how her fellow-workers would take the news she was to be their overseer. She didn't have to wait long to find out. Making her way to the work-room, she heard Cora's indignant protest and the mutterings of the other ladies. As she hesitated in the doorway, Mrs Bodney looked up and smiled reassuringly.

'Come in, Lily,' Mrs Bodney said, beckoning to her. 'Ladies, you are to co-operate and make Lily's job as easy as you can. She has my authority to dismiss anyone who makes trouble or breaches the working conditions I set out on your first day. Do I make myself clear?'

'Yes, Mrs Bodney,' they intoned, and with a brisk nod of her head she left the room, her skirts bustling in her wake. Lily swallowed nervously.

'Well, get you, Lily Rose, all dolled up like a donkey's thingummy,' Nell sniggered.

'You needn't think we're taking orders from you,' Cora snorted.

Lily stared at their hostile faces and felt like fleeing.

Peasants persist, Lily. It's up to you to lead the way, not run away. You can do it.

She heard her father's words of encouragement and squared her shoulders, determined not to let him down.

'Right, ladies,' she said firmly. 'As you heard, Mrs Bodney has appointed me to oversee the work here. And, with your co-operation, that is all I will need to oversee,' she said, smiling at them.

'Oh, yeah? How do you make that out?' Cora spat, her green eyes glinting like a cat's.

Lily swallowed but refused to be intimidated. Striving to keep her voice calm, she smiled and looked at each of them in turn.

'You are skilled lace makers and I trust you to work diligently. However, if anyone requires help they only have to ask. Mrs Bodney has already outlined our schedule and we know the deadline we are working to.' Lily paused, endeavouring to meet their glares with a friendly smile. Although silence greeted her words, she continued to smile until her face was as stiff as the washing on a frosty morning.

'Well, I'm pleased it's you who's overseeing us, Lily,' Mary said eventually. 'And I'd just like to say how sorry I was to hear about your mother.'

'Thank you, Mary,' Lily answered and, feeling tears welling, she swallowed hard. Then, to cover her emotion, she said in her best imitation of Mrs Bodney, 'Well now, let's get on with our work, shall we?' Picking up her bobbins, she began weaving the threads under and over, following the pattern she'd pricked out. There were a few mutters but, to her relief, everyone followed her example.

Halfway through the morning, she was disturbed by the sound of clattering followed by muffled giggles. Looking up, she saw Cora and Nell rolling their bobbins across the floor to each other.

'Stop that this instant,' she ordered, jumping to her feet. Cora stared at Nell and then deliberately sent another spinning towards her. As Nell giggled, Lily marched over and snatched up the offending bobbins.

'If you wish to behave like children, then take yourselves outside,' she instructed. As Cora and Nell stared at her defiantly, the others looked up, from their work. An undercurrent of excitement rippled around the room as they waited to see how Lily was going to handle the situation. Well, there could be only one outcome, Lily thought. Carefully she inspected the thread remaining on the bobbins.

'Cora and Nell, luckily for you the thread hasn't soiled otherwise I would have had to deduct the damages from your wages,' she said.

Their looks of amusement turned to outrage.

'You wouldn't dare,' Cora spluttered while Nell's pale complexion turned ashen.

'As I said, it won't be necessary this time, Cora. However, if you don't return to your work immediately, I shall deduct money for time wasted.'

Nell promptly sat down and after a few moments Cora followed. The other ladies resumed their work and Lily breathed a sigh of relief.

The rest of the morning passed uneventfully and when the church clock chimed noon, Lily rang the little bell signalling it was time for their break. As the lace makers filed outside into the yard, there were a few baleful looks cast in her direction but Mary smiled at her reassuringly.

'Give them time, Lily,' she whispered.

Lily nodded, and was just wondering whether she should join them when Tilda tapped on the door and announced that Squire Clinsden was waiting to see her. Biting back the retort that sprang to her lips, she followed the maid through to the parlour where the man was impatiently pacing the floor.

'Lily, my condolences on the sad demise of your mother,' he said solicitously, but as soon as the door had shut behind the maid, his demeanour changed. 'I take it you are ready to end this farce,' he growled.

'I'm sorry, sir, I'm not sure I understand you,'

she said, trying to keep her voice level.

'Oh, we understand each other perfectly, Lily, so don't play games.'

'Sir, I have duties to attend to, so please state your business,' she said, looking him square in the face.

'Don't you get uppity with me, young lady; in order to save you and your family from being homeless I offered you a position in my household. I'm here for your answer. You needn't think I made a special visit, though. I had business in Bransbeer and thought I'd see to two birds in one go,' he said, guffawing at what he clearly saw as his wit. She shuddered, guessing the nature of his business only too well.

'Thank you, sir, but, as I've already told you, I am satisfied with my position here,' she answered serenely. Now she knew how a swan felt: all calm on the surface while it paddled furiously under the water.

The squire's face turned redder still. Determined not to be browbeaten, Lily continued looking him straight in the eye.

'Let me remind you that your family will be out on the street come the quarter-day. Do you want to see your brother and sister in the gutters of Coombe? Surely that's not what your dear mother would have wanted?'

Oh, how low, she thought. 'I appreciate your concern, sir, but I assure you it won't come to that. I take my duties towards my family seriously and have already decided what we shall do. Now if, you'll excuse me I have work to see to,' she said, snatching up the little brass bell from the

74

table and ringing it vigorously. As he stared at her in disbelief, Tilda appeared in the doorway.

'Squire Clinsden is leaving. Please show him out.'

'You'll be sorry for this,' he hissed before stomping from the room.

Trembling, she sank onto the chair and covered her face with her hands. She had made a powerful enemy, she knew, but the idea of being friendly with the squire was even more frightening.

Chapter 8

'Are you all right, miss?' Looking up, Lily saw the maid hovering in the doorway, eyeing her anxiously.

'Yes, thank you, Tilda,' she said, forcing a smile. Then, taking a breath to steady herself, she hurried back to the workroom and summoned the ladies in from the yard.

Although they came in willingly enough, she could sense the underlying tension as they settled themselves at their pillows.

'Oops, I think I've put a pin in the wrong place,' Nell announced, not sounding the least bit concerned.

Lily went over to look at her work. 'I can't see anything amiss,' she said, frowning down at the perfect sprig before her.

'Silly me, I must have been mistaken,' Nell giggled, shaking her mane of copper hair.

'Easily done,' Lily said lightly. 'However, I think you should put your cap back on before Mrs Bodney returns. She won't be pleased if she finds red hair over your lace work.'

Nell glowered, muttered something under her breath and then reluctantly did as she'd been asked.

Impatient to resume her own work, Lily hurried back to her stool but as she sat down a flash of grey caught her eye. Bending to see what it was, her eyes widened in surprise when she saw a mouse nibbling the straw that was poking through a hole in her pillow. As she watched, the creature edged closer to the pristine white of her thread. Deftly scooping it up, she hurried to the door and let it go. She watched it scuttle to freedom, fervently wishing she could join it.

Hearing barely suppressed giggles, she turned to face the lace makers. It was obvious from the looks of amusement Cora and Nell were exchanging, that this had been planned in retaliation for earlier. When they saw Lily staring at them, they quickly looked down at their work.

Returning to her stool, Lily stared at her damaged pillow. Pranks she could put up with, wilful damage she could not ignore.

'Who slit my pillow?' she demanded, looking around the workroom, which was now ominously silent. 'Put down your bobbins this minute,' she instructed. The lace makers stared at her in amazement but did as they'd been told. 'I will ask you once more. Who did this?' she asked, pointing to the slit in her pillow and then staring at each of them in turn. Although they fidgeted on their stools, still no one answered. Knowing she needed to gain the upper hand or she'd never command the respect required of an overseer, she ordered firmly, 'No more work will be done until the culprit owns up.'

'But before she left, Mrs Bodney said we had to produce more,' Anna said.

'Precisely,' Lily answered. 'And if those responsible don't own up soon, you will still be sitting here like stuffed dolls when she returns.'

'You wouldn't dare...' spluttered Cora.

Lily raised an eyebrow but remained silent. Although her insides were quivering she was determined to maintain a calm exterior. As one, the lace makers turned and glared at Cora but she studiously ignored them. Defiantly she picked up her bobbins.

'Put those down, Cora,' Lily instructed. 'I said no more work was to be done until the culprit owns up. Do you have anything to say?'

'Yes, I blooming well do, Lily Rose. You think you're so high and mighty but you're no better than us. You only got this overseer job by sucking up to Mrs Bodney.'

'Put down your bobbins, Cora,' Lily repeated, ignoring the outburst. 'Well, it's up to you to decide whether you want to waste what's left of the afternoon or not. However, Mrs Bodney won't be happy if your work is behind schedule when she returns.'

As if to emphasize her words, the clock on the church chimed the hour. The ladies; looking decidedly uncomfortable, started squirming in their seats.

'For God's sake tell her,' hissed Mary. This was greeted with a snort of disgust from Cora.

'All right, it was me,' she muttered, her green eyes narrowing.

'And I had to say I'd gone wrong to distract you,' owned Nell.

'I see,' said Lily. 'Well, in that case, Cora, you will mend my pillow before doing any more lace work.'

'But that will make me even more behind,' she spluttered.

'You should have thought of that before coming up with such a stupid prank, Cora. Nell, you will clear up the droppings our little friend has left and then sweep the floor to make sure it's thoroughly clean. The rest of you can pick up your bobbins. If you have any sense, you will work like weasels to make up for lost time. Then, with any luck, Mrs Bodney won't find out.'

'You mean you aren't going to tell her?' Cora asked, staring at her incredulously.

'If your work is back on schedule by the time she returns, I won't need to, will I?' Lily responded.

Relieved they'd been let off so lightly, Cora and Nell hurried over to Lily's pillow and began clearing up the mess they'd created. The others snatched up their bobbins and fervently resumed their work. As silence filled the room once more, Lily silently let out the breath she'd been holding. Then she walked over to the window and began winding thread onto spare bobbins in order to save time later.

'They were expecting you to scream when you saw that mouse,' Mary whispered.

'What? When I was brought up on a farm?' asked Lily, grinning. If they thought they would scare her off that easily, they had another thought coming.

'I've mended your pillow, Lily,' Cora announced. Lily went over to inspect it and was surprised to find the repair was hardly noticeable. She knew better than to say so, though.

'Yes, that will do, Cora. You may return to your own work now,' she said, but Cora hovered. 'Well, is there something else?' Lily asked, impatient to make a start on her own lace.

'Will you be taking anything out of my wages for the damage?' she asked, her voice unnaturally subdued.

'No, Cora, I won't.' The girl brightened and Lily added, 'but only if you promise me there will be no more tricks like this. We have got to work together for some time yet so we may as well try and help each other, don't you think?'

Cora nodded vigorously and then hurried back to her own pillow. Lily hoped there would be no more trouble but knew she'd need to keep her wits about her.

She glanced around the room, pleased to see everyone was working furiously. Clearly they were anxious to make up for lost time and the workroom was silent apart from the clacking of their bobbins. Settling down to continue the sprig she'd begun earlier, Lily realized she was going to earn every farthing of her pay rise.

It seemed no time at all before the shadows were creeping across the room and Lily picked up the bell to signal the end of the working day.

'Have you all made up the time you lost earlier?' she enquired. Nodding their heads, the ladies eyed her warily. 'In that case you may cover your work and I'll see you bright and early tomorrow.'

As the sound of their voices faded away, Lily sank on her stool, relieved to have made it through her first day as overseer. Then, conscious her employer would soon be returning, she got up and began inspecting their work. Luckily, despite their earlier escapades, the lace appeared to be up to standard. She was just returning to her own pillow when Mrs Bodney bustled into the workroom.

'Well, Lily, I'm pleased to say the ladies at High House have had a productive day. I hope yours have too. Did you encounter any problems?'

'Not really. Everyone has achieved the amount of work required for us to keep to the schedule.'

'And did you experience any difficulty with the ladies accepting you as their overseer?'

'I think they now understand my position, Mrs Bodney,' Lily answered, wishing to be truthful without giving them away.

'Hmm,' her employer said, looking at her closely. To Lily's relief, she didn't pursue the matter, asking instead, 'Did you receive any visitors?'

'Just Squire Clinsden, ma'am,' she answered.

'Did he perchance call to place an order for lace?'

The thought of that unlikely scenario made Lily smile and she shook her head.

'Well, if you encounter any problems, and I do mean any, you must feel free to bring them to me.'

Lily looked at Mrs Bodney in surprise.

'In the short time I have known you, Lily, you

80

have become a valued employee and I should hate to lose you.'

Shocked by the woman's perception, she stammered, 'Thank you, Mrs Bodney.'

'That's all for today, Lily. Just remember what I've said,' and with that she left the room.

The arrangements for her mother's funeral had been made and Aunt Elizabeth, having declined Lily's offer to help, had been tidying and cleaning like a demented demon to ensure the cottage was presentable for those coming back to pay their respects after the service.

Now it was the Sabbath and, while Aunt Elizabeth was enjoying a well-earned rest, Lily and Tom packed a picnic of bread and freshly made brawn and went out to the orchard. It was a beautiful morning. The trees were laden with fragrant, feathery blossom and a skylark trilled overhead. Tom took off his jacket and spread out a blanket on the grass. Then, sitting side by side, he and Lily tucked into their meal, revelling in the rare treat of not having to rush. Afterwards, they lay on their backs watching the fluffy clouds and playing their favourite game.

'That one looks like a fish,' murmured Tom.

'What's that cloud like, then?' she asked.

'A wolf?' he guessed.

'No, it's a dragon,' she laughed.

'Like your Mrs Bodney, you mean?'

'Oh, Tom, she's really nice when you get to know her. By the way, I've been meaning to tell you, I've been made up to overseer and–' But Tom had spotted her brother returning in the donkey-cart and jumped to his feet

'Hey, Rob, we've some food left if you want to join us,' he called. But Robert shook his head, glared at Lily and passed by without stopping.

'What's up with him?' Tom asked.

'He's sore at me,' she muttered.

'What do you mean?' he asked, looking at her sharply.

She sighed. 'He's blaming me for Mother's death. When the squire told her about Stanton moving in here, he said there was a job with a room for me at the manor. If I take it, a hut in the grounds would be made available for them to live in.'

'Yes, but how does that make you responsible for your mother's death?'

'I refused to even consider the proposition and Robert got the notion that's what killed her. Aunt Elizabeth said it was the shock of knowing she was to lose her home, though. It was just too much, it coming so soon after Father's death.'

Tom looked serious for a moment, then shook his head. 'Look, Lily, I know you like this job with Mrs Bodney but it doesn't give you anywhere to live, does it? Surely, it'd be better if you did work for the squire, even temporary like? Leastways, you'd all have a roof over your heads?'

'No, I couldn't work for that pomp– I mean, it makes sense for us to move nearer to Mrs Bodney's so I'll be making other arrangements...' Her voice tailed away as she saw his eyes narrow.

'Has Squire Clinsden done something to upset you, Lily?' he asked, studying her closely.

'Of course not, whatever gave you that idea?'

she asked, jumping to her feet and gathering up their picnic things.

'It was something Molly said,' he muttered.

'Well?' she asked, her voice sharper than she intended.

'What do you mean, well?'

'I mean, Tom Westlake, just what was it that your dear old school friend said?' she asked, glaring at him.

He looked away, shrugging. 'I guess it was nothing. Look, Lily, it's been an awful week and you're exhausted. I need to check the nets before we sail tomorrow, so I'll leave you to get some rest,' he said.

'I will see you for the funeral?' she asked, looking worriedly at him.

'I'll be here first thing Wednesday,' he promised before turning and striding across the orchard towards the cliff path. With heavy heart she watched him go. Just what had that scheming shrew Molly Baker said to him?

Chapter 9

It was a sombre procession, dressed in their best, dark clothes that trudged behind the cart as it wended its way to St Winifred's church that Wednesday morning. Lily, had been up before dawn, collecting the wild violets her mother had loved. Now they sat atop the wooden casket, a tiny splash of colour in the gloom, as it bore her body on its final journey. Lily's hair felt damp as she pushed stray strands back under her black cap. Somehow, though, it seemed appropriate the day was dank and mizzly. Friends and neighbours, their heads bowed, lined the narrow winding street as they passed slowly by. Those fortunate to have curtains at their windows had pulled them shut out of respect.

Lily took a deep breath, determined not to cry even though Robert was still studiously ignoring her. Aunt Elizabeth assured Lily he would come round in time.

To her consternation, as they entered the church, she saw Squire Clinsden seated in his family pew. He rose to his feet, head bowed as the funeral cortège slowly made its way down the aisle. However, as Lily passed, he glanced up briefly, his eyes taunting. Biting back her anger, Lily followed her aunt into the front pew.

The service was pitifully short, and despite Lily having told the parson what her mother's favourite hymns had been he saw fit to substitute his own choice of prayers as he deemed singing inappropriate at funerals. Personally, Lily thought it would lift their spirits. Still it didn't do to question the parson, did it?

Now they were standing in the churchyard that looked down over the rolling valley. As his voice intoned the final blessing, the simple casket was lowered into the freshly dug hole. Lily could smell the damp earth and had to bite her lip to stop herself crying out. It seemed so final. The parson signalled to her to scatter the first handful of soil but, as she moved forward, her legs buckled and it was only Tom's quick reaction that saved her from falling in as well.

'Steady, Lily,' he whispered, squeezing her hand. 'You're doing fine; your mother would be proud of you.'

Grateful for his reassurance, she gave him a wobbly smile. Robert, leaning heavily on his stick, was standing beside them and she saw him wipe a tear from his cheek. Her heart went out to him and, reaching over, she put her free arm through his. He turned, and, for the first time since their mother's death, gave her a lopsided grin. Relief flooded through her and she smiled back. At that moment, a single golden sunbeam burst through the clouds and, although she knew it was fanciful, she liked to think it was their mother showing her approval that brother and sister were on good terms once more.

Then she saw the squire making his way towards them. Quickly turning away, Lily heard him offering his condolences to Aunt Elizabeth and Robert.

'Thank you, sir,' her aunt replied. Then to Lily's horror she added, 'We are holding the funeral wake back at the cottage. It will be a small affair but you'd be welcome to join us.' Lily held her breath, her heart racing.

'That is most kind of you, but I merely came to pay my respects. Mrs Rose was the widow of one of my most valued workers and will be sorely missed,' Squire Clinsden said, bestowing his benign grin. Charlatan, Lily wanted to shout at his retreating back. Really the man was an out-and-out hypocrite. No doubt he'd only attended to look gracious in front of everyone.

'Are you all right, Lily?' Tom asked, concerned.

'Yes, I'm fine, thank you,' she replied, feeling anything but.

'My dear, how lovely to see you, although, of course, I wish it was under happier circumstances.'

Lily turned towards the booming voice. 'Uncle Vincent,' she exclaimed, as the jovial man approached. 'I hadn't realized you were here.'

'No reason why you should, Lily. Please accept my sincere condolences on your sad loss. Your mother was a fine woman.'

'Thank you, Uncle,' she whispered, biting her lip as the tears threatened to spill once more. Then, remembering her manners, she added, 'You remember my betrothed, Tom Westlake, don't you, Uncle?'

'Of course I do,' he responded, shaking Tom by the hand. 'And a man who makes such a fine choice has got to be a sensible one in my books.' As Tom flushed with pleasure, Lily shook her head.

'I think it's time we headed back home,' she said.'

Torn between duty and respect, Lily had made the decision not to return to work that day. Instead she accompanied her aunt back to the cottage, handing out steaming mugs of broth and freshly baked bread to fortify and warm the mourners. A large pound cake, one of Aunt Elizabeth's specialities, had already been cut into generous wedges and was displayed on the freshly polished dresser next to a dish of strong cheese.

Accepting condolences, her face frozen into a

smile, Lily was determined not to break down. At first, the conversation was about her mother, but then it turned to their coming eviction and she felt a rush of panic tightening her chest and tying her stomach in knots. News of Squire Clinsden's offer had spread and Lily's neighbours all assumed she'd be taking up the position at the manor.

She knew they'd be shocked when they found out she intended to continue working in Bransbeer, but today was not the time to break the news. Luckily, Mrs Bodney had consented to her taking these few hours off, though not before Lily had agreed to make up the time, for now they were working to an even more demanding timetable. She just hoped her ladies were working diligently in her absence.

The babble of voices jolted her back to the present and she saw her brother in earnest conversation with Uncle Vincent. Then she noticed her aunt was still scuttling around ensuring everyone's plate was filled.

'Come along, Aunt Elizabeth,' she said, taking the other woman's arm and leading her towards an empty chair. 'You've been on your feet since before daybreak. Sit here and chat to Uncle while I get you some refreshment.'

'Are you bearing up, Lily?' Tom whispered, following her to the dresser.

'Just about, Tom. I really appreciate you being with me today.'

'I'll always be here to support you, Lily my love,' he murmured. She stood there for a few moments, drawing comfort from his presence. Then she heard their visitors preparing to take their leave, and, giving him a rueful smile, she went to say goodbye and thank them for coming.

Uncle Vincent was the last to leave, having issued an invitation for Lily and Tom to visit him in Ilminster whenever they could. When he'd gone Lily leaned back against the door and closed her eyes. She was just gathering her thoughts when Robert hobbled over to her.

'Lily, I'm sorry. I should never have blamed you for Mother's death. It wasn't your fault, I can see that now.' As he stood there looking shamefaced, her heart went out to him.

'It's all right, Rob,' she whispered, going over and kissing his cheek. 'Everything will work out, you'll see.' He smiled, relief spreading across his, face. Then as he opened his mouth to say more, she quickly asked, 'Can you go and help Tom finish clearing away in the scullery?' and without giving him time to answer, she hurried through to the front room where her aunt was banking up the fire.

'I want to talk to you about young Beth,' Aunt Elizabeth said, as Lily flopped into a chair. 'How would you feel about her staying with Grace and Harriet for a bit longer?' Lily stared at her aunt in surprise and the woman continued, 'It might be best, what with things being all up and airy here. Grace has shown them how to pack pillows with straw and they've even started producing some good lace work between them. Little Beth is helping to pay her way, Lily.'

She could see the sense in her suggestion, but Beth was her little sister, for heaven's sake.

'You've done your best for her, I know,' Aunt

Elizabeth continued. 'But now you're away down to Bransbeer before she wakes and most days she's abed by the time you return. She's lost without you, Lily. Oh, it's not your fault,' she added, seeing Lily's frown. 'But think about it. Grace has a tender heart and she looks after Beth like one of her own. I can't deny I'm enjoying seeing more of the child too.'

'But it's not really fair on Mrs Goode to have another mouth to feed, what with her being a widow,' Lily said, feeling uncomfortable.

'Don't you worry about that, my dear, for I've been sharing the stews and brawn I make. Besides, as I said, she wants to help. Remember your mother looked after Harriet when her Walter was so poorly.' Lily nodded. 'And if you're really determined not to take up the squire's offer, it will give you more time to find somewhere to live if you're not having to mind Beth,' her aunt said.

'Yes, you're right, Aunt Elizabeth, but I can't deny that it will be strange without anybody else in there,' Lily said, sighing as she looked towards the next room. Then she noticed lying on the shelf the lace work she'd begun before she went to work for Mrs Bodney. Picking it up, she handed it to her aunt. 'Perhaps Mrs Goode would like to finish this. She can give it to the journeyman when he calls and receive the payment.'

'That's generous of you, Lily. Well, that just leaves us with Robert to sort out now.'

'Rob? I don't think he'd like to share a room with me,' Lily said, looking up in surprise.

Her aunt laughed. 'No, dear, that's not what I meant. That dreadful accident might have left him a cripple, but he's still got a good head on his shoulders. Wandering around here feeling useless day after day's not doing him any good and now, of course, he's fretting about the flitting.'

Guiltily, Lily realized she hadn't given any thought to how her brother must be feeling.

'But what can we do to help?' she asked.

Her aunt smiled. 'Actually, an idea did occur to me when I was speaking to my brother earlier,' she said.

'Oh, what was that?' Lily asked.

'I thought it would be good for Rob to learn a new trade and my brother agreed. But nothing can be decided until he and Rob have had a discussion. I can't say anything more,' she said, yawning. Gathering up the lace work and thread Lily had given her, she got to her feet. 'It has been a tiring day so I'll be away down to Grace's to check on young Beth and then I hope to get some sleep.'

'Thank you, Aunt Elizabeth, for all you've done for us. I don't know how we'd have managed without you.' Impulsively Lily threw her arms around the woman and kissed her cheek.

'Oh, get away with you,' Aunt Elizabeth clucked, flushing with pleasure. 'But just you think hard about your own future, young Lily,' she said, wagging her finger as she left.

'All well between you and Rob again then?' Tom asked, coming into the room a few moments later.

'Yes, thank heavens,' she said, smiling with relief.

'He's still worrying about the eviction,' Tom said frowning.

'So Auntie was saying. Look, Tom, my head's spinning like a top and I can't think straight at the moment.'

'Poor thing, it's been quite a day, hasn't it? I know you'll never forget your mother but I wanted to make you something particular to remember her by,' he said, flushing as he handed her a small package.

She opened the brown paper, and carefully folded back the small piece of linen within, then had to blink back the tears when she saw the bobbin he'd fashioned out of fish bone. It was delicately etched with the name of her mother, Sarah Rose, and the dates July 1802–May 1839, her pitifully short life span.

'Thank you, Tom, I'll treasure it always,' Lily whispered, trying to swallow the lump that was threatening to choke her. 'I'll keep it with the one you made for our betrothal.'

'Well, we've been stepping out for over a year now and I'm still working hard to get you that ring, like I promised. Then everyone will know you're my intended.'

'Oh, Tom, they know already. Anyway, it's you that matters to me, not fancy baubles.'

'It's important to me that you have a betrothal ring, Lily,' he said firmly.

'Let's go for a walk,' she said, anxious to break the tension.

The mizzle of earlier had cleared and the afternoon air smelled fresh. Swallows swooped low, catching insects, and the crickets were chirping in the meadow. Everything seemed normal, and yet everything was different.

'It's strange to think we won't be living here after next month,' she said, sighing.

'I suppose I'll have to get a pass from the squire to come visiting,' Tom teased. She tensed. Why hadn't she kept her mouth shut?

'There'll be no need for that, Tom. Oh, don't worry,' she added quickly, seeing his sharp look. 'I have an alternative plan.' And she vowed she would make enquiries as soon as she returned to Bransbeer.

'Oh?' he asked, breaking away from her and frowning.

'Now I've been made up to overseer it will make sense to live near to where I'm working. This is a fine opportunity to earn extra money for our wedding.'

'That's as may be, but you're being evicted in less than a month and if you're not careful you'll all be out on the streets, Lily.' She suppressed a shudder. 'Remember, this job, however good, is only temporary,' he added.

'It's for six months and I can always find another position after that. The status of overseer is far superior to that of a maid in service. Why, it could set me up for the future,' she declared.

'Pardon me, your ladyship. I suppose you'll not be wishing to walk out with a humble fisherman now,' he mocked.

'Idiot,' she said, laughing as she linked her arm through his. 'You know I love you and the extra money means we can marry as soon as I'm out of mourning.'

'Lily, love, that's a wonderful idea but the little extra you'll be getting won't make that much difference,' he scoffed.

Irritated by his condescending attitude, she

stopped walking and turned to face him. With great delight, she told him just how much she was now earning. His eyes widened in surprise and he stood there gaping like a freshly caught fish.

'Come along or we'll never reach the water,' she said, laughing.

They continued on their way, but Tom remained quiet, seemingly lost in thought. Then, reaching the cliff edge, they stood side by side gazing at the huge rollers breaking on the beach below. Although it had been sad to lay her mother to rest, Lily couldn't help feeling she was now at peace and hoped that she and her father had indeed been reunited.

The setting sun was painting the bay a glorious riot of gold and scarlet. Lily closed her eyes and wished that their future would be as rosy as the scene before them. It was some moments before she noticed Tom was still unusually quiet.

'Farthing for them?' she asked.

He grinned wryly. 'Funnily enough, it's money I'm thinking about. Simon's been finding it hard managing the lobster pots now his feet are bad, so I've taken them over. I was hoping the extra would help with our wedding, but even now, I'll not be earning anything like you, Lily.'

'So?' she demanded, puzzled.

'So, it means you'll be bringing in more than me, and that's something my pride won't allow. It's the husband's duty to provide, so I guess I'll just have to come up with a way of earning even more.'

'But you work all the hours as it is, Tom.'

'But it isn't enough, is it?' he insisted, his voice louder and echoing off the cliffs.

'Surely, it doesn't matter who brings in the money? It will all go into the pot, won't it? A lobster pot, even,' she said, laughing up at him. But, for once, he remained serious.

'It matters to me Lily,' he said firmly. 'Especially as you seem to have developed a taste for wearing finely fashioned gowns. Though I must say, it does make you look right comely.' Lily opened her mouth to say that it was one Mrs Bodney had lent her, but Tom was speaking again. 'Anyway, I'd better be on my way, tide's early tomorrow.'

Watching as he strode down the path towards Bransbeer, she sighed. She knew he was a proud man, but surely – it didn't matter a prawn who earned the most? He was so old-fashioned.

The sun had finally dipped behind the horizon, but it wasn't only the gathering shadows that caused her to shiver. What did her future hold? She so wanted to continue working for Mrs Bodney, she just had to find suitable lodgings she could afford. Of course, the choice seemed easy to him but he didn't realize the consequences if she went into service. She could remember her father telling her you didn't get anything for nothing in this life. Well, she wasn't afraid of hard work, but surely she had the right to choose where she did it, and for whom?

Chapter 10

Entering the workroom the next morning, Lily set about uncovering the pillows, keen to have everything ready for the ladies' arrival, for she knew each minute saved was an extra minute's lace making. She also wanted to inspect the work they'd done in her absence, but as she looked down at the lace pinned up on the first pillow, a frown creased her face. It was in exactly the same state as it had been when she'd left to go to the funeral. Quickly she moved to the next pillow, then the next, her frown deepening. Unable to believe her eyes, she checked the pillows again but not one sprig of lace had progressed.

'Morning, Lily. How was the funeral?' Mary asked, entering the room closely followed by the rest of the ladies, chattering together.

'The funeral service went well, thank you, Mary, which is more than I can say about your work here. Will someone please tell me the meaning of this?' she asked, pointing to their pillows.

The room fell silent, as the puzzled ladies stared at her.

'Before I left, did I or did I not remind you of the quota you had to achieve before you took your leave?' she asked. They nodded in agreement. 'Is this another of your pranks?' she asked, turning to Cora.

'No!' the girl protested, looking bewildered.

95

'Then why has no progress been made?'

The ladies looked at each other and then back to Lily.

'Well?' she asked, hearing her voice rising and fighting to control her emotions.

As usual, it was Mary who spoke. 'What's wrong, Lily? We only did like we'd been told.'

'What do you mean, you did as you were told...' Lily began, but Nell butted in.

'We just did what that lady said.'

'What lady?' Lily asked.

'The one you sent to tell us the pattern had been changed and we was to go home,' Nell said slowly, as if she was talking to a child.

'But I didn't send anyone. What was she called?' Lily asked.

'She didn't say. Just said you'd told her to deliver the message straight away. As she was wearing a black veil and long black gloves, we guessed she'd come from the funeral.'

Now it was Lily's turned to look confused. Casting her mind back to the small group gathered in the church she was sure no one there had been wearing a black veil.

'She spoke all genteel, like Mrs Bodney does when she receives the merchants,' piped up Anna.

'But I didn't send anyone here and, as far as I know, no change has been made to the pattern. I'll go and check with Mrs Bodney straight away,' she said snatching up her shawl. 'In the meantime, please get on with your work.'

'Tilda, did you let a lady wearing a black veil into the workroom yesterday?' she called out to the maid once she'd closed the workroom door.

Startled, Tilda looked up from her duties and nodded.

'You've been told that only Mrs Bodney and the lace makers are permitted to enter that room, Tilda, so explain yourself.'

Looking scared now, the maid explained that the lady had told her that Lily had instructed her to speak to the workers.

'Were you with her the whole time?'

'Yes, but she was only here a moment.'

'Did she look at the ladies' work?'

'Oh, no, she wasn't interested in that at all. She just stood in the doorway and told them that as the pattern had been changed, you'd said they were to stop work straight away and go home. Then she rushed out like she'd been stung by a bee. Am I in trouble, miss?' she asked, her lip wobbling.

As Lily looked at the worried girl, she felt her anger evaporating.

'No, Tilda,' she sighed. 'Tell me, is Mrs Bodney working at High House this morning?'

'Yes, she is,' she said, nodding frantically.

'I'm going to see her right away. No one is to enter the workroom in my absence. Should any-one call, they are to wait in the parlour until I return. Is that clear?'

'Yes, Miss Lily.'

Rushing up the lane, her thoughts in turmoil, she didn't see the women washing their clothes in the brook, or the parson waving to her from the church steps. She was in such a state that her breath was coming in noisy gasps by the time she reached High House. Rapping briskly on the door, she could hardly contain her anxiety.

'Is something wrong, Lily? I trust all went well at the funeral?' Mrs Bodney asked, as soon as the maid had withdrawn.

'Yes, well, no. What I mean is...'

'Calm yourself, Lily. Take a deep breath then start at the beginning. It's the best way, I find.'

'Mrs Bodney, something terrible has happened. Whilst I was at my mother's funeral, a stranger visited the workroom. She told the ladies that as the pattern had been changed, they were to stop work and go home immediately.' There was a moment's silence as the older lady digested what she'd said.

'Well, the pattern's certainly not been changed. Our dear Queen's known the exact design she wanted from the start, I can assure you of that. Now, can you think of anyone who would want to put a bobbin in our works, so to speak?'

There was only one person Lily could think of but he didn't wear a veil. Anyway, as far as she was aware, it was only Lily he had it in for, so she held her tongue.

'Well, if you do think of anyone, please let me know. Now you must make haste and get those ladies back to work. They will be well behind schedule but you may assure them they won't have any money deducted from their wages provided they've recovered output by my next visit.'

Back in the workroom, the concerned lace makers were relieved to hear they weren't going to lose any of their much-needed money. As they were due to receive their first month's wages shortly, they knew they'd have to work flat out to make up for all the time lost. Gloom descended upon the workroom like a blanket of sea fog.

'I don't mind staying on, but the trouble is, the later I'm away at night the more the kids play up,' Anna muttered, and the others nodded in sympathy.

'What about us cutting our noon break?' Mary suggested. Lily knew Mrs Bodney wouldn't approve but she couldn't see any other solution.

'Just until the schedule is back on track then,' she agreed.

For the rest of the day they worked as fast as they dared, fearful as ever of making mistakes; so that by the time she told them they could cover their pillows they were boggy eyed with tiredness. However, that didn't stop them speculating as to who the mysterious lady with the veil had been as they hurried from the room.

Lily watched them go, then, determined to start making up for the time she'd missed, resumed her work. It seemed only moments later that Tilda popped her head around the door.

'Pardon me, Miss Lily, but Mr Mountsford wondered if you could spare him a moment. I've shown him through to the parlour.'

'Thank you, Tilda. Tell him I'll be with him shortly,' she said, striving to keep her voice pleasant, for she really could do without any interruptions this evening. Stretching her back to ease her aching muscles, she straightened her cap and hurried through to the parlour.

Rupert Mountsford rose to his feet, greeting her with such enthusiasm that she found her exasperation disappearing.

'Miss Lily Rose, I hope I find you well?'

'Indeed you do, Mr Mountsford. I trust you are keeping well yourself?'

'Rupert – please call me Rupert,' he insisted. That idea didn't sit well with Lily at all, but Mrs Bodney had insisted she was to keep him happy when he visited.

'Well, Rupert,' Lily said, blushing as she stumbled over his name, 'how may I help you? I'm afraid Mrs Bodney isn't here at present but I'll be happy to convey a message to her.' She swallowed.

'That's most kind. However, I saw Mrs Bodney yesterday. The fact is, Lily... I may call you Lily?'

She nodded, impatient for him to come to the point.

'My business today took longer than anticipated and as it's too late for me to begin my journey back to the city, I've decided to stay overnight at a hostelry nearby. I was wondering if you would do me the honour of joining me.'

Shocked by his suggestion, her eyebrows shot right up to her cap and she could feel heat burning her cheeks.

'I beg your pardon, Mr Mountsford, I can assure you I'm not...' Outraged, she stammered to a halt.

'Forgive me, Lily, I've been clumsy in my proposal. I was merely suggesting you might care to join me for a bite of supper. My carriage would convey you safely home afterwards.'

'Oh,' she muttered, looking down at the floor and thinking how stupid she was. 'I thank you for the invitation, Mr Mountsford ... erm, Rupert, but that will not be possible. We have experienced a delay here and I must work on this evening.'

A glint hardened his eyes, but it was gone so

quickly she thought perhaps she'd imagined it.

'That is most unfortunate. Forgive my intrusion. I'll detain you no longer. Perhaps I shall be luckier on my next visit. Good evening, Lily.' And with that he bowed and made his exit, remembering just in time to duck to avoid hitting his head on the door frame.

Eager to make up the hours she'd lost and grateful for the longer hours of daylight the summer afforded, Lily worked on each evening after the others had left. By the end of the following week, although her lace had grown nicely, she thought that if she saw any more white thread she'd go crazy. It was a relief to tidy her things away that Saturday night, and after checking the workroom was neat for work to resume on Monday, she snatched up her shawl.

Arriving at the stables, she was glad to find Doris in her usual place. Having hitched up the cart, she was about to climb in when something caught her eye. Lying on the seat was a black veil and a black glove. Remembering the visitor to the workroom, she shivered. Whoever had placed them here obviously knew this was her donkey-cart and was expecting her to find them. But why only the one glove? she thought peering around. The cobbled yard, however, was empty.

In church the following morning, Lily looked to see if there were any strangers present. Suddenly a ripple of excitement ran around the congregation and her eyes widened in surprise when she saw Squire Clinsden ushering his wife into their family pew. What were they doing here, she wondered. Usually they graced the village church only when propriety dictated, preferring instead to worship in the far grander cathedral of Exeter.

All through the service she could feel the squire's eyes upon her. No matter how hard she tried, she couldn't refrain from glancing up over her hymnal at him. Two hazel eyes mocked her back and his thin lips twisted into a leer, making her feel so sick she could hardly concentrate for the rest of the service.

As the final blessing was given, the Squire and Lady Clinsden rose and swept regally up the aisle. The parson hurried after them, bowing and thanking them for honouring his service with their presence. Aunt Elizabeth was busy talking to Grace and didn't notice that Lily hadn't followed them out. She was hoping that if she waited the squire would have left, but to her horror, he was waiting for her by the yew tree opposite the lich-gate.

'Ah, Miss Rose, the very person I was hoping to see,' he said, his lips curling upwards whilst his eyes taunted.

'Lady Clinsden and I have decided to host our customary summer ball at the manor. You did such an excellent job at the Harvest Supper, my wife would like you to serve at table on this occasion also. You'll be happy to, I'm sure,' he said, giving his supercilious grin.

What, after his behaviour last time? Like hell she would. She'd rather ride Doris naked through the streets of Coombe than serve at his table again.

'In that case it would be courteous of me to reply to her ladyship in person,' Lily said, realizing it would be easier to make her apologies to Lady

Clinsden, for she, at least, was reasonable. Lily peered around, her heart sinking when she saw the lady was already seated in her carriage.

'We'll expect you on the afternoon of the 24th,' said the squire, turning to go. Then, as if it were an afterthought, he stopped and turned back. 'Of course, that will be quarter-day and you'll already be installed in the servants' quarters. Won't that be convenient? I shall give instruction for the game-keeper's hut to be made ready for your family.' He gave another smirk, and she was tempted to slap it clean off his face and into the sea. Instead, taking a deep breath, she forced herself to look him straight in the eye.

'I'm afraid your lordship will be disappointed. As I've already said—'

He leaned closer towards her, eyes narrowing so his brows joined in the middle like a worm, making him look very much the low life she always thought him to be.

'I'm never disappointed, Lily, of that you can be sure. I know what I want and intend to get it. Soon,' he added, ogling her body so that his meaning was clear. 'Oh, and I shall be sending my land agent over to conduct an inventory before quarter-day. It wouldn't do for you to leave with anything that wasn't yours, would it?' Then with-out a backward glance, he strode towards his carriage.

How dare the man? Lily thought, tempted to pick up the dung his horse had deposited on the path and hurl it after him.

Chapter 11

As Lily went over and stood by the freshly turfed mound of her mother's grave, she was shaking with anger, tinged with sadness.

'Lily, Grace has invited us to share a bite with her,' Aunt Elizabeth called. Not wishing her aunt to see her in such turmoil, she turned and forced a smile.

'That's kind of her, but I have things I need to do,' she answered. She wanted to be at home for she was hoping Tom would visit.

'Well, we'll collect the girls from Sunday school on our way,' her aunt said, eyeing her speculatively.

Lily nodded and then watched as the two women hurried up the lane, jabbering like the crows on the church tower.

All the way back to the cottage, Lily fumed over her confrontation with the squire, and her resolve not to go into service for him hardened like glue.

By the time she had finished her midday snack of bread and cheese, her wrath had subsided, leaving her feeling empty and tired. She was clearing away when there was a tap at the door.

'Well, how's my pretty petal today? Still going to make us our fortune, are you?' Tom asked.

Instantly her mood lifted. 'Well, I've had nothing else to do, seeing as how my betrothed hasn't seen fit to visit recently,' she quipped, showing him into the living room.

'Not through choice, I can tell you,' he said frowning. 'When I was out baiting up the pots I spotted several rows of corks bobbing close to the caves, and you know what that means? Someone's been out sowing the crop.'

'Sowing the crop? It sounds like you were in a field, not on the water.'

'Oh, Lily,' he said, shaking his head, 'sometimes I can't believe how naïve you are. It's an expression smugglers use when it's not safe for them to land their cargo. They pitch it overboard, having first weighted down the casks so they bob just beneath the surface of the water. Then they lay out rows of corks as markers. Word is, this time it's kegs of brandy from France.' Lily wrinkled her nose and Tom shrugged.

''Tis the way of things, Lily, what with taxes being so high. Anyway, the kegs haven't been there long but I reckon they'll be wanting to reap the crops soon. That's bringing them ashore to you, land lubber.'

She made a face. 'So, what's this sowing and reaping the crop got to do with you not visiting me? Smuggling goes on all the time. Everyone knows that. Terrible men,' she said, shuddering.

'Yes, but things have changed since they installed those naval officers in the coast station down at Coombe Mouth. Now the Preventatives spend their time looking out over Lyme Bay and when they spot any suspicious activity, they tip off the Revenue.'

'Well?' she asked, trying to follow what he was saying.

'The smugglers try to fool the excise men by

acting as decoys and rowing out in empty boats. While their attention's diverted, the carriers load the goods onto their mules and transport them overland. I've heard the most popular route they use is up over the cliff path from Bransbeer.'

'But that's the path I use to get to Mrs Bodney's,' she gasped in dismay.

'I know, but you needn't worry, they only travel under the cover of darkness which, thank heavens, doesn't fall until late this time of year. I wouldn't want you using that path come the winter, mind,' he said, so protectively that Lily felt a warm glow inside. 'I can't understand why you won't take the position up at the manor,' he said, looking at her closely. 'Still, I'll get to the bottom of it one of these days.'

'I still don't see why that stopped you from coming to see me?' Lily said quickly. The last thing she wanted was another inquisition about the squire. 'You would never get involved in anything illegal like that, would you?'

'Of course not, but the smugglers aren't choosy whose boats they steal so I'm keeping a close watch on mine. That's why I've painted the spars on my lugger white, so they show up in the dark. I'm hoping that'll deter the smugglers from using it.'

'Oh, Tom, you hear such dreadful things. Promise me you'll keep away from those frightful villains?' she asked him, her eyes wide with worry.

'Course I will,' he said, patting her shoulder reassuringly. Then getting to his feet, he added, 'Anyway, can't stop now, I've something to sort out.'

'But you've not long arrived,' she said, looking disappointed.

'Look, Lily, I'm as keen as you that we be wed the minute we can and I think I've found another way to make a bit extra. If it works out, I'll be bringing in at least as much as you, if not a bit more besides,' he said, looking excited.

'Tom, I thought you'd got over that silly nonsense,' she sighed, shaking her head.

'It's not nonsense for a man to want to provide for his future wife, Lily Rose,' he replied. As he stood in front of her, chin tilted upwards and that steely look in his eye, she smiled inwardly, for was it not his spirited manner that had attracted her to him in the first place?

'Besides, as I've said before, it seems you've acquired a taste for wearing those grand frocks, and right nice you look too,' he said quickly, as she made to protest.

'You know Mrs Bodney's only loaned me this. She said, as overseer, I need to look respectable when the merchants call.'

'Then I'll need to earn enough to buy you one of your own, though I hear you're good at the hobnobbing, Lily,' he said giving her a wry grin. The tone of his voice puzzled her but before she could ask him what he meant, he'd gone. His choice of words worried her. Was it merely coincidence that Molly had said the selfsame thing?

The cottage seemed quiet after Tom had left and, feeling restless after his talk about the smugglers and her job with Mrs Bodney, she decided to go to the barn and see if Rob was there. Perhaps he could have a word with Tom about this obsession of his to earn as much as she. They were good friends, after all.

As she went outside, she remembered how they'd met at the Cuckoo Fair the previous April. She'd been gazing at the brightly coloured ribbons set out on one of the stalls and thinking how beautifully the cornflower blue would trim her Sunday bonnet, when a portly gentleman, well the worse for liquor, had bumped into her. Suddenly, this tall, fair-haired man had reached out and steadied her and the attraction had been instantaneous. Then her brother had made the introductions. When Tom had called at their cottage the next day and presented her with the ribbon, she'd been touched at his kindness, especially when Rob told her he looked after his widowed mother and didn't have much money to spend. He'd also, bravely, asked her father's permission to step out with her.

Smiling at the memory, she hurried round to the barn. However, it was empty and she wondered where Rob could be. Oh, well, he'll turn up, she thought. Thinking it was time she paid Beth a visit, she went back to grab her shawl and then hurried down the lane to Mrs Goode's cottage.

Beth squealed with delight when she saw Lily, throwing herself into her arms and chattering so quickly she could hardly make out what the little girl was saying. She was pleased to see her little sister looking so happy, though.

'Come and look at my lace, Lily,' Beth said, pulling her into the living room with its homely smell of baking.

'Hello, Lily,' Mrs Goode greeted her. 'Elizabeth and I have been having a lovely old chat about when we were young uns.'

'Now then, Grace, don't you go giving away any secrets,' her aunt said, blushing as she got to her feet.

'Look, Lily,' Beth said, tugging at her skirt and holding out a sprig of lace for her to see.

'Why, that's beautiful, Beth,' she said, genuinely surprised at how good the work was.

'Yes, she's got the makings of a fine lace maker, just like her dear mother, God rest her soul,' said Mrs Goode. Lily felt a pang. Surely, she should have been the one to teach her little sister the art of lace making. Pushing aside her feelings, she smiled and patted Beth on the head.

'Well, come along, Lily, we'd best get back before Rob returns and wonders where we've got to,' her aunt chivvied. Feeling guilty that her visit had been so brief, she turned to say goodbye but her sister had already disappeared. Through the window, Lily could see her playing outside with her little friend Harriet and she guessed her visit had already been forgotten.

'Beth seems happy but I still feel guilty about not being around more for her,' Lily said to her aunt as they made their way back up the lane.

'Well, you shouldn't. We have to make the best of circumstances in this life, as I should know only too well.' Lily looked at her sharply but her aunt, seemingly oblivious, continued, 'Beth is settled and it's no good bringing her back to the cottage then having to find somewhere else for her to go in a couple of weeks. That is, unless you've changed your mind about working for the squire?'

Groaning inwardly, Lily shook her head.

'I couldn't help noticing he was waiting for you after church this morning. I have to say I didn't like the way he was gawping at you, young Lily, so you be careful. Happen I was wrong not to listen to what you said about him after all.'

'Yes,' Lily said, with feeling. 'I'm no liar, I promise you.'

Her aunt turned to look at her. 'I realize that now, Lily, and I apologize for thinking otherwise. I've heard talk about the squire since I've been back. Men like him grab what they want then off they go, leaving the likes of you to pick up the pieces.'

Lily stared at her aunt in amazement.

'Oh, I may be a spinster, young Lily, but I'm not as green as I'm lettuce-looking. I'll have you know I had my fair share of attention in the past, and not all was welcome, so I know what I'm talking about.' As her aunt stood there imparting her pearls of wisdom, Lily could not help noticing what a fine-looking woman she was with her tumble of dark hair, similar to her own, curling around her shoulders.

'I'm sure you did, Aunt Elizabeth. I bet you were quite pretty when you were young...' Her voice tailed off as she realized how rude she sounded.

'I got by, young lady. As I said, I know what I'm talking about so you'd do well to listen. These things can have far-reaching consequences.'

Lily pushed open the door to the cottage then waited, feeling there was something else her aunt wanted to say, but the woman hurried inside and began poking the fire. 'There, that's better,' she said, holding up her hands to the flames that now blazed. 'Anyway, you haven't told me what it was the squire wanted this morning.'

'He asked me to serve at table at the summer ball he's holding up at the manor. Oh, yes, and he said something about an inventory being carried out before we leave here. I mean, as if we'd take anything that's not ours. By the way, I haven't seen Rob this morning. Do you know where he is?'

Before her aunt could answer, the door clattered open and her brother stood there, his face wreathed in smiles. As he crossed the room, though, Lily couldn't help noticing his limp was more pronounced than usual. Aunt Elizabeth grinned.

'Judging from the look on your face, young man, I'd say your journey was successful?'

'It was indeed, Aunt, and I can't tell you how good it feels. Although I must confess I'm tired out now,' he said, sinking gratefully into the chair.

Lily looked from one to the other. 'Will someone please tell me what's going on?'

'Oh, Lily, it's simply the best news. I've been offered a position with Uncle Vincent. You know he runs a fancy repository in Ilminster? Well, he's moving to larger premises in the town and needs an assistant. I'm to be his apprentice in the clock and watch making business.'

His face was flushed with excitement and Lily's heart gladdened. His whole demeanour seemed to have changed and, with a flash of insight, she realized it was because he now had a purpose in life.

'Congratulations, Robert, that's wonderful news,' she said, crossing the room and kissing his cheek. 'I wondered where you'd gone.'

111

'Yes, it is. I was speaking to Uncle Vincent after Mother's funeral and he asked what I intended to do with my future. When I said I had no real plans, he suggested I should visit him at his repository. I caught a lift with the carter first thing this morning.'

Lily turned to her aunt and smiled.

'I believe I spoke to you about this before, Lily. After his wife died, my brother threw himself into his work and as a result his business has become very successful.' She coughed, adding quickly, 'He also needs a housekeeper and has asked if I would consider the position.'

'Is that what you want, Aunt?' Lily asked.

'Well, with Rob going to Ilminster and Beth, happy living with Grace, what reason do I have to stay?' she asked, looking sad for a moment. 'After all, you'll be moving on soon, won't you?'

Lily knew what her aunt was saying was true.

'We'll always be grateful for what you've done for us, Aunt Elizabeth, especially as you insisted on paying for Mother's funeral. It was a good send off, wasn't it?'

'Yes, Lily, it was and believe you me, my dear, that was the least I could do for your poor mother. She was a fine woman, God rest her soul.' Feeling tears pricking the back of her eyes, Lily nodded. 'Of course, I'll stay and help you with the packing up. You'll need to decide what's to be done with your mother's things, though from what I can see, she had precious few. It's been a very distressing time recently, and I reckon a fresh start will be good for all of us. The only worm in the wood pile that I can see is that we'll need to take Doris and the cart with us when we go.'

Lily's heart sank. After spending many hours worrying how she was going to find a new home for her family, it now appeared she was the one who would be left without a roof over her head. As she looked at her aunt and brother standing happily before her, their new lives beckoning brightly, she suddenly felt very alone.

Chapter 12

Lily blew out the candle, then lay in her bed listening to the familiar sounds of the cottage settling for the night. A hoot sounded nearby, but whether it was from the bird or an owler, she couldn't be sure, for those devious wool smugglers who plied their trade by night had perfected their call so that it was only discernible from that of the real thing by another owler. Shivering, she snuggled further under her cover and thought of the surprises Aunt Elizabeth and Robert had sprung earlier. She was pleased for them, of course, but she couldn't help feeling a bit sorry for herself. Soon they'd be going their separate ways, and for the first time in her life she wouldn't have her family around her.

With her mind whirling like the sails on a windmill, she thought she'd never sleep, but must have dropped off eventually for the next thing she knew, the sparrows were chirruping in the thatch above. Dressing quickly, she went through to the living room where she found Robert stirring a pot of oats.

'I've prepared you something to eat, Lily. It's raw out there this morning and you'll need something warm inside you before you leave. I take it you do intend to brave the elements?' he asked, handing her a bowl of steaming porridge.

'I must, Rob; Mrs Bodney wants to discuss the project's progress before the others arrive. It's kind of you to prepare this for me, though.' She smiled at him as she picked up her spoon.

'Truth is, Lily, I'm feeling a mite guilty.'

Puzzled, she stopped eating and looked up.

'Well, I was that excited about my new position, I didn't think to ask how you're going to manage. I know you're betrothed to Tom but it will be some time before you're wed. I'd feel happier knowing you had a roof over your head and that's a fact.'

'Don't worry, brother. I intend to find somewhere in Bransbeer close to where I work. I really like my job as overseer; it's interesting and I feel I'm doing something worthwhile,' she said, pushing her half-empty dish aside. 'And when you're mastering your new trade, you'll understand what I mean. Now I must go, it doesn't do to keep Mrs Bodney waiting.' She leaned forward and kissed his cheek. 'Everything will work out, you'll see.'

Snatching up her shawl, she let herself out of the back door where, to her dismay, she was met by a bank of chilling mist. It swirled around her so that she couldn't see a thing and her fingers froze as she carefully felt her away along the damp cob wall of the cottage. Finally, she reached the barn door and Doris brayed as Lily attached the cart, clearly reluctant to leave the warmth of her straw bed.

Fearful of being late, Lily gave the donkey a good slap on her withers and urged her out onto the track.

Although it was June, the east wind was biting, stinging her ears and making her eyes water. Shivering, she pulled her shawl up over her head and peered into the mist, trying to make out where she was going. She could hardly see Doris, let alone the track ahead. Far below, to her right, she could hear the surf pounding against the rocks of the undercliff, and she had to fight her instinct to steer Doris further over to the left, but that was where the ruts were deepest. It was like riding inside a cold, grey cloud and she shuddered, remembering Tom telling her the smugglers used this very path.

How she wished he was by her side now to keep her safe. Thoughts of him made her smile, and she remembered her resolve to buy material for a new dress. Although, she'd have to wear black for a while longer, she could make one in a bright fabric and put it away in her betrothal drawer.

She was deliberating between blue or green when a prickle of unease crept up her spine, and she got the distinct feeling she was being followed. The donkey's ears, were pinned back as if she'd heard something and Lily shuddered, wishing she was safely indoors. It was foolhardy being out in this weather but she had no choice; Mrs Bodney was relying on her. Convinced she could hear the muffled sound of hoofs behind her, she tightened the reins and risked glancing over her shoulder. But all she could see was the mist swirling in sinister shapes, like ghouls suspended from the branches over the track.

To raise her spirits, she started singing one of the songs her father had taught her and as the lively tune of 'Bobby Shafto' rang out against the murk, she felt her mood lift. Then, as the cart began its descent, she again felt that tingling creeping up the back of her neck and her voice tailed off. She could hear the rattle of wheels now, and knew for certain someone was following her. She couldn't understand why they didn't try to overtake her, for Doris was hardly the speediest beast on four legs.

By the time she reached the sweep of Lyme Bay, the mist was beginning to lift and she took a quick look behind her, but there was nobody there. She shivered and tightened her grip on the reins. Then she noticed Tom's lugger pulled up on the pebbles alongside the other boats. Its red sails were tightly furled so he wasn't intending putting out to sea this morning. Her heart flipped and she peered around hopefully, but apart from the gulls scavenging, the beach was deserted. Fighting down her disappointment, she turned Doris away from the bay, and headed towards the stables of the hostelry.

Having ensured Doris was safely tethered and that she had a plentiful supply of hay, Lily pulled her shawl tighter round her and, head down against the buffeting wind, she carefully picked her way through the piles of seaweed that had been blown up off the beach and so to Mrs Bodney's cottage. To her surprise, her employer was already in the workroom.

'Good morning, Mrs Bodney,' she said, hurriedly shrugging off her wet shawl.

'Is it?' her employer replied so curtly that Lily's heart sank. 'I've been inspecting the sprigs that have been made for the flounce. The work is good but we still need lace for trimming the neck and cuffs as well as the back panel. Then, of course, there's the veil.'

'We have a lot of lace still to make,' Lily answered.

'Yes, you do. Our Queen is having the silk satin for her dress woven in Spitalfields as we speak and it's imperative everything's ready for sewing up by the time it's completed. Your ladies will be able to finish their part of the design on time, won't they, Lily?' her employer asked, looking at her searchingly.

'Yes, of course we will,' Lily, said, crossing her fingers behind her long skirts and hoping it was true.

'Good. Now, my services are needed in Honiton, so for the next two days you will be overseeing both groups of lace makers. It will mean dividing your time between here and High House but that shouldn't pose any problem. I've told the maid there to expect you today,' Mrs Bodney said.

As Lily didn't appear to have any choice in the matter, she nodded dutifully, although when she'd have time to begin her search for lodgings, she really didn't know.

'Oh, and when I return I shall need your help writing up details of our work to date and the materials used.'

'Pardon, Mrs Bodney?' Lily said, frowning.

'The Queen's Mistress of the Robes will require this information. Don't worry about it now,' said her employer, waving her hand in the air. 'I'll bid you good day and good work. Remember to weave happy thoughts through your threads.' With a brisk nod of her head, she swept out of the room.

Watching through the window as Mrs Bodney climbed into the waiting carriage, Lily wondered if the day could get any worse. At that moment she couldn't think of one single happy thought. However, there was no time to dwell on her worries for the ladies were filing in ready to start their day's work. As soon as they were settled at their pillows, she checked they knew what they had to do that morning and then made her way to High House.

Arriving outside the building, with its squared limestone frontage and tall casement windows, she climbed the three steps and knocked on the heavy panelled front door. The maid let her in and led her through to the high-ceilinged room the ladies were using.

To her relief, they were all competent lace makers, used to working without supervision. As she walked around the room, checking everything was all right, she noticed that the sprigs they were making were patterned with leaves. Her own ladies back in the workroom were making sprays of flowers. Immediately, she could picture what the lace for the Queen would look like when it was joined together. Now she could understand why Mrs Bodney had kept the work separate.

Satisfied that the ladies were happy and knew what they had to do next, she retraced her steps, impatient to resume her own work. But, as she hurried back down the lane, trying unsuccessfully to dodge the puddles that had pooled between the uneven cobbles, she felt moisture seeping through the soles of her boots. The wodge of straw she'd stuffed inside them the previous week had disintegrated; and the cold water was soaking her woollen stockings. Stamping her feet to try to restore some feeling, she was tempted to call at the cobbler's before returning to the workroom. But that would delay her and she had far too much to do. With any luck his door would still be open when she'd finished work.

Relieved to be back at Mrs Bodney's cottage, she emptied the water from her boots and hurried through to the workroom. Immediately, she could sense excitement in the air. Although apparently busy with their bobbins, the ladies were covertly watching her as she made her way round the table. She was about to ask them what the matter was when she noticed the posy of pale pink lilies bound with a contrasting blush silk ribbon, lying beside her pillow.

'Oh,' she exclaimed, 'what beautiful flowers. Where have they come from?'

'Tilda said they arrived by carriage. You lucky duck, they must have cost a fortune,' Cora observed. 'So who have you been pleasing to be sent such gifts?'

'I don't know what you mean,' Lily spluttered.

'Why don't you see who they're from?' said Mary quickly.

Looking at the eager faces staring at her in anticipation, Lily smiled nervously. Then she realized they had stopped work. Knowing it wouldn't do to fall further behind schedule, she adopted the brisk manner of Mrs Bodney.

119

'Right, come along now, everyone, back to work. We have a deadline to meet, remember.' Then, pointedly ignoring their whispers and murmurings, she picked up the flowers and carefully set them on the sill of the window. Settling herself at her pillow, she picked up her bobbins and hoped the other lace makers would follow her example.

Although her hands worked calmly, inside, her thoughts were gathering pace. The flowers were beautiful, but what did they mean? Who could have sent them? And why? Although she could feel the curious glances that were being cast her way, she studiously ignored them. They all had enough to do without added distractions. With luck, they'd forget about the flowers.

The church clock struck noon and relief flooded through her as she rang the little bell. But instead of filing outside as they normally did, the ladies remained on their stools looking at her expectantly.

'Go on, Lily, open your card. We're dying to find out who the flowers are from. Or are you too grand to share things with the likes of us now?' Cora challenged.

'Please do, Lily. Nobody's ever sent me flowers,' pleaded Anna, wistfully.

Seeing they weren't going to move until she'd satisfied their curiosity, Lily got up and carefully detached the envelope from the flowers. Then, drawing out the card, she stared at the black letters but they blurred before her like scattering ants.

'Come along, everyone, we mustn't intrude upon our overseer's privacy,' Mary said, noticing her concern. 'Let's all go outside and have our break. I don't know about you, but I'm famished.'

As they clattered out to the yard, Lily went over and picked up the flowers. They were beautiful, their subtle fragrance reminding her of something she couldn't quite put her finger on. Gently, she traced a finger over the bell-shaped petals, marvelling at their silky softness. Then she gasped. Lying in their midst was a single blood-red rose. Suddenly, the lilies no longer smelled fragrant. Instead the room was suffused with cloying sweetness, and she snatched up the bell.

'Tilda, please put these in water and take them through to the parlour,' she ordered. Then before the girl could ask any questions, she hurried outside, breathing in the fresh air to clear her lungs.

Chapter 13

All afternoon, Lily ignored the curious stares and whispered exchanges that stopped whenever she looked up. Finally, when the shadows had lengthened, and she could call a halt to the day's work, she breathed a sigh of relief.

Still hoping to catch the cobbler, for she knew he too worked very long hours, she waited until the last of the ladies had left the workroom and then followed them out into the street. To her surprise, Tom was sitting on the wall outside and all thoughts of getting her boots repaired vanished. He seemed oblivious to the lace makers huddled in a group nearby, throwing speculative glances their way. Obviously they'd deduced he was unlikely to have sent the flowers, for a fisherman's wages would never stretch to such luxuries.

His eyes lit up when he saw Lily and, taking hold of his arm, she led him down the hill, away from the others.

'It's nice to see you, Tom,' she said, snuggling closer, breathing in the mixture of salt and sea that was him.

'I was wondering if you'd time for a cold drink before you return to Coombe?' he asked. She glanced down at her boots. Oh, what the heck, they'd last another day or so.

'That would be lovely, Tom,' she said, smiling up at him.

They sat together looking out over the harbour and for the first time that day Lily felt herself relaxing.

'This fruit drink's really refreshing,' she said, having almost drained her jug in one go.

'That it is. Eliza makes it herself. Says the recipe's been handed down in her family for generations. You should ask her how it's made, then you could make us some when we're wed.'

She nodded then, remembering her news, began telling him about her aunt's housekeeping position and Robert's apprenticeship.

'The trouble is they'll be moving to Ilminster and taking the donkey-cart with them,' she finished.

'Well, Lily my love, I'm right pleased for Robert. It would've been hard for him to go from being man of the house to nothing when you move out.'

'I must confess I hadn't thought of that,' she replied, feeling guilty.

'You've had a lot in your bowl recently. Will Beth be staying with Mrs Goode when they go?'

Another stab of guilt pricked her. 'Aunt Elizabeth says as she's settled so well it's best to leave her. I called to see her after you left yesterday and she was really happy. She showed me the lace she'd made and it's really good. Mother would have been so proud of her,' she said, looking sad for a moment. 'Perhaps we could take her down to the beach at Coombe Head for a picnic one day soon?' she suggested, brightening.

'Don't see why not, Lily. It would do us all good. We could take young Harriet as well and give Mrs Goode a break.' Lily smiled fondly at him, thinking how thoughtful he could be. But his next words shattered her good mood. 'Still, going back to what we were talking about. That just leaves you. It's not long until your eviction notice expires, is it?'

'I know, and I am giving careful consideration to what I'm going to do,' she said, smiling sweetly at him.

He took a long swig of his drink, then looked at her speculatively.

'I don't know what's been going on up at the manor, our Lily, but you can rest assured I'll get to the bottom of it.'

She took a breath to calm herself and then forced a smile.

'And I don't understand why you should think anything's been going on, Tom. Isn't it reason enough that I want to stay working for Mrs Bodney?'

'All I want is your happiness, Lily, but I can't

123

help feeling you are keeping something from me. Without complete trust between us, we cannot have a true relationship. Promise you'll tell me if anything's wrong?' he asked, peering at her so earnestly she had to look away.

'Maybe you could look for lodgings here in Bransbeer now you have only yourself to worry about. Just think of all that travelling you'd save each day. I'll ask Mother if she knows of anyone with a room to rent,' he continued, looking pleased with his suggestion.

'What a good idea, Tom,' she exclaimed, as if the thought had never occurred to her. If his mother knew of anywhere, that would be such a help.

'Oh, Lily, if it wasn't that you was in mourning, I'd suggest we marry right now for I'm sure we could scrape enough together to get ourselves started.'

Lily grimaced. There was nothing she'd like better, but people would say it was disrespectful and she didn't want to begin their married life with a cloud hanging over them.

All the way home, her thoughts raged as turbulent as the weather was becoming. Tom's words about trust kept going round her head.

Involuntarily her thoughts went back to the Harvest Supper. She shuddered, remembering how she'd been ferrying dishes along the dingy hallway towards the scullery, when the squire had pounced out from behind the linen cupboard. Laden down with crockery, she'd ducked and dived as his slug-like hands reached out, attempting to paw her private places while making the most lewd suggestions. How she hadn't dropped one of his precious plates she'd never know. Steely determination to avoid both his advances and having her wages docked for any breakages had been uppermost in her mind. It was later that the feelings of revulsion had really hit her. It was the squire who'd made the advances, ensuring he'd caught her when she was alone. Never ever had she given him one ounce of encouragement. Her conscience was clear, she thought, remembering Tom's words about trust.

It was only as she was leading Doris into the barn that she remembered she hadn't mentioned the flowers. But as she let herself in through the scullery door all thought of Tom vanished.

'Have you had a good day, my dear? Aunt Elizabeth asked as she continued stacking crockery. Then before Lily could answer, she said, 'Oh, before I forget, Lady Clinsden is delighted you've decided to accept the position at the manor and wishes to discuss details of the summer ball. She'd be obliged if you would call upon her first thing on the morrow. I must say I was surprised. I didn't know you'd changed your mind.'

Lily's heart sank.

'I haven't. In fact, I've already told the squire I'll be continuing to work for Mrs Bodney and won't be accepting his position. Nor will I be serving at table at their summer ball.'

'Well, her ladyship seems to think otherwise, Lily, so you'll have to make your intentions plain,' her aunt continued.

Lily nodded, distracted by the delicious aroma wafting from the pot over the fire. As often seemed to be the case these days, she'd quite forgotten to eat her noon piece.

'I'm famished and need something to eat before I drop dead on the flags.'

'Davey called by with a rabbit for the pot so I've made a nice soul-sticking stew for supper. They say poachers always make the best gamekeepers,' Aunt Elizabeth laughed, giving a roguish wink. Impatiently, Lily watched as her aunt ladled a generous amount into a dish and cut her a hunk of bread. Good old Davey, she thought. Many a time, when their larder had been bare, he'd called by with a rabbit or pigeon he'd chanced upon.

'Robert's been clearing out the barn and chicken coup. He's taken the fowl up to Grace as we'll not be able to take them with us,' Aunt Elizabeth said.

'That was a kind thought,' said Lily, as she mopped up the last of the savoury juices with her bread.

'He says he wants to leave everything as neat as a needle,' Aunt Elizabeth continued, and Lily smiled to herself. She was going to miss her aunt with her mixed-up sayings.

'I've put your mother's things in a pile on your bed. There's not much of any use. Even her dresses are all worn through, though you might find the material useful for rag rugs.'

Lily had a sudden vision of her and Tom sitting in front of the fire, hooking strips of material into sacking, then realized her aunt was still speaking.

'You'll want to keep her wedding ring and Bible, of course.'

Lily looked up in surprise. 'Surely, she was wearing her ring when she was buried?'

'What, so that the gravies could filch it? I think

126

not, our Lily,' her aunt snorted. 'What those thieving scoundrels get up to after a body's been buried is nobody's business.'

Lily shivered and was pleased that she'd finished eating her stew.

'Anyhow, you'd best write a note to Lady Clinsden so she knows what's happening.'

Robert, hobbling into the room at that moment looked at Lily meaningfully.

'It's all right, Aunt Elizabeth. I'll see her ladyship gets the message first thing. You look tired, Auntie, why not get on home now?' he said.

'You're right, Rob, I am, so I'll bid you both good night,' Aunt Elizabeth said, pulling her shawl around her.

When she'd left, Lily smiled at her brother.

'Thanks, Rob. I think I'll take a look at Mother's things before I turn in. Good night,' she said, going over and pecking his cheek.

Walking into the bedroom where her mother had spent the last few months of her life, Lily saw the little pile of clothes with the Bible and wedding ring lying on top. Picking up the golden band, she caressed it gently. Although it was now thin and slightly misshapen, she knew it had been her mother's most precious possession. Gently she touched it to her lips then slipped it onto the third finger of her right hand Standing alone in the dark room, her throat tightened and hot tears flowed like lava down her cheeks. 'Goodbye, Mother dear,' she whispered, for only now had it sunk in that she would never see her again.

She woke next morning feeling drained yet somehow cleansed inside. The air was bracing and by the time she trundled the donkey-cart into the hostelry stable yard at first light, her spirits were lifted. She knew her mother would want her to be happy. Having been a proficient lace maker herself, she'd have been proud her daughter had been chosen to make lace for the Queen, especially as she'd been the one to teach her the craft. Although Lily preferred working in the company of others to sitting by herself for long hours at a stretch, all this travelling was very time consuming. If she could find lodgings in Bransbeer, she and Tom would have more time to spend together.

Feeling brighter than she had for a long time, she handed the reins to Ned who, as usual, was looking the worse for wear, and hurried towards Mrs Bodney's cottage.

'Lily!' Hearing her name, she turned and saw Mary puffing along the lane behind her.

'Morning, Mary, isn't it a beautiful day?' she said brightly and the other woman eyed her sharply.

'Aye, now the blow's cleared. Look, I wanted to speak to you about the card that came with those flowers. It's been playing on my mind all night...' But Lily had seen Tom hurrying towards them and waved.

'Tom. What a nice surprise,' she exclaimed. 'I don't usually see you at this time of day.'

'I'll go on then, shall I?' snapped Mary, annoyed at being interrupted, but Lily was smiling up at Tom and didn't hear.

'I've not got long. The pots need baiting up,' he said, catching his breath. 'I spoke to Mother last night and she mentioned Miss Chicke has a

128

room coming vacant. She runs the lodging house next to High Field up on Long Hill. Mother says it's respectable so her rooms get taken quickly.'

Lily's spirits rose higher still. 'That's just past High House, isn't it? That could be very convenient. Thank you, Tom,' she said, clapping her hands together excitedly. 'I'll see if I can pay Miss Chicke a visit during the noon break.'

It was a quiet morning, and whilst the ladies worked diligently at their pillows, Lily walked over to the table and began counting the pile of finished sprigs. To her relief, the lace makers' hard work had paid off and she calculated they were back on schedule at last.

As the church clock chimed noon, she rang the bell for their break and was just snatching up her shawl when she noticed Anna was screwing up her eyes, a worried frown creasing her face.

'Is something wrong, Anna?' she asked, but the older woman shook her head and scuttled outside. Anxious to be on her way, Lily hurried from the workroom.

As she made her way up the main street, past the church and on towards the lodging house by High Field, she prayed the room hadn't already been taken. Fighting down the butterflies that appeared to be enjoying a summer ball of their own in her stomach, she knocked on the door of the lodging house.

A small, mouselike woman with tawny hair tied up in a bun answered almost immediately. However, there was nothing mouselike about her manner.

'Yes?' she barked, looking Lily up and down.

'Good afternoon. Miss Chicke? My name is Lily Rose and I understand you have a room to rent.' There was silence for a few moments whilst she was subjected to intense scrutiny from the woman, whose dark eyes reminded Lily of the black flints that jutted out of the chalk cliffs. Finally, she sniffed then motioned her inside. Lily followed her down a narrow passage that clearly never saw any daylight. However, the room she was shown into, although sparsely furnished, was neat and clean.

'Someone recommend the room?' Miss Chicke asked.

'Yes, Mrs Westlake. Her son, Thomas Westlake, is my betrothed.'

Miss Chicke sniffed and looked as if she was sucking on a lemon. 'I'll have you know I run a respectable establishment and don't tolerate any goings-on. No men are allowed in these rooms at any time. Do I make myself clear?'

Lily nodded, wondering what this sour little woman could possibly know about men and 'goings-on', as she put it. She must be naïve if she thought they were confined to the bedroom. Besides, that tiny bed would surely only accommodate one body, and a small one at that. With a start she realized Miss Chicke was still speaking and quickly turned back to face her.

'Front door is locked prompt at 10 o'clock each night. Meals, by arrangement, no cooking in rooms, and facilities are shared. Laundry's extra. How old are you and why are you seeking accommodation?'

'I'm seventeen years of age, Miss Chicke, and the cottage we rent went with my father's job. He was killed when the byre collapsed earlier this year. Squire Clinsden's hired someone new to help on the farm, which is why I need to find somewhere to live.'

'I see. Sorry about your father, I'm sure. Right, I'll take a look at your testimonials then.'

'My what?' she asked.

Miss Chicke sniffed. 'Testimonials. Guarantees of your qualities and virtues. You could be anyone, for all I know.'

'Oh, I see. I'm sure my employer, Mrs Bodney, will provide one.'

'Right, and I'll need one from your present landlord too.'

Lily's heart sank, although she knew there was no reason for the squire not to provide one. Their rent had always been paid on time and they'd been good tenants. However, the thought of having to ask him for one didn't sit well with her. In fact, the idea of having to ask him for anything sickened her stomach.

'Are you sure the one from Mrs Bodney won't suffice? I'm an excellent worker and although I've only been with her a matter of weeks she's already promoted me to overseer.'

'That's as maybe, but the rules of my house dictate two must be provided,' the woman sniffed, then led Lily back down the corridor. 'If you want the room, bring me two testimonials. Otherwise there'll be others glad of the opportunity, I'm sure,' she said, sniffing again as she pushed the door firmly shut.

Out on the street, Lily took a deep breath. Goodness, the woman was a right shrew – and

Lily had thought Mrs Bodney was a tartar. Still, she'd been told respectable rooms were hard to come by and if she wanted this one she'd have to bottle her pride and ask the squire for a testimonial. She grimaced, imagining the supercilious sneer on his face when she did.

Chapter 14

As Lily hurried back to work, the sun blazed overhead and it wasn't long before her black dress was clinging to her legs, hampering her movement. Beads of perspiration trickled down her back, making her corset stick to her body. She stopped to tuck a lock of hair back under her cap, and saw a mob of youths huddled alongside the brook, goading a small boy. She smiled, remembering Tom telling her jumping the brook was regarded as a rite of passage and that no male could be regarded a man of Bransbeer until he'd fallen in at least once.

As she watched them frolicking, she couldn't help wishing she was that young again. Not that she'd ever enjoyed the luxury of such freedom; as far back as she could remember her days had been spent making lace. However, the sun sparkling on the water looked inviting, and she had a sudden urge to take off her clothes and jump in.

A burst of raucous laughter brought her sharply back to the present. Spinning round she realized she was standing outside High House. The door was open and she ran up the steps and followed the sound of merriment through to the work-room. She stood there for a few moments, but the ladies were so engrossed in their fun they didn't notice her. Rapping sharply on the table, she waited until silence descended.

'What is the meaning of this?' she asked, trying to keep her voice steady as their questioning looks turned belligerent.

'We was doing no harm,' muttered a woman she recognized as Cora's sister.

'And no work either. I'm surprised at you. Return to your pillows and I will check your work.' She watched as they slunk back to their stools and then went around the room inspecting each pillow in turn. To her relief all the lace was beautifully worked, although under the circumstances, she knew better than to remark on the fact. Walking to the front of the room, she addressed the now silent lace makers.

'You are all aware this job is confidential, are you not?'

'Course we are,' they chorused, looking af-fronted.

'Then why was the front door open? Anyone could have entered the building and with the noise you were making, you'd have been none the wiser.' There was silence.

Then a timid voice squeaked, 'It was me, miss. I went outside to relieve myself and must've forgot to shut the door when I came back. Will you tell the missus?' A young girl, not much higher than her stool, was staring at her wide-eyed. The mood of the room was sombre now as they stood there waiting for Lily's response. Instead of answering, though, she had a question for them.

'Are you going to reach your quota of work before Mrs Bodney returns?'

As one, they nodded vigorously. Fixing them with her fiercest glare, and leaving the question hanging in the air, she turned and walked out of the room. The silence behind her was palpable, and she trusted they would make up the time they'd wasted. With employment at a premium and money short, nobody in their right mind would incur the wrath of Mrs Bodney and risk losing a well-paid job like this.

On legs that wobbled like jelly after her confrontation, Lily made her way back through the village. Being an overseer wasn't easy and she hoped she'd handled the situation correctly. She just trusted her ladies weren't misbehaving in her absence.

She quickened her step, but when she entered the workroom, everyone was busy at their pillows. Gratefully she sank onto her stool but as she worked, she wondered. How could she obtain a testimonial from the squire? And if she didn't get one, how could she secure the room?

By the time the shadows had lengthened and she was able to dismiss the ladies, her head was pounding. Grateful for the sudden silence, she walked round the room inspecting their work. It all looked satisfactory and she was just breathing a sigh of relief when she reached Anna's pillow, and saw the sprig she'd been working on was badly distorted. Further examination revealed that two of the pins had been enclosed in the wrong place, and the lace was wrongly tensioned.

She then remembered that the woman had seemed to be having trouble with her eyes earlier. Why on earth hadn't she checked her work when she'd returned from High House? Sinking onto the stool by the woman's pillow, she began the arduous task of weaving back the threads. It would take her an age to rework the sprig, but she had nobody to blame but herself. The light was failing now but she daren't light a candle for Mrs Bodney would be sure to ask why it had been necessary to use one. Besides, all materials had to be accounted for. She moved her pillow directly under the window and was thankful the moon was full.

As ever, the reworking took much longer than she'd anticipated and by the time she left the workroom she was dropping with exhaustion. Clouds had covered the moon and she had to pick her way carefully over the ruts in the back lane as she made her way to the hostelry. Everywhere was sinister and silent, everything cloaked in darkness, and she could feel the hairs on her neck prickle. She couldn't help wishing Tom was with her. Suddenly, a piercing screech stopped her in her tracks. Then moments later an answering one sent her scuttling. Owlers? She wasn't hanging around to find out. Heedless of the potholes and detritus, she lifted her long skirts and ran as fast as she could towards the stables.

Finally, she gained the safety of the tumbledown building. Quickly closing the door behind her, she scrambled into the donkey-cart and pulled her shawl over her head. Her heart was beating faster than the clappers on the church bell while her stomach churned like butter. As she lay shivering in the darkness, she could hear the sound of activity outside: the sound of muffled hooves crossing the yard and the murmur of lowered voices. She jumped as something heavy hit the ground, setting the cart rocking. Then she heard the sound of casks being rolled over the cobbles. Disturbed by the noise, Doris gave a loud bray and Lily stuffed her hand in her mouth to stop herself from crying out in fright as she crouched in the darkness, waiting for the door to creak open. She was certain someone would come and investigate. Then, as suddenly as it had started, the noise ceased. Still she didn't dare move. Instead she lay there listening to the sound of her heart thumping and Doris munching her hay.

Next morning, bleary-eyed, she entered the cottage to be greeted by Tilda informing her Mrs Bodney was waiting to see her. Her stomach lurched and, worried her late night's work had been discovered, she hurried through to the parlour. Her employer was sitting in her comfy chair, staring at the tall glass vase of lilies and the familiar fragrance tugged at Lily's throat. Mrs Bodney looked up and smiled, gesturing for her to be seated.

'Good morning, Lily I trust everything went well in my absence?' she asked.

'Yes, Mrs Bodney.'

The other woman gave her a searching look. 'Then why, my dear, do you look deadly pale and have bags like pillows under your eyes?'

'I had to work late, Mrs Bodney,' Lily muttered, looking down at the floor.

'Yes, I understand even the moon had retired by the time you finally left here last night. Surely, the schedule I've set does not require you to work to such a late hour?' Lily shook her head. 'You were working, I take it, and not here for any other reason?'

Her head jerked up and she stared at the older woman perplexed. 'Any other reason? Sorry, I don't understand.'

'You were entertaining Mr Mountsford, perhaps?'

Lily swallowed, staring at Mrs Bodney as if she'd grown another head. 'Entertaining Mr Mountsford?'

'Lily, will you stop parroting me? I'm not accusing you of anything. Quite the reverse, actually. It is I who owe you an apology.'

'You owe me an apology?'

'Indeed I do. When I returned and saw those beautiful flowers, I had reason to think they were for me. I've been … that is to say, I too have an admirer.'

Lily watched in amazement as a flush swept across the older woman's cheeks. It made her look softer somehow, and with a shock she realized her employer wasn't nearly as old as she'd supposed. Then something else struck her.

'But, Mrs Bodney, you're married,' she spluttered

'Of course I'm not, Lily. The "Mrs" is a courtesy title. It commands respect from the people I trade with.'

'Oh, I see,' she said, although she didn't really.

In her book you were either married or you weren't.

'Anyway, as I was saying, I thought the flowers were for me so when I saw the card propped up against them, naturally I read it. Only then did I realize they'd been sent to you. Silly of me really as cleverly they comprise lilies and a rose. And as for that beautiful poem; who'd have thought our merchant so eloquent?'

Eloquent? What did that mean? Lily's head was spinning.

'Well, Lily, you're a lucky young lady, though I'm not sure your young man would think so. Tom, isn't it? Still, some things are best kept secret,' she said, tapping the side of her nose with her finger. 'I'm not sure why Tilda set the flowers in here, but it's probably best you put this somewhere safe,' Mrs Bodney added, handing her the card.

So the flowers were from Rupert Mountsford, she thought, placing the card in her apron pocket and cursing herself for not having listened to Mary the other morning. She started to say that she'd asked Tilda to put them in here, but Mrs Bodney was speaking again.

'Right, now back to business. Perhaps you'd care to tell me why you were working so far into the night?'

Didn't the woman ever forget anything? Lily explained how she'd seen one of her ladies blinking repetitively and looking upset; how she'd meant to check her work upon her return but after calling in to see the other ladies when she was passing High House, she'd forgotten.

'Lily, High House is right on the outskirts of

Bransbeer on the way to Seaton. How could you be passing?'

'Somebody told me of a room to let in a lodging house by High Field and I went to visit during the nuncheon break yesterday. Then on my way back I heard, um, noticed... I was outside High House and called in to see how things were going there. I was later getting back than anticipated and needed to catch up on my own work.' She could feel Mrs Bodney's eyes boring into her as she related the events of the previous day.

'And?'

'I forgot to check An– erm, this lady's work until she'd gone home and when I did it was, erm, slightly wrong.'

'So you sat up half the night reworking it?'

Lily nodded, gazing down at her boots and wondering if she was going to be sacked.

'Lily, my dear, I might be a taskmaster but I'm certainly no slave driver. The problem could surely have waited until today. Whatever did your aunt say when you arrived home halfway through the night?'

Again, Lily stared down at her boots.

'Lily, you did go home last night, didn't you?' Mrs Bodney was watching her closely and her words came out in a whisper.

'I was really tired and afraid the owlers would be on the road to Coombe, so I slept on my donkey-cart in the stable.'

'Lily, you didn't!' Mrs Bodney exclaimed, shuddering. 'But, my dear, that's quite ghastly. Anything could have happened. Why ever didn't you stay here in the cottage?'

Not liking to admit she thought the other woman would have had apoplexy, Lily kept quiet.

'Have you broken your fast this morning?'

'Don't worry, Mrs Bodney, I'm used to missing meals. I washed in the brook before I came here, so I am clean.'

'That's as maybe, but your clothes are creased. Nourishment is fuel for the body, Lily. You can't work on an empty stomach and I don't suppose you have anything with you for your noon break either?'

She shook her head and Mrs Bodney picked up her little bell and rang it. Tilda appeared so quickly she must have been standing outside the door, and when Lily looked at her she could see the girl was agog. However, Mrs Bodney's next instructions had her positively gawping.

'Tilda, take Lily upstairs to my room and set out my spare working dress and cap. Then please bring tea and toast for two in here. Lily, when you've changed into clean clothes, Tilda will take those to the wash house. Mrs Maggs can see to them when she comes on Monday. When you return we will break our fast together and then discuss the ledger we need to set up.'

Remembering the steam and backache of the Monday wash she and her mother had struggled with, Lily smiled gratefully.

The clatter of boots on the cobbles and snatches of cheery chatter heralded the arrival of the ladies for their day's work. Lily looked at Mrs Bodney.

'Don't worry, Lily, I'll see to them whilst you change,' she said, sweeping from the room.

Lily followed Tilda up the stairs and waited

140

while she laid out the black dress and cap Mrs Bodney had specified. Then as the little maid hovered in the doorway, clearly hoping Lily would confide in her, she smiled her thanks and firmly pushed the door closed.

Gazing around the little bedroom, she noticed it was clean and tidy but as sparsely furnished as the room at Mrs Chicke's had been. To her surprise, there was no evidence of any personal effects other than a hairbrush lying next to the washstand. It was in stark contrast to the parlour downstairs.

Hurriedly she changed her clothes before returning to the parlour, where she noticed the vase of flowers had been removed and a tray piled high with toast and preserve set in its place. Embarrassingly, her stomach growled but Mrs Bodney merely smiled and gestured for her to help herself whilst she poured tea for them both.

Hungrily, snatching up the toast, she bit into it. It was only after helping herself to a second piece that she noticed Mrs Bodney had cut hers into triangles and was daintily nibbling at the edge of one. Not wishing her employer to think she had the manners of a street urchin, she made a supreme effort to take smaller bites. Picking up her cup, Lily marvelled at how dark Mrs Bodney's tea always was. At home, their tea got weaker by the day as the leaves were mashed and then remashed until they were virtually drinking hot water, although she thought it would be rude to mention this. Finally, when their plates were empty and they'd drunk their tea, Mrs Bodney summoned Tilda to clear away. Then she turned to Lily.

'Right, now to work. First of all, you are right in

your assumption that Anna has something wrong with her eyes. Oh, I know you didn't name names,' she said as Lily looked worried. 'However, I have been working in the lace business long enough to recognize the signs of someone losing their sight.'

'Oh, that's terrible,' Lily gasped. 'I didn't realize it was that bad.'

'As you know it is a hazard of our trade,' her employer said, shrugging. 'Naturally, I will help her all I can. Even though it's summer, I'd let her light a candle if I could justify the expense. However, every penny I spend is vetted by the Palace.'

Lily sighed, thinking how tragic it was. It was so unfair that some had so much whilst others had to struggle.

'I will arrange for her to see Dr Trimble, but in the meantime I will let her wind thread onto the bobbins and do any other jobs we can find for her. We simply cannot afford to get behind schedule.'

'No, Mrs Bodney,' Lily agreed, knowing her employer was right, yet feeling nothing but sympathy for poor Anna. It was harsh that a woman who'd worked long hours at her lace making to provide for her family should be losing her sharp sight and yet it was indeed a hazard of their trade.

'Now are there any other problems I should know about?' Lily thought of the ladies at High House and, as if she'd read her thoughts, Mrs Bodney asked, 'What about the other ladies you've been looking after in my absence? Are they working well?'

'I think they should be on schedule. I was only able to pay a couple of visits as it takes so much time out of the working day.'

'Yes, that's true,' said Mrs Bodney, studying her thoughtfully for a few moments. Then, as was her way, she became brisk again. 'Now, we need to start making our account ready for the Queen's Mistress of the Robes. The cost of the lace for the wedding dress is estimated to be around £1,000.'

'One thousand pounds for just one dress?' Lily gasped.

'Yes, it's a royal sum. We will spend this morning setting up the ledger detailing the materials used, and then this afternoon we will work out the wages paid to date. From then on it will be your responsibility to update the necessary information on a monthly basis.' So saying, she took out a huge book, along with numerous slips of paper, which she proceeded to separate into different piles. She passed the first set to Lily.

'Now these are the purchasing invoices. You read them out and I'll enter the figures into the ledger. Then this afternoon I'll read out and you can write up the ledger.'

Lily stared at Mrs Bodney in dismay.

'Well, come along, Lily. Don't stand there gaping like a fish out of water.'

'I'm really sorry, Mrs Bodney, but I can't do this.'

'Don't be stupid, of course you can.' Mrs Bodney snapped. Time was of the essence and she was fast losing patience.

'But, Mrs Bodney, I *am* stupid. I can't read,' she wailed.

143

Chapter 15

As Mrs Bodney stared at her aghast, Lily lowered her eyes, blinking back the tears that were threatening. Determined not to cry, she concentrated on the rug on the floor, tracing its pattern with her boot as she waited for the other woman to speak. Despite her best efforts over the past few weeks, she knew she'd be asked to leave and would end up having to go into service after all. She shuddered, for wasn't the squire just waiting to make her life a living hell?

'Lily, did you hear what I said?'

She started back to the present. As if she wasn't in enough trouble she'd been caught woolgathering yet again. Her day, was going from bad to worse.

'Sorry, Mrs Bodney, I'll get my things and leave right away. Don't worry; I'll see your clothes are washed before I return them.'

'Lily, what are you wittering on about? If you'd been listening, you would have heard what I asked you. I don't suppose you can write either?'

'No, Mrs Bodney. There wasn't a charity school in our hamlet and Mother and Father couldn't afford for me to take the time to journey to the nearest one like some of my friends did. Besides, they needed the money I could bring in helping Mother with the lace making.'

'Evidently I've been away too long. I'd quite

144

forgotten things were different in these parts,' Mrs Bodney said, shaking her head. 'You're such a bright girl, Lily. And you speak so well, I'd assumed you'd been educated to charity school standard, at least. Presumably you are not the only one here who can't read or write?'

Lily shrugged. 'I really couldn't say, Mrs Bodney,' she whispered.

'Well, it's not too late to learn.'

Lily stared at her employer in disbelief. 'But I'm seventeen. Could I really learn my letters, Mrs Bodney?' she gasped.

'Yes, Lily, you could. It's something we can discuss later. In the meantime, I have no desire to lose a good lace maker and overseer. I must confess this is an inconvenience, but nothing we can't work around. It just saddens me that here we are, well into the nineteenth century, and a bright young lady like yourself has been denied the chance of even a rudimentary schooling.' She shook her head, looking up at the lilies, which Tilda had now placed on the mantel over the fire. 'Lily, the message that came with your flowers, has anyone read it to you?'

'No.'

'Did you know who had sent them to you?'

'Not until you said,' she answered quietly, bending her head in shame.

'Oh, Lily, how awful it must be not to be able to read or write,' Mrs Bodney exclaimed. 'Not only did Mr Mountsford send you these beautiful flowers, he penned a delightful poem to accompany them. If you'd like to give me the card, I could read it to you.'

Lily still couldn't understand why Mr Mountsford had sent her flowers but she was curious to know what his poem said, so, delving into her pocket, she brought out the now crumpled card and handed it over.

Mrs Bodney cleared her throat then read:

*I send these flowers to make amend, perchance my
candour did offend.*
*Oh Lily Rose of fairest face, with speedwell eyes and
dainty grace*
*Take pity on a merchant's plea; that I may take you
out to tea?*
R.M.

Lily's lips twitched and then she burst out laughing. 'Why should he want to take me out to tea when he can have a cup here?'

This time, it was Mrs Bodney's turn to shake her head. 'Lily, dear, it's terribly unkind to mock someone who clearly wishes to spend time in your company. For the sake of my business, I beg that when he next calls, you receive him courteously.'

'Yes, Mrs Bodney.'

'Now, whilst I'm certainly not asking you to compromise yourself in any way, you must understand that relations with our merchants and customers are, well, that is to say, they can be somewhat sensitive. Any suspicion that you find his approach amusing would offend him deeply and could cause him to take his trade elsewhere. Not that I'm suggesting you should encourage any improper advances, you understand,' her employer added hastily.

146

'Oh, I wouldn't. I'm betrothed to Tom, after all.'

'Indeed you are, Lily, and he is a fisherman, is he not?'

'It's a respectable living, Mrs Bodney,' she said, her chin jutting up defiantly.

'Of course it is, Lily, and apologies if I inadvertently implied otherwise. Now when Mr Mountsford next calls, I suggest you entertain him to tea here in the parlour. It's a comfortable room away from prying eyes,' she said, nodding her head in the direction of the room next door where the ladies were working. 'I know he is a respectable merchant; however, should you at any time feel uncomfortable in his presence, you have only to ring the bell and Tilda will appear.' She nodded towards the little brass bell on the table.

Like I did before, Lily thought, thinking back to the squire's visit.

She glanced around the room, taking in the comfortable furnishings and colourful rugs on the floor, appreciating for the first time how much it contrasted with the rest of the cottage. As ever, Mrs Bodney was ahead of her.

'In order to gain a good reputation and trade profitably, it is vital to appear successful. That is why I always entertain my merchants and clients in here.'

'Sort of all fur and no frock, as my dear mother would have said.'

'Appearance and perception are all,' said Mrs Bodney, pursing her lips. 'Now let's return to our earlier conversation. You've been to see a room that's become vacant so can I take it you're intending to move to the village sometime soon?'

'Yes, Mrs Bodney. We've been served an eviction order by our landlord, Squire Clinsden. Aunt Elizabeth and Robert are moving to Ilminster and Beth is staying in Coombe with our neighbour Mrs Goode. Harriet Goode is her best friend.'

'Indeed. Robert is your brother and Beth your sister?' Lily nodded. 'Your parents had just the three of you?'

'Oh, no, Timothy was born frail. He got the consumption and died when he was three, and then the twins were born sleeping. They're all buried in the churchyard along with Father and Mother,' she sighed. 'Still, at least they're together now. Do you believe in heaven, Mrs Bodney?' she asked.

'Indeed I do, Lily. It can be a comfort to think we'll be reunited with our loved ones when our time on this earth is over. Now, you need to find somewhere to live?'

'Yes.'

'And you managed to secure this room you went to see yesterday?'

'The landlady insists she needs to see two testimonials. I said you would provide one...' Lily stuttered to a halt. 'Sorry, Mrs Bodney, it would have been good manners to ask first.'

The other woman, a stickler for propriety, nodded in agreement.

'I shall of course furnish you with one, and presumably your present landlord, the squire, will as well?'

Lily was about to tell her that the squire might be difficult but, remembering it was her employer she was talking to, checked herself. 'Yes, that's right, ma'am.'

'Well, I'm sure that won't pose any problem. Now we really must get down to business, we've a lot to sort out today and I must see how the ladies at High House have been faring.'

'The lace is going to look absolutely beautiful when all the flowers and leaves are joined together. Imagine having a wedding gown as detailed as that,' Lily said, sighing.

Mrs Bodney smiled and then put a finger to her lips.

'Confidentiality; remember, Lily. Although it is becoming increasingly difficult to keep what we are doing a secret. Still, we owe it to our dear Queen to try our best. With that in mind, I think it will now probably be safer to have all the ladies working together.' Lily looked at her employer in surprise but the woman waved her away. 'You'd better return to your duties in the other room. Remember, it's your job to encourage the ladies to be as productive as possible.'

'Yes, Mrs Bodney,' she replied getting up to leave. 'Thank you for the tea and toast. It was quite delicious.' Her employer's lips twitched, though Lily couldn't think what she'd said to amuse her.

As she entered the workroom, Mary looked up and whispered, 'Your Tom was looking for you earlier. He wanted to check you were safe and said he'll be by the stables when you finish this evening.'

'Thanks, Mary. Is everything all right in here?'

The other woman looked disappointed at the change of subject but nodded and resumed her

149

work. Glancing around the room, Lily saw Cora and Nell, heads bent, deep in conversation. She coughed and they looked up quickly. When they saw her, they raised their eyebrows at each other then resumed their work. Wistfully, Lily remembered the early days when she would have been included and thought again that her job hadn't come without its price. Pulling herself back to the present, she noticed Anna was measuring out thread and winding bobbins and was pleased to see the woman humming softly to herself and looking calmer. Sinking onto her stool, Lily pulled her pillow towards her.

As she worked, her thoughts turned to Tom. It sounded as if he'd found out she'd not been back to the cottage the previous evening and wanted to know why. No doubt she'd be in trouble with her aunt too. How good it was going to be having her own room where she could come and go as she pleased – well, at least until 10 p.m., she thought, remembering Miss Chicke's stern face as she'd reeled off the rules of her house. For Lily, the day she and Tom wed and got a place of their own couldn't come quick enough.

Lost in thought and lulled by the rhythm of the bobbins, it seemed no time at all before the shadows had lengthened, darkening the room until it was impossible to work. She stood up and rang her bell indicating the day's session was at an end. Relieved, the ladies covered their pillows then stretched their stiff limbs. Calling good night, they hurried outside, their companionable chatter carrying back to her on the evening air.

Heavy-hearted, she watched as they laughed and

joked their way down the lane. They were still friendly, but their actions made it clear that now she was overseer she was no longer one of them. Moving swiftly from pillow to pillow, checking their work, she was pleased to see that the lace was perfect, and the pile of sprigs in the middle of the table growing satisfactorily. Now that Anna was winding the cotton onto their empty bobbins, the ladies could work almost continually. Thanking her lucky stars that things were going well for once, she checked the door to the workroom was bolted.

Breathing in the early evening air, laced as ever with the tang of salt, her mood lifted as she made her way towards the stables. When she'd been lace making with her mother, they'd often taken their pillows outside and worked in the fresh air.

She'd just reached the hostelry when Squire Clinsden staggered out of the door, almost falling onto the cobbles in front of her. He treated her to one of his lecherous leers, letting his gaze rove deliberately over her body as he leaned over her. Instinctively, she recoiled but he was too quick for her, his clammy fingers grasping her wrist and pulling her towards him. She could smell the liquor on his breath and for one dreadful moment she thought he was going to kiss her. Then, as if remembering he was in a public place, he let go of her so abruptly she nearly fell.

'Not long until the summer ball, young Lily,' he sneered. She was tempted to spit in his eye then remembered she needed his testimonial.

'Indeed it isn't, sir,' she replied, smiling up at him.

Encouraged by her friendly response, he grinned, clearly wondering whether to push his luck a bit further.

'Squire Clinsden, I wonder if you could please provide me with a testimonial? As you know, we shall be leaving the cottage this month and I need to secure a room in a lodging house here in Bransbeer.' He looked down at her, taking so long to reply that she wondered if she should have waited until he was sober. Then, in a snap, his manner changed.

'A testimonial can only be given once the premises you rent have been inspected and the inventory checked. Of course, had you accepted the position I so generously offered, you wouldn't be requiring one. It pays not to upset your landlord, Miss Rose, as you will soon find out.'

Before she could respond, Ned appeared, leading his lordship's bay. As he helped the squire into the saddle, Lily took the opportunity to slip away. Loathsome man, she thought. And although it was uncharitable of her, she couldn't help wishing he'd fall off and break his neck.

Chapter 16

'Lily, are you all right?' She spun round to find Tom hurrying towards her. 'I saw the squire galloping off like the devil was after him. Gosh, girl, you're trembling. Did he upset you, 'cos I'll have something to say to him if he did?'

She noticed he was bunching his fists as he spoke, and quickly reassured him. 'Heavens, no, he was three sheets to the wind.'

Tom stared at her, opened his mouth to say something, then shrugged.

She'd do her best to get her testimonial, although goodness knew how, and then have nothing more to do with the squire, she vowed.

'Did you go and see Miss Chicke?' Tom asked.

She nodded.

'And was the room still vacant?'

She nodded again, deciding she'd had enough questions for one day. 'Fancy a stroll along the shore?' she asked.

Tom gave her a searching look. 'Why not?' he said, and grinned.

But as they walked side by side along the water's edge, the events of the past few days caught up with her and she could feel her anger rising. Stopping to lean against a rock, she pulled off her boots and stockings, hitched up her skirts and stepped into the water. Ignoring Tom's startled look, she paddled around, enjoying the feel of the waves as they lapped over bare skin. As her feet cooled so did her temper.

She was damned if she going to let the sordid squire and his empty threats spoil her evening. Turning towards Tom, she saw he was frowning.

'Is something wrong?' she asked, climbing out of the, water and shaking the drops from her feet.

'Your aunt was going frantic this morning. She said she hadn't seen you last even and that your bed hadn't been slept in.'

'When did you see her?' she asked as she pulled

153

on her boots.

'First thing,' he said, frowning as he remembered. 'There I was walking past your cottage when out she came like a whirling dervish, accusing me of spending the night with you.'

'Oh, she didn't?' Lily groaned.

'Well, you can rest assured your reputation is safe, for I put her right on that score. Couldn't tell her where you were, though, 'cos I didn't know meself, did I?' he said, giving her a searching look.

'Come on, I'd best be getting back. I'll tell you what's been happening as we walk.'

When she'd finished filling him in, he was silent for a few moments.

'Lily, I know you're a kind-hearted girl but aren't you taking this all a bit seriously? You're paid to make your own lace, not other people's, and as for sleeping in the donkey-cart, well, anything could have happened. I've already warned you about those owlers, haven't I?'

'Well, nothing did, and I wouldn't expect you to understand, Tom. Anyway, what were you doing up at Coombe first thing?' she asked, as it struck her that it wasn't the first time he'd visited whilst she was away in Bransbeer.

'Ah, well now, happen that's for me to know,' he said, tapping the side of his nose. 'Let's just say I have a surprise for you, my lovely Lily. If all goes to plan, it means we can be wed as soon as you are out of mourning for your mother, God rest her soul.'

'That's wonderful, Tom, but what is the surprise?' she asked, tugging at his arm.

'Not telling you,' he chuckled. 'But as soon as

154

you've settled into your new room, I'll take you to dinner at the finest hostelry in Bransbeer to celebrate.'

'Hmm, that'll give us lots of choice then,' she teased. Well, I suppose I better get back home and face the music,' she said as they reached the stables.

'Oh, so you've remembered where your home is, albeit not for much longer.'

Lily looked up from unlacing her boots, to see her aunt standing in front of her, hands on hips, two bright spots staining her cheeks.

'I'm sorry I didn't make it home last night, Aunt Elizabeth, but I had to rework one of the lace maker's pieces. By the time I'd finished, it was dark and I was too scared to come home by the cliff path in case the owlers were out, especially with all the sheep having been sheared. Tom told me they always move the wool on as soon as they can.'

'Spent the night by yourself, did you?' Aunt Elizabeth asked sharply.

'Yes,' Lily answered, looking puzzled.

'And I was born yesterday, was I?'

'If Lily says she was working, then she was, Aunt. She's no liar,' Robert declared, coming into the room. Lily shot him a grateful look.

'It's the truth all right, Aunt Elizabeth. I always tell the truth, remember? Besides, Tom said he spoke to you this morning.'

'It wasn't him I was thinking of, young Lily. Word on the street says a certain merchant's taken a shine to you. Spend the night with him, did you?

Become his dolly mop, have you?'

Lily's eyes widened as she stared at her aunt in disbelief.

'I've no need to make extra money like that, thank you very much,' she retorted, wondering why her aunt was being so nasty. Crossing the room, she held her hands out in front of the fire to warm them.

'Are you all right?' Robert asked, following her.

'Just bone weary,' she said stifling a yawn. 'I can't say I'd recommend sleeping in the donkey-cart, though.'

Robert grimaced. 'Reckon you'll not have spent a comfortable night.'

'No, it took a while to get to sleep,' she answered, shuddering as she recalled the scary noises and how she'd cowered under her shawl. 'But I was that tired, I nodded off eventually...' Her voice tailed off as she sniffed the air appreciatively.

'Hungry? You'll not say no to some pea soup then,' he said, smiling.

'Well, don't think I'm about to wait on you, young lady,' her aunt shouted through from the scullery. 'I'm away to Grace's and my bed.'

'Good night, Aunt Elizabeth,' Lily called, but the only reply was the slamming of the back door.

'Don't fret, Lily,' Rob soothed as she stood there openmouthed. 'Aunt Elizabeth was that worried when you didn't come home that she stayed here last night. She'll have calmed down by the morning.'

'I hope so. I felt awful realizing she'd worry; but there was no way I could let her know. I could hardly call to her from Bransbeer, could I?'

156

'You've got aloud enough voice, our Lily, but happen even you couldn't shout that far.'

'Cheek!' she said, pretending to be outraged.

Chuckling, he leaned forward and ladled out some soup from the pot hanging over the fire. 'That used the last of the dried peas from our stores, but I reckon we've just enough potatoes to last until we move out,' he said, handing the cup to Lily. 'Now, tell me, why did you have to stay up half the night working on this lace? Couldn't the woman redo it herself?'

'Anna, that's her name, made a right mess of it. She's having trouble with her eyes and may be going blind, poor thing,' she said sighing. With lace making putting such a strain on the eyesight it's not an uncommon occurrence, but it would be a real tragedy for Anna. She has a hard life as it is, with a drunkard for a husband and six young kiddies to feed. If I hadn't reworked the lace she would have been in trouble, we would have been behind schedule, and Mrs Bodney wouldn't have been pleased.'

'It's a really important job, this one, then?'

'Yes, it is. When it's finished and you find out who we're making it for, you'll be amazed, Rob.'

Gently easing himself up from the chair, he patted her shoulder. 'I'm sure. Now sup your soup and I'll fetch some bread. I hid a heel in the cupboard in the scullery,' he said, grinning as he hobbled from the room. She smiled and took a sip. As the liquid slipped down her throat, warming her insides, she felt herself relaxing at last. Then, when Rob returned with her bread, he sat quietly watching the fire whilst she ate it. But as soon as

157

she'd finished, she heard him clearing his throat. A sure sign he had something on his mind

'Lily, this merchant Aunt Elizabeth was talking about. Is there anything between you?'

'Robert, what is all this? Mr Mountsford is just a merchant who deals with Mrs Bodney.'

'Did he send you flowers?' he asked, watching her closely.

'How do you know about those?' she gasped.

'Aunt Elizabeth took some clean clothes down for Beth earlier. Apparently, when Mrs Goode went to Bransbeer to collect her provisions, Molly thought it her duty to pass on what she'd heard.'

'Molly. I might have known. Honestly, I swear I'll silence that tattle-tale permanently one of these days,' she burst out, remembering the girl had delivered Mrs Bodney's victuals the day before. Clearly, she'd taken advantage of the woman's absence and snooped around. Robert stared at her in surprise and, shocked by her outburst, Lily stared down at the floor.

Robert cleared his throat again. 'Look, Lily, I don't mean to pry; but I worry about you. This Mr Mountsford is obviously a man of the world and you, well, you've led quite a sheltered life here at the cottage.'

'I know how many beans make what, though, and I swear there's nothing between us. Yes, he did send me flowers,' she said, 'but only because he thought he might have offended me.' Seeing the look of relief spreading across his face, she smiled. It was nice having her big brother looking out for her. 'Besides, you know Tom's the one for me.'

'Tom's a fine man and a good friend, but he

158

cares that much for you, Lily, he'd get mighty mad if he thought anyone had eyes for his betrothed.'

'Rob, you do worry so,' she said, patting his arm.

'As I said, people like to talk and now with this Mountsford on the scene, well...'

'Mr Mountsford is just a merchant who deals with Mrs Bodney,' she repeated.

'He's a merchant who likes you well enough to send you flowers. His kind lead a different life from ours, Lily. He might try and tempt you with the finer things of life. But then he'll expect you to—'

'Oh, Robert, don't you start,' she said, sighing. 'Mrs Bodney was saying something similar earlier. Fishing's an honest way to earn a living, and now Tom's baiting up the pots as well he's bringing in more money for when we wed.' Eager to change the subject, she asked, 'Are you looking forward to going to Ilminster?'

'Oh, Lily, I can't wait to feel useful again. I never dreamed I'd get the opportunity to learn a new trade. Who knows, I might even make you and Tom a clock for your wedding present.'

She smiled fondly at him. 'That would be something to treasure, Rob,' she said, stifling a yawn. 'Now, if you don't mind, I'll bid you good night. As you reminded me earlier, it's less than three weeks till we flit, and I haven't even begun packing my things.' She bent and kissed his cheek. 'You will keep in touch when you move, won't you?'

'Nothing will keep me away from your wedding, little sister,' he said, his eyes bright with emotion.

When Lily was alone in the room she used to

share with her mother and Beth, the events of the day caught up with her. Undressing quickly, she sank thankfully into bed. However, sleep eluded her and she lay in the darkness thinking back over the past few days. Should she have told Tom about the flowers? Surely, he would understand they were given as a peace offering? There again, Molly was a troublemaker and might make it her business to tell Tom before Lily next saw him. She would get up early and see him before he sailed. How much easier it would be when she was living in Bransbeer and they could spend more time together. But would the squire give her a testimonial? And if he did, would the room still be available?

Finally, she fell into a restless doze, only to be plagued by busy dreams where the squire was chasing her around the cliffs, his slug-like fingers greedily reaching out to grab her. He was being chased by Rupert Mountsford, who was being chased by Tom. Round and round the cliffs they all ran, faster and faster, until she was so dizzy she spun off the edge and fell into the sea.

Chapter 17

Next morning, Lily woke later than she'd planned and by the time she arrived in Bransbeer Tom's boat, along with the rest of the fleet, was already heading for the deeper waters off Lyme Bay.

Promising herself she'd tell him about the

flowers the next time they met, she stabled Doris and made her way to Mrs Bodney's cottage. She had a lot of work to catch up on so the extra time would be well used. However, she hadn't long been at her pillow when the maid popped her head round the door.

'Mr Mountsford wonders if you could spare him a moment?' she whispered.

'Oh, Tilda,' she groaned. 'Can't Mrs Bodney see him?'

But the girl shook her head. 'Madam's out this morning.'

'Very well,' she said, smothering a sigh as she smoothed down her skirts and hurried through to the parlour.

'Mr Mountsford, what a pleasant surprise. How can I be of help?' she asked briskly. He jumped up, smiling at her so brightly, she couldn't help smiling back.

'Rupert, please,' he reminded, then nodded towards the mantel where the lilies were in full bloom. 'I see you received my flowers. I trust they were acceptable?'

'They are beautiful, Rupert, thank you,' she said, still feeling awkward at using his personal name.

'I felt I must ask because, to be honest, I'm puzzled to see them here in Mrs Bodney's parlour,' he said, frowning.

Remembering her employer's instructions to keep him happy, Lily thought quickly.

'My journey home from work entails riding in a donkey cart. Alas, all that bumping would cause the petals to fall and I thought it would be a shame to ruin such beautiful flowers.'

'I understand,' he said, looking relieved. 'And the card that accompanied them?'

'I have it right here in my pocket,' she said, slapping her apron.

Positively beaming now, he continued, 'Then may I ask if you've had time to consider my invitation to join me for tea?'

'Oh, yes. I'd be delighted to offer you tea here in the parlour,' she said quickly and although he smiled politely, his eyes sparked with mischief.

'That would be most agreeable. That is, if you're sure I won't be keeping you from your work.'

'I'm sure Mrs Bodney won't mind, as long as we are not too long,' she said, ringing the little bell. Tilda appeared, seeming unusually flustered.

'A tray of tea for two, please, Tilda,' Lily said, frowning at the maid, who seemed to be studying the floor with unusual interest.

However, Rupert proved to be an entertaining visitor, and she soon forgot Tilda's curious behaviour, as he regaled her with amusing tales of his travels between London and Devonshire. The moment he'd finished his tea, however, he jumped to feet, declaring he had kept her from her work long enough.

'Before I forget, please could you see that Mrs Bodney receives this?' he said, handing her a small package.

'Yes, of course,' she said, setting it down on the table.

'I'd be obliged if you'd hand it to her personally, Lily,' Rupert said frowning.

'Why, yes, of course,' Lily said, surprised at his insistence. Picking up the package she popped it into her apron pocket.

'It's something she particularly likes and I'd hate for her not to receive it,' Rupert explained, smiling. 'Thank you for your kind hospitality, Lily. I hope you will let me return it by joining me for supper one evening.' A knowing grin spread across his face and she knew that not for one moment had he been taken in by her ploy of entertaining him here in the parlour. However, Mrs Bodney's instructions were to keep him happy, so she coaxed her lips into a smile.

'Thank you, Rupert,' she said, ringing the little bell. Relieved when Tilda appeared, she hardy noticed that once again, the little maid kept her eyes averted.

That evening, as soon as the ladies had left the workroom, Lily followed them out, bolted the door and hurried to the donkey-cart. She was concerned that Rupert might appear and she had no wish to make excuses to him or her aunt. As she began the descent into Coombe, it suddenly struck her that in her haste to avoid Rupert, she'd forgotten about seeing Tom.

'Oh, well, Doris, it seems another early morning's called for,' she said. The donkey brayed, but whether it was in response to her statement or because she'd spied the cottage and knew supper was waiting, Lily couldn't he sure.

Drawing up outside the cottage, Lily was surprised to see the squire's bay tethered to the fence. Her heart sank. Was there no escaping the man? Then she saw Rob, looking grim, hobbling towards her.

'Squire Clinsden's inside. He's in a right old

163

temper and going through all your things,' he cried.

'What?' Lily gasped. 'Why?' Looking up, she saw Aunt Elizabeth wringing her hands as she hurried. towards her.

'Oh, Lily, what have you done?'

'What on earth's the matter?' Lily asked, rushing into the cottage. Her heart beat faster as she heard banging and cursing coming from her room. Then, the squire burst out, brandishing something aloft.

'Thief!' he hissed at Lily, but it was the look of pure malice in his eyes that made her blood go cold. He was almost beside himself as he marched right up to her. 'Miss Rose, I came here to carry out the inventory prior to you and your miserable family leaving and what do I find? Stolen property, that's what!'

Bewildered, Lily stuttered, 'But you said you were going to send your agent.'

'Isn't it just as well I came myself then?' he retorted. 'Miss Rose, I order you to attend the courtroom at noon tomorrow where you will be tried and sentenced. You will then see what happens to common thieves.'

'What?' she gasped. It was then she noticed what it was he was holding. 'Oh, those were on the donkey-cart when I came out of work one evening. I was going to find out who left them there but, with all that's happened in the past week, I forgot.'

'You forgot. How convenient,' the squire sneered. Well, you can explain that to the Justice of the Peace tomorrow.'

'Now come on,' Rob began, but the squire

whirled around. 'And as for you, you are to be off these premises by sundown tomorrow or I'll set my dogs on you.'

'But there's still over two weeks until quarter-day. Where will we go?' he gasped.

'I neither know nor care about you or her,' the squire snarled, pointing at Aunt Elizabeth. Turning to Lily he gave, a mocking laugh. 'However, you, Miss Rose, being a common thief, won't have to worry for you will be housed in a secure cell,' he declared. Then, before they could answer, he stalked from the room, his cruel laughter following after him.

They stood there in stunned silence for some moments before Lily finally found her voice.

'A common thief, am I? Well, I'll show that Justice of the Peace. You wait and see,' she declared bravely, although she felt sick inside.

'But, Lily, Squire Clinsden *is* the Justice of the Peace,' her aunt cried.

'Well, he's lying and he won't get away with it,' she said. 'The truth will out, isn't that what they say?'

But Rob looked at her pityingly. 'I remember when old Miss Keys upset him. He accused her of stealing from him and had her sentenced to sixty days...' Aunt Elizabeth gave him a warning look and Rob stuttered to a halt.

Lily sank into the chair and buried her head in her hands. 'You will be there to support me, won't you?' she whispered.

'We'll do what we can, Lily, but we've to clear this place of our things, remember?' Rob said. Looking up, she saw the grim expression on his face and the full implication of the squire's visit hit her. Suddenly she felt very afraid.

'You do believe me, don't you, Tom? I didn't steal those things, really I didn't. I was up all night worrying about it.'

Tom slumped back against his boat, shaking his head as if he couldn't take in what she'd told him. Lily searched his face, anxiously waiting for him to say something.

'Of course I believe you. There's no one more honest than you, Lily,' he said, squeezing her arm. Leaning against him, she willed his warmth to stop the shakes that had been racking her body since the previous evening. No matter how hard she blinked, the tears still coursed down her face. Gently, he took out his kerchief and wiped them away.

'Hush, now, don't go getting yourself into a state again. Your eyes are all red and puffy as it is, and fretting ain't going to help none, is it?'

'I know, but if I'm found guilty, the squire could send me to gaol. Oh, Tom, I'm so scared. Why didn't I take that veil and glove into the hostelry when I found them on the donkey-cart?' she cried. 'And if I'd begun packing my things for the move when I should have, I'd have come across them.'

'Now, now, Lily, you've had more than enough to worry about recently. What I'd like to know is who put them in the cart in the first place?' He glanced up and saw they were attracting attention from the other fishermen. 'Come on,' he said, taking her arm, 'let's get something hot inside you. I bet you've had nothing to eat or drink this morn?'

'Oh, I couldn't. I'd be sick,' she grimaced but, ignoring her protests, he took her arm and led her up the beach.

'What about your boat?' she asked, glancing back at his lugger. With its red sails half hoisted, he'd obviously been preparing to put out to sea.

'Bugger the boat, Lily, this is more important. First of all we'll go and see Mrs Bodney and tell her what's been going on. Then I'm taking you home, young lady. No, don't look at me like that,' he said as she opened her mouth to protest. 'You can't think on an empty stomach, and you'll need your strength to defend yourself. Don't worry, Mother's out visiting so we won't have to tell her anything.'

She let out a sigh of relief. Much as she liked Tom's mother, she really didn't have the strength for any more questions this morning. And what if she thought Lily really was a thief?

Tom called to a wizened man who was sitting atop a lobster pot, giving the impression of mending his nets, although Lily knew he'd been watching them keenly.

'Hey, John, tell Michael to skipper the boat. Something's come up.'

'Right ye are, Tom,' he answered. He was about to say something else but, seeing the scowl on Tom's face, shrugged and turned back to his nets. Tom took Lily's arm and together they trudged back up the beach.

Mrs Bodney took one look at Lily's tear-stained face and ushered them straight into the parlour. Then, instead of ringing her bell as was her wont, she called through to Tilda to bring them cups of strong sweet tea immediately.

'Do sit down and tell me what's happened,' she said, looking enquiringly at Tom.

'Forgive our intrusion but Lily's in a spot of bother.'

Mrs Bodney turned to Lily, smiling encouragingly, 'Come along, my dear, it can't be as bad as all that surely, unless you've spilled the beans on what we are making here?' she said, only half joking.

'Of course not, as if I would,' Lily spluttered. 'No, it's the squire. He came to the cottage yesterday to take the inventory himself. He's accused me of stealing.'

'Surely, there must be some mistake. I'd stake my life that you are an honest person, Lily Rose.'

'That's what I said,' Tom declared.

'I am, really I am but...' she stuttered to a halt as hot tears trickled down her cheeks once more. Tilda, appearing at that moment with the tray of tea, looked quite alarmed.

'Thank you, Tilda, that will be all,' Mrs Bodney said firmly, and the maid scuttled away.

'Right, Tom, tell me exactly what this is about.' Her calm manner encouraged him to repeat what Lily had told him earlier. When he finished, the room was silent apart from the tick of the clock on the mantel above the fireplace.

Then Mrs Bodney said, 'Lily, I want you to think hard. Are you absolutely certain that you'd never seen this veil and glove before you found them on the donkey-cart?'

'I swear it. Oh, why didn't I take them straight

into the hostelry?' she wailed, dabbing at her eyes with Tom's kerchief.

'Introspection's a wonderful thing,' her employer replied. Then, seeing the puzzled look on both their faces, added, 'It means that if we knew what the future was going to bring, it would save us a lot of trouble. The mystery is, who put these things on your donkey-cart and why?'

Mrs Bodney glanced in Tom's direction before continuing. 'Lily, may I ask you something delicate?' Puzzled, Lily nodded. 'Have you in any way upset the squire?' Mrs Bodney's eyes were boring into Lily. She felt her cheeks burn.

'Ay, I've been wondering that,' Tom said, staring at Lily as well.

'Well, erm, er...' Lily stuttered, wringing the kerchief between her fingers.

'Look, Lily, if we're to get you acquitted, we need to find a motive.'

'We?' she said, looking at Mrs Bodney in surprise.

'Yes, Lily. I, for one, am anxious to get to the bottom of this and I'm sure Tom is too.' He nodded vigorously. 'But in order to do that, you need to answer my question. Now think carefully and then start at the beginning. It's the best way, I always find.'

'Yes, you've told me that before, Mrs Bodney,' she said. 'It was at the Harvest Supper. I'd been serving at table and the squire, he...' she shuddered to a halt.

'Yes, go on, Lily,' Mrs Bodney encouraged.

'He, well, he jumped out on me from the linen cupboard and tried to touch my–'

'I knew it!' Tom shot to his feet, fists clenched. 'I'll see that bast–'

'Tom, please sit down,' Mrs Bodney interrupted. 'I can understand you being upset but we need to ascertain the facts. Now, Lily, did anything actually happen?'

'No. Other than I had to keep dodging his blinking hands. Like an octopus, he was. I called him a few choice names, I can tell you.'

'Did anyone see or hear you?' Mrs Bodney asked, watching her closely.

'No, I don't think so,' she said.

'Well, I think Molly might have,' Tom said. 'She's been insinuating about you and the squire for ages now. Goes on and on, she does; has a right thing about it.'

'That's 'cos she wants you back,' Lily blurted out.

'Wants me back where?' he asked, looking puzzled.

'She wants you to step out with her again, like you did before you met me.'

'What?' he spluttered. 'Me and that fat, gossiping besom? Oh, Lily my love, you do have some weird ideas in that woolly head of yours. The only time Molly and me was together was when we attended lessons at the charity school. Even then I kept well away from her, I can tell you.'

'But she said–'

'Look, excuse me for interrupting, but I think this is something you two can sort out between yourselves later on,' Mrs Bodney stated. 'If we are to have our strategy worked out by noon we must stick to the matter in hand.' She got to her

170

feet and began pacing the room. 'You say you refused the squire's advances, Lily. Has he made any since?'

Lily looked down at the floor and nodded. 'He wanted me to accept a position at the manor when I leave the cottage.'

'And you declined?'

'Oh, yes, Mrs Bodney. I wanted to stay working here on the ... well, you know. Anyway, the position he offered meant living in and that would mean ... well, I'd be on hand, as it were, if he were to...'

'Yes, quite,' replied Mrs Bodney, sighing and sinking back into her chair. 'I think we get the picture.'

'Oh, Lily, my love, why ever didn't you tell me?' asked Tom. 'I'd have had it out with him and made sure he didn't bother you again. I said we was to have no secrets between us.' He shook his head sadly, and sat there twisting his cap in his hands.

'I know, Tom. But you know what they say about there being no smoke without spark, and I couldn't take the risk that—'

'Quite,' said Mrs Bodney. 'Does Lady Clinsden know about the squire's behaviour towards you, Lily?'

'I don't know but he's not exactly subtle. Poor woman, whatever made her marry a swine like that? She seems such a nice lady.'

'She is, Lily, but things aren't always straightforward for the upper classes. Surprising as it may seem, life can be more complicated for them. They have to satisfy parental requirements, especially where the matter of estates is concerned. Now,' she said briskly, jumping to her feet, 'I have some enquiries to make, so I suggest you go and get some fresh air. I shall see you at the courtroom at noon.' And with that, she ushered them out of the door so quickly they didn't see the worried look on her face. She knew only too well how the squire stopped at nothing to get his own back on anyone who crossed him.

Chapter 18

As Tom and Lily made their way to the courtroom, they may have been walking side by side but the gap between them was wider than the brook. Suddenly she could stand it no longer.

'I'm sorry I didn't tell you about the squire, Tom,' she burst out, turning towards him. He stopped walking and looked at her so sadly her heart seemed to hit the cobbles.

'So am I, Lily, love,' he said, giving a deep sigh. 'It pains me to think you didn't trust me enough to confide in me.'

Hearing the anguish in his voice, her heart sank. Desperate to heal the breach, she smiled tentatively up at him.

'Heaven help the squire if he pesters you again, that's all I can say,' he muttered, then gave her a wry grin. 'Come on, let's get this over with, eh?'

'Oh, Tom, it will be all right, won't it?' she asked.

'You'll be fine, Lily,' he said, trying not to think of what had happened to others who'd crossed

172

the squire. 'Come on, chin up,' he urged.

Despite the sun being overhead, Lily shivered and when she saw the crowd gathered outside, her legs nearly buckled beneath her.

'Steady, Lily,' Tom whispered, taking her arm and leading her inside.

'I bet they're all hoping I'll be found guilty so they'll have something to gossip about later,' she whispered.

A stern-faced official showed her to a seat at the front of the dingy room, but when Tom made to follow, he shook his head and pointed to the seats directly behind. Wondering how it was possible to feel so alone in a room packed with people, Lily stared down at her boots. The holes in the toes seemed to have grown even larger and the soles were coming away. She would see the cobbler as soon as she left here. Unless she was sent to gaol – the thought came unbidden, making her feel sick. Then Tom leaned forward and patted her shoulder and she nearly jumped out of her skin.

'Good luck, my love,' he whispered, and she nodded.

Nervously, she took a quick peek around and was disappointed not to see her aunt and Robert there to support her.

The voice of the court official boomed out, 'Please be upstanding.' Everyone rose to their feet as Squire Clinsden strutted regally into the room looking as if he owned the place, which, of course, he did.

'Call Lily Rose,' bellowed the official, which she thought unnecessary as she was sitting right in front of him. She stumbled to her feet and Tom

173

leaned forward, whispering to her to be strong.

'Do you, Lily Rose, swear solemnly to tell the truth?' the official demanded importantly.

'Of course, I do. I always have and always will,' Lily retorted. The squire, pompous in his role as Justice of the Peace, glared at her and she made a supreme effort to stare him straight in the eye.

The court official read out the charge that she, Lily Rose, had stolen goods belonging to Lady Clinsden, namely a black veil and one single calfskin glove. Then he held up the items cited as evidence so that everyone could see.

'I never stole anything from anyone, and I didn't know these things belonged to Lady Clinsden. They were on my donkey-cart when I went to collect it,' Lily said indignantly.

'Silence,' barked the squire, banging his gavel on the desk. 'Miss Rose, you are required to speak only when spoken to. It is not your place to question the charge brought against you.'

She glared at him, thinking how ridiculous he looked in his lopsided wig and with his face powdered. But, even from where she was standing, she could see the jubilant look in his eyes and realized he was enjoying her discomfort. Refusing to be intimidated, she continued glaring at him.

'Call my wi– Lady Clinsden,' he barked.

As Lady Clinsden walked regally to the stand, she gave Lily a reassuring smile.

'Can you identify these items, my dear?' the squire asked, smiling benignly at her as the official held up the veil and glove.

Lady Clinsden took the veil and glove, studied them carefully, then shook her head.

174

'I've never seen these items before in my life.' There was a gasp from the room as the squire clattered to his feet and turned on his wife.

'Of course you have, you stupid woman. They are yours,' he snapped.

'They most certainly are not. Besides, there is only one glove here and I would never be so careless as to mislay any of my clothing, especially when I have such a hard job getting it in the first place.' She smiled sweetly at her husband, who was turning redder by the moment.

'Of course they belong to you. I took them out of your dress–' the squire stuttered to a halt. Then, making an effort to compose himself, he forced his lips into something resembling a smile. 'My dear, clearly you are mistaken. Why, I remember purchasing these very items for you only recently.'

'You purchased these for me, recently? No, I think not, for I would have remembered such a phenomenon, husband, dear,' she said, shaking her head, 'and, for the record, I feel I must state that my dear husband is not given to generosity.' A titter rippled around the courtroom, for it was well known that the squire parted with as little money as he could get away with, unless it was for his own enjoyment. Lady Clinsden grimaced at her husband, eyes glinting like steel. 'Husband dear, I think you are rather more concerned with what a lady does not wear rather than what she does.'

At this, the courtroom was rocked by gales of laughter. The folk of Bransbeer had never seen or heard anything like it. They were in their element, looking from squire to lady, eagerly lapping up all the personal details that were being revealed.

They seemed to have forgotten it was Lily, who was on trial.

'Now, husband dear,' continued Lady Clinsden, 'if you observe the size of this glove, you will see that it fits my hand perfectly. However, it would never stretch over Miss Rose's capable working hand, so I ask you, what possible use could it serve her?'

Lily looked from the glove Lady Clinsden was holding out to her own broader hand and shook her head. Why hadn't she noticed that herself? The squire, realizing his wife was determined to outwit him, was almost beside himself with anger. His face was so suffused with colour Lily thought he would have apoplexy at any moment.

'I feel in this case, dear, you have clearly been mistaken, and Lily Rose should be found innocent forthwith.' Lady Clinsden smiled sweetly at her husband.

Seeing he had been bested by his wife and that further interrogation would only make him look more foolish, he banged his gavel, announced the case dismissed and stormed out of the court.

As Lily shook her head in bewilderment, she noticed Mrs Bodney following after him.

'Well, my dear,' Lady Clinsden said, appearing at Lily's side, 'that certainly showed him.'

'So those things weren't yours, then?' Lily asked, bewildered.

'Of course they were,' Lady Clinsden replied, laughing. 'As well the old bugger knows, and that makes it an even finer victory.'

'Now I'm really confused.'

'Well, don't be. Let's just say it's retribution.'

Her tinkling laugh echoed around the courtroom, which was rapidly emptying now the drama was over.

'Gosh, Lady Clinsden, if you don't mind me saying, you seem too nice to be married to someone like him,' Lily said, staring at the other woman, who sobered immediately.

'I agree with that sentiment entirely. Regrettably, some of us have little choice whom we marry. However, my dear, there's more than one way to skin a cat. Now if you'll excuse me, I must take my leave. The squire is sure to be drowning his sorrows in the strongest liquor known to man, and I think it would be wise if I went to stay with my sister in Sidmouth until he gets over it.' She swished her way elegantly out of the courtroom leaving Lily staring after her in admiration. She wasn't sure about her skinning a cat, though. Surely she wouldn't dirty her hands in such a manner?

'Blimey, Lily, that was a right fine turn-up.' Tom appeared at her side, a huge grin nearly splitting his handsome features. Then, heedless of the people still milling around, he leaned forward and kissed her on the cheek. Feeling dizzy from his affection and the realization she was free, she slumped against his shoulder.

'I still don't understand what that was all about.' But, at that moment, Mrs Bodny reappeared, triumphantly brandishing a piece of paper.

'Look, the squire has kindly furnished you with a testimonial, Lily,' she said, laughing as she stressed the word 'kindly'. 'Now why don't we all go back to the cottage, and I'll get Tilda to provide some refreshment.'

Lily sat in Mrs Bodney's parlour sipping her lemon drink, having declined anything stronger, for she felt quite giddy enough as it was. She couldn't believe how the events of the past hour had turned out. Not only had she been acquitted, she had the vital testimonial to secure her a room. Slumping back in her chair, she watched Tom laughing at something Mrs Bodney was saying. It struck her then how lucky she was to have their support.

'Are you all right, Lily?' Mrs Bodney asked, looking up.

'I'm fine, though still a bit puzzled by Lady Clinsden's actions.'

'Well, don't be. She has a lot to contend with, putting up with the squire. She can certainly hold her own, though.' She leaned forward, adding in a hushed voice, 'Do you know every time she sees her dressmaker she instructs her to make two identical dresses but to bill them as one item? Then, when the squire checks the account he assumes his wife has done as he's said and had only one made. As she always appears to be wearing the same dress, he has no reason to doubt her. A clever ruse, don't you think?'

'Yes,' Lily giggled, 'that's quite the smartest thing I've heard.'

'Well, you'd better not be getting ideas for after we're wed, our Lily,' said Tom, looking so affronted the two ladies laughed.

'I'm sure having such a splendid fellow as you for a husband, Lily won't have to resort to such trickery,' said Mrs Bodney, and Lily watched in amazement as Tom, normally so unassuming, puffed up like a peacock at her words.

'And I'm sure my husband will want me to do him proud when he takes me out, so he'll always make sure I have a new dress to wear,' she teased. Tom shook his head, understanding for the first time why, as his father had once told him, it was usually wisest for a man to remain silent.

'Well, Lily, I've made out a testimonial for you so I suggest you take it, along with the one from the squire, up to the house at High Field and secure that room. In the meantime, I will go and check that our lace ladies have had a productive day.'

'Oh, Mrs Bodney, I've not done any work at all today,' she said. 'I reckon you should be deducting my wages.'

But the other woman's eyes twinkled mischievously. 'That won't be necessary, Lily. You'll be pleased to hear the squire wouldn't hear of my being out of pocket for today's events.' Winking at them, she put her hand in her reticule and drew out a handful of golden coins, which she laid in a neat pile on the table in front of them. As they gasped she added, 'Let's just say, he understood it would be prudent to make some recompense for the error of his ways.'

'Oh,' said Lily, her hand flying to her mouth. 'You talking of pockets has reminded me, Mr Mountsford asked me to give you this when he called. I was going to leave it on your table but he said I was to hand it to you personally.' Fumbling in her apron, she withdrew the package and handed it over.

'Thank you, Lily,' Mrs Bodney said, not meeting her eyes. 'In future, should he have anything for me, I'd be obliged if you'd hand it over immediately.'

Lily opened her mouth to remind her she'd been away from the cottage but Mrs Bodney was waving them away.

'Right, off you go and secure your room,' she said, her composure restored.

'Yes, Mrs Bodney, and thank you,' Lily said as they took their leave.

This time their steps were lighter as they made their way through the village, but Lily's head was spinning. In less than twenty-four hours she'd been both accused and acquitted of theft.

'I can't believe how kind Lady Clinsden and Mrs Bodney have been, can you, Tom?'

'No, they've been right dandy. Though, you know, I have a feeling they were both getting their own back on that scoundrel today. Mrs Bodney seemed put out you hadn't given her that package, Lily. What was in it?'

'I've no idea. Rupert Mountsford didn't tell me.'

'Hmm, just you be careful, Lily,' he said.

She was about to ask him what he meant, but they'd reached the lodging house. Clutching her precious testimonials, she took a deep breath and rang the doorbell.

'You'll be fine, love,' encouraged Tom. 'Just think what fun we'll have when you've got your own room.' He winked suggestively at her, but before she could respond the door opened and Miss Chicke stood there glaring at them.

'Good afternoon, Miss Chicke. I've brought

the testimonials you requested,' Lily said, but the woman's eyes narrowed and, turning up her nose, she sniffed.

'Oh, have you indeed?' she said, putting her nose even higher into the air.

Lily glanced at Tom.

'I believe you said Lily could have the room if she provided two testimonials, Miss Chicke,' he said quietly but firmly.

'Yes, but that was when I thought she was decent,' Miss Chicke said, narrowing her eyes at Lily. 'You can sling your hook, missy, I'll not be having any criminals in my house, thank you very much,' she spat and slammed the door in their faces.

Chapter 19

'Well, of all the bare-faced...' Tom began, but the words died on his lips when he saw Lily's white-faced look of disbelief. He raised his fist ready to bang on the door, determined have it out with the old biddy, but she shook her head.

'No, don't bother arguing with her. I wouldn't want to lodge with a sour-faced, prejudiced woman like that anyway.'

'But she called you a criminal and that's not right. You were acquitted fairly and squarely.'

'I know. It does rather prove my point about folk thinking there is no smoke without spark, though, doesn't it?' she said, taking his arm and urging him away from the house. The sun was lowering in the sky and she shivered.

However, he wasn't ready to let it go.

'But this is different, Lily. It's your character we're talking about here,' he declared, turning to face her.

'Precisely, Tom, and as I said earlier, people like to think the worst.'

'Maybe some, but not me, Lily,' he told her. 'I love you and know you're an honest woman. If you'd trusted me enough to tell me about the squire's improper behaviour, I'd have gone to see him and then it mightn't have come to this.'

As she listened to his declaration of love, a warm feeling curled its way through her body, melting the ice that had encased her insides since she'd first heard the squire's accusations. Relieved that everything was going to be all right between them, she couldn't resist teasing him.

'And what would you have done? Challenged him to a duel at dawn?'

'No, that would've been too good for him,' he grinned. 'I'd have punctured his privates with my fishing hooks.'

'Heaven forbid,' she giggled, and Tom, relieved to see she was feeling better, pulled her into the shade of a spreading oak tree and kissed her on the lips.

'Oh, Lily, my love, if only we could set up home together right now, I'd be able to look after you properly.'

She sighed and, forgetting about propriety, snuggled into him, enjoying the feeling of being cherished.

'It's right torture being this close to you, yet not close enough, if you get my drift?' he murmured.

Feeling the heat of a blush spreading up her cheeks, she moved away, but her heart was pounding so crazily he must surely hear it.

However, instead of the pounding easing, it seemed to be getting louder. It was only when Tom pointed down the hill that she realized the noise was Doris, clip-clopping towards them. Robert was holding the reins with Aunt Elizabeth sitting alongside, and the cart looked laden as it laboured towards them. Then, when it drew alongside, she saw it was piled high with all their belongings.

'Oh, Lily, we're so sorry we couldn't make it to the court in time. The squire sent his land agent to the cottage to carry out another inspection and make sure we left. By the time he decided we hadn't taken anything that wasn't ours, it was too late,' Robert explained.

'Odious man!' Lily exclaimed, looking indignant.

'Hush, Lily,' her aunt chided, mindful of the curious stares they were attracting.

'We were glad to hear you were rightly acquitted, Lily. Mrs Goode had already heard the news when we called in to say goodbye to Beth,' Rob said.

'Yes, Grace says you're not to worry about Beth. She'll take fine care of her and you are welcome to visit any time you can. You will go and see her soon, won't you?' asked Aunt Elizabeth, looking troubled.

'We'll go and see her on the Sabbath, won't, we, Lily?' replied Tom. 'We could take her and young

Harriet down to the beach for that picnic.'

Aunt Elizabeth brightened and Lily smiled at Tom gratefully.

'Thank you, Tom, that sets my mind at rest. I'm sure Grace would appreciate a break from the girls, although she assures me Beth's no trouble. Now, we've decided to make our way directly to Ilminster earlier than planned. I've already sent word to my brother by the stagecoach that, God willing, we should be with him by tomorrow. It will take poor Doris some time to pull this laden cart. We've detoured via Bransbeer to say farewell and to give you the few things I managed to pack for you.'

Her aunt turned and rummaged behind her, then handed Lily a small parcel wrapped in sacking. 'It's just some necessities to see you all right for a night or two. The rest of your things are stored in the barn by the orchard. I'm to tell you they'll be kept safe for the next seven days. If you haven't collected them by then, they'll be disposed of.'

'Mercy me,' Lily whispered, shaking her head in disbelief.

'Well, of all the callous–' Tom burst out but Robert gently cut in.

'I know, Tom. I feel that bad myself, but we were in no position to argue. I'm just so glad Lily has you to look after her. You will take care of my little sister, won't you?' he asked, his voice thick with emotion as he looked at Lily.

'Of course I will, Rob,' Tom answered, putting an arm protectively around her shoulders and drawing her closer.

'We were relieved to hear that justice was done, Lily.' Blinking back the tears, Lily nodded before reaching up to kiss her aunt goodbye. 'I'll be back to see you as soon as we're settled. There was so much I wanted to say to you before we left,' Aunt Elizabeth said, her eyes suspiciously bright as she pressed a few coins into Lily's hand.

'But you have already been so kind, Auntie,' Lily said.

'It's not much, my dear, but perhaps you can treat yourself to some of that bright material you were talking about. I reckon you deserve a treat after all you've been through,' said Aunt Elizabeth, attempting to smile.

'Oh, Auntie, thank you,' Lily said.

'And I'll not forget that clock,' her brother said, pulling his cap back on. Then with a rueful smile, he picked up the reins and urged Doris to walk on.

Lily and Tom stood watching as the donkey-cart rattled its way up the hill. Then, as it turned the corner and was lost from view, the tears finally fell. Hiding her face in Tom's shoulder, she sobbed uncontrollably. Once again those she loved had left her.

'Come on, chin up, Lily, my love,' he said gently, taking her parcel. Choking back her tears, she smiled bravely. Lost in their own thoughts, they trudged down the hill.

As they were nearing Mrs Bodney's cottage, they heard a shout.

'Hurry up, Tom. We can't wait the boat any longer,' called Mikey, beckoning urgently.

Tom was about to answer that they could sail

without him, but Lily shook her head.

'You go, Tom. You've missed one trip already today. Anyway, I'd best go and see Mrs Bodney or she'll think I've vanished off the face of Bransbeer.'

He eyed her doubtfully, torn between staying with her and skippering his boat.

'Go on,' she urged, quickly kissing his cheek.

'Well, if you're sure,' he said, looking relieved as he handed over her things. She nodded, watching as he raced down to the boat and set about hoisting the sails. The sun, now a crimson globe, was sinking behind the horizon, its fire-spun fingers spreading out to hug the bay.

'Godspeed and come safely home, my love,' she whispered before letting herself into the cottage.

Expecting all to be quiet at this time of the evening, she was surprised to hear shouting coming from the workroom. Then the door burst open and a figure rushed, out, pushing past her and sending her package flying.

'Whatever's wrong, Abigail?' she asked, noticing the tears streaming down her cheeks. But the girl ignored her and shot out of the door.

'There you are, Lily,' said Mrs Bodney, bustling out of the workroom. 'Come through to the parlour, please. I'd like a word.' Stopping only to retrieve her things, she followed the older woman through to her inner sanctum.

'Sit down,' her employer instructed. Noticing the woman's heightened colour, Lily carefully placed her things on the floor and perched on the edge of a chair.

'The court case earlier set me thinking, Lily. If

it wasn't you who took Lady Clinsden's things, then who did? No one in their right mind would steal just the one glove, would they? No, please don't interrupt,' she said, holding up her hand as Lily made to speak. 'I knew you were innocent of the charge. That was never in doubt. However, someone entered my cottage on the day of your mother's funeral and ordered the ladies to stop work.'

Lily looked up in surprise. In all the turmoil of the past few days, she'd completely forgotten about that.

'And that person was wearing a black veil and leather gloves. Two leather gloves. That much I know for I questioned Mary, who, in your absence, has taken the initiative in overseeing the work, and very competently she's gone about it too.' Mrs Bodney paused and sat staring gravely at her. Oh no, I'm going to lose my job, Lily thought.

'Don't look so worried, Lily, you're not about to lose your position, if that's what you're worried about. No, Mary has nothing but admiration for the way you run the workroom. She said everyone looks up to you.'

Lily blinked in surprise. 'Oh, that's all right then,' was all she could utter, but Mrs Bodney was continuing her story.

'A few days ago, Tilda was brushing the steps when she found a leather glove behind the boot scraper and brought it to me. It made me think about something Mary had told me and the two things connected. Anyway, I took the glove to the courtroom this morning and, as I'd suspected, it matched the one exhibited there.'

Lily frowned, not sure where the conversation was going.

'It appears that Abigail has got herself into, shall we say, a predicament. Because of that, she was turned out of the position she took when I dismissed her from here and, in desperate need of money, she agreed to assist the squire in his little ruse. Wearing his wife's veil and gloves, she was to turn up at the workroom saying she had a message from you. The idea, of course, was to stop the work in your absence and then you would lose your job and have to go to work for the squire. It was a clever scheme, too, for it being the day of the funeral no one questioned her arriving attired in black. Remember what I said about appearances and perception, Lily?'

'Yes, Mrs Bodney,' she duly answered, not really understanding at all.

Anyway, the girl was supposed to return the clothes to the squire but, in her haste to get away, she carelessly dropped a glove. Apparently, the squire was livid when he found out and threatened to tell her parents of her predicament if she didn't retrieve it. But before she had time to do that, he'd hatched another little plan, getting old Ned to plant the other glove and veil on your donkey-cart.'

'Goodness, is no one to be trusted around here?' gasped Lily.

'Not where money's concerned. Most people hereabouts scratch a living and will seize any opportunity to come by extra. You've led a somewhat sheltered life, Lily, and need to learn to trust at your discretion.' Remembering her brother's similar words, she looked down at the ground; then, seeing the state of her boots, tucked them under her skirt. Glancing up, she checked in case Mrs Bodney had noticed, but the other woman was still intent on her story.

'I heard voices in the parlour, and when I went to investigate I found Abigail asking Tilda if she'd found a black glove. When I confronted her, she broke down and, after explaining everything, rushed out of the cottage. Upon reflection, I should have realized Abigail might bear a grudge for being dismissed, and she is slender in stature with hands to match; hands that fitted the gloves.'

As she sat trying to take in everything Mrs Bodney had said, Lily realized she had a lot to learn about life outside the cottage. How she wished her father and mother were still alive. They'd been such a happy family. Reminded she had nowhere to live, she stared down at the parcel and testimonials and wondered what she was going to do.

'Well now tell me how you got on with Miss Chicke? Did you secure the room?' Mrs Bodney asked, as ever seeming to tune into her thoughts.

Lily shook her head.

'What happened then?'

Lily told her about Miss Chicke's reaction, and her employer clicked her tongue in exasperation.

'She's a stupid, bigoted old woman. Well, it's too late to find anywhere tonight. You'd better sleep in my spare room. It's the door opposite mine. At least it will be more comfortable than that donkey-cart,' Mrs Bodney said, smiling.

Lily shuddered, thinking that was an experience she never, ever wished to repeat. Nor was she likely to now. She had no home and no mode of transport either.

'Go on, Lily, up you go; I'll get Tilda to bring you a tray of food and a candle. Get a good night's sleep and make an early start in the morning. We have a deadline and, as overseer, it is your duty to ensure that it's met.' She picked up her bell to summon the maid and Lily knew she'd been dismissed.

Chapter 20

The little room was sparsely furnished but neat as a pin, with a bed set under the window and a washstand in the corner. As she put her things down on the bed, her feet hit the chamber pot beneath it, sending out a ring. Lily smiled; no rushing outside to the thunder box for her tonight. Carefully, she untied the parcel her aunt had given her. Inside there was a change of petticoat and stockings, her mother's Bible and a letter. For long moments she sat looking at it, her fingers tracing the outline of the words that meant nothing to her. She recognized the writing as Aunt Elizabeth's, for sometimes they'd received a letter by the stagecoach from her, but, of course, it had been Rob who'd read it out to them.

Frustrated by her lack of learning, she put it aside, wondering if she really would be able to learn her letters. Perhaps Mary would read it to her in the morning, she thought yawning, grateful that her friend was one of the few ladies she worked with who knew their letters, having been to the local charity school.

It had been a long, eventful day and all she wanted was to curl up and go to sleep. The wind had risen and was howling around the cottage like a banshee. It felt more like January than June, she thought, shivering in the gathering gloom. Her stomach growled and she hoped Tilda would soon arrive with the promised food.

A thundering on the front door downstairs, made her jump. She heard a man's angry voice followed by muffled whispering and then all went quiet again, but her nerves were shattered by the events of the day and it was some minutes before her heartbeat returned to normal. She sat in the darkness thinking back over Mrs Bodney's revelation. That the figure in the veil had been Abigail surprised her, but she could remember her mother telling her that people resorted to desperate measures when hunger knocked at their door.

Her musing was interrupted by Tilda arriving with the promised candle and tray of food, and Lily's mouth watered as the aroma of chicken broth wafted temptingly towards her. She smiled her thanks.

'Gosh, there was a right old argument out there earlier. Picky Pike–'

'Thank you, Tilda,' Lily said firmly, ignoring the maid's disappointed look. Clearly the girl was longing to chat, and whilst Lily was curious to know what the earlier outburst had been about, she knew Mrs Bodney deplored gossip. Besides, it was hours since she'd eaten, and her insides were gnawing like rats in a grain store.

She sat on the bed, supping the broth and listening to the rain lashing against the window, as the wind soughed down the chimney. She thought of Tom out in his boat and prayed he'd be safe, and that her aunt and brother had found somewhere comfortable to shelter for the night Finally, supper finished, her eyelids began to droop. Undressing quickly, she climbed under the cover and blew out the candle. Lying down, she breathed in the wonderful scent of lavender that fragranced the bed linen and smiled. When she and Tom were married and had a place of their own, she was going to collect wild flowers and dry them. Then their room would smell as sweet as the countryside too.

To her surprise, although she was comfortable she didn't fall asleep immediately. The noises of the night seemed unusually loud in the darkness and they unsettled her. She could hear the pounding of the waves and the push and drag of the shingle, a boat being hauled across the pebbles. Then a hoot sounded close by. Her ears picked out the sound of muffled hooves on the cobbles and she turned to face the wall. Shivering in the darkness, she was convinced she'd never sleep. But eventually everything went quiet and she felt her body relaxing under the warm coverlet.

Waking to the pale light of dawn, Lily jumped out of bed determined to make an early start. While Mrs Bodney had been good about the time she had missed yesterday, the fact remained that the work still needed to be done. Quickly dressing, she rinsed her face with water from the ewer then tiptoed downstairs with her pot, letting herself out into the early morning air.

The gale from the night before had blown itself out, and a watery, white sun was peeping from behind the cliff. Looking down to the harbour she was relieved to see Tom's lugger pulled up on the beach. Hastily she cleaned her pot into the brook and then scurried back indoors.

The peace of the empty workroom was balm to her spirit, and she set about her work with renewed vigour. She had almost completed a sprig when the ladies began to arrive.

'We was glad to hear you was acquitted yesterday,' Mary said, settling onto her stool.

'Thank you. I can't deny I'm relieved to be proved innocent but now I shall have to work like ten men to make up for the time lost.'

But she'd no sooner bent back over her pillow, than Tilda appeared.

'Mrs Bodney wishes to see you in the parlour, Lily.' Fighting down a sigh at the interruption, and hoping nothing was wrong, she followed the little maid out of the room. Mrs Bodney was sitting in her chair looking as fresh as an oxeye daisy and Lily, smoothed down her apron, hoping she looked neater than she felt.

'Good morning, Mrs Bodney,' she said, looking anxiously across at the other woman.

'I trust you slept well, Lily?' her employer asked.

'Yes, thank you.'

'I see you made an early start this morning,' she said, smiling.

'Well, it was only fair I should catch up on some of the work I missed yesterday.'

'Yes. However, you cannot work for long on an

empty stomach, so we shall break our fast together,' Mrs Bodney said, motioning for Lily to help herself to toast from the silver rack that was set on the table. Then she passed her a dainty cup of strong tea. Lily was so thirsty, she couldn't help thinking longingly of the large mugs they'd supped their morning drinks from back at the cottage. Remembering the previous meal she'd eaten here, she carefully cut her toast into quarters, making herself nibble as daintily as she could manage. She was concentrating so hard that it was some moments before she realized Mrs Bodney was speaking.

'Honestly, Lily, I don't believe you've heard a word I've said. I was outlining my plans for bringing all the workers together. Yesterday, I negotiated a deal with Agent Pike. Those premises of his are ideal for us to use.'

Lily stared at her employer. The thought that someone could do a deal with the agent astounded her.

'However, he's a greedy man,' her employer continued. 'He came knocking on my door last night, demanding I increase my offer. Much to his chagrin, I refused. A deal's a deal, as I hastened to point out to him.' She grinned delightedly and Lily found herself smiling back.

She couldn't help marvelling at her employer's nerve, for although the journeyman had sold most of her lace to the agent, there'd been times when Lily had had to deal with him herself, and she knew how difficult he could be. He wasn't known as Picky Pike for nothing.

'Did he object?' Lily couldn't help asking.

'Don't worry, even Pike will come to his senses. He won't turn down the opportunity to make a bit of extra money. As I told him, a little bit of something is better than a lot of nothing,' said Mrs Bodney, chuckling. 'He has until first thing Monday to accept what I'm offering or I'll find other premises.' Lily shook her head but her employer hadn't finished. 'Time is ticking by at an alarming rate and I need your total concentration on our Queen's lace, so until things are settled, you may continue to sleep in my spare room.'

'Oh, thank you, Mrs Bodney. That really is kind of you. I can't tell you how relieved I am,' Lily exclaimed for she'd wondered when she'd have the time to seek somewhere to stay.

'However, I really can't have you being seen in a dress that has more creases than the wise woman's forehead, so please ensure you smarten yourself up before returning to the workroom. It will do my reputation no good whatsoever to have my over-seer parading around like a crumpled clod. I myself have business to attend to elsewhere so will see you here first thing on Monday morning. We will break our fast together and see what has transpired in the meantime. Do you have any plans for the Sabbath?'

'Yes,' Lily replied. 'Tom and I plan to take my little sister and her friend to the beach at Coombe for a picnic.'

'Good, good,' said her employer, her mind already on other things. 'Well, unless you require more tea or toast, I suggest you make yourself respectable then get back to the workroom. Remember, it's your responsibility to ensure the ladies stay on schedule.'

Lily smiled as she watched Beth and Harriet searching the beach for the brightest ribbons of seaweed. Tom had helped them build a fairy castle out of the shiny pebbles and they were now decorating it while Tom fetched water for the moat.

'Hurry up, Tom,' they squealed, as he stood in the shallows filling his pail. How happy and relaxed he looked, Lily thought, leaning back against a rock and revelling in the warmth of the sun on her skin. Tom duly obliged and emptied the water into the channel he'd dug, then pretended to be outraged when it seeped through the stones and disappeared. The girls dissolved into peals of laughter and sent him back to collect more. He was going to make a good father, she thought. Her stomach growled and she realized the fresh air had sharpened her appetite.

'Time to eat,' she called, bending to spread out the picnic Mrs Goode had insisted on packing for them.

'I'm really hungry,' Beth said, running over.

'Me too,' Harriet squealed, joining her.

'And me,' Tom said, grinning.

'Well, sit down,' Lily answered, patting the horsehair blanket she'd spread out for them.

They fell on the delicious feast of bread with pickled eggs, and silence descended. Lily glanced over at Tom and he winked back. It was a long time since she'd felt so happy.

Food finished, Tom instigated a game of hide-and-seek behind the rocks. The sound of the little girls' delighted squeals of laughter when he found them echoed around the beach. All too soon, though, the sun was lowering in the sky and it was time to pack up and make their way home.

'I've had the bestest time ever, Tom,' Beth said, tucking her hand into his as they walked along the track.

'Me too, Tom,' Harriet added, not to be outdone.

'Then we'll just have to do it again soon, won't we?' Tom said, grinning at Lily.

'Ooh, yes, please,' they chorused and then ran off. Pretending to be a monster from the deep, Tom spread out his arms and chased after them along the path towards the cottage.

'You look as though you've had a good time,' Mrs Goode said, scooping up the girls in her arms.

'We have, and thank you for that delicious picnic, Mrs Goode,' Lily said.

'Yes, those pickled eggs were the best I've ever tasted. You must give Lily the recipe when we're wed,' said Tom, rubbing his stomach appreciatively.

'Glad you enjoyed them. And I must say, I've enjoyed the rare treat of having a lazy few hours to meself,' Mrs Goode said, beaming. 'Would you like to come in for a drink?'

'That's kind of you, Mrs Goode, but we really must be getting back,' Tom said politely, as Lily stifled a yawn. 'As you can see, this one definitely needs her beauty sleep.'

'Cheek,' Lily retorted. 'It's all this fresh air, and we still have the walk back to Bransbeer so I guess we'd better get going.'

'Yes, and I'd best find those two rascals and get

them ready for bed,' Mrs Goode said.

They said their goodbyes and made their way back down the cliff path. The evening was balmy, with crickets chirping and the birds swooping low to catch the rising ants.

'If only we could have more days like this, Tom,' said Lily, sighing contentedly.

'We will, my love, we will,' he said, kissing her gently on the cheek. 'Mind you, when we've got thirteen nippers of our own, I guess it'll take a bit of organizing,' he added.

'*Thirteen?*'

'Well, got to keep you out of mischief somehow, girl, haven't we?' he said, winking. 'By the way, I had a word with the carter about collecting your things from the barn next time he's this way.'

'That's kind of you to arrange that, Tom. I was wondering how I'd get them to Bransbeer. How much will it cost?'

'For you, my sweetest love, not a farthing.'

'But he must be charging something,' she protested.

'Think of it as a small gift from your betrothed, Lily,' Tom said.

'I can't expect you to–' she began; then, seeing the look of pride on his face, kissed his cheek instead.

Chapter 21

As Lily entered the parlour on Monday morning, Mrs Bodney signalled for her to be seated.

'Whilst we break our fast, I have several things to acquaint you with.' Lily sat looking at her employer expectantly. Mrs Bodney, however, calmly poured their tea before continuing.

'Unsurprisingly, Mr Pike *has* agreed to let me rent his premises for the sum I originally offered,' she said. 'Conveniently for us, it seems he has an important deal to broker further west. He is leaving this morning and will be away for some time. Whilst I've already engaged the best lace makers in Devonshire, I feel it would be prudent to have a few extra standing by in case of sickness or incapacity. I myself do not have the time available to test the quality of their lace making, so this job will now fall to you, Lily.'

'Yes, Mrs Bodney,' Lily said, carefully cutting her toast into four, then biting into it daintily. Really this preserve was so delicious, she thought, savouring every mouthful.

'...so Mr Mountsford has offered his services. Is that not kind of him?'

Quickly looking up, Lily saw the other woman waiting for an answer.

'Lily, dear, whilst there is no doubt as to the quality of your work I rather think you need to improve your listening skills,' her employer rebuked.

'Sorry, Mrs Bodney,' she said, looking down at her cup.

'I was saying that Mr Mountsford has gallantly offered his services. He is calling for you in his carriage at 10 of the clock. You can direct him to Coombe and he will be happy to transport your belongings from there to Pike's place.'

'But I ... the agent's premises?' she said, surprised.

'There is a room in the attic there, which will afford you comfortable accommodation. In return, you'll have responsibility for ensuring the work gets completed on time and that it is up to standard. Of course, if you encounter any problems you can and must come to me. Now do I take it you are agreeable?' Stunned, Lily could only nod, quite forgetting Tom had already arranged to have her belongings, moved.

'Oh, and, Lily, it would serve you well to be an entertaining companion, for I rather think Mr Mountsford has taken a shine to you.'

Promptly at 10 o'clock, Rupert Mountsford drew up outside Mrs Bodney's cottage. As Lily clambered inside the carriage and settled back onto the squabs, she became aware of an unfamiliar smell. It was rather pleasant, vaguely reminding her of Christmas. She turned to ask Rupert what it was, but he was calling to the driver. Then, they pulled away and her attention was diverted by what was passing by the window.

'Goodness, this must be how the Queen feels,' Lily said, leaning forward and waving to her friend Sally, who'd just emerged from the dairy and was staring at her incredulously. Rupert smiled indulgently, but a few minutes later he wrinkled his nose as a noxious stench pervaded his nostrils.

'What on earth is that disgusting smell? And what are all those people doing?' he asked, pointing to the huddle of women hunched over the brook.

'Village folk draw their water from there and do their washing. It's a kind of meeting place where they catch up on the gossip at the same time as doing their chores.'

'But there are ducks and geese swimming in it,' he said, shaking his head.

'That's why the canny go up the top of the village, Rupert. By the time the water reaches here it's full of slops and whatnots,' Lily informed him, laughing as he shuddered. 'It's clearly a different way of life where you come from.'

'Indeed it is,' he agreed with feeling.

At that moment the carriage tilted as it turned sharply into the lane and she clung on tightly, watching as the steeply pitched roofs of the almshouses flashed by the window. Then they turned again and she shook her head. This carriage was already travelling much faster than Doris ever did.

'I wish Tom could see me,' she said, looking down at the sea shimmering beneath the cliffs. Gulls screeched and wheeled on the breeze. 'There's his lugger pulled up by the fish hut.' Rupert stared in the direction of her pointing finger. 'That one with the white spars. He painted them so they'd show in the dark and no smugglers would want to use his boat,' she said proudly.

Rupert looked quickly across at her but she was busy staring out of the window.

201

'He'll be going out to bait the pots soon,' she added, and Rupert duly looked down at the boats drawn up on the beach.

'Tom – he is a special friend?' he asked.

'Oh, Rupert, you know full well he's my betrothed.'

'Indeed?' he asked, furrowing his dark eyebrows as he glanced down at her left hand. Well, Lily, I must say that I'm surprised. If I were lucky enough to have such an attractive young lady as my betrothed, I'd want everyone to know she belonged to me.'

'How would you do that?' she asked, puzzled.

'I'd buy her a ring with a stone as big and bright as her speedwell eyes,' he replied, looking at her meaningfully.

She felt her cheeks burn and, cursing inwardly, turned to stare back out of the window. Would she never grow out of this childish blushing? Then, sensing he was waiting for her to respond, she turned back towards him.

'Well, Tom and I don't need showy baubles to seal our relationship,' she retorted.

'Sorry, Lily, I always seem to be putting my foot in it with you. Let's just enjoy the ride, shall we?' he asked, smiling.

She nodded, relaxing back on the leather squabs once more. Truth to tell she'd have been delighted if Tom had gone down on one knee and proffered a ring, but that was the stuff of fairy tales, wasn't it? There again, he had said he was saving up for one. She didn't think Rupert would understand, though. If he wanted something, he could probably just go and buy it.

They were cresting the cliffs, the dark red soil from the adjoining fields showing through the bright green of the early summer crops. The warmth from the sun shining through the window, combined with the gentle swaying motion, restored her equilibrium. But as they began their descent into Coombe, the carriage started to rock precariously from side to side. It was going too quickly for the rutted ground and the driver appeared to be having difficulty keeping the horses to the track. She peered out of the window and saw that he was using his whip vigorously. Feeling compelled to say something, she looked across at Rupert, who, seemingly unaware, was staring at the tumbledown cottages they were passing.

'Good grief, just look at those topsy-turvy huts clinging to the cliffs,' he said, grimacing. 'Don't tell me people really live in them?'

'Yes, Rupert, they do, and they call them cotts or cottages,' she said, sighing. 'I guess all the houses in London are grander.' But before he could answer, the coach lurched again, sending her sliding towards the other side of the carriage. Unable to stand it any longer, she shouted, 'Look, I really don't like the way your driver is whipping the horses. It's not necessary.'

Surprised at her outburst, he stared at her for a long moment.

'You're right, of course, Lily,' he agreed, pulling down the window and shouting to the driver to desist. However, they were now passing alongside a pigsty and hastily he put a hand up to cover his nose before snapping the window shut. Collapsing back on the squabs, he looked so affronted she had to stifle a giggle.

'Good healthy smell of the country, that, Rupert,' she couldn't resist saying.

'Yes, I see,' he said politely, clearly not realizing she was pulling his leg.

Feeling a pang of remorse, for he was loaning her his carriage, she smiled sweetly at him.

'Not much further now,' she said, as they passed the church. Excitement bubbled as she looked out at the familiar scenery. 'We're here,' she announced as they reached the orchard. Peering around, she could see no sign of the new tenant and, as Rupert shouted to the driver to stop, she got ready to jump out. But Rupert was staring from the muddy path leading to the barn down to his grey flannel trousers and shiny shoes.

'You stay here,' Lily laughed. 'It will only take a moment to collect my things and my boots are used to the muck.' Before he could answer, she jumped down from the carriage.

'Good job we don't still have our pig or the ground by the barn would be a quagmire,' she couldn't help shouting over her shoulder.

Rupert, however, was gingerly climbing down after her and staring aghast at the cottage, the lean-to linny and then the pig pen.

'Did you really live in this ramshackle building?' he asked in disbelief.

'This was our home, and very happy we were here too,' Lily retorted, marching towards the barn. Carefully picking his way around the puddles, Rupert followed after her.

'Mind the rats,' she warned, smiling to herself as he visibly paled. That would teach him to be rude about their family home. The barn door creaked as she pulled it open, and to her relief she saw her things safely stacked on the clean straw.

'Is this all you have?' he asked, staring at the small bundle that constituted her worldly goods.

She nodded. 'Don't need much to live,' she said, picking it up, but he reached out and took it from her.

'Here, allow me.'

'Thank you, Rupert.' She peered around, surprised not to see signs of activity. 'Could I just have a quick look inside the cottage? I'd like to say goodbye.' Understanding – or maybe sympathy – flashed in his eyes and he nodded.

'Take as long as you need, Lily. I'll wait in the carriage.'

Making her way round to the back, she lifted the latch, giving the door the necessary shove to open it. Slowly, she wandered through the cold, empty rooms, hearing the echoes of her childhood, remembering happier times. The fuss their parents had made of them on their birthdays and Christmas, with specially made cakes, fruit pies and a feast of succulent roast chicken or pork. Their living room would smell fragrant with cooking for hours after the meals had been eaten. Then there were the egg hunts at Easter, each child desperate to be first to find the biggest, which their mother would have coloured with onion skins. She could almost see Rob chasing her from room to room, hear their squeals of laughter. That was before the accident, of course.

She sighed, remembering her grandmother saying that a life took an age to live, yet the memory could skip down through the years in moments. She hadn't understood what she meant at the time but she did now. Her chest tightened painfully and she feared she might choke.

'Goodbye, Father, goodbye, Mother,' she whispered. Then, blinking back the tears, she hurried outside. As she pulled the door shut for the last time, a skylark flew up from the adjoining field, its joyous song floating on the breeze. Vowing not to cry, she bit down hard on her lip and hurried back to the carriage.

Rupert smiled as she settled on her seat.

'Are you all right?' he asked gently, concern clouding his eyes, but she felt too emotional to speak. Nodding briefly, she turned and stared out of the window.

They travelled back through Coombe in silence, passing the church with the graveyard where her parents and siblings were buried, the rickety forge, red sandstone inn and cob cottages with smoke rising in plumes from their chimneys. Lost in her memories, she forgot Rupert was sitting opposite, until he reached over and gently covered her hand with his. Looking up, she caught a waft of lemony citrus from his cologne. It was quite pleasant, she thought, but a different smell from the one she'd noticed when she'd first got into the carriage. There was something reassuring about the warmth of his touch and she found herself staring in fascination at his silky smooth skin and neatly manicured nails. Such a contrast to Tom's work-roughened hands, she thought. Guiltily she snatched her hand away. What was she doing letting another man touch her?

Rupert just smiled and said nothing.

It could have been minutes or hours before he broke the silence; Lily had completely lost track of time.

'We're nearly there now,' he said, pointing out of the window. To her surprise, she saw the carriage was making its way up the main street of Bransbeer.

'Will you be all right?' he asked, as they drew to a halt outside the agent's imposing premises. 'I'm sure Mrs Bodney will understand if you need to partake of a little refreshment before you resume your duties, and I'd be delighted to escort you to the hostelry.' At the mention of her employer's name, Lily snapped back to the present.

'Thank you, Rupert, but I have missed almost a morning's work as it is.'

'That's as maybe, but I'm sure Mrs Bodney would permit you time to recover from what has obviously been an upsetting experience for you.'

Lily smiled at his understanding. 'You have been most kind but I dare not neglect my duties; I appreciate your assistance, though. Perhaps, I could offer you afternoon tea once we are settled in our new place of work.'

'Thank you. I'd like that,' he said, beaming, and despite her recent low mood she found herself smiling back.

She was still grinning as she jumped down and went to collect her things from the driver, only to find her way blocked.

'You're looking mighty pleased with yourself.'

'Tom, what are you doing here?' she asked, her smile growing wider.

'I might well ask you the same question, Lily Rose.' The sharpness of his voice wiped the smile from her face.

'Whatever's wrong, Tom?' she asked, noticing now the set of his jaw, fists clenched by his side.

'Didn't believe it, did I, when Molly came down to the boat as soon as we landed, shouting she'd seen you riding through the village in a posh carriage sat alongside your fancy man? Ran here as fast as I could and what do I see? That she was telling the truth, that's what,' he shouted.

'But, Tom, Mr Mountsford kindly escorted me back to Coombe in the carriage to collect my things,' she said, bemused.

'Oh, so my arranging for the carter to pick them up wasn't good enough for you?' he growled, his eyes narrowing.

Before she could reply Rupert appeared at her side, asking, 'Is something wrong, Lily?' Realizing they were now drawing curious stares from passers-by, she shook her head and forced a smile.

'No, everything is fine, thank you, Mr Mountsford. I was just explaining to Tom how you kindly escorted me back to Coombe this morning so that I could collect my things.' She turned to Tom.

'Wasn't that kind of Mr Mountsford, Tom?'

But he was too busy glaring at Rupert to reply.

At that moment, Mrs Bodney's strident voice cut through the crowd that had gathered to see what the fuss was about.

'Miss Rose, come inside immediately.' Turning quickly, Lily saw the furious look on her employer's face and groaned. Muttering to Tom that she'd see him later and nodding to Rupert, she grabbed her bundle from the driver and hurried after the irate woman. She was for it now.

'Well, Lily, what excuse can you possibly have for making such an exhibition of yourself in public?' As Lily looked into the formidable face of Mrs Bodney, her legs began to tremble and she was grateful for the cover her long dress afforded.

'There was a slight misunderstanding, Mrs Bodney.'

'It looked more than that to me. I'm a respectable businesswoman, Lily, and cannot – no, I will not – have my overseer causing such a disturbance in the street.'

'But I...' Lily was shaking all over now and was afraid if she didn't soon sit down, she'd fall down.

'There are no buts, Miss Rose,' Mrs Bodney said, banging her fist on the table. Bobbins crashed to the floor and Lily watched helplessly as they scattered in all directions, their threads unravelling on the stone flags. She waited for Mrs Bodney to rant about them getting dirty, but intent on delivering her diatribe, her employer seemed not to notice. 'As you are aware, Mr Mountsford is a reputable merchant with whom I conduct a considerable amount of business, and I distinctly remember instructing you to treat him with courtesy and respect.'

'But I did, it's just that Tom'd already arranged–'

'My dear Mrs Bodney, please forgive my intrusion,' Rupert Mountsford said from the doorway. 'It would appear that in my efforts to be of assistance to Miss Rose I neglected to consult with her betrothed. Regrettably, having already made arrangements himself, he jumped to the wrong conclusion. However, we now – how shall I put it? – understand each other perfectly.' Although his voice was serious Lily could see his eyes twinkling with amusement.

'I see,' said Mrs Bodney, struggling to regain her composure. 'Well, Miss Rose, I dare say it has been an unsettling morning for you. As long as you remember I have a reputation to uphold, we will say no more about it. There will be half a dozen ladies arriving shortly to sit the ability test. I suggest you go through to the room behind this one, which is to serve as the workroom. You can set out the requisite materials and when I have finished my business I'll be through to check everything is in order. Rupert, perhaps you would care to take a seat? I have made a number of changes I need to acquaint you with.'

Before Mrs Bodney could change her mind, Lily hurried towards the door. However, in her haste to get away, she caught the toe of her boot on the corner of the step. Clutching at the doorpost for support, she watched in horror as a loose nail came away from the sole, spun across the floor, and came to rest by Mr Mountsford's foot. Solemnly, he picked it up and held it out to her. As she moved to take it, he gave her such an outrageous wink she had to bite down on her lip to stop herself from bursting out laughing.

'Do hurry up,' Mrs Bodney commanded.

But Lily's spirit had returned and, with head held high, she walked out of the room in what she hoped was a dignified manner. She only hoped Mrs Bodney hadn't noticed the sole of her boot flapping as she went.

Chapter 22

Lily stood staring around the unfamiliar room, then spotted, stacked on the dresser, the patterns, bobbins and threads the ladies would need to make their test samples. She was about to set them out on the large round table when she noticed it was covered in a thick layer of dust. Snatching up a cloth, she gave it a brisk polish and had only just finished setting out the materials when Mrs Bodney bustled in. As usual her beady eyes had missed nothing, and she gestured impatiently to Lily's boots.

'How long have they required repair?'

Ashamed, Lily looked down at the floor. 'Only a short while, Mrs Bodney.'

'Well, this simply will not do, Miss Rose. Not only have you made an exhibition of yourself outside my establishment, you've also seen fit to turn up for work slovenly attired. Can you think of one good reason why I shouldn't dismiss you on the spot?'

She gasped. 'Oh please, Mrs Bodney, I promise to do better. Time hasn't been on my side lately...' She stuttered to a halt as the other woman held up her hand.

'As it happens, Mr Mountsford has already appealed to my better nature, which he assures me I have hidden somewhere about my person.' Mrs Bodney shook her head as though not quite believing what she was saying. The thought of Rupert Mountsford having the audacity to tease her employer in such a manner made Lily widen her eyes in astonishment. Mrs Bodney, though, was looking around the room, taking in the shining table and neatly laid out materials. Turning back to Lily, she shook her head.

'You work well and your attention to detail is second to none. If you would only exercise a little more self-restraint, I'd be entirely pleased with you.' She shook her head again. 'Mr Mountsford also saw fit to point out that you've had a lot to contend with of late, so on this occasion I will overlook your earlier behaviour.'

'Thank you, Mrs Bodney. I'll work really hard and–'

'As I've said, I have no concerns regarding your work,' her employer cut in. 'However, from now on you must promise to conduct yourself with decorum when you are about my business.' Nodding vigorously, Lily breathed a sigh of relief. 'And for heaven's sake get yourself a decent pair of boots made. I suggest you take yourself to the cordwainer later and get sized.'

Lily looked at her employer in despair. 'But I was going to get the cobbler to repair these,' she said, pointing down to her boots.

As if she hadn't heard her, Mrs Bodney continued, 'Tell Albert only his finest work will do and that you require them to be ready in three days' time.'

'Why, he'll never have a new pair made that quickly,' Lily said, amazed at the assumption.

'Oh, he will, Lily, believe you me. And, if you are

212

worried about the cost, I will make an advance on your next month's wages.' There was a pause.

'Thank you, Mrs Bodney,' Lily said, when she saw her employer was waiting for her to say something.

'Now, I'll get Tilda to prepare your room and have your belongings taken upstairs for you. You'll see she has already set your pillow over there,' she said, pointing to the chair by the window. 'I suggest you get on with your own work whilst the ladies are sitting their test, Lily. You will be on hand in case they need any help.'

'Thank you, Mrs Bodney, but I can take my own things up to the attic,' she replied. However, the other woman was already bustling from the room. Lily let out a sigh of relief. Mrs Bodney was no longer referring to her as Miss Rose so it seemed she still had employment.

Moments later, a young woman with a mop of curly fair hair popped her head around the door.

'I've come to sit the test. Mrs Bodney said it was all right to come through,' she said, her trembling voice indicating how nervous she was.

'Come and take a seat,' Lily said, smiling to put her at ease. Then, before she could say anything else, the door opened again and an assortment of ladies, armed with their pillows, entered the room.

Once they were seated, Lily explained what they had to do. Then she went over to her own pillow and began work.

'Oh, no.' A plaintive wail broke into Lily's thoughts. Looking up she saw the curly-haired girl shaking her head and madly reversing her bob-bins. Poor thing, Lily thought. She's clearly nervous. Her thoughts went back to the time she'd sat her own test. She knew just how stomach-wrenching it was. She looked around the table but the other ladies were working away quite happily.

When their allotted time had passed, Lily stood up.

'Right, ladies, if you will put your test samples on the table before you, I shall come round and inspect them.'

'Oh, no, I need a few moments more,' the girl pleaded.

'No, I'm afraid you must put what you've done on the table now,' Lily insisted, trying to ignore the look of desperation on her face. She circled the table, inspecting the work as she collected it up, her heart sinking when she saw the distorted mess the girl had made. Before she could say anything Mrs Bodney appeared in the doorway.

'Report your results to me, please, Lily,' she commanded.

'Yes, Mrs Bodney. I'll be as quick as I can,' she said, turning back to the ladies, who by now were desperate to hear if they had passed.

'Well, Lily, how have they fared?' Mrs Bodney asked, as soon as she'd closed the door.

'Two are fine, Mrs Bodney, but the rest...' Lily shrugged, holding out the sprigs for the other woman to see, but her employer waved them away.

'Dismiss those not up to standard, and tell the others to report here at first light tomorrow.'

'But don't you want to check–'

'Lily, it is your job as overseer to inspect their work,' her employer said, looking down at the papers on her desk. Then as Lily turned to go, she looked up again. 'Don't forget to go to the cordwainer when you've dismissed the ladies,' she said, then looked down at her desk again before Lily could answer.

As she entered the room, six pairs of eyes turned anxiously in her direction. Gently, she gave them the results, her heart sinking as the curly-haired woman burst into tears.

'But I need the work. Please give me another chance. I was so nervous I got the bobbins mixed up...'

Much as Lily sympathized, for she herself could have easily been in the same position, she knew she had to harden her heart or Mrs Bodney would take her to task.

'I'm really sorry,' she said, opening the door. She wished she could give the poor girl another trial, but time was of the essence and the lace for Queen Victoria's dress had to be perfect. Mrs Bodney was relying on her and she couldn't afford to let her down.

After they'd gone, Lily sank on one of the chairs the women had vacated. She hated disappointing people. Her job as overseer definitely had its downside. Then remembering Mrs Bodney's order to be sized for new boots, she jumped up and grabbed her shawl.

Hurrying to the outskirts of the village, where Albert's cottage was situated, she wondered just how much a new pair of boots was going to cost. Passing the cobbler's, she was tempted to get him to repair her old pair instead, but realizing Mrs Bodney would be furious if she found out, Lily continued on her way.

Albert's door was open, and she could hear hammering coming from within. Smoothing down her skirt, she stepped inside. The room was gloomy after the bright sunshine, and the air heavy with the smell of leather and glue. Lasts of varying sizes were lined up along one wall and lying next to the workbench was the most exquisite pair of boots she had ever seen. They were in the latest fashion, decorated with dainty stitching in cherry red. She'd seen similar footwear on the ladies when she'd served at table at the manor, but never anything as fine as these.

'Be liking a pair like those would ee, young lady?' Spinning around, she saw the cordwainer staring at her with a gleam in his eyes.

'Oh, wouldn't I just,' she burst out. 'If I owned a pair like that, I'd think I'd died and gone to heaven.' She gave a heartfelt sigh. 'No, begging your pardon, Mr Albert, it's a sturdy pair of hobnailed ones I'm in need of.'

The old man looked at her feet with practised eyes, taking in the well-worn boots and their flapping sole.

'Sit ee down and we'll get ee sized. Ee'll have to wait the best part of a month for them, mind, for I've never been so busy.'

Lily groaned. 'A month? But Mrs Bodney said my new boots were to be ready in three days.'

'Ah, she would,' Albert muttered. 'Well, likes I says, my order book's full to overflowing. Seems like I've no sooner finished making folk their fancy footwear for one ball up at the manor, than they're back again ordering new for the next.' He threw up his hands, grinning. Lily's stomach lurched at the mention of the manor; then she realized the money she now earned meant she'd never have to serve at the squire's table again.

'Course, I shouldn't moan 'cos it means more business, but the missus mithers on about the time I spend in me workshop,' he continued, holding out his hands for Lily's boots. Moments later the vagrant nail was back in place, he then added a couple more to secure an offcut of leather over the hole in the sole. Quickly applying black sealing wax to the scuffed toes, he then handed them back. 'There now, these should last ee till ee new ones are ready.'

Lily was amazed at the transformation, but before she could answer, he'd turned back to his bench and was busy hammering again.

She'd just arrived back outside the agent's when someone tapped her on the shoulder.

'Tom, you made me jump,' she said, spinning round. 'What are you doing here?'

'I was going to ask the same of you, Lily. I thought you'd be making up the time you missed earlier when you went out riding in that fancy coach.'

'I've just been to the cordwainer's,' Lily said, her heart sinking when she saw him frown.

'And why would someone like you be seeing a cordwainer and not the cobbler? Your fancy merchant's not treating you to a pair of new boots, is he?' he asked, his eyes narrowing.

'Of course not,' she gasped. 'And Mr Mountsford is not my fancy merchant, Tom, so I'll thank you to watch your tongue.'

'Oh, aren't we hoity-toity now we've been

riding out in a fancy carriage?'

As he stood there looking indignant, the fight went out of her. She'd had enough of being at loggerheads with him.

'Look, Tom, it's like I said earlier. Mr Mountsford offered me a trip in his carriage so that I could collect my things from the barn. I'm sorry, it all happened so quickly, I completely forgot you'd made arrangements with the carter.'

He shrugged.

'Not only are we working at the agent's premises, I've got a room in the attic,' she said.

Immediately his mood brightened. 'A room here at Picky Pike's? Well, that is good news. So when do I get to see it?' he asked, grinning mischievously.

'Even if I wanted to, I couldn't possibly allow you up to my room, Tom. Mrs Bodney would die of shock.'

'I doubt it. From what I heard, she has a fellow on the go herself.'

'Tom, that's a terrible thing to say.' Then Lily remembered Mrs Bodney had told her she had an admirer. She wondered if she should mention it, but before she could say anything, he continued.

'Sorry, it's just that I hardly see you, and have been going spare as a sprat having to make do with these chance meetings,' he said, moving closer so that she got a waft of fish. She couldn't help comparing it to Rupert Mountsford's tangy aroma of lemon cologne.

Shocked by her disloyal thoughts and reminding herself Mrs Bodney would probably be waiting for her, she said, 'I must go in, Tom. All the ladies will be working together from tomorrow and I've so much to get ready before then.'

'It'll make life easier for you if they're all in one place. Well, I'd better go and check the pots. Now the weather's calmed I'm hoping there'll be lots of lovely lobsters and crabs waiting to greet me,' he said, making clawlike motions with his fingers and thumbs as he reached out and pretended to remove her cap.

'Tom, someone might see,' she rebuked, tapping his hands away.

'Well, I guess now you're living here in the village, we'll be able to spend more time together. What say we take a walk along the beach later then?'

Her heart flipped but then she remembered that she'd spent the best part of the morning away from her work.

'Sorry, Tom, but like you said, I must make up for the time I was in Coombe. I'll meet you by your boat after I finish work tomorrow,' she promised. Then with a cheery wave, she hurried inside the agent's house.

Tilda came out to greet her. She was carrying a plate of bread and cheese.

'Mrs Bodney says you can eat in the workroom, as you're by yourself, but you're to be sure to wash your hands before doing your work afterwards.'

'Thank you, Tilda. I hadn't realized I was hungry until now.'

Whilst she ate, she looked around her new surroundings, noticing the big windows, which would afford them good light in which to work, the wide wooden floorboards and the rest of the ladderbacked chairs set out along the walls. It was a large room and would be perfect for them all, she thought, getting up and rearranging the chairs ready for the following morning. Then, heeding Mrs Bodney's orders, she went outside and washed her hands at the pump. Staring around, she was pleased to see the enclosed yard was bigger than the one at Mrs Bodney's cottage. No doubt, her employer would expect all the ladies to partake of their nuncheon here and they would need the extra space.

She was just making her way back to the workroom when Mrs Bodney came through to the hallway.

'Did you see Albert and get sized for new boots?' she asked, putting on her gloves.

'Yes, but he said I might have to wait a month for them.'

'We'll see about that,' said Mrs Bodney, frowning.

'You should have seen these boots he's made,' Lily burst out. 'They're beautiful with fine stitching the colour of cherries. I'd do anything to have a pair like that.' Her employer looked at her for a long moment and then cleared her throat.

'You are now mixing with a different class of man, some of whom like to treat a lady to little luxuries in return for the delight of their company.'

'Really?' Lily asked, looking perplexed for a moment. 'Oh, you mean like Mr Mountsford brings you packets sometimes?' she asked.

Immediately her employer's demeanour changed.

'I'm sure you are anxious to get back to your

work, Lily,' she said brusquely, before opening the front door and disappearing into the street.

Doing as she'd been bid, Lily settled down to work. Her mind was spinning as she thought how much had happened over the past few days. It had been sad saying goodbye to the family home, the only one she'd known, and she hoped Aunt Elizabeth and Rob had arrived safely in Ilminster. She thought of Beth and the lovely time they'd had on the beach. Tom was going to make a really good father when they had their own children, and she couldn't help grinning at the thought. It had been kind of him to arrange with the carter to collect her things too. She hoped he hadn't been too offended that she'd accepted Mr Mountsford's offer. After all, it was her employer who'd arranged it.

Dusk descended into darkness, casting eerie fingers of shadow around the room and Lily covered her work. Making her way up the steep stairs to the attic, she stood in the doorway looking around the large, airy room. She couldn't believe she had all this space to herself. There was a decent sized bed covered with a pretty yellow coverlet and a little table and chair set beside it. She noticed her things had been placed neatly beside a tin chest set under the eaves. Then she spotted the skylight and went over to push it open. Standing on tiptoe, she found herself staring over the thatched roofs, with plumes of smoke rising from the chimneys into the air, and could just glimpse the silver of the bay beyond.

Quickly she stowed her things in the chest, then, eyelids drooping with tiredness, she kicked off her boots and slipped out of her dress. Sinking thankfully under the coverlet, she thought she'd fall asleep straightaway, but the creaking of the house was unfamiliar and she could hear the waves pounding the beach and the shooshing sound as the water was sucked back out again. As she lay in the darkness her thoughts drifted back over the past hours: the ride in Rupert's carriage, visiting her home for the last time, collecting her things, those beautiful boots and the curious thing Mrs Bodney had said.

Finally, she drifted off to sleep and dreamed that she was dressed in a fine gown and wearing dainty boots with stitching the colour of red cherries.

Chapter 23

Lily woke with a start, her heart racing as fast as a galloping stallion. Snatches of her dream were playing in her head. She'd been in an elegant drawing room festooned with chandeliers. There'd been soft music playing, arms holding her gently as she'd danced. She shivered, remembering how she'd looked up into her partner's face only to find it had no features, no expression. It had been as blank as a ghoul's mask at Samhain. Shaking her head, she tried to dispel the disturbing image. There was no time to dwell on its meaning, for already the soft grey of morning was filtering through the skylight. Dressing quickly, she let herself out into the freshness of the morning and, after drawing water from the pump, quickly rinsed her face and hands.

Aware the ladies would shortly be arriving for their first day's work on these premises, she hurried to their new workroom. She hoped they'd all get on together and there would be no problems. All these thoughts vanished, when she saw Mrs Bodney was already waiting for her. Remembering their last meeting, she looked anxiously at her employer.

'Ah, Lily, I trust you slept well?' her employer asked.

Relieved that the woman seemed in a good mood this morning, she nodded.

'I see you have already prepared for the ladies' arrival, so take yourself through to the next room, which I have turned into my parlour. Tilda will bring you in some refreshment to break your fast. I have urgent business to attend to but will be back later to see how you are all getting on.'

'Yes, Mrs Bodney,' Lily replied, her spirits lifting at the thought of being amongst friendly faces again. She must remember to ask Mary if she would read her the letter from Aunt Elizabeth.

'I hope you've thought about what I said, Lily,' said Mrs Bodney, pausing in the doorway. 'Mr Mountsford will be visiting again shortly so remember to be good company for my best merchant,' she said, winking as she hurried out of the door.

Before Lily could reply, her employer disappeared from the room, leaving her more confused than ever.

As she entered the parlour, Tilda appeared with her food and Mrs Bodney's comment went from her mind. She was just devouring the last crumb of toast when she heard the clatter and chatter of the ladies making their way into the building and hurried back to the workroom.

'Morning, Lily. I see we're going up in the world,' Mary puffed as she offloaded her pillow onto the table with a thud and peered around the room.

'I bet Picky Pike was none too pleased to lose his domain,' giggled Cora, making Lily smile.

'I heard the Revenue's after him and he's got to lie low,' Nell whispered.

'I understand he has business to attend to further down the country,' Lily said hastily, not wishing to encourage gossip. Hearing more hustle and bustle in the doorway, she looked up and saw the ladies from High House crowding into the room with their pillows and bundles.

'Find yourselves places around the tables, ladies, and unpack your work,' said Lily with a welcome smile. When they had settled themselves, she introduced everyone. Then she noticed the two lace makers she'd recruited the previous day were hovering nervously in the doorway.

'Come in and take a seat,' she encouraged. 'It's lovely to see you again and, of course, you will all have time to get to know each other better at nuncheon. Meanwhile, I'm sure we will enjoy the benefit of working together. Before we begin, there are a couple of things I need to tell you. Those of you who have been working with me have been making sprays of flowers, whilst those who have been with Mrs Bodney at High House have been working on leaf patterns.' She paused, as a ripple of surprise ran around the room. 'This was to ensure the design was kept a secret, but Mrs Bodney now feels it would be more convenient to have you all working under one roof. As we are working to a strict timetable, for speed and efficiency you will continue with the designs you have been making until sufficient have been made.'

'Thank heavens,' Mary said. 'Me poor brain couldn't take the pressure of learning any more patterns.' There was a burst of laughter and Lily smiled.

'Mrs Bodney is really pleased with the progress you have made so far. Remember, though, we are already approaching the third month of this commission so please work diligently whilst maintaining your highest standards. Weave happy thoughts through your work, ladies,' she said encouragingly, and then made her way over to the two new recruits. 'Now these are the patterns I want you to prick out,' she said.

'Getting hoity-toity now and speaking like Mrs Bodney, are we?'

Glancing up in surprise, she saw Molly standing in the doorway, a large bag of groceries in her hand. 'Guess you'll be thinking you're above us now, riding out with that toff in his fancy carriage.'

'It wasn't like that,' Lily protested, feeling the heat creeping up her cheeks.

'Well, you must have let him have something. A gentleman like that wouldn't give the likes of you a second look else.'

'Really, Molly, that's downright nasty. It's a good job Mrs Bodney isn't here...' Mary's voice tailed off.

'Ah, but Mrs Bodney is here.'

Molly spun round, her jaw dropping as she saw the woman standing in the doorway. 'And a dog knows its own tricks. Kindly remove yourself from my premises.'

'But–'

'No buts. Get out this instant and you can tell your father I'll be making other arrangements for my victuals in future.' With that, she pushed the gaping Molly out onto the street, slamming the door behind her. The lace makers looked at each other in amazement.

'Right, ladies, it's nice to see you all here, but the show is over, so back to work,' Mrs Bodney ordered. 'Lily, I'd like a word, if you please.'

As the ladies bent their heads over their pillows, Lily swallowed hard and followed Mrs Bodney into the adjoining room.

'Don't look so worried, Lily. There will always be those who resent others getting on in life. You mustn't ever let another person's jealousy get to you.'

'But I never did anything, you know, improper,' she protested.

To her astonishment, Mrs Bodney burst out laughing.

'Oh, Lily, I never for one moment thought you did. The secret of dealing with people like Molly is not to rise to their bait. Just smile sweetly, then, when they see their taunts are having no effect, they'll back off. Do you understand?'

Lily nodded.

'Good. Now, as you know, Anna has been waiting to see if anything can be done about her eyesight. Poor woman, it's not good news, I'm afraid, and I can no longer employ her here. Oh, don't worry,' she said, as Lily gasped in dismay. 'Someone I know requires domestic help, so she will still be earning a wage. We now need to think about how we can protect our lace makers' eyesight in the future, Lily. I know it's summer and we have the longer hours of daylight but we shall have to encourage employers, myself included, to let the ladies light candles earlier in the year.'

Lily gasped. 'Really? That would be helpful and save many a headache too,' she said, speaking from experience. 'I'm pleased you have been able to find a position for Anna, but having her winding the thread onto the bobbins has made a huge difference to our daily output.'

'Yes, and that is why I've engaged someone to take her place. When I left earlier, there was a girl waiting outside. Although she failed the test yesterday, she pleaded with me to find her work. I like a person who doesn't give up easily, so I've engaged her to take over from Anna. Come in please, Emma,' she called, and Lily looked up to see the curly-headed girl looking shyly at her.

'Emma is prepared to work hard and do anything asked of her, so please take her through to the workroom and explain what her duties will be.'

By the time Lily had shown Emma what she was to do and then checked everyone's work, it was well into the morning. Drained from her restless night and setting up the new workroom, she sank onto her chair. Being an overseer was certainly demanding, but she mustn't grumble. The extra money she was earning would help swell her betrothal fund, she thought, before remembering the new boots. One step forward, three back, as her mother used to say when she was trying to eke out their meagre funds.

Picking up her bobbins, she resumed work on the sprig she'd started the previous day and before long the rhythm of her work restored her equilibrium. As often happened, she began day-dreaming about the lace she would make for her own wedding dress and how long it would be before she and Tom were wed. Tom was right: they didn't spend enough time together. Now she was living here, she would have more free time to see him and make plans for their future. As he was baiting up the pots as well as fishing, they'd be able to save more money to marry. Time was passing quickly and it was exciting to think that soon they could look for their own place. She couldn't wait.

The lace makers worked through the long days of high summer, only too aware of the deadline looming. Mrs Bodney took to popping in for on the spot inspections but Lily's exacting leader-ship meant their work was never found wanting. They adopted the mantra of tongues still, bob-bins moving and Lily used the resulting quiet of the workroom to foster her happy daydreams.

'Damn and blast.'

Rudely roused from her reverie, Lily was about to rebuke Cora for her bad language when she noticed the girl was distressed. Huge tears were rolling down her face and it was only Emma's swift intervention with a scrap of material that saved them from landing on her lacework.

'It's ruined anyway,' Cora wailed. 'Oh, I hate it here,' and with that she fled from the room, leaving the other lace makers speechless. Even when her friend Nell called after her, she didn't stop.

'All right, everyone, back to your work,' Lily said, rushing to the door and peering out. But Cora had already disappeared. Puzzled at the girl's unusual behaviour, she went over to Dora.

'Do you know what's up with your sister?' Lily asked.

Two green eyes stared up at her and the girl shrugged. 'She never talks to me,' she muttered.

'Oh?' Lily said, surprise showing on her face.

'We don't even like each other. Closest we ever got was our names. Mother was having a right laugh, I reckon. 'Spect Cora's got man trouble. That's usually it with her,' the girl added, then looked down at her pillow. Seeing the matter was closed as far as Dora was concerned, Lily went over to look at Cora's lace.

It was in such a mess that she could have cried herself. It would take an age to undo and then rework the threads. For two bobbins she'd cast the wretched sprig aside and start on a new one but, of course, that wasn't an option because all the thread had to be accounted for.

Breaking Mrs Bodney's golden rule, she didn't stop for her noon break but set about putting Cora's work to rights. She hoped the girl would return once she'd calmed down. Although they'd got off to a bad start, once Cora had accepted that Lily was overseer, she'd proven to be a good worker.

However, the afternoon wore on and Cora didn't

reappear, leaving Lily no option but to carry on and finish the sprig. If Cora didn't turn up on the morrow, she'd have to let Emma work the lace, and employ another girl to replenish the bobbins and keep the workroom tidy. It would mean watching Emma closely, but working to time was critical if all the lace were to be ready for sewing up by November.

Although they had benefited from the summer hours of daylight, they were past the longest day, and the shadows were lengthening earlier in the evening. Before Lily realized it, Mary and the others were covering their work. Despite there being so many more lace makers together now, they'd been working so quietly she'd forgotten they were there. Smiling her thanks as they filed out of the room, she returned to her own pillow. She'd never make up the time lost, but at least she could finish the piece she'd been working on.

It was twilight by the time she'd caught up sufficiently to stop working. Letting herself out into evening air, she lifted her skirts and hurried towards the harbour, hoping Tom would be waiting, as he was each evening that the tide allowed. But he wasn't there. Apart from the boats drawn up on the beach, the bay was unusually deserted. Dejected, she trudged wearily back up the hill, pulling her shawl tighter around her against the stiffening breeze. Then as she passed the grocer's store, a voice called through the open door.

'Let you down, has he?' Molly jeered.

Remembering Mrs Bodney's advice of a few days ago, Lily ignored her and carried on walking.

'Happen Tom got tired of playing second fiddle

to yon fancy man. Got himself another girl, maybe,' Molly's cackle taunted. But Lily remained silent and the other woman slunk back indoors.

It wasn't like Tom not to turn up, Lily thought, making her way back to Picky Pike's. What if he *had* found someone else? The idea made her stomach churn and she vowed she'd make more time for him in future.

Having had her supper, she felt too restless to sleep, so she went through to the workroom and settled herself at her pillow. Although it was almost dark, she knew the pattern by heart and thought she'd use the time to catch up with her own lace. For once, though, her work failed to soothe her. As her movements increased so did her fretting. Where could Tom be? Was he with some other girl? Or had Molly been getting her own back for the other day? He'd never failed her before. Why, he'd always been as reliable as the tide. So where was he then?

'Lily, what are you doing in here at this time of night?' Startled out of her thoughts, she looked up to find Mrs Bodney standing in the doorway.

'I was just inspecting the work, Mrs Bodney.'

'Hmm,' said the other woman, frowning at Lily's pillow. 'I may be a taskmistress but I'm no slave driver, Lily. Cora may have jumped ship but that doesn't mean you have to do her work as well as your own.'

She stared at Mrs Bodney in surprise. Surely, the woman was a witch.

'No, I'm not a mystic, Lily, if that's what you're thinking. I may have been living in London but I was born and raised here in Bransbeer and know

231

only too well how juicy gossip spreads faster than lightning. Come through to my parlour, time is marching on and we need to discuss how much lace still needs to be made,' she ordered, before disappearing in a flurry of skirts.

Lily quickly put down her bobbins. Getting up, she stretched her body to ease the tiredness from her back.

'What a delectable vision to greet a humble merchant.' She froze, as Rupert Mountsford dipped his head and stepped into the room.

'I'm sorry if I took you by surprise. Seeing you execute such an elegant movement fair made my heart beat faster. Please forgive my intrusion.' His voice sounded sincere, but the gleam in his eyes confirmed he was anything but sorry.

'Why, Mr Mountsford, er, Rupert, I fear you jest,' she answered, smoothing down her dress and trying to recover her composure. But he continued standing there, staring at her so intently, her heart skipped a beat. She really couldn't understand why his presence should affect her so but she wouldn't be human if she didn't find his obvious admiration gratifying Remembering her employer's words, she smiled up at him. His look of surprise turned to one of pleasure.

'Well, well, young Lily, it seems you are blossoming before my very eyes,' he said, grinning delightedly.

Chapter 24

'How much longer do you intend to keep me waiting, Lily?' Mrs Bodney snapped, bustling back into the room. Then she saw Rupert standing there and her demeanour changed in an instant. 'Oh, I do beg your pardon, I had no idea you were here, Rupert. I hope Lily has been attending adequately to your requirements?'

He turned to Lily, beaming.

'Indeed she has; more than adequately, in fact. Forgive my intrusion at this late hour, Mrs Bodney, but I find I have to return to London tonight and was hoping we could discuss business before I leave.'

'Yes, of course. Please come through to the parlour. Lily, ask Tilda to bring us some refreshment, then I suggest you retire for the night. I'll see you in my parlour at first light for we have much to go through before the ladies arrive tomorrow.'

'Yes, Mrs Bodney,' she answered. Then with a quick nod in Rupert's direction, she turned to leave.

'I'll bid you good evening then, Lily,' Rupert murmured. She could feel him staring at her, and felt compelled to return his look.

'Good evening, Rupert. I trust you have a good journey.'

'And I trust you will not forget this humble merchant in his absence,' he replied, bowing slightly.

'Well, Lily, I have good news,' Mrs Bodney said as they sat in the parlour breaking their fast the next morning. 'Rupert Mountsford has increased, his business with me. Personally, I think it's so that he has more of an excuse to return to Bransbeer, but who am I to complain?' She took a sip from her cup and then smiled. 'In fact, he has a surprise for you, which I'm sure you will find most acceptable.'

'Oh, and what might that be, Mrs Bodney?'

'I really cannot say, for if I tell you it won't be a surprise, will it? Suffice to say you can prepare to be impressed by his generosity. Now, if you've finished your meal, let's get down to business. You can confirm the work is on schedule?'

'Yes, I counted the sprigs last evening to make sure.'

'Good, that means the ladies can now move on to making the tulips. The pattern maker delivered these this morning,' she said, handing Lily the new patterns. 'Make sure they master it quickly, Lily,' she instructed.

Lily hurried through to the workroom where, instead of being at their pillows, the ladies were huddled together in a corner of the room. They were chatting so earnestly, she had to clap her hands in order to get their attention.

'Ladies, please, we have a new pattern to learn,' she said briskly, only to be met with their surprised stares.

'Have you not heard the news?' Emma asked.

'What news?'

'There's been a wrecking,' Mary said. 'Those evil men, they shone their lights along the cliffs until the vessel foundered on the rocks. At least eight dead, so I was told. Poor souls; may they rest in peace,' she stuttered to a halt, shaking her head and crossing herself.

Remembering Tom's words about sowing and reaping crops, Lily felt her heart sink to her boots and she hoped he and his lugger were safe.

'Brought their spoils in at Seaton Hole, they did. Plundered all manner of brandy, silks and gold, even some jewels, so I heard. By the time the Preventatives got wind, there was only bodies and wreckage left floating on the tide,' added Emma, eager to impart what she'd heard.

'It's a terrible thing, wrecking. Smuggling I can understand, what with the taxes being so high, but wrecking is a different barrel of fish. Tricking innocent men onto dangerous rocks then leaving them to perish is an unforgivable sin in my book,' exclaimed Mary, almost beside herself.

'Yes, that is terrible,' Lily agreed. 'I suggest we say a prayer for those poor lost men and their families and then we must begin the day's work before we get any further behind.'

Obediently, the ladies bent their heads and the room fell silent. To think such barbaric things still went on in this day and age, thought Lily. Quietly, she prayed for the souls of the dead to be safely delivered to heaven. Then, after a respectable silence, she brought the ladies back to the present by asking if anyone had seen Cora. They looked at each other then shook their heads. Lily looked at Dora.

'We ain't seen anything of her. Father's hopping like a frog,' she muttered.

'She hasn't been to see me even though she said

I was her best friend,' Nell said sadly.

It seemed Lily had no choice but to set Emma to work at the absent girl's pillow. Lily fought down a groan, knowing she'd have to keep a careful watch over her work.

'Gather round while I show you the pattern to be pricked out,' Lily said.

'I'll be right pleased when we can go back to doing our own ones, I can tell you,' Mary groaned, shaking her head. 'I'm too old for all this new learning.' The others nodded in agreement.

'Come on, ladies, this is for our Queen's wedding,' Lily said, smiling her encouragement.

'Bet the old pattern maker's been in a right old how's yer father. You knows how pernickety she is about her creations,' Mary said, shaking her head. 'By the way, Lily, I saw your Tom this morning.' Her heart skipped a beat. If Mary had seen him this morning, then he was safe. 'He said to tell you he waited till the clouds covered the moon, and he's mighty mad you didn't show.' She looked at Mary in surprise.

'But I did. It was Tom who wasn't there,' she protested, her cheeks burning as she remembered Molly's caustic remarks.

'Well, he says he'll be waiting outside for you when you finish work. He has a surprise for you so I'd spruce yourself up, girl. It sounds like you're in for a treat,' Mary said, winking at her. It seemed it was to be a day for surprises, she thought, going over to check how Emma was doing.

To her delight, Emma had taken to the new pattern immediately, and Lily was gratified to see her working steadily. Perhaps she really had been suffering from nerves after all. However, some of the others were struggling with the change, and she was kept busy all day rectifying their mistakes. By the time everyone was confidently working the tulips, the day was drawing to a close.

As they covered their work, the mood in the room miraculously lifted. Tomorrow was the long-awaited Sabbath when they could forget their lace making and spend time with their families.

Determined not to keep Tom waiting, Lily tidied herself up as best she could. Staring down at her sober dress, she frowned. How she longed for her period, of mourning to be over so she could wear bright colours when she went out.

Tom was perched on the wall outside and he gave her a wry grin when she appeared.

'Thought I'd make sure you weren't going to keep me hanging around again,' he said, jumping down.

'But I waited for you on the beach as we'd arranged.'

'The beach? But I asked Molly to tell you there'd been a change of plan and I'd meet you up by the top field instead. Didn't she speak to you?'

'Oh, yes, she spoke all right, but she didn't give me your message.'

He stood there scratching his head and looking perplexed.

'Never mind, Tom, let's not waste our precious time arguing. Mary says you have a surprise for me,' she said, smiling up at him. Immediately he brightened.

'I want this to be a special night for you, Lily, and first of all, I'm going to treat you to that supper I promised you.'

'Goody, I'm so hungry I could eat a sheep,' she said, laughing and feeling carefree for the first time in ages.

'Well, you might have to make do with mutton pie,' he answered.

'Delicious! You said first, so what are we doing after that?'

'You just wait and see my girl,' he said, tapping the side of his nose and then laughing at her indignant look. 'Tonight, Lily Rose, you are going to eat your fill and then, if you are very good, well, we'll have to see, won't we?'

Seeing the barely suppressed excitement in his eyes, she smiled up at him, happy to go along with his game.

The landlord had lit a fire as the evening was cool, and the scent of burning apple wood mixed with the aroma of good food made the room welcoming. Tom paid her special attention, listening intently as she recounted the events of her day. He even cracked a few jokes as they tucked into their pies washed down with a jug of small beer each. Lily relaxed, enjoying her meal and the rare treat of their having time to spend together. Then Tom's mood changed and, looking serious, he leaned across the table.

'Lily, you do still want to marry me, don't you?' he asked.

'Why, Tom Westlake, what kind of question is that?'

'I need to be sure now that you're mixing with men finer than me.'

'Don't be daft, Tom. You're a fine man yourself.

The one I want to marry.' she said, smiling across at him.

A raucous cackle erupted from the next table and Tom flushed as red as the flames in the fire.

'Come on, let's get out of here,' he muttered, rising to his feet.

Outside, he took her hand and led her away from the bustle of the hostelry. They made their way to the beach, deserted now after the activities of the day. The tide was high, the waves slapping against the boats. She listened to the swishing of the sea being sucked in and out of the pebbles. An owl hooted, and with Tom beside her, she didn't care whether it was a real one or not. Lost in thought, it was some moments before she realized he'd stopped walking and was looking at her strangely.

'Did you hear me, Lily, or have my incredibly handsome looks knocked you out yet again?'

'Sorry, Tom, what were you saying?'

'Oh, nothing important, only that I love you and I'd like you to wear this so everyone knows we're betrothed,' he muttered. Her eyes widened as she gazed at the ring he was holding before her, its ruby gleaming like fire in the gathering darkness.

'Why, Tom, it's beautiful,' she gasped, holding out her left hand. Gently he placed it on her finger. It fitted perfectly; as if it had been made especially for her.

'You like it then?' he asked, his voice teasing.

'I love it and I love you, Tom Westlake, but this must have cost a king's ransom. How on earth did you manage to buy me something so special?'

'Only the best is good enough for you, Lily,' he said, gazing at her so lovingly, she couldn't help but throw her arms around him. He pulled her closer and she felt desire flame, like the fire of the ruby. Making a supreme effort, she pushed him away and then stood looking up at the night sky with its blanket of winking stars, her heart beating erratically.

'The weeks are flying by and it'll not be long till we can wed, Lily,' Tom murmured, putting his arm around her shoulders. She smiled contentedly.

'I can't wait, Tom,' she said, snuggling closer. Together they stood, staring up at the silvery moon, making plans for their future together.

The crunch of pebbles further up the beach brought them rudely back to the present. Reluctantly they broke apart and strolled back towards the village.

'It's been a lovely evening, Tom,' she sighed.

'Yes, it has. You truly are my betrothed now, and everyone will know it,' he said, stopping and kissing her cheek.

'I love your surprise,' she said, running her thumb along the smooth band of the ring. Even though it was dark, she could feel him smiling. 'Red's my favourite colour, you know.'

'Goes with your passionate nature, my girl,' he responded. He lifted her left hand to his lips and she saw the ruby twinkling in the starlight.

'Hey, Tom, saw you over Seaton way last night,' a voice boomed, making them jump. As Lily peered into the darkness, trying to make out who was standing there, Tom snatched up her hand and hurried her up Sea Hill.

Chapter 25

'Hold on a minute,' Lily puffed, trying to keep up with him. What was all that about?'

'Nothing,' he muttered tersely, not relaxing his stride. However, she was thinking back to her earlier conversation in the workroom. Seaton Hole? Wasn't that where they'd said the wrecking had taken place, and hadn't one of them mentioned jewels being plundered?

'Tom Westlake, stop this very minute,' she ordered.

'Sorry, gal, I wasn't thinking,' he said, duly slowing down and smiling at her.

Lily stared him straight in the eye. 'Tell me honestly, Tom, this ring you've given me, did you buy it from a jewellery shop?'

'Why do you ask?' he said, looking down at the ground.

'Well, it seems mighty funny you've not been able to give me a betrothal ring before today.'

'What do you mean, funny?' he said, peering back down the beach.

'Well, I don't mean funny ha ha, Tom Westlake. I mean funny peculiar.' She was getting cross at his evasiveness.

'I'm not with you.'

'No, and you weren't last night, were you?'

'Stop talking in daft riddles, and explain what you mean.'

241

'I mean, Tom Westlake, it's funny peculiar that, after all the months we've been betrothed, you suddenly produce a ring the night after a vessel was wrecked. A vessel that was plundered at Seaton Hole, and only a minute since someone called out that they'd seen you there.' Her voice sounded shrill in the night air, and when she came to a halt there was an ominous silence.

'What are you insinuating, Lily?' Tom asked, his voice dangerously low.

'I'm saying, Tom Westlake, that I have no wish to associate with someone who stoops as low as stealing. So you can take your ring back, you wrecker, you,' she shouted, tearing it from her finger and throwing it to the ground where it lay winking up at her like a drunken eye. He stood looking at her for a long moment, and even in the darkness she could see his lips were set in a tight line.

'If that's what you think of me, Lily Rose, then there's nothing more to be said,' he retorted as he bent down and snatched up the ring. Before she could answer, he stormed off into the darkness.

She stood watching his receding figure and the tears coursed down her cheeks. How could he be involved with anything so horrible? She'd always thought he was an honourable man. Angrily, she wiped her cheeks with the back of her hand and made her way to Picky Pike's. How could such an exciting evening have ended this way?

Letting herself indoors, she crept up the stairs to her room, hoping Mrs Bodney had returned to her own cottage, for she desperately needed to be alone with her thoughts. Throwing herself on her bed, she stared at the stars twinkling through the skylight. To think just a short time ago she was feeling on top of the world. She closed her eyes, but the image of Tom's hurt expression haunted her.

Knowing she would never sleep, she peered round the room; noticing her things strewn about the floor. She'd been in such a hurry to meet Tom earlier she'd left her clothes where she'd stepped out of them. Slowly, she got to her feet and began tidying them away in the tin chest. As she smoothed out the material, her hand touched something hard. It was her mum's Bible, and lying inside was the letter from Aunt Elizabeth. She'd forgotten to ask Mary to read it to her. Tomorrow was the Sabbath so it would have to wait until Monday now.

The church clock chimed one and she realized that it was the Sabbath already. Remembering her vow to visit Beth, she thought about setting out early, but the idea of walking along the track used by the owlers before honest folk were about made her shudder. It wasn't as if Tom was there to protect her. Her heart twisted as if she'd been stabbed with a knife, but she could never marry a wrecker and a thief. It was morally wrong and she had her pride.

Peasants may have pride, Lily, but remember pride cometh before a fall, young lady. As she heard her father's voice, she jumped. He sounded so angry.

'You were the one who taught me right from wrong, Father, so I don't know why you are cross,' she whispered, peering up at the stars.

I warned you about making impulsive judgements. Look before you leap, Lily.

As his voice petered out, she sat back on her bed, mulling over what he'd said. She lost all track of time, so it might have been minutes or hours later that she heard a rustling noise outside her door. She shivered. Was someone lurking outside? Then a branch dashed against the window and she chided herself. It was only the wind freshening. Diving under the covers, she pulled them right up over her head.

'Why did you do it, Tom? It wasn't as if I needed a ring,' she cried, the salty tears dampening the loose tresses of her hair.

She must have fallen into a restless sleep, for streaks of grey and yellow were filtering through the skylight when she opened her eyes. Feeling heavy-headed as well as heavy-hearted, she rose, and tidied herself as best she could.

Then, thinking to freshen her face at the pump, she threw open her door, nearly, tripping over a package on the landing. Frowning, she pulled at the tie, gasping in amazement when she saw inside the most exquisite pair of brown boots with cherry-red stitching.

'Oh my,' she murmured, picking them up and caressing the soft skin. She heard a chuckle and saw Mrs Bodnney smiling at her from the bottom of the stairs.

'There, didn't I tell you Rupert had a surprise for you?'

'You mean these really are for me?' she asked, hardly daring to believe her good fortune. They were fashioned from the finest-quality leather and would have cost more than she'd ever be able to afford.

'Well, put them on and come and show me,' Mrs Bodney said, laughing at the bemused expression on Lily's face. Obeying, she gently eased her feet into them, marvelling at their softness. Then, fingers fumbling with excitement, she tied the laces and took a few steps along the landing. They fitted like gloves and felt so comfortable she almost floated down the stairs.

'Well, Lily, there's no denying you've landed on your feet, as it were, pardoning my pun, of course. It will be good to see you properly attired in my workroom tomorrow.'

'But I couldn't possibly keep them. The ones Albert sized me for should be ready soon.'

'I think you misunderstand, Lily. These are as well as the hobnailed ones you ordered. When Rupert heard how enchanted you were with the boots Albert had made for her ladyship, he gave instruction that a similar pair be made for you. He has already settled his dues so there can be no argument.'

'Oh, but I couldn't possibly accept–' Lily began.

'Fiddlesticks,' said Mrs Bodney, waving her hands in the air. 'The dear man wants to treat you, and my advice is that you act like a lady and accept his gift graciously. And, of course, be extra nice to him when next you meet,' she added, winking at Lily.

Remembering how he'd beamed when she'd smiled at him, Lily thought this would be very easy to do.

'Now,' Mrs Bodney said briskly, 'how are you spending this Sabbath? Off somewhere nice with Tom, no doubt. It's probably best if you're discreet

245

about those boots, if you know what I mean,' she added, tapping the side of her nose with her finger.

At the mention of Tom's name, Lily's good mood vanished.

'I'm going to visit Beth in Coombe,' she said carefully, but there must have been something strange in her voice for Mrs Bodney studied her closely.

'Ah, your little sister; you must miss her.'

'Yes, I do,' Lily agreed. 'But as Aunt Elizabeth said, she's better off with Mrs Goode. She's at home all day and then, of course, Beth has Harriet to play with.'

Mrs Bodney was nodding her head but her mind was already on other matters. 'Well, don't let me keep you. I'll see you bright and early to-morrow in the workroom then; complete with new boots.' She looked meaningfully at Lily's feet.

'Yes, Mrs Bodney,' Lily answered, fleeing back upstairs to the safety of her room.

Now she was committed to keeping the boots. Exquisite they may be, but it didn't sit well with her that Rupert had paid for them. Heedless of the expensive leather, she kicked them off and stepped into her old ones. Men – why did they make life so difficult?

As she made the arduous trek to Coombe, she fretted and fumed so that by the time she reached Mrs Goode's cottage she hardly knew how she'd got there.

'Lily,' Beth shrieked, as she was shown inside. 'Come and see what I've made,' she hopped up and down excitedly so that, despite her low mood,

Lily couldn't help smiling. She duly admired the lace her sister had made, which, for a four-year-old, was very good indeed and of saleable quality.

'Well done, Beth,' she said, trying to inject some enthusiasm into her voice.

'She'll be earning her keep before much longer,' said Mrs Goode, smiling and ruffling the little girl's hair. 'Which is more than can be said for this little rogue,' she added fondly as Harriet appeared carrying Tiger the tabby cat.

'I do wish you'd let me give you something for looking after her, Mrs Goode. I feel mean when I'm earning good money. I could afford to pay you something on a regular basis,' she said, putting her hand in her pocket and drawing out her money pouch.

Mrs Goode shook her head. 'Put it away, Lily. You know right well that neighbours help each other out, not take money. Besides, you gave me that lace job, which I got paid nicely for, thank you. No, you keep your wages for when you're wed.'

Lily sighed and sat down on the hearth beside Beth.

'So what's up then, Lily?' Mrs Goode asked, eyeing her shrewdly. 'Do you want to tell me what's weighing you down, apart from that heavy money pouch of course?' she said, jokingly.

Lily shrugged. 'Men, they're just no good,' she burst out, then flushed guiltily as she remembered the other woman had lost her husband the previous year. Yet, Mrs Goode just smiled knowingly.

'They're not all bad, ducks. Whatever your Tom's done, happen it'll all come out in the wash,' she said, patting Lily on the shoulder. 'Now come through to the kitchen, I've a nice bit of stew cooking. Time for nuncheon, girls,' she shouted over her shoulder and, cat following, they came charging, almost knocking Lily over in their haste.

Listening to their incessant chatter as they wolfed down their food, Lily realized that Beth was truly happy here and was amazed at how much she ate. Although she had little appetite herself, for the sake of good manners she forced down a few mouthfuls. However, Mrs Goode wasn't fooled.

'Whatever's ailing you, Lily, you'd best get it sorted, and soon, for that frown on your forehead will turn into a huge wrinkle if the wind changes–'

'Sorry, Mrs Goode, I'm a right wet rag, I know,' she said, sighing and getting to her feet. 'I'd best be getting back. I need to get everything sorted for the morrow.'

'Remember, if you want to talk, well, I'm a good listener and one that can keep her mouth shut,' Grace Goode added, smiling gently.

'You'll come and see me again soon, won't you, Lily?' Beth asked, hopping up and down.

'Of course I will,' she said, tweaking the girl's silky hair. 'Maybe I'll even bring you a little present, if you're good.'

'Now, don't you go worrying about young Beth,' Mrs Goode said, showing Lily out. 'She's settled in now and, like I told your aunt, she does a fine job of keeping Harriet out of my hair whilst I'm working.'

Lily smiled. 'You're very kind, Mrs Goode. It's a relief to know she's happy and being so well looked after. Aunt Elizabeth said she would be better off living with you, and she was right. I'll visit again as soon as I'm able, though,' she added, throwing her shawl around her and beginning her journey back to Bransbeer.

The next week passed in a blur as Mrs Bodney, worried the commission wasn't going to be completed in time, had taken to appearing suddenly in the workroom. The ladies, already working as diligently as they could, became restless and tempers were frayed. To make matters worse, the weather had been humid and the workroom was stifling, Mrs Bodney had said a storm was in the offing and as she wearily made her way to the workroom on the Saturday morning Lily could hear raindrops pattering on the roof. Thank goodness it was nearing the end of the week, she thought. At least they'd get a break from each other.

Then she noticed the hem on her skirt was hanging down. Cursing silently and not wishing to incur the wrath of her employer, she sat down, hitched up the material and began sewing. Lost in thought, she didn't notice Mary coming into the room.

'That rain's getting heavier. Have you seen those clouds? They be as black as Old Nick himself. Reckon we'll be in for a right old blow later. Oh…' she said, her voice tailing off when she saw Lily's boots.

'Goodness, Lily, just look at you,' she exclaimed, her eyes widening. 'I'm sure even the extra money you get as overseer wouldn't pay for quality like that.' There was a pause, then she frowned. 'Hey, you're not giving favours to that fancy merchant, I hope. 'Cos if you're getting gifts like that, your mother would be turning–'

'No, of course not, Mary,' Lily retorted, turning away. So that was what Mrs Bodney had meant about her getting luxuries for being nice, she thought, going hot with embarrassment.

Just then, the others came clattering in and Lily breathed a sigh of relief. Greeting them quickly, she set them to work. Then, careful to cover her boots with her long skirt, she settled on her stool. As her bobbins gathered pace, so did her thoughts. She'd have to tell Mrs Bodney she wasn't like that. The only man she wanted was Tom, but he hadn't called to see her. On Sunday she'd been certain that when she returned from Coombe, he'd be waiting to reassure her he had bought that ring. She wiped her burning forehead with the back of her hand. Last night, unable to sleep yet again, she'd tossed and turned so that now her head ached as much as her heart. If Tom hadn't called to see her, it could only mean one thing, couldn't it?

'Lily, I've gone wrong somewhere.'

Emma's plaintive wail roused her from her thoughts and, sighing, she made her way across the room. Relieved to find the girl had merely missed enclosing a pin on the previous round, she quickly rectified her mistake and then made her way back to her own pillow.

But she'd only just picked up her bobbins when she heard a giggle. Looking up, she saw the ladies were grinning and nudging each other as they stared at her feet under the table. Oh, fish bones,

250

she thought, they'd spotted her boots. Quickly she picked up the brass bell and rang it vigorously.

'Time for your break, ladies,' she called out. Thankfully, it had stopped raining and a watery sun was peeking out from behind some ominously lowering clouds. Just be dry for half an hour, she prayed, returning to her pillow and her thoughts. Grinning, as they picked up their pieces, the ladies filed outside. Although she could do with some fresh air herself, there was no way she was joining them, for she could well imagine the questions they'd ask.

The afternoon passed slowly with the quiet of the workroom broken periodically by the rising wind soughing like a lost soul around the building and down the chimney. Then the heavens opened and the rain came down like pebbles, lashing against the windowpanes. The room grew so dark they could hardly see their work and Lily had no option but to send the ladies home.

'Be sure to be here early on Monday,' she called as she watched them hurrying on their way, trying to dodge the puddles. She returned to her pillow, but before long, she too had to admit defeat. Slowly she made her way upstairs, dreading being alone again, for thoughts of Tom plagued her, constantly. However, she'd no sooner thrown herself, still fully dressed, onto her bed than tiredness caught up with her, and she sank into an exhausted sleep.

She could hear banging. She could hear shouting. She wished it would stop. Her head felt so heavy.

251

'Lily, Lily.'

Disorientated, she opened her eyes and peered up at the skylight, but it was dark as pitch. There wasn't one single star to be seen. Her eyes closed and she was just drifting back to sleep when the banging started up again.

'For God's sake, Lily, will you open the door?' Mary's angry voice called again.

Getting groggily to her feet, she ran downstairs, opened the door and saw the other woman, drenched and dishevelled, hopping from one leg to the other.

'Thank God. I thought you'd never hear me. You'd best come quick. This blow's a big one all right, and there's a sea fog so thick no one can see a thing,' she wailed, almost beside herself.

'Well, we've got through blows before,' Lily answered, surprised at the other woman's open distress.

'But the fishing fleet's out there. They set sail first thing and haven't returned.'

'Why didn't you say? What's the time?' Lily gabbled, grabbing her shawl from the peg by the door.

'Nigh on midnight. They should have been back hours since.'

Lily's heart flipped so hard she thought it was going to come right up into her throat. 'Tom?'

'It was your Tom's boat leading them.'

'Oh, no,' she gasped.

'That's one heck of a storm raging out there. The sea's frothing like a cauldron and with the fog they'll not be able to see the lights from the Preventatives' station.'

But Lily didn't wait to hear any more. Pushing past the woman she clattered down the front steps and out into the street.

Chapter 26

Lily gasped as the bank of swirling mist engulfed her, muffling the sound of her boots on the cobbles as she hurried towards the cove. With her heart pounding and her breath ragged, she joined the huddle of women hugging the shoreline. As one, they peered into the gloom, their faces etched with worry. The wind was whipping the waves into rollers, lashing them against the rocks and sending sprays of salt water over their already drenched bodies.

''Tis no good us standing here, we can't see a blooming thing in this,' shouted the woman beside her, grabbing her arm.

'Let's go up to the headland. It's higher and we might catch sight of something there,' Lily murmured in agreement. One by one, the forlorn little group picked their way over the mounds of stinking seaweed and retraced their steps back up Sea Hill. Her father would soon make use of that for fertilizing his beloved vegetables, she thought, then felt a pang when she remembered he was no longer with them.

Heads down against the rain, the little group trudged up the well-worn cliff path. Lily pulled her already drenched shawl tighter around her and sent up a silent prayer for Tom to be safe, for she didn't think she could bear it if someone else she loved was taken from her. And love him she did, whatever he might have done. She knew that now.

Buffeted by the wind, which at times threatened to propel them right off the cliff, the little group clung together as they kept their vigil, the older women muttering they'd never seen a blow like it. Then a cry went up. The woman Lily had met on the beach earlier was jumping up and down, shouting she'd seen a shape in the swirling mist. Hopes rose as they all peered into the murk, only to be dashed when it turned out to be debris tossing on the spume. Unwilling to voice their fears, the women fell silent, but it was all too much for one waiting wife and she crumpled to the ground. Lily moved to help her but already the woman was being comforted by those standing closer. Then Lily spotted Tom's mother, tears glistening like diamonds in the gloom, standing amongst them. Hurrying over to her, Lily reached out to embrace her, but the woman stared at her as if she were a stranger.

'It's me, Lily, Mrs Westlake,' she said softly.

The woman gave a heartfelt sigh. 'I know full well who you are, Lily. I'm just surprised you're wasting your precious time here.'

'Wasting my time? But I'm waiting to see Tom safely home like you are,' she said, assuming worry was affecting the older woman.

'Oh? And why would you concern yourself about him this day, when he wasn't good enough for you on the last weekend?' she demanded.

'What do you mean, not good enough?' she

asked, shaking her head. But Tom's mother was glaring at her so fiercely that even if Lily hadn't been able to make out her features in the swirling mist she'd have felt the hostility emanating from her.

'All excited he was when he went out last Saturday night. Then home he came with a face like a beached bass. Seemed his nana's ring wasn't good enough for you. And after he'd walked all the way to Seaton to beg her to let him have it sooner rather than later, if you get my drift.'

'You mean that ruby ring belonged to his grandmother?' Lily gasped, staring at her future mother-in-law in horror.

'Of course it did. It was her most treasured possession. Only wore it high days and holidays, mind. Tom's father, bless his soul, wanted it for me when we got betrothed, but she wasn't having any of it.'

'Oh, Mrs Westlake, I had no idea,' she whispered, thinking of Tom's set face when she'd hurled the ring back at him.

'No, well, you wouldn't. Tom always was the apple of her eye. Can't think why it wasn't good enough for you, though. I'd have given my eye teeth for it. Still, there we are. There's no accounting for taste.'

'But I thought...' Lily's voice tailed off. She could hardly admit to Tom's mother what she had thought, could she? Oh, Tom, please hurry home so I can make amends, she prayed silently. Then she realized Mrs Westlake was still speaking.

'And pray, just what did you think, young Lily Rose?'

'But Mrs Westlake, it was all a terrible misunderstanding,' she said, wringing her hands in despair.

Mrs Westlake shrugged. 'I don't think Tom saw it that way. Oh, why isn't he back yet?' she groaned, and this time when Lily put her arm around her shoulder she didn't pull away.

There, Lily, didn't I say you'd been impetuous? her father's voice whispered in her ear.

Yes, Father, she agreed silently for, as ever, he was right. Please, please make him come home soon, she beseeched him. I promise I'll never judge anyone like that again.

But there was no answer, only the screaming of the wind and the sobbing of the waiting women.

'Mercy me, the fog seems to be lifting at last,' Tom's mother said, her voice rising in hope.

'Was Tom terribly upset, Mrs Westlake?' Lily asked.

'Aye, Lily, he was. He's been working himself into the ground, literally, what with harvesting them potatoes up on the platts as well as going out in the boat fishing and seeing to the pots. Just dug up his second crop this year, he had. He was that proud of the money he was putting by, and all so you two could wed as soon as you're out of mourning for your mother, God rest her soul.'

Lily turned towards the other woman in surprise. 'He's been working the platts?'

'That's what I said. You really should learn to listen properly, my girl.'

Lily fought back the retort that sprang to her lips. That explained why Tom had been shifty when she'd ask him what he was doing up at Coombe. He'd been earning as much as he could to match her wages, even if it meant him doing three jobs to her one. Her heart swelled in admiration. Just wait until he returned and she told him how proud she was of him, she thought, her heart lifting.

Always supposing he did return. Her heart sank again. Oh dear God in heaven, please let him be safe, she prayed. Supposing he perished before she had the opportunity to tell him how much she loved him? She couldn't bear his being out there, thinking she didn't care for him. How she regretted accusing him of being mixed up with the wreckers at Seaton Hole. She should have known he wasn't like that. Why hadn't she accepted his ring in the spirit in which he'd given it? She looked around at the huddle of fisher-women waiting and hoping, in the time-honoured way, and prayed again that the fishing fleet would return safely.

Grey was lightening the sky when the cry went up. Anxiously the huddle of women moved closer to the cliff edge, squinting towards the horizon. Lily stared until she thought her eyes would glaze over. Then she saw them: tiny specks in the distance. Too far to see for sure that it was the fishing fleet but, hope in heart and heart in mouth, the women watched and waited until they were sure it was them. A cheer went up and, tiredness and frozen feet forgotten, they hurried down to the beach. There they stood watching and waiting again, as with agonizing slowness, the boats drew closer to the shore.

Suddenly women were hurrying home to make sure their fires were burning and pots of broth bubbling, ready to welcome their menfolk. Mrs

Westlake bustled off, promising she'd be back before the first boat touched land, and Lily was left alone with her thoughts. Her father had been right when he'd told her she should be sure of her facts before casting judgement, and she vowed she would in future. It had been a terrifying night, but now she could see Tom's red sails with white spars inching closer, and she couldn't wait to put things right between them.

It was still another hour before the first boat hit the pebbles and the weary men clambered out, dragging it clear of the breaking seas. One by one their womenfolk had returned, silently reforming in their little group and waiting until, as tradition decreed, the last man had touched land. Then as one they swarmed down the beach, throwing their arms around their loved ones, hugging them tightly as if they'd never let them go.

Lily hopped up and down impatiently as Tom clambered wearily from his boat and helped his crew drag it clear of the surf. Then she could wait no longer.

'Tom, oh, Tom,' she cried, racing down the beach towards him. Looking up, he glared at her then deliberately turned away. Shocked, Lily stood rooted to the spot before going over and taking his arm.

'Tom, please, I need to talk to you. There's been a misunderstanding.'

Shaking off her arm, he turned towards her, his expression grim.

'Too right there's been a misunderstanding. I thought you was a sweet young woman, Lily. Instead, I find out you're a suspicious, mistrustful shrew,' he barked, before striding up the beach, leaving her gaping after him like a fish out of water.

'But, Tom, your mother told me about the ring being your nana's and I want you to know I'll be proud to wear it,' she shouted after him.

'Huh, don't think you'll be wearing any ring of mine 'cos I'll not be offering one. As for my dear nana's ruby, you're not worthy even to touch it,' he spat out over his shoulder as, taking his mother's arm, he made his way home.

'Tom, please, let's talk,' panted Lily, running after him and catching hold of his arm again. 'I've been thinking all through the long night and–'

Snatching his arm away, he turned and snapped, 'I've been thinking all through the long night too; thinking that anyone who could accuse me of the treachery you did, Lily, is not worth getting out of bed for, let alone spending time with. Go back to your fancy merchant. He's welcome to you.'

'He isn't...' she began, but he'd already turned on his heel and she was talking to the wind.

The haulers and handlers were calling to each other as they dragged the storm-torn fishing boats further up the beach to safety; but Lily hardly noticed. She was watching Tom embrace his mother; and as the two of them made their way up the hill she didn't know whether to scream or cry. Perhaps he'd see reason when he'd calmed down and had some rest, she thought, picking up the largest cobble she could find and hurling it into the water. Then, squaring her shoulders, she made her way back towards Picky Pike's. Lost in thought, she barely noticed, even though there was now full daylight, that her boots were filled with salt water, seaweed and goodness knew what else.

'Well, Lily Rose, doesn't that prove you can't keep your fellow? He's better off without the likes of you. Go and suck up to your fancy merchant and leave Tom to someone who knows what a real man needs,' cried Molly.

As Lily looked at the girl hanging out of the shop door, her round face beaming with malicious glee, something snapped inside her. Quickly scraping the caked mud and seaweed off her boots, she threw it over the taunting woman, and then continued her journey.

'I'll get you for that. You see if I don't, Lily Rose,' Molly screeched after her.

'Well, well, that was hardly fitting behaviour for an overseer.'

Spinning round, she nearly collided with Squire Clinsden stumbling out of the alehouse. Of all the rotten luck, she thought.

'Perhaps I should escort you back to your place of employment,' he said, clearly enjoying her discomfort.

'That isn't necessary, thank you.' Somehow she managed to force the words out between clenched teeth.

'Oh, but I think it is. After all, Mrs Bodney is a stickler for propriety. What would she say if she heard her overseer had been acting like a common gutter snipe?' he sneered, moving closer to her.

Although she managed to evade his touch, the smell of liquor on his breath was so strong it made her recoil. Thinking it better not to rile him when he was under the influence, she turned to continue her journey.

'Not so quickly, young Lily,' the squire said, grabbing her wrist. 'Now if you're nice to me and make it worth my while, I might just ignore what I saw earlier. What do you think?' He stood leering at her, his bloodshot eyes roving over her body in such an intimate way, she wanted to jump straight into the brook and scrub herself clean.

'I think you spend too much time in the alehouse and that it's mighty funny you're always coming out of it just as I pass by,' she answered.

'I'll have you know I have been busy conducting my business, which is more than can be said for you, judging by the state of you,' he sneered.

The events of the past hours caught up with her and she snapped back without thinking, 'What about the state of you? You're always so full of liquor you couldn't possibly conduct business.' His eyes narrowed and she stepped quickly backwards.

'Not so quickly, young Lily,' he snarled. 'You're going nowhere until you tell me what you meant by that remark. Have you been spying on me?'

'Of course not,' she retorted, cursing herself for rising to his bait.

'Then what do you know about my movements? Tell me, Lily, or it will be all the worse for you. It's about time someone taught you some good manners,' he snarled, tightening his grip on her arm.

Chapter 27

Desperately, Lily looked around for a means of escape, but his other arm caught her round the waist. Before she knew it, he was dragging her into the deserted alley leading to the stables behind the hostelry. She kicked out, managing to make contact with his ankle, but this only served to excite him.

'Playing hard to get, my lovely? Come on, you know you want it.' His guttural grunting made her skin prickle with revulsion. She could feel the bile rising in her throat as she fought back. 'Oh, I love a spirited filly; they always give the best ride I find,' he chortled, leering down at her. 'Come on, you little hussy. You've been teasing me for months, taunting me with that nubile body of yours.'

Desire as well as drink seemed to be lending him some extra strength, and inch by inch, she was dragged closer to the stables. She spat at him but he just laughed, tightened his grip and carried on pulling. Then she tried going limp so that her body was a dead weight. But even that was no good for he was as excited as a rampant bull. Summoning the last of her strength, she screamed as loudly as she could but his hand clamped over her mouth. The stench of horse and tobacco invaded her senses, making her retch.

'No good screaming, there's no one to hear you. Your fisher friend's not around to help, is he?' Squire Clinsden hissed in her ear, tightening his grip once more as he pulled her ever closer to the stables. Turning her head, Lily managed to sink her teeth into his hand. He swore, letting her go so abruptly she almost fell to the ground. As she steadied herself, a figure appeared out of the shadows.

'There you are, husband,' Lady Clinsden said, her silky soft voice belying the flinty glint in her eyes. 'I wondered where you'd got to.'

'My dear, this is a surprise. I had no idea you were visiting Bransbeer today,' the squire stammered struggling to regain his composure. He gestured towards Lily. 'I was just finalizing arrangements for our Harvest Supper. Knowing how much it means to you, my dearest, I've been trying to persuade Lily here to serve at table,' he simpered.

'Now if that were true, I'd be delighted,' Lady Clinsden cut in, giving Lily a knowing look. 'However, Jean Bodney confided in me only yesterday that her ladies are all working every daylight hour to get her commission completed by the November deadline. I will be most surprised, therefore, if Lily will have any spare time available.'

At the mention of her employer's name, Lily's heart skipped a beat. Seizing the opportunity to escape, she muttered, 'Forgive me, Lady Clinsden, but I really must be getting back.'

'Of course, my dear, but before you do, might I suggest you clean yourself up a bit?' she said, pointing to Lily's dress.

Looking down, Lily saw it was dishevelled and spattered with mud and weed, while her feet were streaked with salt and slime. Seeing sympathy and understanding in the other woman's eyes, she couldn't help wondering again why this refined lady was saddled with such a despicable man.

'Come with me, Lily. You can use the room I've hired at the hostelry and tell me what's been going on.'

'You've hired a room here? But why?' the squire asked, visibly paling, but Lady Clinsden just smiled sweetly. 'There's no need for you to concern yourself my dear,' the squire blustered, looking decidedly uncomfortable. 'I'm sure young Lily can take care of herself.'

Ignoring him, his wife took Lily's arm and led her back through the alley and into the safety of the hostelry. As they entered, Lady Clinsden called to the landlord for refreshment to be sent upstairs, and moments later Lily found herself being shown into a large airy room. She stared around, taking in the comfortable chairs, embroidered antimacassars draped over their backs, the highly polished table and dresser.

'I didn't know you had accommodation here, Lady Clinsden,' she said, surprised.

'I hire it to use on the days I visit the almshouses. I rather think it will have come as quite a shock to my husband, though,' she said, laughing. 'Especially as he uses this place for entertaining his ... well, I was going to say lady friends, but that would be a misnomer if ever there was one.'

'Pardon me, Lady Clinsden, but I don't know how you put up with him,' Lily burst out, then covered her mouth with her hand. 'Sorry, that was dreadfully rude,' she whispered, sure the other woman would be cross.

Instead Lady Clinsden smiled sadly. 'He wasn't so bad before consumption took our eldest son. Charles was his favourite, you see. After that he began visiting the grave each day, which led him on to the alehouse.' She sighed. 'He said it was the shock of losing an heir that turned him to drowning his sorrows in drink.'

'Oh, Lady Clinsden, that's terrible,' Lily said.

'Yes. Now, you go and get freshened up,' she said briskly, gesturing to the washstand discreetly placed in the far corner of the room.

As Lily was rinsing her face, Lady Clinsden said, 'I was pleased to hear the fishing fleet returned safely. You must be relieved to have your Tom back on dry land.'

Remembering the cold look in her beloved's eyes and the harsh words he'd used, Lily felt her heart sink. However, she was saved from answering by a sharp rap on the door.

A buxom woman entered the room bearing a laden tray. Lady Clinsden smiled her thanks and then turned to Lily.

'You finish tidying up, whilst I pour our tea.'

'But I should get back; Mrs Bodney will be wondering why I haven't appeared this morning.'

'Remember it's the Sabbath, Lily, so surely you don't have to hurry. Besides, you are in no state to go anywhere until you've had some hot tea and toast. You look terribly fatigued, if you don't mind my saying so.' As she settled herself on the chair and began pouring tea into dainty china tea cups, Lily did as she'd been told.

She then did her best to clean up her mud-spattered clothes. Finally, she used the cloth to wipe over her boots, and as she bent down to put them on, she couldn't help thinking how fortunate it was she had not put on her new ones by mistake in her haste to get down to the beach. Having smoothed down her dress and apron, she straightened her cap and went over to where Lady Clinsden was waiting.

'That's better, Lily. Now sit down and partake of some breakfast,' the other woman said, passing her a plate of buttered toast.

Remembering to eat in a ladylike manner, Lily ignored her rumbling stomach and nibbled daintily. They sat in companionable silence until they'd finished and then Lily jumped to her feet.

'That was delicious, thank you, Lady Clinsden, but I really must be getting back to the workroom. I have to prepare all the materials ready for tomorrow. We are working against the clock, as Mrs Bodney says, and if we don't get this commission finished for Queen Vic...' Her voice petered out as she put her hand to her mouth in horror.

'Queen Victoria,' Lady Clinsden finished for her.

Lily stared aghast. 'You know who the lace is for?' she asked in amazement.

'Indeed I do. Jean is a dear friend. She often confides in me, knowing I'm discreet.' Realizing that she hadn't given away the secret, Lily breathed a sigh of relief. 'I have to confess to sharing things with her too,' Lady Clinsden added, smiling conspiratorially.

'She often gives me advice as well, especially about dressing correctly,' Lily said, looking down wryly at her crumpled clothes. 'It's so depressing

266

having to wear black all the time.'

Lady Clinsden nodded, then peered into the looking-glass. 'Now, that I can empathize with,' she said, sighing at her reflection. Lily remembered Mrs Bodney telling her the squire insisted Lady Clinsden always had her dresses made to the same pattern. She had been so kind, Lily wanted to help her now.

'I had a thought, Lady Clinsden, if you won't think me too disrespectful mentioning it.' Emboldened by the other woman's encouraging look, she went on, 'Were I to make you some lace collars and cuffs in various designs you could attach them to the dresses to change and enhance their appearance.'

Lady Clinsden pondered for a moment and then smiled. 'That's a splendid idea, Lily, and when you have finished working for Mrs Bodney, I shall commission you to do just that. Now, if you're sure you've had enough to eat, I shall walk you back.'

'You don't need to come with me, Lady Clinsden,' Lily said quickly.

'I think it would be better if I did. You still look dreadfully pale, and besides, I need to speak with Jean,' Lady Clinsden replied.

Tiredness was indeed threatening to overwhelm Lily but she managed to stifle a yawn.

No sooner had they entered Picky Pike's than Mrs Bodney came bustling out, all concern.

'Lily, dear, I hear you were out all night waiting for the boats to come in. You look exhausted. I suggest you go to your room and rest,' she said firmly.

Gratefully, Lily nodded and went up the stairs.

Sinking onto the edge of the bed, she wearily kicked off her boots then lay back on the covers. She closed her eyes and sank into oblivion.

Then arms were holding her, shaking her. 'Leave me alone, you brute,' she screamed, trying to struggle free

Chapter 28

'Hush, Lily dear.' As the softly spoken words penetrated her fuddled brain, she opened her eyes to find herself staring into the face of her employer.

'I'm sorry, Mrs Bodney. I thought you were someone else,' she muttered, embarrassed.

'Evidently, my dear, and after my discussion with Lady Clinsden yesterday I think I know whom.'

'Oh,' she whispered. Then, realizing what Mrs Bodney had said, her eyes widened in alarm and she struggled to sit up. 'Yesterday?' she repeated.

'Yes, it's Monday morning, Lily. I sent Tilda up earlier with some broth, but she couldn't rouse you. The silly girl thought you were dead and came crying to me. Clearly, thank heavens, you are not. However, since you didn't wake to eat your broth, your body must be in need of nourishment. I suggest you change your dress and then come down to the parlour.'

'But my work...' Lily tried to protest, but she was feeling light-headed, almost as if she was floating.

'No buts. Tilda has laid out a clean dress, and your new work boots are ready,' she said, gesturing to the shiny black hobnailed boots by the chest. 'And not a moment too soon,' she added, shaking her head at the salt-encrusted pair beside the bed. Even Lily could see they could no longer be worn.

When Mrs Bodney had left, Lily gingerly clambered out of bed. She stared down at her crumpled dress and groaned. Not only had she not woken in time for work, she'd gone to bed without undressing Mrs Bodney would never put up with an overseer who had such slovenly ways. She sank back onto the mattress, covering her face with her hands. If she lost her job, she'd have no home. Tom; she'd go to Tom. Then she remembered his bitter outburst, and the tears fell.

Peasants aren't pessimists, Lily. They don't give up; they get on.

She heard her father's voice in her ear and warmth crept through her body like a burst of sunlight. He hadn't deserted her, after all.

'You are right, Father, and I will,' she whispered, getting determinedly to her feet. Stepping into her new black leather boots, she smiled. They fitted perfectly, and although they were sturdy and not a bit like the dainty ones with cherry-red stitching she felt a bubble of excitement inside that they were brand new and she could wear them every day.

Minutes later she was in the parlour, dressed and tidied. Mrs Bodney nodded down at her feet. 'At last you look worthy of the post of overseer.'

'You must tell me what I owe, Mrs Bodney, for I do have some savings put by.'

'We will talk about that some other time, Lily. Now we have business to attend to.'

'I'm very sorry for not waking at dawn, especially with the deadline...' She stuttered to a halt as the other lady held up her hand, then pointed to the steaming bowl and chunk of bread on the table beside her.

'First you must eat. I shall go and check that the ladies are all present, and when I return we will talk.' As her employer bustled from the room, the fragrant aroma of vegetable broth wafted in Lily's direction. She picked up the spoon and ate ravenously. By the time Mrs Bodney returned, her bowl was drained.

'Feeling better?'

'Yes, thank you, Mrs Bodney. I'm ready to work like ten men, well, women. That is, if I still have a job?' she asked, hardly daring to look up.

'Yes, you do for I understand you needed to ensure Tom had returned safely. Now, we must discuss our schedule. I've been informed that the silk for Her Majesty's dress is nearing completion and that she will require all the lace not only made but to be sewn up and ready by the 25th of November.'

'St Catherine's Day,' Lily said.

Mrs Bodney smiled ruefully. 'I can't deny it's appropriate, what with her being the patron saint of lace makers. However, whilst we've finished making the lace for the flounce, we still have the veil and other adornments to finish, plus the Bertha collar, of course. Then it will all require sewing up and attaching to the netting. Being positive, the designs of tulips, leaves and scrolls left to make will be the same only smaller and, as Cora has seen fit to return, we have an extra pair of hands.'

'You've taken her back?' Lily asked, her eyes widening in surprise.

'I had little choice. We mustn't look a gift pony in the mouth, as they say. Now before you resume your duties, tell me how Tom is.'

'He ... well, I ... that is, I really need to speak to him.'

'Hmm,' her employer said, giving her a penetrating look. 'What about the,squire? Have you ever complained about his behaviour towards you?' Mrs Bodney asked. Lily stared at the other woman in surprise.

'The likes of me are hardly in a position to complain about the squire, Mrs Bodney. He would make my life a misery...' Her voice tailed off. Surely her employer knew that peasants were in no position to complain.

'Well,' Mrs Bodney said, pursing her lips, 'as Lady Clinsden is fond of saying, there's more than one way to skin a cat.' Blimey, there was that cat again, Lily thought.

'Right, Lily, it's time you got back to the workroom. I want you to encourage the ladies to work as fast as they can without compromising the quality of their work. You also need to make up for the time you've lost on your own work so I'm sure I can trust you will not leave here until it is back on schedule.'

Relieved she still had her job, Lily nodded. But as her employer left the parlour, she couldn't help wondering when she'd be able to see Tom. For see him she must, and very soon.

271

As Lily entered the workroom, the ladies looked up from their pillows, hardly able to contain their curiosity. As ever, though, it was Mary who spoke.

'Morning, Lily; here, I'll move and let you have your rightful place.' But as the woman struggled to get to her feet; Lily noticed she had a large bandage covering the lower part of her leg.

'What's the matter with your ankle, Mary?' she asked.

'Oh, 'tis nothing,' the other woman answered, shrugging.

'She tripped going after you in that murk,' Nell burst out, 'and you didn't even stop to see if she was all right.'

'Hush now, Nell,' Mary admonished.

'Well, I think it was right selfish of her leaving you like that,' spluttered the normally mild Nora.

'But I didn't know...' Lily began, shaking her head.

'Course you didn't, Lily, don't worry yourself. You was in a hurry to make sure your Tom and the fleet came home safe. And they all did, thank the Lord,' Mary said, making the sign of the cross in front of her.

Hearing Tom's name, Lily felt a pang and was torn between duty and desire. However, desperate as she was to see him, she knew she had to produce some work before she could even think of leaving the workroom or she'd be out on the street, sure as sprats were sprats. Mrs Bodney would only tolerate so much.

'Thanks, Mary. I really am sorry about your ankle, though, and I hope it's not too painful.'

'I've suffered worse.' But as the woman sat there smiling ruefully, Lily remembered that in her desperation to get to the harbour she had pushed past Mary on the front steps.

'Oh. Mary, tell me it wasn't because of me you fell?' she asked, taking the woman's hand.

'Dearie me, no, Lily,' Mary answered, looking quickly, away.

Not convinced the other woman was telling the truth, but at a loss to know what to do, Lily shrugged, saying, 'Well, I'm sorry if it was because of me. I feel dreadful that I didn't know you'd fallen. Has everything else been all right?' she asked, looking anxiously at the woman.

'Yes, I think so. We've been working that hard since Mrs Bodney poked her head in this morning,' she said, then pointed to the sprigs heaped on the dresser. 'At least we are onto the smaller pieces now.'

'That's as may be,' Emma piped up, 'but do you know how many we need?'

'Mrs Bodney is very pleased with your work but we are under even more pressure as the Queen now wants her lace delivered earlier than originally planned,' Lily told them.

A groan went round the workroom but they knew they were being paid well and bent their heads over their pillows.

'I'm sure it will be worth it when we see the Queen in all her finery,' Lily said, smiling.

'As if that's likely to happen,' Cora snorted.

'It'll only be Mrs Bodney who'll get to see her on her wedding day,' Nell said, shaking her head. The others murmured in agreement. Realizing she'd inadvertently distracted them from their work Lily bowed her head over her pillow and hoped they'd follow her example. Luckily they did, and silence descended on the room.

As her movements gained pace, so did her thoughts. When would she see Tom? Would he forgive her for the terrible things she'd said? Maybe it was exhaustion that made him speak to her so harshly yesterday. In her heart, though, she knew she'd wronged him terribly, for hadn't he always told her that trust was at the heart of a relationship?

'Ooh, me stomach thinks me throat's cut.'

Jolted from her musing, she looked up to see Cora running her hand across her throat, clearly intent on letting Lily know it was time for their break. Despite her worries, she couldn't help but be amused at the girl's theatrics; obviously she was back to normal, Lily thought, feeling strangely relieved. Quickly, she got up and rang the little bell.

As the ladies eagerly hurried out into the sun-filled courtyard, Lily let out a sigh. The urgent need to see Tom was gnawing away at her like a terrier tormenting a rat. Did she dare risk leaving the workroom now, whilst the ladies were having their nuncheon? Before she could decide, Mrs Bodney appeared.

'Lily, I'd like you, as overseer, to take responsibility for making the Bertha collar. You will see from this pattern that it has the design of crowns and needs to be worked to a depth of 5½ inches. I suggest you make a start on pricking out the pattern now whilst it's quiet.' Then, before she could answer, her employer swept from the room. Lily groaned under her breath. There was no way she could leave the workroom now. It was almost as if Mrs Bodney had known what she'd been contemplating, she thought as she duly began pricking out the new pattern.

All afternoon she worked without stopping. Aware that time was racing by and Mrs Bodney was keeping an eye on them, the ladies hardly lifted their heads and the workroom was unusually quiet. However, as soon as Lily rang the bell at the end of the day, they jumped up, covered their work and all but ran out of the door. The long hours were taking their toll and they were eager to get back to their families.

As soon as the last lady had left, Lily hurriedly covered her own pillow and made her way outside, bolting the workroom door behind her. Although her conscience was pricking, she just had to see Tom.

Pulling her shawl tighter round her, for the air was cooler now the nights were drawing in, she ran down to the beach. Her heart leaped when she saw him bent over his lugger.

'Tom,' she shouted, running towards him. He turned, but the face that stared back at her was not his. 'Hey, that's Tom's boat,' she cried.

''Tain't no more,' the stranger muttered. 'Sold it to me last night, he did.'

'What? He can't have,' she gasped.

'Bought it fair and square with my hard-earned money, I did. I'm preparing to sail out on the morning tide with the rest of the fleet,' the man said.

Dumbstruck, Lily stared at him but his open face and clear eyes told her he was telling the truth.

In frustration, she kicked at the pebbles then, heedless of her new boots, crunched along the, water's edge. When she reached the spot where, only a short time ago, they'd stood together making plans for their future, it all became too much. Throwing herself down onto the beach, she let loose the tears that had been threatening all day. Finally, overcome by exhaustion, she fell into a troubled sleep.

As if from a long way away, she heard the crunching of a boat being dragged over the pebbles. Groggily she opened her eyes, wondering why she wasn't in her bed. Trying to sit up, she grimaced. Her body was stiff and her left arm numb where she'd been lying on it. Then with her heart feeling as heavy as her pillow, she trudged back up the beach.

'Hey, Lily, come on or you'll be late.'

Looking up, she saw Mary beckoning to her.

'Gosh, you'd give a scarecrow a run for his money,' the other woman laughed. 'You look like you've been up all night,' she added, giving Lily a level look as she caught up with her. Lily blushed. 'Love a duck, you have, haven't you?' she gasped. 'Well, you'd best hurry and freshen up before Mrs Bodney sees you. Don't worry; I'll cover for you,' she added when Lily hesitated.

Fearful that someone might see her if she went round to the yard, Lily kicked off her boots then stood in the brook, letting the cold water cascade over her. Where was Tom? Had he really sold his lugger? She found it hard to believe, for it had been handed down from his father and was his pride and joy. She'd have to call at his mother's house and find out, she thought. Then hurriedly rearranging her dress, she bent down to pull her boots back on. But when she saw the state of them, she gasped. The sea water had stiffened the new leather and they were now streaked white with salt. There was also a dark stain on the toe that looked suspiciously like tar. She'd have to ask Albert how to remove it, she thought.

She was pulling down her skirt as far as she dared, in the hope of covering her feet, when she heard the clatter of wheels. Looking up, she saw Rupert's carriage coming down the street towards her. Not wishing for him to see her in such a dishevelled state, she drew back into the shadow of the cliff. To her dismay, the carriage pulled up outside Picky Pike's premises.

Thinking quickly, she decided that, rather than risk bumping into him, she'd make her way to Mrs Westlake's cottage straight away. Lily knew full well she should be working, but the urge to find out about Tom was too great to ignore. Promising herself she'd work on after the others had finished for the day and trusting Mary would be true to her word and cover if Mrs Bodney came looking for her, she hurried off up the path.

It proved to be a futile journey, for when she reached the Westlakes' cottage there was no answer to her knock on the door. She tried again, and was just taking a peek through the tiny window for any sign of life when a voice called out, making her jump.

'Can I be helping yer, lass?' Spinning round, she saw a wizened old man with a shock of white hair peering over the low wall that separated the gardens.

'I'm looking for Mrs Westlake or Tom, sir,' she answered.

'Gone away, so they have. Left the key with me, so they have,' he said in his singsong voice.

'Oh, no, did they say where they were going?' Lily gasped in dismay.

'Why bless yer, child, calm yerself. They've only gone as far as Seaton, so they have. To stay with the old lady, they said.'

'Oh,' she said, relief flooding through her. 'Do you know when they'll be back?'

The old man shook his head. 'Ah, 'tis disappointed they're gone, so yer be?' he guessed.

'Yes, I am,' she answered, trying not to break down. He must have heard the tremor in her voice for he got to his feet, opened his little gate and beckoned her towards the bench that was set on his neat square of grass.

'Like a barley drink? I made some earlier, so I did,' he asked gently, looking concerned.

'Oh, please,' she answered, suddenly realizing how thirsty she was. He scuttled indoors, reappearing moments later with two filled tumblers. The barley water was so cool and delicious she drank it down in one gulp.

'Well, that was worth making it for, so it was,' he said, laughing. 'Now tell me what's ailing thee, young Lily.' Seeing her surprised look, he continued, 'Thought I recognized yer earlier. I knew yet father, so I did. Fine man he was. It was a

278

sorry thing, that accident.'

The old man looked down at Lily's feet and frowned.

'Yer've made a fine mess of they boots. A good bit of leather that, too, so it is.'

'I know. I shall be in right trouble with Mrs Bodney when she sees them,' she said, grimacing.

'Mrs Bodney, eh? Well, lass, happen I can help yer.'

She looked at him in surprise. 'That's very kind of you but I'm pretty sure that's tar,' she said, sighing and pointing to the thick black stain on the toe. To her surprise the old man laughed.

'"Taint nothing a spot of eucalyptus oil won't fix or my name's not Bobby Fixit, so it is.'

'Oh, Bobby Fixit, can you really get rid of that?' she asked, her eyes widening in surprise and hope.

'Take them off and let's see, shall we?' he said, chuckling as he disappeared indoors again and by the time she'd done as he'd bid, he was back carrying a bowl and cloth. Sitting himself back down on the step, he worked in silence, concentrating so hard she didn't like to interrupt him. Finally, he sat back, held out the boots at arm's length and smiled.

'There, young Lily, if these aren't as good as new then my name's not Bobby Fixit, so it's not,' he said, handing them to her. She stared down at them in amazement for indeed they did look as good as new.

'Bobby Fixit, I'm that grateful I could hug you,' she squealed, and to her surprise the old man burst out laughing.

'Let's just say if we've beaten the old harridan

it's made my day, so it has. Now it's time for my nap. Good day to yer, young Lily,' he said, nodding to her. Then, leaning back, he put his hat over his face and promptly began to snore.

Whilst she hadn't got a clue what he'd meant about beating the old harridan, she felt relieved that Tom had only gone as far as Seaton. She'd visit him when he'd had a chance to calm down, she thought, as she made her way back to Agent Pike's house.

To her dismay, she noticed the sun was already warm. How could she have been away for so long? Haring back down the hill as if the devil was after her, she prayed her absence hadn't been noticed and, if it had, that Mary had been able to cover for her, otherwise she was in deep trouble.

Chapter 29

The church clock chimed ten as Lily arrived back in the workroom. Mary shot her an enquiring look but Lily shook her head and then picked up her bobbins. Determined to produce a fair amount of lace; she worked furiously.

The day sped by so quickly, Lily could hardly believe it when the ladies began tidying away their things. She stared around the workroom, gratified to see the pile of sprigs had increased significantly. Stretching to ease her cramped muscles, she bent back over her pillow and picked up her bobbins.

Absorbed in the lace for the collar, she lost

track of all time. Only when the shadows had lengthened so that she could hardly see her hands in front of her did she put down her pillow. She was just making her way up the stairs, when Mrs Bodney's voice rang out from the parlour.

'A word, if you please, Lily.' Smoothing down her dress, she made her way back down the hallway.

'Come in, Lily. Rupert is here to see you,' Mrs Bodney said, her eyes twinkling.

'It's good to see you again, Lily,' Rupert said, rising to his feet and looking down at her black work boots quizzically. Noticing his glance, Lily quickly gave him her best smile.

'Good evening, Mr Mountsford, I see you noticed I'm not wearing those beautiful boots you kindly gave me. They are so delicate they would be quickly ruined if I tramped round in them all day, therefore I am saving them for a special occasion.'

'Well, that's opportune then, for our dear merchant craves a boon,' said Mrs Bodney.

'A what?' Lily looked at her employer in bewilderment.

'A boon is a favour, Lily,' Mrs Bodney said, shaking her head. Then, leaning forward in her seat, she said, 'Lady Clinsden has invited Rupert to her Harvest Supper and he would like you to accompany him as his guest.'

'Me? Be a guest at the Harvest Supper?' Lily spluttered.

'For heaven's sake, Lily, stop parroting,' Mrs Bodney snapped. 'Considering the squire's outrageous behaviour towards you, I rather think it would be the perfect reprisal.'

'Not that that is the reason for my invitation,' Rupert hastily intervened. 'What do you say, Lily? Would you do me the honour of escorting me?' he asked, looking at her so expectantly she couldn't help smiling up at him. 'I think that would be an eminently suitable occasion for showing off the cherry-red stitching,' he added.

'Well, Lily looks suitably appreciative, so I think we can safely say she accepts your kind invitation, Rupert,' Mrs Bodney said, smiling like a cat that had discovered a churn full of cream.

'Oh, but I don't ... I mean I can't...' she stammered to a halt as she saw his crestfallen look.

'Why can't you, Lily?' Mrs Bodney exclaimed, looking affronted.

'Because I'm betrothed to Tom,' she said. But even as she uttered the words, she wondered if they were true.

'We understand that, don't we, Rupert?' said Mrs Bodney, looking at him for confirmation.

'Indeed,' he replied.

'And, as I said earlier, it would be the perfect way of getting our own back on the squire,' Mrs Bodney added, grinning.

'But, I've not got a suitable gown and–'

The other woman waved her hand dismissively. 'Then I shall loan you one. Let me see, the evenings will be a little nippy by then, so the sapphire velveteen, perhaps? There, that's decided then. Now, after your recent traumas, I'm sure you are ready to retire. You may leave it to us to finalize the arrangements.'

'Good night, Lily, I trust you will sleep well,' Rupert said, smiling at her so charmingly, her cheeks began to burn and she had to look away. As she did, she noticed a package similar to the one he'd recently asked her to give Mrs Bodney lying on the table. He was clearly a generous man, she thought. But Mrs Bodney had followed her gaze and was frowning.

'Good night, Rupert, Mrs Bodney,' Lily said quickly and left the room.

In the sanctuary of the attic she sank onto the bed, her thoughts reeling. How could she, Lily Rose, accompany. Rupert Mountsford to the squire's Harvest Supper? She'd only ever attended functions at the manor in the capacity of servant. She couldn't possibly go as a guest. Could she? Imagine the surprised look on the squire's face. He'd be livid, she thought, smiling.

Why shouldn't she go? She was as good as any toff. Besides, she hadn't heard from Tom, who could have resolved never to see her again, for all she knew, and Rupert seemed to like her company. Mrs Bodney had offered to lend her a suitable dress, hadn't she? The more she thought about it, the more she liked the idea.

All that week Lily was at her pillow as soon as dawn broke, determined to make progress on the Bertha collar before Mrs Bodney could accuse her of shirking. The empty workroom was peaceful and as she moved her bobbins over the pillow, she couldn't help thinking of the Harvest Supper. She couldn't believe it was approaching that time of year already. They'd been so busy the summer had passed in a blur.

Her resolve to attend had wavered in the cold

light of day. She wouldn't have the audacity to go up to the manor house, would she? A whole week had passed and she was still undecided. Before long, though, the peace of that early morning was broken by the clattering of the ladies on the cobbles outside.

'Good morning,' she called brightly as they settled themselves down to work, conscious of their ever-approaching deadline.

By the time the day was darkening, the piles of sprigs on the dresser had greatly increased. Lily was just pondering who would have the job of sewing them onto the netting backing, when Tilda appeared in the doorway.

'Mrs Bodney wants to see you, Lily,' she said.

'I'll be right through,' she answered, hastily tucking the hairs that were escaping their braid back under her cap, and smoothing down the folds of her dress.

'Lily, please sit down. I need to speak with you on a serious matter.'

She felt her throat tightening as she glanced anxiously at Mrs Bodney, who, unusually, was pacing the room. Lily perched nervously on the edge of the chair and waited. Then, to her surprise, Mrs Bodney drew up the other chair beside her.

'Lily, this is a somewhat delicate matter. You remember the time you took to your bed without undressing?'

Perplexed and embarrassed, she could only nod.

'Well, when Tilda took your dress for laundering, she found this letter in your pocket and handed it to me. In all the recent upheaval, I quite forgot to return it to you and must apologize for my tardiness. Now do you recognize this?' she asked.

Lily looked at the creased paper she was holding out and, seeing Aunt Elizabeth's writing, nodded again.

'Lily, I have taken the liberty of reading what your aunt has to say and can only assume she is not aware that you are unable to read.'

'The subject never really came up,' she answered, looking down at the floor. 'We never saw her much when we were growing up, as she had a position in Exeter...' Her, voice petered out as, she saw her employer frowning. 'Why, Mrs Bodney, has something happened?'

To her surprise the other woman reached out and covered her hand with her own. 'My dear, what I have to tell you is going to come as a shock. I've thought about whether to reveal the contents of your aunt's letter, but reasoned she wouldn't have written it if she hadn't wanted you to know.'

'Know what?' Lily asked, wriggling impatiently in the chair. Would she never get to the point?

'Did your parents ever speak of why your aunt went to Exeter?'

'No,' she said, shaking her head. 'I presumed it must have been because of her job.'

'Well, yes, in a way it was,' Mrs Bodney said slowly.

'What did you used to call your parents, Lily?'

'Mother and Father,' she said, shaking her head at such a ridiculous question. 'Why? What does that have to do with anything?'

Mrs Bodney sighed. 'I think it would be best if I just read out her letter. But, my dear, you must prepare yourself.'

And Lily watched in amazement, as the ladylike Mrs Bodney cleared her throat before she began to read.

'My dearest daughter, for indeed, Lily, that is who you are,

Now that the woman you always believed to be your mother has departed this earth, I feel it is my duty to inform you of your true parentage. Sadly the only man I ever loved, your father, Ernest, was lost at sea before we could be wed.

To save me from disgrace, your mother, my dear sister, and her husband offered to raise you as their own, provided I removed from Coombe. You can believe me, Lily, when I tell you that it was the saddest decision I've ever had to make, but what kind of life could I offer you? I hope you will find it in your heart to understand and forgive me, Lily dearest. You may rest assured I have followed your progress from when you were a baby and wish you to know that I am truly proud of the fine woman you have grown up to be.

I know I can never hold a candle to the wonderful woman who raised you as her own, but pray you can find it in your heart to forgive me, and that we shall meet again soon.

God Bless You always, my darling daughter.

Aunt Elizabeth'

As Mrs Bodney finished reading, Lily sat there, shaking her head.

'Are you all right, my dear?' the other woman asked gently, patting her hand.

'I think so,' she answered, her voice shaking. Vaguely, she was aware of Mrs Bodney getting up

286

and ringing her bell. Then Tilda appeared with a tray of tea and Lily was being urged to take a sip of the hot, sweet liquid. But all the time her mind was spinning faster than her sister's toy top as she tried to take in what her employer had just told her.

The woman she'd always thought was her mother wasn't. Aunt Elizabeth was. Her father wasn't her real father. That meant Rob and Beth weren't really her brother and sister. It was unbelievable; too much to take in. Suddenly, she felt as if the walls were closing in on her and could hardly breathe. Desperate for fresh air, she jumped up, sending her cup and saucer flying as she fled the room.

Instinctively, she headed for the harbour and Tom's boat. Except, of course, he wasn't there and nor was his boat. She stood on the pebbles staring at the distant horizon, her thoughts as turbulent as the tide in full flood, as she tried to make sense of what Mrs Bodney had told her.

How could Aunt Elizabeth, a comparatively rare visitor in her life, be her mother? She'd had a mother, Sarah. A gentle woman, who'd raised her, loved her and passed on her own skill of lace making. Lily shook her head, trying unsuccessfully to clear the thoughts that were whirling around her mind like a spinning top. To think, the life she'd always known and thought normal, sometimes even humdrum, had been a sham. Her family was not really her family at all. The woman she'd thought was her aunt was actually her mother. A mother who'd abandoned her, no less. Just like Tom had. Nobody wanted her. Everybody left her. She stared at the huge breakers rolling ever closer and then slowly took a step forward.

Don't even think about it, Lily Rose.

His voice came so sharply, its energy sent her reeling backwards. Shocked, she could only watch as the waves broke on the very spot where she'd been standing.

You always did forget there were spring tides on a full moon, daughter dear.

'But I'm not your daughter and you're not my father,' she screamed into the night air.

Don't be silly, Lily, of course I am. Always have been, always will. You might not be of my flesh but you are my daughter, I can promise you that.

'But why didn't you tell me?'

Your mother and aunt thought it best that way. Besides, we always thought of you as our own. 'Tis a shock you've had, but when you've had time to think, you'll see nothing's really changed. We always loved you and always will, Lily, remember that.

As his loving words penetrated her thoughts, they filled her heart with warmth, melting the ice that had encased it since Mrs Bodney had read out that letter. It was still a terrible shock, but knowing she'd been loved and wanted was some comfort.

'Thank you, Father,' she murmured, but the only response was the sighing of the wind. He'd gone again. But he had restored her faith. Of course he was still her father and his spirit was guiding her, even though he was no longer here. She wished she'd known the truth before he'd died, then she could have asked him all the questions that were still buzzing around in her mind like wasps at a picnic.

Then she remembered her grandmother, a wise woman, telling her that it didn't do to dwell on the past. Her grandmother! Her mother and her aunt were sisters so she must have been her real grandmother, she thought, drawing some comfort from that fact.

She'd concentrate on the present, for wasn't she lucky enough to have a good job with her own little room in the attic? And an employer who seemed to care about her?

Hearing noises coming from the headland known as The Hall, she shivered. Tom had told her that there were several rift caves at the base, which smugglers used as temporary stores. Suddenly eager to be back in the safety of the house, she hurried up the beach, fervently hoping she wouldn't bump into any menacing men of the night.

Relieved to be back at Picky Pike's without any unpleasant encounters, Lily let out the breath she'd been holding. Remembering her hasty exit and the cup and saucer she'd sent clattering to the floor, she hoped they weren't broken and the tea hadn't stained the chair covers. She knew only too well that her employer set great store by how things looked. But then her family hadn't been at all how they'd looked, had they?

Chapter 30

Peering through the open parlour door, she saw the room had been restored to its pristine condition and breathed a sigh of relief. As far as she could tell no damage had been done to the carpet or chair covers.

'There you are, Lily,' exclaimed Mrs Bodney, looking up from the table in the corner, where she was writing in the dreaded ledger. 'Are you all right?' she asked, frowning when she saw Lily was shivering. 'I was beginning to worry about you.'

'I'm still shocked and angry that Father and Mother never told me the truth when I was growing up,' she answered, feeling her stomach tighten into a knot.

'My dear, if they'd promised your aunt they would raise you as their own, then I don't suppose it was their secret to share,' Mrs Bodney said.

Lily thought for a moment and then nodded her understanding.

'Well, I'm much better now that Father's explained everything to me,' she said.

Her employer shot her an anxious look. 'I do hope you're not feverish; you've had quite a shock.' Skirts rustling, she got up and hurried from the room, reappearing moments later with a small glass.

'Drink this, child. It's ginger wine and will help settle your system.'

Lily took a tentative sip, grimaced then gasped as the amber liquid hit the back of her throat.

'All of it, Lily,' encouraged Mrs Bodney, as she made to place the glass on the table.

Knowing better than to disobey, Lily took a deep breath, swallowing the rest down in one gulp. It brought tears to her eyes but then she felt warmth flooding her body.

'That's better. You've got some colour back in your cheeks.'

'Thank you, Mrs Bodney,' she replied.

'I've been thinking, Lily. Your Aunt Elizabeth, as you know her, will have been wondering about your reaction to her letter. It's a delicate secret to disclose, after all, and she was obviously expecting to discuss it with you before she left.'

'I'm not sure how I really feel at the moment,' Lily said, frowning.

'No, I'm sure it has come as a considerable shock. However, when you have had time to get used to the idea, I think we should pen a letter to her, between us,' Mrs Bodney said, leaning over and patting her hand. 'You could also let her know you've been to see Beth and that she's well.'

'You'd help me do that? Do you have the time?' Lily asked, knowing her employer was a busy woman.

'It's about priorities,' she said. Seeing the puzzled look on Lily's face, she added, 'I mean, making time for the important things in life.'

'Thank you, Mrs Bodney. Would you be able to help me learn my letters too? It would make such a difference if I could write.'

'Yes, Lily, I will. It will take time, though, so we

will probably have to continue your lessons after the commission for the Queen is completed. The clock is ticking and that must take precedence. In the meantime, I suggest you keep this safe,' she said, holding out the letter from Aunt Elizabeth.

'Right, off you go or you'll be of no use to me in the workroom, and I don't want the ladies taking liberties.' Mrs Bodney's voice resumed its usual brusqueness as she waved Lily away.

Up in her room, Lily's thoughts were reeling so fast, she never for a moment thought she'd sleep.

This morning she'd woken not giving the life she'd had as a child a second thought. Now, she'd discovered it had been built on a lie. She wondered if Rob had known the truth. Probably not, she thought, sighing into the darkness as she got undressed. As Mrs Bodney had said, it hadn't been her parents' secret to disclose.

She lay in her little bed, thinking back over the events of the day. How she wished she could discuss the letter with Tom. She missed him so. Finally, she fell into an exhausted sleep only to dream she was a little girl again. She was sitting beside her mother in the sunshine, learning how to make lace. Mother was smiling and patient, no matter how many mistakes Lily made, sharing in her jubilation when finally she'd mastered the craft. Her father laughing as they strolled through the orchard, inspecting the crop, holding her high above his head so she could pick the first ripe apple of the season. Aunt Elizabeth, strict but kind, offering to stay in Coombe so that Lily could work for Mrs Bodney.

Then the dream changed. The sun no longer shone. It was her aunt teaching her to make lace, a stranger who walked beside her in the orchard, but he was holding her hand too tightly and smelled strongly of liquor. She was trying to escape but he turned and brought his lips down on hers. It was the squire, his slug-like fingers trying to paw her body.

She woke with a jolt, her heart pounding like the waves in a storm. Peering around, she breathed a sigh of relief when she realized she was safe in her bed. She sank back onto the pillow, closing her eyes and willing her heart to calm. Once again, she wished Tom was here so that she could discuss her aunt's revelation with him. Dearest Tom. She wondered how he was. Was he thinking of her?

Come the Sabbath she would visit him at his nana's house in Seaton, she decided. She was that impatient to see him, she even toyed with the idea of missing church. Reluctantly, she opened her eyes. She had work to do before she could even think of the Sabbath.

It was Saturday evening when, at Mrs Bodney's gentle insistence, they sat down together at the table in the parlour. True to her word about protecting their eyes, she'd insisted on lighting a candle. In the flickering glow, Lily watched as her employer showed her how to write the first two letters of the alphabet. But as Lily went to copy them Mrs Bodney shook her head.

'Not tonight, Lily. You can practise them later but first we have to decide what you want the letter to your aunt to say.'

'I'm confused. Am I meant to call her Mother

293

or Aunt Elizabeth?' Lily asked.

The other woman's brow furrowed. 'I think you should decide what you feel most comfortable with.'

'Well, Mother was my mother and it would be disrespectful to call Aunt Elizabeth that, somehow. She has always been my aunt in my eyes.'

'Then we shall begin with "Dear Aunt Elizabeth",' said Mrs Bodney, dipping her pen into the ink. Lily watched as the words flowed onto the page.

'Will I really be able to write like that?' she asked in amazement.

Mrs Bodney stopped writing and, pen poised, looked at Lily. 'If you practise, there is no reason why you shouldn't. Now listen, whilst I read this back to you.

Dear Aunt Elizabeth,

I trust this letter finds you well and you are settled in your new life in Ilminster. As you can imagine, your letter came as a shock. I am still trying to take in the news that you are my birth mother and await the opportunity of discussing this with you. In the meantime I trust you will understand if I continue to address you as Aunt Elizabeth for, of course, this is how I have always thought of you.

I have been to see Beth and she is happy and well. Please give my love to Rob.

With sincere affection, Lily Rose

'Does that say everything, Lily?' Mrs Bodney asked, looking up from the letter.

'Yes, thank you, although I will feel better when

294

I've spoken to my aunt. It's such a big thing to take in.'

'Yes, it is. However, with time it's surprising what we can become used to, and I'm sure they did what they thought would be best for you. Now, I shall seal this ready to be dispatched with the next stagecoach.'

'Thank you so much, Mrs Bodney. I can't believe I will ever be able to write like you do.'

Her employer smiled, handing her the precious piece of paper on which she'd written the letters.

'You may borrow this pen and ink for the time being. Take them up to your room but on no account must they get anywhere near the workroom. Ink and lace would make sorry bedfellows. I'll look out a slate and some slate pencils when I return to my cottage and then you can practise regularly. When you have mastered these letters, we will go on to the next.'

'Are there many, then?' Lily asked.

'There are twenty-six letters to the alphabet,' Mrs Bodney said, smiling as Lily's eyes widened in disbelief. 'Don't worry, as I said, all it takes is practice,' she assured her. 'Now that's quite enough for one night, so I'll bid you good night.'

Lily all but skipped up the stairs. To think she, Lily Rose, would soon be able to write her own letters. She couldn't wait to tell Tom.

The Sabbath dawned and as Lily made her way outside she noticed the autumn air was damp with chill mist rolling in from the sea, spreading in ghostly ribbons throughout the hamlet. She pulled her shawl tighter and hurried towards the church. At the last moment, her conscience wouldn't allow her to miss morning service, but at least by attending the one here in Bransbeer, her journey to Seaton wouldn't take long. As she walked down the aisle, two hazel eyes turned in her direction. Fighting down the urge to turn tail and leave, Lily made her way to the pew furthest away from where Squire and Lady Clinsden were sitting. Why were they worshipping here, she wondered. Then the parson climbed into the pulpit and began his sermon. As his voice droned on interminably, Lily couldn't help thinking back over the events of the past few days. Then Lady Clinsden rose to read the lesson and Lily's question about why they were attending the local church was answered. Fighting down her growing impatience as the parson then beseeched them all to repent their sins, she sighed. It was Tom's forgiveness she needed.

At last, the service ended and she jumped up quickly, hoping to make a speedy exit but the press of people hindered her progress. As she made her way outside, blinking in the sudden brightness, the squire stepped in front of her.

'We look forward to you serving at our Harvest Supper next weekend, don't we, my dear?' he said, turning to his wife.

'We are indeed looking forward to seeing you there,' Lady Clinsden replied, winking at Lily behind her husband's back.

'And I am looking forward to being there,' Lily said sweetly, trying not to laugh at the squire's surprised look. 'If you'll excuse me, I am on my way to Seaton,' she said.

Thankful for the comfort her new hobnailed boots afforded, Lily made her way up Long Hill, on through fields festooned with stooks of golden corn, until she reached the common. Then, as she gained the outskirts of Seaton, the mist lifted as it often did this time of year, and she could see the sea shimmering below her. It being the Sabbath, there were no boats out fishing, and the outline of Portland Bill rose like a whale's back in the distance. Catching sight of Seaton Hole below, where the remains of the wrecked ship perched like a skeleton on the rocks, her heart lurched. Hastily averting her eyes, she hurried on her way. Almost before she knew it, she was standing outside old Mrs Westlake's cottage. But, as she raised her hand to lift the knocker, the door flew open and Tom's mother stood there glaring at her.

'Hello, Mrs Westlake. I'd like to see Tom,' she said, her voice trembling when she saw the hostile look on the woman's face.

'Wouldn't we all,' Mrs Westlake snapped.

'Isn't he here?' Lily asked, her heart sinking.

'And why would he be?' his mother asked, folding her arms.

'Bobby Fixit said he was.'

'Oh, he did, did he? Well, that's right. He was,' Mrs Westlake growled, making to shut the door.

'Please, Mrs Westlake, I really need to talk to him,' Lily begged.

'Seems to me like you've said enough already. Broke my boy's heart, you did, with your doubting ways. It's 'cos of you he sold his boat. The family boat that his father worked his fingers to the bone to pass onto him. Taken the money he got and

297

disappeared. I hope you're pleased with yourself, Lily Rose, you doubting Thomasina, you.' With a final glare, she slammed the door in Lily's face.

Shocked, Lily stood there for some moments then realized she was being watched. Looking up, she saw a group of women staring at her from across the lane. Clearly they'd heard what had been said and were waiting to see what would happen next. Biting back tears of frustration, she put her chin in the air and marched back down the road. Her heart might be breaking but she had her pride.

It was only when she reached the common that she slowed down. Perching on a tree stump and idly watching the scarlet poppies swaying in the breeze, she thought of Tom. How could she make things right between them now? Before long, she felt a prickle of awareness snake up her spine. Spinning round, she stared towards the row of trees beyond. Tom was there, she knew he was. She could feel it. Jumping to her feet, she cupped her hands to her mouth.

'Tom!' she called. But apart from the bleating of a sheep there was silence.

'Tom, please come and talk to me,' she called, hearing the desperation rising in her voice. But, still there was no answer.

Chapter 31

Ignoring the pang that jolted her insides, she straightened her cap and hurried on her way. How could they sort things out if he wouldn't even speak to her? If this was love, then she didn't think much of the misery and hurt it inflicted. Such were her thoughts that by the time she found herself back at Picky Pike's, she'd convinced herself she was better off without him.

'Good afternoon, Lily.' Glancing up, she saw Rupert Mountsford alighting from his carriage. Immaculately dressed in a crisp dark suit with blue silk cravat, he was smiling at her in such an admiring way that she clean forgot her wounded pride.

'Mr Mountsford, er, I mean Rupert,' she acknowledged, giving him her brightest smile, and hoping she didn't look as dishevelled as she felt.

'I was about to partake of some afternoon refreshment. Would it be very forward of me to ask if you would care to join me?' he enquired.

'Oh, yes. I mean that would be nice but I'm not sure if I should. Mrs Bodney might have something she wishes me to do...' She stuttered to a halt.

'Indeed, she does, Lily,' and as if someone had conjured her up, her employer appeared on the doorstep before her. 'I have something to attend to back at my cottage, and now, it seems a visitor who requires looking after here. Regrettably, I cannot manage both at the same time, so I'd be obliged if you would take Rupert through to the parlour and ask Tilda to bring you some afternoon tea. Her presence should be sufficient to quieten any no-good gossipers on this Sabbath day,' she added, her lips twitching.

'If you are sure, Mrs Bodney, then I would be delighted to accept your kind invitation,' Rupert said, bowing respectfully.

'Rupert, please accept my sincere apologies for not being able to join you. Although, something tells me my presence will not be missed too much,' she said, giving him an outrageous wink and hurrying on her way.

'Well, Lily, is that agreeable with you?' asked Rupert, solicitous as ever. 'I wouldn't wish to inconvenience you if you have other plans.' He was gazing at her so intently her heart began beating like the clappers on the church bells. As she stood there feeling attractive and appreciated, the hurt of the morning vanished like the mist.

Smiling coyly up at him, she opened the door. Then, completely forgetting the propriety of ringing for the maid, she called to Tilda to bring a tray of tea for two through to the parlour. Rupert folded his lean frame into the comfortable chair beside the fireplace, and then sat looking intently at her. The atmosphere felt charged, as though something exciting was about to happen, and although Lily didn't fully understand, she was enjoying the tingly feeling she was experiencing when he smiled at her.

'Lily, it has been an age since we were last together, though I must confess to thinking of you often whilst we've been apart.'

'Mr Mountsford, you do say such funny things. You must have a very busy life in London.'

'Rupert, please, Lily. And yes, I am kept busy. However, my dealings in Bransbeer ensure I return on a regular basis and I can't think of anything nicer than spending time with you.' Not knowing what to say, she looked down at her boots.

'The weather is still quite clement so perhaps, when we've had our tea, we could take a stroll through the village?' he asked, smiling at her. Lily looked at him in surprise but the moment was broken as Tilda came bustling into the room carrying a laden tray.

'Here we are, Miss Rose, your tea – and I've taken the liberty of adding slices of Mrs Bodney's best pound cake,' she proudly announced, flushing as she looked at Rupert.

Once the little maid had left, Lily turned her attention to her duties as hostess. But Rupert was watching her closely and her hands trembled as she poured their tea. Whatever was the matter with her? If he noticed, he was too polite to show it, reaching out and helping himself to a slice of cake. Why was she flustered, she wondered.

'Relax, Lily dear,' he said, grinning at her so roguishly she felt her cheeks growing hot. Should he be saying such things, she wondered. Seeking refuge in her drink, she endeavoured to sip it in the ladylike manner of Mrs Bodney and tried to think of something to say.

'This tea of Mrs Bodney's is deliciously strong,

301

isn't it? Ours at home was always as weak as water.'

Her comment was met with silence. Looking up, she was surprised to find Rupert had gone quite red in the face. Suddenly, the rhythmic ticking of the mantel clock seemed inordinately loud. Then, seeming to have regained his composure, he smiled across at her.

'Indeed,' was his only comment, and she wondered what on earth she'd said. Picking up her cup again, she sipped her drink.

He then asked, 'Are you not having any cake?'

She shook her head, knowing that she being so nervous, the fruit would stick in her throat. He, however, had no qualms and ate heartily. When he'd finished, he returned the plate to the tray and extracted a snowy handkerchief from his pocket. She watched in fascination as he delicately wiped first his lips and then his long, neatly manicured fingers. Again, she couldn't help comparing them to Tom's work-roughened skin, but now Rupert was rising to his feet.

'Thank you for your kind hospitality, but regrettably I must take my leave for I have urgent business to attend to before my journey back to London. However, I will ensure I return in time for the Harvest Supper. Until then, Lily,' he said, bowing, and before she had even had time to draw breath he'd gone.

Well, I never, she thought. He treated me just like a lady. But then she remembered he'd left so quickly, they hadn't gone for the walk he'd suggested.

Mrs Bodney bustled into the room, cradling a

parcel in her arms. Placing it on the chair, she looked around.

'Rupert gone already?' she asked in surprise.

'He said he had business to attend to before he returns to London, but will be back in time for the Harvest Supper.'

'Did he indeed?' her employer asked, raising an eyebrow. 'Well, it gives us time to see about your outfit for that evening. It is imperative you look the part and I've the very thing.' She untied the parcel and held a swathe of sapphire material in front of Lily. Cocking her head to one side, she studied the effect and then nodded. 'A few nips here and tucks there and this will be perfect. I do envy you your sylphlike form, but then you are a few years younger. Now slip this on while I get my pins.' Lily took the gown, running her hands over the velvet nap, marvelling at its softness.

'It's only velveteen, as I said earlier, but it should suffice,' Mrs Bodney said, sweeping back into the room.

'It's very kind of you, but I can't possibly wear this.'

Mistaking her concern, the other woman brushed her worries aside with a shake of her hand. 'Of course you can. I don't mind you borrowing it in the slightest. I even have a reticule that complements it perfectly. As I said earlier, it's imperative you look the part, Lily.'

'But it's blue, and I'm still in mourning for my mother.'

'Oh, Lily, I'm sorry; I'd quite forgotten,' Mrs Bodney said, looking concerned. She was quiet for a moment. 'I know it's not yet six months

303

since she died, and then you'll be free to cast off those dark garments, but I'm sure the Good Lord will forgive us being slightly premature for one night. It is in a good cause, after all. Yes, I'm sure that will be all right,' she added as if to convince herself as well as Lily. 'After all, you can go back to wearing black after the Harvest Supper. Come along, let's get you fitted.'

Seeing further protest would be futile, Lily clambered out of her sober black then gently stepped into the brilliant blue. Immediately, she felt brighter, and as she moved around the soft folds clung to her like a second skin.

'Why, it doesn't need altering at all, Mrs Bodney,' she exclaimed.

'Believe you me, a little adjustment here and there will make it look as if the dress was made for you. Perception is all, Lily, remember that.' She kneeled down and began pinning the dress.

'Yes, Mrs Bodney,' Lily answered, not having a clue what the other woman meant, but not wishing to appear rude. It seemed to be an age before the other woman finally got to her feet, telling Lily to turn around slowly. Then, after a few more pins were added here and there, she finally seemed satisfied.

'Right, you may now step out of the dress. But gently, Lily, you don't want to go undoing my hard work.'

Carefully, slipping out of the dress, Lily held it out to her employer.

'Goodness, child, do you expect me to do everything for you?' Mrs Bodney asked, shaking her head. 'Your stitches are as neat as any I've seen, so away and make the adjustments yourself. Take a candle through to the workroom. You can lay the dress out over the big table so that it doesn't touch the floor. Here's my sewing basket; you'll find thread to match the material inside,' she said, waving her hand at Lily. 'I'll be in to see how you're getting on later.'

In the workroom, Lily settled to her task. Nervous in case she made a mess of the fine material, she carefully followed the line of the pins. Then, as she saw the new outline taking shape, her confidence grew so that by the time Mrs Bodney returned, she was just finishing off the final stitches.

'Well, Lily, this is superb work,' Mrs Bodney said, holding the material up to the light of the candle to inspect her stitching. 'Well done. You will do Rupert proud.' She stood back, eyeing Lily critically. 'We must do something with that hair, though. A chignon will suit, I think.'

'A what?' Lily asked, shaking her head.

'It's an elegant knot, Lily. It will show off your shoulders to perfection. I'll get Tilda to press the dress ready for Saturday. Now it's getting late, so I'll bid you good night and see you back here first thing in the morning. We have but a few short weeks left to finish making the Queen's lace. I trust everything is in order?'

'Yes, Mrs Bodney. It's coming along...' But she was talking to an empty room, her employer having left as soon as she'd heard the word 'yes'.

That night her dreams were of dresses, dancing and desire. When she woke she felt hot, as if she were on fire. Easing open the skylight, she breathed in the cool morning air, smelling the tang of the sea. Her senses seemed heightened and yet she felt strangely unsettled. It must be that time, she thought, removing clean rags from her chest in readiness, then taking herself down the stairs.

'You look feverish,' Mary remarked, walking into the workroom sometime later. 'Your eyes are bright as beacons. Are you feeling quite well?'

Lily looked up from her pillow. Although she'd been sitting here since first light, she'd had great difficulty concentrating, and consequently the lace for the collar was not progressing as quickly as it should have been.

'I'm fine, Mary, thank you. Well, actually, I'm worried we'll not get all the lace finished in time.'

'It will be a close thing, I'll admit, but we can only do our best,' Mary said, shrugging.

'That's not good enough, though, is it?' Lily sighed.

'Well, wasting time fretting is not getting the work done,' Mary pointed out.

Realizing the truth in the older woman's words, Lily bent her head back over her pillow. Forcing herself to concentrate, she hardly noticed the others arriving. It took all her willpower to stop her thoughts from wandering, but she was determined that by the end of the day she'd have made enough lace to finish the collar. She bet Her Majesty had no idea how much sweat and toil was going in to the making of all this lace. Though, no doubt the seamstresses at Spitalfields were under the same pressure too.

'Have you seen your Tom recently, Lily?' She looked up to see Cora hovering beside her, clearly dying to impart some tittle-tattle. 'What about you, Nell, have you seen him?' she asked, turning to her friend. But for once the other girl didn't answer.

Trying to appear casual, Lily said, 'No. Why, have you?'

'I heard he'd sold his boat and gone off on his travels.'

'Yes, I heard something like that too. Now please return to your pillow, it's time I inspected the lace and I'll begin with yours.' Trying not to smile at Cora's obvious disappointment, she snapped into overseer mode.

It took her some time to check all their work, and there was no chance of further conversation. By the end of the day, she was surprised to see that they were on schedule after all.

Feeling heartened and relieved that she hadn't lied to Mrs Bodney the previous evening, she bade them good evening, and then sat there in the gathering dusk going over what Cora had said about Tom and his boat. It appeared Mrs Westlake had been telling the truth, so where had he gone?

Chapter 32

'Stand still, for goodness' sake,' scolded Mrs Bodney as she put the finishing touches to Lily's hair.

'Sorry, Mrs Bodney, but I'm really nervous and it's uncomfortable with all these pins in my hair.'

'That style makes you look sophisticated and it shows off your shoulders to great effect. Men like that, Lily.'

'Oh. Must I really wear gloves, though? It's not winter yet,' she asked, as Mrs Bodney placed a pair next to her dress.

'A lady wears gloves regardless of the season. Now stop fussing. Rupert will be arriving any moment. Do you want him to see you in your under things?'

'Goodness me, no,' Lily gasped, shuddering at the thought.

'Well, step into your dress and I'll fasten it for you. Good, now for the gloves,' Mrs Bodney said, slipping the silky material over her hands. 'Right, hold the reticule and I'll pop a touch of rouge on your lips.'

'On my lips?' Lily exclaimed.

'Well, you certainly don't need any on your cheeks now, do you? There, that's better,' Mrs Bodney finally pronounced, taking a step back to check her handiwork.

But Lily was too excited to stand still. Swishing the beautiful dress from side to side, she smiled, then caught sight of her boots. They were beautiful but the cherry-red stitching poking out from under the delicate material looked all wrong.

'These are lovely but they don't really go with the dress, do they?' she asked, frowning.

'You look charming, and if I'm not mistaken the carriage is pulling up at the door right this very minute. Have a good time and remember to look the squire right in the eyes as you are presented,' Mrs Bodney instructed.

'Presented?' Lily squeaked, horrified.

'Indeed you will be, but remember it's all about

perception. If you act like a lady, you'll become one.'

'Me? Become a lady?' Lily laughed, but the other woman was already disappearing down the stairs. As she stood there gulping like the goldfish she'd once won at the travelling fair, there was a knock on the door.

'Mr Mountsford is waiting for you in the parlour, Miss Rose,' Tilda announced.

Taking a deep breath, Lily descended the stairs.

As she appeared in the doorway, Rupert rose to his feet. He seemed transfixed, staring at her for a full moment before moving towards her and shaking his head.

'Lily, I can't believe it's really you. Why, you look wonderful, utterly charming. Not that you don't always look beautiful,' he added quickly, holding out a corsage of tiny rosebuds. Bewildered, she stared down at the yellow flowers. What was she supposed to do with them? Seeing the uncertainty in her eyes, Rupert gently took them from her.

'May I?' he asked, bending and pinning them to her dress; then gently taking her arm he led her outside. 'My carriage awaits you, Cinderella,' he announced.

'As long as it doesn't turn into a pumpkin before we get there,' she laughed, feeling like a princess in the sapphire velveteen gown. If only she had glass slippers to wear instead of her boots, she thought settling back on the leather squabs and sniffing gently. There was that odd smell again.

Before she could dwell on it, Rupert had climbed in and called to the driver. As the carriage began to move, she sat watching the flickering lights from the candles in the cottages and the wood smoke pluming into the inky sky. The scenery looked sort of hazy mauve and very different from the last ride she'd taken in the carriage. Just then, Rupert rapped on the window and the coach drew to a halt.

'What's the matter?' she asked, but he was busy retrieving something from under his seat and didn't answer. Then, with a flourish he handed her a parcel tied with a red satin bow. Surprised, she sat looking down at it.

'Well, don't you want to see what's inside?' he asked.

Slowly, she pulled at the ribbon then, curiosity getting the better of her, flipped off the lid. Inside, nestling amongst the softest paper, was a pair of blue velvet dancing slippers. They were encrusted with diamond-like gems that twinkled in the twilight.

'Why, they're beautiful,' she gasped.

'Yes, they are rather,' he said, smiling at her bemused look. 'Aren't you going to try them on?'

'You mean they're for me?' she asked, her eyes widening in amazement.

'Well, I rather think they'll be a bit small for me,' he teased. 'Of course they are for you, Lily. When Mrs Bodney let slip what colour dress you'd be wearing, I took the liberty of having these made to match.'

'And she knew? No wonder she didn't think my wearing these boots would be a problem,' she said, eagerly pulling them off.

'May I?' he asked, taking the slippers from her, then bending down and gently placing one on each foot.

Speechless for probably the first time in her life, Lily could only gaze in wonderment at her new footwear.

'They are simply exquisite,' she said eventually.

'Well, I do pride myself on knowing what ladies like,' said Rupert, rather smugly.

'I guess Albert must have remembered my size,' she murmured.

'Ah,' he said smiling. 'Whilst Albert is undoubtedly a skilled cordwainer, I don't think he would have had the materials for these. I commissioned them to be made in London.'

'But how did you manage that? You only knew what I'd be wearing a few days ago,' she asked.

He tapped the side of his nose, the way Mrs Bodney did when she was being secretive.

'As long as you are pleased, Lily, then that's all that matters. May I say how delightful you look wearing them?' he complimented, as she held her feet out in front of her.

'Thank you,' she murmured, still bemused at such a wonderful gift.

'Now, it's time we were on our way,' he said, rapping on the window again, whereupon the carriage began to move. As she sat there admiring her new slippers, she heard her father's voice in her ear.

Careful, Lily, you don't get anything for nothing in this life.

'Oh,' she gasped.

'Is something wrong?' Rupert asked, looking concerned.

'Well, nobody gives you things for nothing, so will you, erm, expect...?' her voice stuttered to a

311

halt and she felt her cheeks growing hot.

'Lily, really,' he spluttered, quickly staring out of the window. There was silence for a moment and then having recovered his composure, he added, 'I enjoy your company, and am lucky to have the means to give you a present from time to time. Now stop fretting and enjoy the rest of the ride.'

She relaxed back, thinking what a really nice man he was. Then, as they continued their journey, her insides fizzed excitedly as she thought of the evening ahead. The image of Tom popped into her mind, but she pushed it away. Why should she worry about him when it was obvious he no longer cared for her?

Lamplight illuminated the courtyard as the driver drove up the gravelled carriage sweep, bringing the horses to a stop outside the imposing pillared portico of the manor house. Jumping down, Rupert helped her from the carriage then, keeping a light hold on her arm, led her inside. She gazed in wonder at the grandeur of the hallway, for of course, in the past, she'd always used the servants' entrance.

'Mr Rupert Mountsford and Miss Lily Rose,' the butler announced, and before she knew it, she was standing before Squire and Lady Clinsden.

'What in heaven's name is the meaning...?' spluttered the squire, his face growing redder by the moment.

'Lily and Rupert, how kind of you to join us this evening,' Lady Clinsden welcomed, cutting swiftly across her husband. 'Please do go through. Dancing is about to commence and supper will be served in the dining hall later. I trust you have an enjoyable evening. Oh, and Lily, Rupert here dances a very good quadrille so if I were you I'd get him to teach you,' she laughed. Before Lily could ask her what a quadrille was, she'd turned away and was greeting her next guests.

'It seems my secret is out,' Rupert said, beaming, and holding out his arm, he guided her through the thronging guests into the ballroom where a string quartet was playing.

Lily didn't know what was affecting her most, the blatant stares of the other guests or the heat from Rupert's arm. She could hear whispers of astonishment as they passed by, but if Rupert noticed he gave no sign. He stopped beside a table that was set back from the floor.

'I think this will suit us well. We'll be near enough to enjoy the music but far enough away to hear each other speak,' he was saying, but she was aware of the sudden chill as he withdrew his arm. 'Would you care for some refreshment?' he asked as a servant hovered beside them.

Lily nodded. Words were beyond her at the moment, and she busied herself studying the glass of sparkling pink liquid that was placed before her. Should she or should she not remove her gloves before picking it up? As the bubbles rose and popped, she surreptitiously glanced around, trying to ascertain what the other ladies were doing.

'It's only mildly intoxicating, Lily. Take a sip; it might fortify you,' Rupert urged, mistaking her hesitation.

Oh, what does it matter? she thought as, throwing caution to the wind, she did as he bid. She was pleasantly surprised to find it tasted of summer berries, and smiling, she took another sip.

'Gently does it, Lily. We've yet to partake of supper,' Rupert chided gently. Much to her embarrassment, her stomach rumbled, reminding her she'd been too excited to eat anything since breaking her fast that morning. If Rupert heard, he showed no sign as he sat there gently tapping his fingers on the table in time to the music. There was a sudden flurry of activity around them, as guests began making their way onto the dance floor. Smiling, he rose and held out his hand.

'They're forming squares for dancing. Come on, let's have some fun.' And before she could answer, she found herself being led onto the floor. Her movements were hesitant at first, but she followed his lead and was soon caught up in the rhythm of the music. Curious stares were cast in their direction but, following Rupert's example, she ignored them. He was clearly enjoying himself and she intended to as well. By the time the quadrille was announced she had forgotten her nerves and was having fun herself.

'You dance well, Lily,' Rupert said, breathlessly, as they finally left the floor to take a break.

'I just followed you, really,' she said, sinking onto her seat, then remembering where she was, sat up straight again.

'Then you are obviously a natural,' he said, smiling at her so engagingly she found herself responding. Heedless of the others around them, he continued gazing into her eyes until she felt quite light-headed and that tingle began creeping up her spine again.

The dinner gong sounded, shattering the

moment and bringing them rudely back to the present.

'Ladies and gentlemen, please make your way to the dining hall where supper will be served,' the butler announced.

Rupert grinned at her ruefully. 'I have to admit I could eat the proverbial horse. What about you, Lily?'

'Oh, I could only manage a pony, I'm afraid,' she quipped, sending them both into fits of laughter, bringing more disapproving looks their way.

'Lily, we must behave ourselves or I fear we shall be cast out on the streets, cold and hungry,' murmured Rupert gravely. Then with a wicked smile, he jumped to his feet, holding out his arm for her to take.

The dining hall was lit by myriad candles and, as they were shown to their table, Lily couldn't get over how splendid the chandeliers looked, casting their flickering glow around the room. Of course, she'd never had time to look around and appreciate the grandeur when she'd been serving at the tables. A guffaw of raucous laughter caught her attention and she shivered as she saw the squire sitting close by. Quickly, she looked down, hoping he wouldn't notice her.

'Is anything wrong, Lily?' Rupert asked, leaning towards her. Again, she felt that tingling sensation. Seeing the tender concern in his eyes, she thought again what a nice man he was.

'No, everything is fine, thank you, Rupert,' she answered, trying not to squirm as the squire turned and shot her a look of loathing. Remembering Mrs Bodney's advice, she coolly returned his stare but it made her feel uncomfortable. Then his attention was diverted as his first course was served and she could relax. Saved by the soup, she thought, trying not to giggle.

'Will there be more dancing after the meal?' she asked, racking her brains for something to say as she turned her attention back to Rupert. Before he could answer, there was a ripple of anticipation as their soup was brought to the table. As a delicious aroma wafted her way, she looked up eagerly and then froze. The maid serving this table was Molly, and the look she was shooting Lily was one of pure venom. She slapped the bowl of soup before her, deliberately placing it right on the edge of the table, where it wobbled precariously. Before Lily could reach out, it toppled over, tipping its entire contents into her lap. She heard a collective gasp from the guests seated around her and, looking up, she saw a malicious grin splitting Molly's face.

'Oh dearie me, I seem to have missed the table,' she cackled as Rupert sprang to his feet and began dabbing at Lily's dress with his napkin.

'And you will find yourself missing from all my tables in future,' said Lady Clinsden, appearing at Lily's side. 'Remove your presence from my establishment this instant,' she continued, her voice so sharp it could have carved through the joint of ham on the salver on the sideboard. Silence hung heavy in the air as the sulking Molly slunk out of the room.

Turning to Lily, Lady Clinsden put her hand on her arm. 'Come with me and we'll attend to your dress,' she said softly.

Rupert made to follow, but Lady Clinsden shook

her head. 'Thank you, Rupert, but there's no need for you to miss your supper. Don't worry, I'll bring her back safely,' she added, and Lily followed her from the room, trying to ignore the stares of the other guests. If she'd had any doubt at all that it had been an accident, the gloating smirk on the squire's face told her it had been anything but.

Chapter 33

'Molly did that on purpose,' Lily burst out as soon as she was alone with Lady Clinsden.

'I fear you may be right, Lily dear, and my husband was behind it, as usual,' she said, sighing. 'He was furious when you turned up as Rupert's guest and must have thought up the ruse to get his own back; knowing, of course, that Molly would do anything he asked.'

'Why would she do that?' Lily asked.

Lady Clinsden's sigh was deeper this time. 'Some women will do anything for money. Come along, let's get your dress clean,' she said, summoning her maid.

However, no matter how hard they tried, nothing would shift the stain. In fact the more they rubbed the more it seemed to settle into the nap of the material. Finally, when Lily's lap was all but saturated, they admitted defeat and Lady Clinsden dismissed the maid.

'Whatever shall I do? Mrs Bodney will kill me,' Lily wailed.

'I doubt that very much. Don't worry, a little specialist attention will put the dress to rights, but not tonight, I'm afraid. I'll loan you one of my gowns, then you can enjoy the rest of the evening.'

Glancing at the rose-pink silk gown Lady Clinsden was wearing, Lily frowned. She couldn't risk wearing something as obviously expensive as that.

Mistaking her look, Lady Clinsden added, 'I know it won't fit properly but at least you'll be presentable and I'll find a cloak to match. Rupert will still think you look delightful. You seemed to be enjoying his company before supper.'

'Oh, yes, he's wonderful, isn't he, Lady Clinsden? I couldn't believe it when he asked me to escort him tonight.'

'But Jean did tell you about our little ruse, didn't she?'

Lily frowned, trying to remember exactly what Mrs Bodney had said.

'And how is Tom?' Lady Clinsden enquired. 'Has he fully recovered from his ordeal at sea?'

'I don't know, my lady. He's not been to see me. Not that I care now,' Lily added dreamily, looking down at her feet where the jewels on her shoes twinkled up at her. Following her gaze, Lady Clinsden frowned.

'Did Rupert give you these?' she asked.

'Yes, my lady,' Lily grinned, and the other woman looked worried.

'Has he told you anything of his life in London?' Lady Clinsden continued, looking concerned.

Lily shook her head, realizing that he'd actually said nothing about his life at all. Silence hung heavy in the room and she began to feel uneasy.

Finally, as if she had reached a decision, Lady Clinsden leaned over and took Lily's hand. 'Lily, I can see from the way you were enjoying yourself this evening that you are becoming fond of Rupert. I would hate for you to get hurt so I feel you should know he is already betrothed to someone, how can I put it, of his own class.'

'What?' Lily exclaimed, snatching her hand away. 'Then why has he been...' her voice tapered off. She'd been going to say, why had he been paying her attention and compliments; giving her presents? Then she remembered what Mrs Bodney had told her about men liking to give presents to ladies in return for the delight of their company, and the farthing dropped. Why, she'd been merely a dalliance, a distraction for him.

'My dear, men like Rupert are utterly charming. However, they do think they can have everything. I'm sure he didn't mean to mislead you in any way, though.' Now the veil had been lifted, Lily couldn't believe she'd been so naïve. Rich men didn't marry ordinary lace makers like her, did they?

Lady Clinsden put her hand on Lily's arm. 'Look, slip out of those wet things, whilst I go and find you something suitable,' she said, disappearing through a door at the back of the room.

Lily looked around her, taking in the satin coverlet on the bed and the heavy damask curtains pulled tight against the night. Crystal perfume bottles adorned the dressing table, along with lotions and potions. So this was how the gentry lived. How could she have been so stupid as to

319

think she could ever be part of it? Quickly gathering up the sodden folds of her dress, she stole out of the boudoir and tiptoed down the stairs. The sounds of laughter and tinkling glasses emanated from the hall. Storming through the servants' quarters and out of the back door, she prayed no one would see her. She'd been taken for a right fool and needed to get her feelings under control before she could speak to anyone.

Outside, using the hedge that sheltered the kitchen garden for cover, she ran towards the carriages that were neatly lined up for their owners' return. Knowing Lady Clinsden's kind hospitality extended to the staff of her guests, she crossed her fingers that Rupert's driver would be tucking into his meal, along with the other coachmen. Locating his carriage, she tiptoed round to avoid the groom, before opening the door and climbing inside. Quickly, she removed the beautiful dancing slippers and placed them back in their box. Then, pulling her boots back on, she clambered out onto the path and sped down the gravelled sweep.

She ran until her breath was coming in ragged gasps, the eerie noises of the night impelling her on. Until, to her dismay, she developed a stitch and the spasms racking her side forced her to stop. Collapsing onto a clome by an old barn, she thought back over her ruined evening, hardly noticing the rain falling around her. Rupert was betrothed. He'd merely been toying with her all along. How he must have been laughing at her expense. How could she have let herself be taken in? She wondered if Mrs Bodney knew. Glancing down at her sodden clothes, Lily dreaded to think what her employer would say when she saw the state her lovely dress was in.

'Why didn't I listen to you Father?' she wailed into the darkness, but the only answer was the plopping of the raindrops as they dripped from the branches onto the fallen leaves, and the barking of a dog fox out on its nightly hunt. Perched like a pixie, her thoughts a jumble, she lost all sense of time.

The hoot of an owl close by brought her sharply back to the present, but it was the answering call that had her jumping to her feet and haring down the hillside. Whatever had possessed her to take a short cut across the fields at this time of night? She knew the answer. It had been to put as much distance between her and Rupert as quickly as possible. The only sensible thing now was to head towards the lane leading to the village. It would take her longer but she hoped at least she'd be safe. Holding her skirts higher, she lengthened her stride.

She was just gaining the hedgerow bordering the lane when she heard the galloping of horses coming towards her. Owlers? She shivered, swiftly stepping back into the shadows and holding her breath. To her relief, a coach and pair went thundering by and she let out a long sigh. With her nerves now completely shot, she ran as fast as she could until she reached Picky Pike's.

To her dismay, Rupert's carriage was drawn up outside. She was just wondering whether she had the courage to confront him when he emerged and called to the driver to head for home. As soon as the sound of horses' hooves had faded,

Lily stole indoors and was just creeping up the stairs when Mrs Bodney's strident tones stopped her in her tracks.

'Running away again, Lily Rose? In my parlour now, please.'

She could have cried but, seeing the set look on her employer's face, she retraced her steps. With her heart racing, she stood in the room staring down at the slate floor.

'I've just had the most unfortunate conversation with Rupert. He was out of his mind with worry, for apparently you left the supper table and simply disappeared. Lady Clinsden couldn't enlighten him either. I trust you have an explanation for such outrageous behaviour?' Mrs Bodney said, turning round and looking at Lily for the first time. 'Goodness, whatever has happened?' she asked, taking in her dishevelled state.

'I'm really sorry about your dress. I'll pay for any damage and—'

'Sit down, Lily,' Mrs Bodney said, her voice softer now. 'Rupert has explained about the unfortunate incident with the soup, but surely that was no reason to abandon him?'

'Lady Clinsden offered to lend me one of her dresses. Then when she saw the velvet slippers Rupert had given me she told me he's betrothed to a lady in London.'

'Ah, I see,' Mrs Bodney said.

'And he was so nice to me tonight, I really thought he cared for me.' She saw her employer frown and her voice tailed off.

'Sometimes, men like to try their chance with young ladies. It's their pride. They see it as some kind of challenge. And, of course, there are those women who, once they get a taste of luxury, are only too happy to oblige,' Mrs Bodney said, so matter-of-factly Lily couldn't help but burst out, 'Well, I think it's horrible that he should pretend to have feelings for me.'

'For what it is worth, I believe Rupert is genuinely fond of you and I did explain that his escorting you to the Harvest Supper was part of our plan to get even with the squire.'

'Yes. I'd forgotten that until Lady Clinsden said. Still, it makes sense; men like Mr Mountsford don't really have relationships with someone like me.'

'It's the way of the world, I'm afraid, Lily. I do think he might have had the decency to explain about his betrothal, though. He probably thought that Devonshire was far enough away from London for word not to get back about any...' Unusually for her, Mrs Bodney stuttered to a halt.

'I was thinking on the way back here and I reckon it's one rule for men and another for women in this life. Men are deceitful wastrels and they can all go and hang themselves. I've finished with them.'

'You are very idealistic, Lily,' Mrs Bodney said, shaking her head.

'If you mean I have principles, Mrs Bodney, then yes I do.'

'Perhaps I was wrong to encourage you to accept his gifts but he so enjoyed treating you, and you work so hard I thought you deserved a bit of spoiling. Never mind, it will all come out in the wash, as they say. Which reminds me, tomorrow is the

323

Sabbath, and after you've attended church, you have my permission to make good my dress before that stain really sets in. Now I'll bid you good night.'

Cursing Mr Mountsford for trying to make a fool of her by playing with her emotions, Lily made her way up the stairs. Tearing off the boots, she flung them across the room, stepped out of the sodden dress and threw herself into bed. She pulled the bedclothes tight up over her head, knowing she wouldn't sleep, but hoping the warmth would penetrate her body and stop the shivers that were convulsing her.

Exhausted, she fell asleep, only to dream of harvest festivities. But it was previous celebrations they'd had back in Coombe, where they'd spend all afternoon decorating the barn with greenery and wild flowers from the fields. Then, they'd sit on hay bales, laughing and drinking homemade lemonade or cider. The trestle would be piled high with hunks of bread, a huge ham, cheeses, savoury pies and apple pies. In the centre would be one of her mother's specially baked loaves, shaped like a sheaf of corn. The men would play their fiddles, Rob would play his mouth organ and they'd dance and make merry until dawn. Best of all, though, was Tom holding her tight, whirling her round and round until she collapsed in his arms. Fun; they'd had such good fun.

When she woke, sunlight was flooding her room. She lay there for some moments before realizing it was the brightness that came with midmorning. Jumping out of bed, she took her chair to the skylight and peered out, dismayed to see everyone streaming out of church. She'd slept right past morning service. When she saw the discarded dress on the floor the events of the previous evening came flooding back. Dressing quickly, she snatched up the offending garment and made her way outside to try to wash off the grease.

'Lily, where've you been, I missed you in church.' Looking round, she saw Mary hurrying towards her.

'Oh, Mary, I've had the most awful time.' The other woman glanced down at the dress she was holding and raised a questioning eyebrow.

'What, in a frock like that? I'd give me front teeth to doll myself up in material that soft.'

'Yes, but I've got soup all down it and it's dried in.'

'Calm yerself, girl. Let's take a gander at it.' Lily watched as the other woman held it up to the light then whistled. 'Someone's been rubbing the nap the wrong way. Soup, you say? Goodness knows what was in it then, 'cos this looks like a grease stain to me. Still, it's nothing a bit of wood ash won't get out.'

'Really?' asked Lily, looking hopefully at the woman who'd become her friend over the past months. 'But someone said it would require specialist treatment.'

'No doubt they did, seeing as them newfangled chemicals cost a week's wage. Want me to take this home and see to it?' she asked, holding up the dress.

'Oh, Mary, would you?'

'Of course I will. It'll take more than a bit of soup to beat me. I'll bring it into work tomorrow with me. Now I'd best get this lot home and fed,' she said as her family swarmed around her, begging for their lunch. She looked at Lily closely. 'You look peaky, love. Why don't you come home and have a bite with us? Who knows, you might even be the lucky one who finds a bit of pig in the broth,' she laughed.

'Thanks, Mary, but I'm not really hungry.'

'Broth not good enough now you're eating fine food up at the manor, eh?' she said, laughing again.

'Of course it is. Anyway, I didn't actually get anything to eat at the supper.'

Curiosity flashed in the other woman's eyes but Lily was still feeling raw about Rupert's deception and didn't wish to talk about it.

Giving a big yawn, she said, 'Sorry, Mary, it was a very late night so I think I'll return to my room and have a lie-down once I've finished washing this muck off the rest of my clothes.'

'That's it, Lily, you get some rest whilst you can. Once you've got a family round you, you'll find yourself lucky to have the time to draw breath, let alone sleep,' Mary said cheerfully, heading down the lane with her brood following after her. Lily was reminded of the song her mother used to sing about an old woman who had so many children she didn't know what to do.

She sighed, for now it was she who didn't know what to do. There was no way she could face Mr Mountsford again without telling him a few home truths, and if she did that Mrs Bodney would be sure to dismiss her.

Chapter 34

Before the first streaks of grey were lighting the eastern sky on Monday morning, Lily made her way to the workroom. As there was no sign of her employer, she busied herself setting out the materials ready for the day ahead. She couldn't help worrying in case Mary hadn't been able to get the stain out of Mrs Bodney's dress. There was no way she could afford to replace such quality, even on the money she was getting as overseer. Fretting made her awkward and in her haste, she knocked over the tray of bobbins, sending them clattering across the floor.

'If there's one thing I cannot abide it's noise, especially at this early hour, Lily Rose. It upsets my equilibrium for the day ahead.'

'Sorry, Mrs Bodney,' Lily replied, cursing her clumsiness.

'I would like to see all the lace that's been made for our Queen,' Mrs Bodney requested, giving Lily a penetrating look. Carefully, she set the sprigs out along the long table, whereupon Mrs Bodney began counting and sorting them into various piles. Finally, she looked at Lily in surprise.

'Well, there's enough here for the flounce and all the various trimmings, and almost sufficient for the veil. The progress you've made on the Bertha collar is quite surprising,' she pronounced.

Lily smiled but her relief was short-lived for then

her employer announced, 'I shall now inspect the work for quality. However, there's no need for you to watch, you can go back to your own work.'

Relieved to have something to focus on, Lily picked up the bobbins, then sat at her pillow. Conscious of Mrs Bodney's presence, she didn't dare look up when the others filed into the room, although she could feel their curious stares, for their employer was seldom seen in the workroom these days. Finally, when Mrs Bodney had finished holding the lace sprigs up to the light she turned to Lily.

'That's a good standard of work. Before I go, did you have any luck with my dress?'

As Lily hesitated, Mary quickly cut in, 'Do you mean this one, Mrs Bodney?' She held up the velveteen material. 'I saw it on the table by the door when I came in and thought how beautiful it is.'

Beaming, Mrs Bodney took the dress from her and held it up to the light. Lily held her breath.

'Well, Lily, it seems there's little wrong with your laundering skills,' she finally pronounced, looking surprised.

As their employer swept out of the room, Lily shot Mary a grateful look.

'Phew,' Emma said, 'we don't often see her ladyship in here, do we?'

'No we don't, so I think we'd best look busy in case she pops in again,' answered Mary, giving Lily a meaningful look.

Nodding in agreement, Lily settled back to her pillow, determined to put all other thoughts to the back of her mind.

As if they were aware of the undercurrents going

on around them, the ladies worked diligently for the rest of the morning, so that when it was time for their nuncheon Lily looked up in surprise.

'Are you coming outside, Lily?' Mary asked, stopping by her chair.

'No, I don't think so. There's still so much to do,' she said.

Well, I think you should. You're still looking right peaky. What's up, our Lil? You can tell me.'

'Oh, Mary, I've really made a mess of things.' The other woman perched on the chair beside her, waiting for her to continue. 'Not only did I get soup on Mrs Bodney's gown, I ran away from the squire's supper dance as well.'

'Don't see that's anything to fret over. Besides, Mrs Bodney's dress came up a dream.'

'Mary, I can't thank you enough for dealing with that. How much do I owe you?'

'Love a duck, you don't owe me nothing. Why, only last year that lovely mother of yours, God rest her soul, sent over a bottle of the violet syrup she'd made especially for my little one. Stopped her colic just like that, it did,' she said, snapping her fingers. 'The old man and me got the best night's sleep we'd had in ages, so call it square, eh?'

'You're so kind, Mary,' Lily said, 'and after I made you fall, as well.'

'Oh, get away with you. Now, why don't you tell me what's really grieving you?' the older woman said, looking at her with knowing eyes.

Unable to keep it to herself any longer, Lily told her about Mr Mountsford's attentions, the boots with cherry stitching and the blue velvet slippers. 'I would never have accepted them if I'd known

329

he was betrothed to another,' she finally declared.

Mary sat silently looking at her for a long moment. 'Look, Lily,' she finally said. 'It's like I told you once before. Fine feathers don't make a fine fellow.'

'But Mrs Bodney told me it was a good way to better myself.'

'Better yourself than what? And who's to say she's right?' Mary asked.

'What do you mean?' Lily asked, puzzled.

'You're doing fine as you are. It's what you feel here that matters,' Mary declared, thumping her heart. 'It's what feels right, Lily, not what looks right. We don't all have ideas above our station like Mrs Bodney, thanks heavens,' she said, shaking her head. 'That woman's got more airs than the weather. Now you ring that bell for the end of break, or you really will have the dragon breathing down your neck.'

'Indeed you will, Mary,' Mrs Bodney said, appearing in the doorway and making them jump.

Flushing, Lily snatched up the bell and rang it vigorously. The ladies filed back indoors, clearly curious as to why their boss was in the workroom for the second time that day. Mrs Bodney nodded to them.

'Continue the good work, ladies,' she instructed before turning to Lily and saying, 'Lady Clinsden called by earlier. She was impressed by the way my dress had been restored and would like to know what you used.'

Lily racked her brains. What was it Mary had said she was going to use? Luckily her friend had seen her predicament and was mouthing the answer behind Mrs Bodney's back.

'Wur dash,' she stuttered, trying to read Mary's lips.

'Wurdash. Thank you, I'll pass that on to her ladyship. I'm sure her maid will know where some can be purchased. Now, everyone, back to work and, Lily, I'll see you in my parlour later.' As she swept out of the room, Mary shook her head and laughed.

'Oh my, that's a good one. She might be a fine businesswoman but she's clearly no housekeeper.'

As peals of laughter rang around the room, Lily joined in, feeling she was one of them again. Settling down to her work, she thought about Mary's earlier comments, and the image of a man with blond wavy hair and cheeky grin they'd conjured up. Her heart felt heavy. Tom obviously didn't care much for her for he hadn't been in touch for weeks now. In fact, nobody seemed to know of his whereabouts. Seemingly, he'd vanished into thin air.

Before she knew it, the sun, which was setting noticeably earlier in the day lately, had disappeared, leaving them struggling to work in the shadow-filled room.

'I can't see a blooming thing,' Nell exclaimed. 'I've reworked this bit twice and it's still not right. We need candles, Lily, or we'll have to go home.'

Privately she agreed, but the thought of her meeting with Mrs Bodney was already filling her with dread without having to ask for what she knew would be regarded as an extra expense, despite her employer's pledge to look after their eyes. Still, it stood to reason the ladies couldn't be expected to work if they couldn't see.

'I think we should call it a day, ladies. You may cover your work and leave.' The early reprieve sent ripples of excitement round the room and there was a scraping of chairs as they shot to their feet, eager to be on their way.

'Be sure to be back at first light, though,' she called after them, but all she heard was their faint laughter as they made their way down the path. Peering around, she realized it was too dark to check the afternoon's work. Knowing she had no excuse to dally, she smoothed down her dress and made her way to the parlour.

'You've finished work earlier than usual. I suppose the ladies are asking for candles to work by now?' Mrs Bodney said, looking up from the ledger she was working on. As always, her employer's shrewdness took Lily by surprise.

'Oh, don't look like that, Lily. I'm not the ogre you all seem to think. I'd like to provide them but it's a business I run here, and cost has to be balanced against profit. However, now it's autumn, the hours of daylight are growing shorter and the work is on schedule so the ladies may continue to leave at this time. Of course, their wages will be adjusted accordingly, so see that they are informed.'

Lily nodded, but her mind was busy working out by how much her own wages would be cut. Mrs Bodney's voice cut through her reverie.

'The reason Lady Clinsden called to see me earlier was because she was concerned about you. She hoped her revelation about Rupert hadn't upset you too much.'

'I'm grateful for her concern, but I won't give up my principles for anyone. I'm sorry if I've let you down, though,' she said. There was silence as her employer studied her for a long moment.

'No, Lily, it is I who should apologize. I should have been aware you thought Rupert was offering something he wasn't. Clearly you are not the sort of woman who is prepared to compromise her standards for the sake of a few luxuries and I admire you for that. I'm sure you will not be taken in again.'

'No, I will not,' Lily stated, with feeling.

'Well, I must continue entering the details of materials used to date in the ledger, so I'll bid you good evening.'

Lily took some bread, cheese and an apple up to her room, where she ate by moonlight and, positioning her paper under the skylight, practised her letters.

There was uproar in the workroom the next morning when Lily explained that working hours were being curtailed for the rest of the contract.

'The stingy old bat could at least provide us with a few candles and we could all bring our flashes,' Cora moaned. 'It's all right for her; she's got pots of money.'

'The stingy old bat could indeed provide you with a few candles and flashes as well,' Mrs Bodney said, appearing in the doorway and making them jump. 'However, if I did that, your work would be finished in less than a month. Do I take it you already have other employment lined up?' she asked, staring at Cora, who at least had the grace to blush.

Everyone knew demand for pillow lace was waning rapidly, and with machine-made lace proving more economical, work was going to be harder than ever to come by. After her conversation with Mrs Bodney the previous evening, Lily had tossed and turned most of the night wondering where she was going to go, and what she was going to do when the Queen's lace was finished. Realizing Mrs Bodney was still speaking, she tried to concentrate.

'And as for the rest of your statement, Cora, I have worked long and hard to get where I am today. You would do well to remember that if I hadn't earned a good reputation I wouldn't have secured this commission from the Queen, and you, young lady, wouldn't have had employment these past few months.' With that, she swept out of the room leaving a sombre little workforce behind her.

As the hours crept slowly by, the mood in the workroom grew ever more sober. Each was lost in her own thoughts, knowing they all would soon be at the mercy of any job they might be lucky enough to come by. Lily was torn between wishing the long day over, and dreading finding out when she'd have to leave. Never had she felt so alone. If only Tom was here to confide in, she thought.

Finally, the afternoon dragged to a close and it was with relief that the ladies tidied away their things. The huge pile of finished sprigs on the large dresser stood as testament to their hard work, yet served also to highlight the fact that the commission was almost fulfilled.

A knock on the door jolted Lily from her musing.

'Mrs Bodney is waiting to see you,' the maid announced.

'Thank you, Tilda,' she said, automatically smoothing down her dress before hurrying through to the parlour.

'I trust all went well today and the ladies have agreed to their new conditions?'

'Yes, although they are concerned as to their future.'

Mrs Bodney nodded, then handed her a letter.

'This was delivered earlier. Well, go on, open it,' she urged, as Lily stood gazing down at it.

'Will you read it for me, please, Mrs Bodney?'

Her employer nodded, holding out her hand for the letter. Then, just as she had done before, she cleared her throat and read,

Dearest Lily,

I was so pleased to hear from you and to know that you do not bear me any ill will.

Of course you may continue to call me Aunt Elizabeth and I trust that when next we meet we shall have the discussion I'd hoped to have with you before our untimely departure. Thank you for letting me know Beth is faring well.

Rob sends his affection, as do I,

Your loving Aunt Elizabeth

PS. I have also received a very interesting communication from Lady Clinsden and will keep you informed should her exciting proposal develop.

'There now, doesn't that put your mind at rest?'

her employer asked.

'Yes, thank you, Mrs Bodney. But what does she mean about a proposal from Lady Clinsden?'

'Lily, despite what you might think, I am not clairvoyant, so we will have to wait and see. Now, off you go and get your beauty sleep,' her employer said, handing her back the letter. 'I'll bid you good night.'

Taking a picnic supper up with her, Lily escaped to her room, then lay in bed mulling over the communication from her aunt and the events of the day. Realizing Mrs Bodney still hadn't said when her work here would be at an end, she vowed to ask her first thing in the morning. She needed to make plans for the future, not least to find somewhere to live. Should she return to Coombe, she wondered.

Finally she fell into a troubled sleep, dreaming a dream she was to have for many nights. She was back in Coombe, a fair-haired man with a cheeky grin beside her. He was vowing eternal love and placing a ruby ring on her finger.

Chapter 35

Lily woke with a start, then lay there feeling restless. Some elusive thought was niggling at the back of her mind. But no matter how hard she tried, she couldn't put her finger on what it was. Jumping out of bed, she tugged on her clothes, ran her fingers through her hair and let herself out into the grey of the early morning. The autumnal air was decidedly chilly and, pulling her shawl tighter round her, she decided to delay her morning wash at the pump until the sun had come up. Hurrying down Sea Hill, her heart leaped when she saw the red sails of Tom's lugger. Then she remembered the boat was no longer his. *Where are you, Tom?* Tears pricked the back of her eyes, but she blinked hard, refusing to give in to self-pity.

Thrusting her hands into the pockets of her apron, she tramped along the shoreline, spray stinging her cheeks, pebbles crunching beneath her boots. Before long, the keen air had worked its magic and her thinking was as clear as the water. She thought back to her strange dream, and was just on the verge of remembering what it was that had been bothering her, when she heard a shout.

'Ouch.'

She spun round but couldn't see anyone.

'Oh, blow it, blow it.' This time the cry repeated, as it bounced off the cliffs and echoed around the bay.

She stood still, then caught a glimpse of movement by the netting hut. Hurrying towards it, she saw Joe the Quarry perched on a rock wringing his hands.

'Joe, whatever's the matter?' she asked.

'I'm a useless old fool, that's what,' the old man muttered, turning his rheumy eyes towards her before glaring down at the pebbles. Following his gaze, she saw the discarded turnip lying where he'd thrown it. 'Can't even make a lantern for me grandson now with these useless mitts,' he spat, holding up his hands, which were squashed almost flat, their misshapen fingers sticking out at awkward angles. She also saw the right one had a gouge where the thumb had been.

Ignoring the nausea that was churning her stomach, she bent to retrieve the turnip and knife, then handed them back to him. She could recall her parents talking about the accident at the quarry, which had claimed the lives of five men, leaving others maimed, Joe amongst them.

'Can't earn me living no more, but thought I could at least make young Jack a lantern for his guising at Samhain.'

Her heart went out to the old man, but instinct warned her to tread carefully. 'I've always wanted to make one of those, Joe, but wouldn't know where to begin,' she said, crossing her fingers behind her back. 'Could you show me?'

Slowly he turned towards her, hope then suspicion flickering in his eyes.

'And why would a pretty young thing like yer be wanting to know how to make a turnip lantern?'

Knowing she had to spare his pride she thought hard. Then an image of Beth sprang into her mind.

'Because, Joe, it would make the perfect present for my little sister.'

The old man studied her carefully then gave her a wizened smile. 'Yer on, lass. I'll get us two more turnips. Yer works for Mrs Bodney now, don't yer? Given yer the day off, has she?'

'Oh my,' she gasped, glancing up at the sky and seeing the first rays of red peeping above the cliffs. 'She'll have my guts for garters if I don't rush. Will you be here later?'

He grinned ruefully. 'Spends most of me time here these days. I'll see yer by the old boathouse when yer've finished yer work. If yer can spare the time, of course,' he added, looking at her hopefully.

'Don't worry, I'll be there,' she promised, before hurrying back to Picky Pike's.

'Ah, Lily, just the person I wanted to see,' said Mrs Bodney, waylaying her as she hurried down the hallway. 'I shall be out for the rest of the day. There are things we need to discuss, so I'll see you in my parlour when you finish work.' She frowned as she took in Lily's windswept appearance.

'I'm afraid that won't be convenient, Mrs Bodney,' Lily stammered. 'I've promised to help a friend.'

'Well, you'd better unpromise then,' Mrs Bodney commanded, turning on her heel and disappearing into her parlour.

'But, I can't,' Lily called after her.

'I beg your pardon, Lily?' asked Mrs Bodney.

'I said I'm afraid that won't be possible, Mrs Bodney.'

'Are you disobeying me, Lily?' asked Mrs Bodney, her voice as icy as a hoar frost.

Staring at her employer, Lily's courage almost deserted her. Then she remembered the hopeful look on Joe's face and stood her ground.

'I'm sorry, Mrs Bodney, I've made a promise and when I make a promise I keep it. Perhaps we could discuss things later this evening or even tomorrow first thing?' But her employer stalked off without answering.

Lily made her way to the workroom, praying

her shaking legs wouldn't give way. She was sure to be dismissed now, but her job appeared to be coming to an end anyway.

'Blimey, Lily, you look like someone's taken your last farthing,' Mary greeted her.

'Wish I could stroll in just when I feel like it,' Cora muttered under her breath, causing Lily to lash out.

'Well, you can't. And I'll have you know, there's been many a night I've worked on after you have all left. Now, you'd do well to remember the work here's nearly completed so your agreement can be ended right now.'

Cora and Nell exchanged glances and an uneasy silence descended on the room. Ignoring them, Lily sat at her pillow and picked up her bobbins. Wary of her mood, the ladies all worked quietly and when noon came, filed outside for their break before she had a chance to ring the bell. Even Mary stayed away from her. A moody maid, her father would have called her, she thought, suddenly feeling unbearably lonely.

The afternoon dragged by and still no one spoke to her, although she did see Mary shooting her puzzled glances once or twice. She knew it was up to her to make amends, but in a peculiar kind of way, she relished being left alone. Finally, she heard the ladies tidying away their things, then their voices fading as they clattered and chattered their way down the lane. No guesses as to what their topic of conversation would be, she thought. Breathing a sigh of relief that she could leave the workroom at last, she covered her pillow and pulled on her shawl.

Hurrying down to the beach, Lily saw it was a hive of noise and activity. The fishing fleet had returned and their luggers and crabbers were beached broadside, whilst their catch and fishing gear was carried up onto the Hard. Gulls circled and screeched, impatient to scavenge the scraps and fish guts they knew would be left on the pebbles.

Then the squire appeared in the doorway of the alehouse and Lily ducked into the shadows, but he was busy talking to the haulers and didn't see her. Then, as he staggered up the hill the others made their way down the beach, ready to haul the boats further out of the water. The fishermen, glad to be back safely on dry land, were laughing as they stowed their nets. Lily couldn't help peering around hopefully, but, of course, there was no sign of Tom.

Joe was waiting by the old boathouse as he'd said he would, two turnips and a knife by his side. He looked so pleased to see her she couldn't help but smile back. 'That's better. Looked like a black tornado, ye did, roaring down the hill. That old dragon given yer a hard time, has she?'

'I haven't seen her all day. Well, not since I refused to do what she wanted.'

To her amazement he grinned wickedly.

'I'd love to have seen her face,' he chortled. 'She's used to getting her own way, that one. What wouldn't yer do, then?'

'Break a promise,' she said. Then, seeing his knowing look, she quickly changed the subject.

'I just saw the squire staggering up the hill. He spends a lot of his time in the alehouse, doesn't he?' she said, wrinkling her nose. 'I guess he's really unhappy inside.'

'Hmm, we all have our crosses to bear,' Joe grunted, staring down at his misshapen hands. 'He'll have been up in the tallet over the kitchen plotting and planning his dealings.'

'Dealings?'

'Yer knows, with them free traders,' he said, tapping the side of his nose with a mangled finger. 'He does all the planning and ordering. Then away he goes, leaving the others to do the risky work of transporting the spoils up to the manor house, with the best going up to London by yon fancy carriage.'

She looked up into the gloom where Joe indicated and thought the vehicle looked similar to Rupert's.

'What kind of spoils?' she asked, remembering the Christmas smell in his carriage.

'Brandy, baccy, tea, spices, silks and whatever else they've brought in,' Joe said, shrugging. Before she could ask any further questions, another group of haulers passed by and he quickly looked down at the turnips.

'Right, show me how to make these lanterns then,' Lily said, taking the hint and changing the subject.

'You whittle, I'll guide,' Joe said.

At first, Lily found it difficult cutting into the hard vegetable, especially in the gathering gloom, but Joe was patient, and under his guidance she soon relaxed. By the time she'd scored out twisted curves for the mouths, she was enjoying herself.

'Well, lass, those will look real scary when

they're lit up. My Jack will be right pleased when I show him what yer've made.'

'No, Joe, what *we've* made. We've done these together.' She saw him look down at his hands. 'Your brains; my labour,' she added. He was silent for a few moments, then nodded.

'Yer real kind, lass. Most people look at my hands and think I'm only fit for the scrap heap, but yer've proved that ain't the case and I'm right thankful.'

'And I'm grateful to you, because now I've got a turnip lamp to take to Beth.'

He put out his hand and, without hesitating, Lily took it and shook it.

'Mrs Bodney says it's the way things look that matters, but you know, Joe, I don't think she's necessarily correct.'

'Aye, that's always been her way, lass, but that don't mean it's the right one for yer. Yer has a heart of gold so yer just go with what yer feel.'

'Thank you, Joe,' she said, feeling as if a weight had been lifted from her. Grinning, she picked up her lantern. 'I know Beth is going to love this.'

Tramping back up the now deserted beach, she wondered if she'd have time to visit Coombe before Samhain. She could remember the fun they'd had last year, Father and Rob had carved out the turnips while she'd helped her mother bake the special apple pie. They'd set extra places at the table so their departed loved ones could join them for supper, for it was that special night of the year when the veil between this world and the next was at its thinnest.

She stopped in her tracks tingling with excitement. Suppose her mother and father were to pay her a visit this Samhain? Or her nana and grandad? Her nana! That was what had been niggling her when she woke, for hadn't the wise old woman told her that problems had a way of sorting themselves while you slept? You simply had to look for the answers in your dreams.

Feeling happier than she had for ages, she let herself into Picky Pike's. She was just placing the lantern on the ledge by the front door when Mrs Bodney came storming out of the workroom.

'How dare you go out and leave the door unbolted?' she spluttered.

Lily stared at her in dismay. 'But I didn't, Mrs Bodney.'

'You did. The door to the workroom was wide open. What if the Queen's lace had been stolen?'

'What?' Lily gasped.

'Luckily Tilda saw you leave and came at once to inform me. I've just this minute finished checking everything's in order and now you come breezing in, beaming like a blooming beacon.'

'But I'm certain I bolted it,' Lily repeated.

'And I'll have none of these heathen things in my house, thank you,' Mrs Bodney snapped, sweeping the lantern onto the floor. 'I shudder to think what would have happened had all that work been stolen. If it'd got into the wrong hands, the Queen would have had my neck on a noose. Your behaviour today has been irresponsible and disappointing to say the least.'

'But, Mrs Bodney, I did bolt the door.'

'You couldn't have done, 'cos it was wide open,' Tilda said from behind them. Both women spun round. 'Mr Mountsford couldn't believe it when he heard and–' At the mention of her merchant's name Mrs Bodney's eyes widened.

'Are you telling me Mr Mountsford has called here, Tilda?' she asked. 'When was this?'

'It was when you were in the workroom, Mrs Bodney. He asked what was going on and I told him about Lily leaving the workroom door open. When I said I'd go and get you, he said not to bother as you was obviously busy. Then he left,' Tilda said, looking very pleased with herself.

'How dare you divulge personal information about my household?' Mrs Bodney exploded. 'I expect discretion at all times, as you should well know. Pack your things and leave this instant.'

'But I was only doing as–'

'I said go,' Mrs Bodney repeated. Then, ignoring Tilda's wails, she swept into her parlour, closing the door firmly behind her.

Chapter 36

Lily turned to the sobbing maid. 'Whatever possessed you, Tilda? We both know the workroom door was bolted so why did you tell Mrs Bodney it wasn't?'

'It was 'cos of Mr Mountsford. He said he'd buy me... I thought if you was gone he... Oh, what am I to do now?' she cried, before turning and rushing out of the front door, leaving Lily staring after her.

'Tilda's run off, Mrs Bodney,' Lily said, hurrying into the parlour. 'Do you think I should go after her?'

'After the trouble she tried to cause you, Lily?' her employer answered, looking surprised.

'Me? I don't understand, Mrs Bodney. I'm sure I haven't upset her in any way.'

'Not directly, perhaps, but the poor girl was sweet on our dear merchant.' As if a candle had been lit, Lily suddenly understood the reason for the girl's blushes on his previous visits. Clearly, he'd been playing with her affections as well. The cad!

'I'd have been dispensing of her services shortly anyway, so she's saved me a job,' her employer said, waving her hands dismissively.

'That seems rather harsh, Mrs Bodney. She's only a young girl, after all.'

There was a pause, as if her employer was choosing her words carefully. Finally she turned to Lily, looking even more serious than she had before.

'Life is harsh, Lily. And as for Tilda being young, don't be fooled. In many ways she's more worldly-wise than you, only too eager to grasp anything that was offered, willing to offer... Oh, never mind. Go and smarten up. You look more like a gutter snipe than my overseer.'

Out in the hallway, Lily looked down at her dress, shocked to see grains of sand and fronds of weed clinging to its hem. Why hadn't she noticed before? Hurrying out to the pump, she sponged down the material, then looking around and seeing the yard was deserted, she dunked her head under the running water. Gasping at its coolness, she let it run through her long tresses for a few moments before squeezing out as much as she could. Hopping up on the wall, she began braiding it. What a day it had been, she mused as she sat gazing down towards the harbour. The rising moon was spreading silvery fingers of light, like the rungs of a ladder, across the inky waters, and she had a sudden longing to hear her father's wise words. A voice sounded behind her.

'Playing at mermaids today, are we? Well, you certainly are a woman of many guises, Lily Rose.'

Her heart sank. The silky tones of the squire did little to hide his intent. Perhaps if she didn't rise to the bait he'd lose interest and go away. Forcing a smile, she turned to face him.

'Good evening, Squire Clinsden,' she answered, trying not to shudder at the lecherous way he was looking her up and down with his bloodshot eyes.

'Prettying yourself up for your merchant, are you?' he asked, placing his hand on her arm. 'How about being nice to me instead?'

'I think you should go home to your wife,' Lily answered, wondering where her daring had come from.

'She spends all her time on charitable works these days,' he said sullenly.

'Well, I think it's wonderful all the things she does for the elderly fisher folk and—'

'Yes, yes, but a man needs his home comforts,' he said, moving his hand up to her hair and attempting to undo her braid. 'You do realize that fancy merchant was merely using you as an alibi? Now, I don't need one, so if you were to be nice to me, I would teach you all you need to know

347

about society,' he leered, his hand digging into her shoulder.

She tried to move along the wall, away from his grasp.

'Still acting the innocent, eh? Well, don't be too hasty, young lady. Beggars can't be choosers, and from what I hear, you'll soon be requiring a new position and somewhere to live. Now, with Molly gone from the manor–'

'Take your hands off her this instant.' Surprised, the squire did as he'd been bid and, seizing the opportunity, Lily jumped to the ground.

'I was only trying to–' the squire simpered.

'On your way, you pathetic excuse for a man. And in future leave Lily alone,' the figure commanded. Then, as Squire Clinsden sloped off and his adversary moved out of the shadows, Lily gasped in amazement.

'Tom, oh, Tom. Where've you been? You came just in time. He was–'

'I know, Lily, don't fret, he's gone now. He'll not bother you again. Bullies never fight those who challenge them. I've learned that if nothing else. Luckily, I was just on my way to see Mother,' he said, giving her the wry grin she remembered so well.

'Good job too,' she said, her smile growing wider as she moved closer to him.

'Aye, and it seems you've come full circle, what with you needing a job again and the squire kindly offering to help,' he said, stressing the word 'kindly'.

'I've still got a few weeks left with Mrs Bodney, but then I'll be seeking work along with all the others. Still, something will turn up,' she said, grinning at him. He was standing so close she could feel the heat emanating from his body. Her senses tingled in response, making her realize how much she'd missed him.

'How've you been, Tom?' she asked softly.

'I've been managing fine,' he answered, his arms reaching out towards her. But then the light went out of his eyes and his arms fell back to his sides.

'Oh, Tom, I've missed you. Haven't you missed me?' she asked, looking at him hopefully. For a long moment time seemed suspended as he stood staring at her.

'Lord knows, Lily, you made me that furious I couldn't bear to see you again. Doesn't mean I've stopped thinking of you, though,' he mumbled.

'Is that why you've come back now?' she asked, brightening.

He shook his head. 'I was passing through on my way from Coombe when I heard the commotion. Couldn't just leave you with that brute, could I?'

'Seems like I'm in your debt then,' she said, smiling. He shrugged and made to turn away. Her heart flopped. Remembering her dreams and determined not to let the opportunity pass, she swallowed her pride and tried again. 'I owe you an apology, Tom. Look, it's a beautiful night, have you time for a walk round the bay, so we can talk?'

'Well,' he hesitated. 'Oh, why not, but you'd best put that bonny hair back up under yer cap,' he said, grinning.

She smiled. This was more like the Tom she knew. He'd always loved her long hair, she thought, twisting it back into its braid then pulling her cap over it.

'Is that better?' she teased.

'Didn't want you to catch cold, that's all,' he grunted, and her heart plummeted. Still she wasn't about to give up.

'Come on then,' she invited, holding out her hand. Ignoring it, he began striding out towards the water. Hurrying to keep up with him, she cast around for something to say.

'I heard you sold your boat.'

'I heard you got yourself a merchant,' he responded.

'Oh, Tom, you always get the wrong end of things. It was all a plan to get back at the squire. It's you I love. Always have and always will, I guess, and anyway, that merchant's actually betrothed to another,' she said.

'Oh, poor you, that's scuppered your chances then,' he snorted.

'But, Tom, I've just tried to explain that it wasn't like that,' she protested.

'Of course it wasn't. Would have solved your problems, though, wouldn't it?'

'What do you mean?'

'It would have given you somewhere to live and a chap of his standing wouldn't expect his wife to work either.'

'Tom Westlake, I can't believe you're saying such things. I thought you loved me,' she burst out.

He sighed. 'Oh, I do; I mean did,' he said quickly, looking out at the sea. 'Think I'll forgo that walk, if you don't mind,' he muttered, stomping off into the gathering darkness.

'Tom, wait,' she called after him, but the only response was the crunch of pebbles. 'Be like that, then. See if I care,' she muttered.

But you do care and so does he. Go after him, Lily. He's hurting badly.

'Oh, Father, you always turn up at the weirdest times,' she cried, her tears mingling with the spray on the breeze. 'If he doesn't want me, so be it. I'll not beg.'

Best not to be pig-headed, Lily, she thought she heard him say but it could have been the soughing of the wind.

'Oh, mangles to all men,' she screamed in frustration, stamping up the beach. By the time she reached Picky Pike's, she was beside herself with rage. How dare Tom mess with her feelings?

'Lily, whatever is going on? Just look at the state of you,' cried Mrs Bodney, hurrying into the hallway.

'Men, that's what's the matter.'

'Oh, is that all,' the other woman replied, waving her hand in the air as if swatting at an annoying fly. 'For goodness' sake control yourself. The hem of your dress is hanging down, your apron is frayed and as for your hair, well, I've seen neater rats' tails. I suggest you go to the workroom, repair your dress and then retire for the night. Things will look better in the morning. They always do.'

Not trusting herself to answer, Lily stomped off to the workroom. Looks, looks, looks. The woman was obsessed with them. Snatching up needle, thread and scissors, she plonked herself down on her stool before realizing it was too dark to see. Muttering under her breath, she gathered up her things and stamped up to her room.

Silvery light from the moon was filtering through the attic window as she squatted on the end of the bed and began to snip. At first she worked with a vengeance; then, as her hot anger abated and cool calmness washed over her, she worked more methodically. It took her a while but finally, she was finished. Stifling a yawn, she hung her dress on the nail, checking the hem was straight. Next she held up the apron to the window, giving a satisfied nod when she could find no loose threads. Finally, she ran her fingers through her hair. Definitely no rats' tails there!

Thoroughly spent, she climbed into bed and fell asleep, only to dream of being snatched from the clutches of the evil squire by a fair-haired fisherman with a cheeky grin.

Chapter 37

When Lily woke, her cheeks were sticky with dried tears and she felt like a wrung-out rag. She was tempted to close her eyes again, but forced herself to get up. Then, after checking her handiwork, she dressed quickly. Running her fingers through her hair, she smiled. Definitely no rats' tails, she thought, securing her cap.

All was quiet in the workroom as she set about inspecting the previous day's work. The sprigs were sorted according to their various designs, and she was surprised to see just how many they had made over the past months. Then she noticed a pile of something on the floor and gasped in horror. The patterns had been cut into shreds.

Rushing through to the parlour where Mrs Bodney was sitting at the table breaking her fast, she was almost incoherent with shock.

'Mrs Bodney, something terrible has happened,' she gathered herself to gasp.

The other woman frowned over the top of her cup. 'Lily, kindly compose yourself, then tell me exactly what has occurred.'

Seeing her employer's look of disapproval, she took a deep breath to steady herself.

'It's the patterns. They've been cut up.'

'Indeed they have,' Mrs Bodney responded mildly.

'But they were the ones we used for the Queen's lace,' Lily said, trying to make her employer realize the seriousness of the situation.

'Precisely, Lily, and that is why they've been shredded.'

Lily stared at her in amazement. 'You mean you know?'

'Of course I know. I cut them up myself. The Queen ordered them to be destroyed so that no one can copy them. She wants her wedding outfit to be unique,' Mrs Bodney explained. Then, when she saw Lily's puzzled look, she sighed. 'Unique means the only one of its kind. Our work here is nearly finished so we won't have any further use for them, will we?'

'No, I suppose not,' Lily answered, wondering if she dare ask how much longer she'd have work. But Mrs Bodney was peering at her head.

353

'Is there something wrong with your cap, Lily?'

'No,' she answered, quickly sliding it back into place. The other woman stared at her for a long moment.

'With Tilda gone, I need someone to answer the door and serve refreshment. It's not worth engaging someone new at this stage, so choose which lady you think will be most suited to the job and send her to me.'

'Someone from the workroom, you mean?' Lily asked, frowning.

'Of course I mean someone from the workroom. You are hardly going to be rushed off your feet, are you? In fact, I shall now be asking some of the ladies to leave. Please advise them accordingly.'

Slowly, Lily made her way back to the workroom. How would the ladies take the news? Who should she choose to replace Tilda? She shook her head, cursing as her cap slipped over her eyes. Just as she was pushing it back in place, Mary walked into the room, yawning.

'Morning, Lily, I hope this day finds you in better humour.'

Remembering her bad mood of the previous day, Lily felt herself colouring up.

'Sorry, Mary. I had no right to be so rotten,' she apologized.

'That's all right, ducks. We all have our off days. My little un was up all night so I thought I might as well come in ... oh, love a dead donkey,' she exclaimed, looking down at the shredded patterns.

'It's all right, Mrs Bodney cut them up. She said that as the lace is almost completed we won't be requiring them. The Queen herself ordered them to be destroyed so they can't be copied.'

'Do we know how long we've got left here?' Mary asked, looking worried. 'Only we've got a bit behind with the rent, what with that chump of mine and his aversion to work.'

'Mrs Bodney says she'll be starting to dispense with our services from now on.'

'Oh, love two dead donkeys,' the other woman moaned.

'Listen, Mary, quickly, before the others come in. Mrs Bodney needs someone to serve refreshment and answer the door now Tilda's gone–'

'Tilda's gone?' the woman interrupted. 'Where?'

'I don't know,' Lily shrugged. 'The point is that from today Mrs Bodney is going to start getting rid of people, but the person who takes the maid's job will be the last to go, so–'

'Morning, ladies,' Emma said, breezing into the room and looking warily at Lily. Then, she too spotted the pile on the floor. 'Whatever's that mess?'

'I was just about to tidy it up,' said Lily, bending to scoop up the pieces, then cursing as her cap slipped over her forehead.

'What's up with yer head?' Mary hissed in her ear.

'Nothing,' she said, pushing the offending cap back in place, then whispering, 'Look, if you want that job then go and see Mrs Bodney now before the others get here.' Mary nodded and hurried from the room.

'What was all that about?' Emma asked, but the arrival of the others saved Lily from having to answer. Quickly, she disposed of the shredded patterns. Then, standing at the front of the room, she held up her hand for silence.

'Ladies, as you know, our job here is nearing completion. Mrs Bodney appreciates the fine work we've done but regrets that from today, she'll no longer need to employ us all.'

There was an indignant protest, followed by sighs of resignation. They all knew their days here were numbered.

'Bet you know who will be last to go,' Cora said to Nell, jerking her head in Lily's direction.

'Regrettably, Cora, I know no more than you. I'm merely repeating what Mrs Bodney told me so that you can make alternative arrangements as soon as possible.'

There was a snort of derision, for they all knew they'd be lucky to find anything at all let alone quickly. Even if they did, they'd probably have to return to the trucking method of payment. A gloomy silence descended.

'Well, if we are going to go, I don't have to wear this,' Nell said, snatching of her cap and shaking her fiery mane free.

'That will only encourage Mrs Bodney to get rid of you first,' Cora said.

'Oh, see if I care,' Nell retorted.

'Hey, where's Mary?' Cora suddenly asked. 'Don't tell me Mrs Bodney's asked her to go already?'

'I understand she has another job for Mary to do,' Lily said. 'Now there are still some sprigs to be made, so I suggest we make a start.'

The tension in the room was palpable as they wondered who would be the first to go and when.

Lily bent over her own pillow, cursing silently as her cap slipped yet again. Suddenly her bright idea of the night before didn't seem clever at all. What was it her father had called her? A hothead – that was it. Well, she certainly wouldn't be now, she thought, tugging at her cap and praying it would stay in place. The mood was sombre as the ladies pondered their future, and the workroom fell eerily silent.

Lily tried to concentrate on her lace making, but her thoughts kept returning to her encounter with Tom the previous evening. Why had he gone off like that? Where had he gone? More to the point, when would she see him again or, heaven forbid, would she see him again at all? As the morning dragged on, the questions whirled around her head.

Finally it was noon, and everyone sighed with relief when she rang the bell for nuncheon. Lily, having had enough of being alone with her thoughts, joined them outside. But the mood was sober as they stood there discussing rents that had to be paid, hungry mouths that needed feeding. And the most important thing of all, where were they going to find work?

'Do you think any of us will have to go today?' Emma asked.

'I truly don't know,' Lily answered, shaking her head and righting her cap. We knew this job was for six months so...' She shrugged, leaving the sentence unfinished. Six months had seemed a long time back in May.

'Mrs Bodney says you're to go through to the parlour, Lily,' Mary announced, appearing at the door, dressed in the maid's attire. There was a gasp of surprise from the others.

'Acting as her ladyship's maid now, are we?' Cora scoffed.

'Indeed I am, thank you for asking,' Mary answered, holding her head high and strutting back inside.

'Well, I'll be, Mary working as a maid,' muttered Emma. 'Heaven knows what things are coming to, and that's a fact.'

'Yes, but she's got a safe job, hasn't she? And I wonder how that came about?' Cora remarked, looking pointedly at Lily.

Sensing trouble brewing, Lily quickly rang the bell to signal the end of their break.

Then, as the ladies filed back inside, Lily straightened her cap yet again, and made her way to the parlour. Her stomach plummeted when she saw Mr Mountsford sitting talking to Mrs Bodney, but when he saw her, he sprang to his feet.

Mrs Bodney also rose and murmuring she had an appointment to go to, quickly left.

'Lily, I've come to see you because I owe you an apology.'

'You owe me nothing, Mr Mountsford,' she said.

'On the contrary; I've been talking to Mrs Bodney. She explained about your misunderstanding of my intentions and–'

'Misunderstanding? Offering me fine things whilst you were betrothed to another? I don't call that a misunderstanding,' Lily retorted, unable to contain her pent-up anger any longer. 'I bet you'd a right good laugh at my expense. Well, let me tell you, Mr Mountsford, you may have fine possessions but it is me who has the morals. Oh, and that reminds me...' she said hurrying from the room.

A few moments later, she returned, clutching the boots with cherry-red stitching. Angrily, she threw them at his feet.

'Here, have your boots back. You can give them to the next poor girl you set out to charm. Now, if there is nothing else I'll bid you good day,' she said, turning to go.

'Your friend Tom–' he began, but she cut him off.

'Tom might not have the riches to buy me expensive presents, but he has principles and has always treated me with respect,' she said quietly, realizing that everything she'd said was true.

'He's a lucky man to command your respect,' Rupert replied. Then when she didn't reply, he bent and picked up the boots. He turned to leave and then hesitated in the doorway.

'Lily, I just want you to know that under different circumstances...'

'You still wouldn't have any principles,' she spat.

'Here we are, ducks, a nice cup of tea with cake, no less,' Mary announced, bursting into the room with their refreshment. 'Oops, sorry, have I interrupted something, only Mrs Bodney said I was to bring in a tray?' she asked.

Stifling an exclamation, Rupert turned and left.

'Mary, your timing was perfect,' Lily said, surprised at the feeling of relief she was experiencing. 'You've just saved me from a most embarrassing situation,' she added, sinking into a chair.

'Has that fancy merchant upset you, Lily? 'Cos if he has, I'll go after him and give him what for.'

'Oh, Mary, you're like a tonic,' she laughed, imagining the older woman chasing him down the street.

'I don't think Mr Mountsford will be back to see me again, thank heavens,' she added, grinning.

'Well, if that's the case, you'd best drink this fine tea whilst there's some left as we won't be getting any more from that source,' Mary said, winking.

Lily looked down at the rich dark tea in her cup, the penny dropping. How could she have been blind to all that had been going on around here?

'Is there anything else, Lily,' Mary asked, breaking into her thoughts.

Lily looked up and saw her gazing longingly at the cake.

'Go on, take it and enjoy it. I won't tell,' she said laughing, as Mary, hardly able to believe her good fortune, scuttled away with her prize. Settling back in the chair, she looked at the tea then shook her head. She'd never touch any again, if that's where it came from, she decided. But as she leaned forward to put the cup on the table, her cap slipped to the side of her head.

'Good grief, Lily. Whatever, do you look like?' Mrs Bodney asked, bustling into the room. 'You look more like a street urchin than ever.'

'Oh, Mrs Bodney, it's never that bad,' she said, but the other woman was looking around the room.

'Has Mr Mountsford gone?'

'Yes, thank heavens,' Lily answered, with feeling.

Mrs Bodney gave her a penetrating look. 'You didn't accept his apologies then?'

'No, I did not. Why should I? I may have had to entertain him as part of my duties but they are all but finished now so it doesn't matter if I never see or speak to him again, does it?'

'Well, there is still some work left for you to do but no, you don't have to see Mr Mountsford again. Did he leave anything for me, by the way?' she asked, looking down at the table and frowning.

'Yes, he left two small packets on the dresser, and Mary took them through to the kitchen. Unfortunately, though, he didn't stay long enough to sample any of his lovely strong tea,' she said, staring meaningfully at her employer.

'Thank you, Lily, I think you should return to the workroom now,' Mrs Bodney said, quickly lowering her eyes.

Chapter 38

Not feeling up to meeting the inquisitive stares of the others and in dire need of fresh air, Lily went to fetch her shawl. On her way back down the stairs, she spotted the turnip lamp lying under the ledge where it had fallen. Picking it up, she decided to take a walk to Coombe to see Beth.

To her surprise, as she walked down the path, she saw Tom sauntering towards her and, despite herself, her heart flipped.

'Afternoon, Lily. It's unusual to see you out at this time of day,' he said, politely, doffing his cap.

'Afternoon, Tom. It's unusual to see you at all

round these parts,' she countered, only to see his lips twitch.

'You always were a ready wit,' he said, stopping and giving her the cheeky grin that made her heart somersault. 'Where are you off to, anyway?' he asked.

'I'm going to Coombe to see Beth and give her this,' Lily said, holding out the turnip.

'Hey, that's a great lamp. It'll look right spooky when it's lit for Samhain tomorrow. Did you carve it?'

'Yes, with old Joe's help. We made one for his grandson too,' she said proudly.

Tom looked at her quizzically. 'You're still an old softy,' he said gruffly.

Her heart started thumping furiously, but he didn't appear to hear.

'I meant what I said about still loving you, Tom,' she said. 'I know you'll probably never forgive me but I want you to know that I'm truly sorry for disbelieving you about the ring.'

'Yeah, well, water down the brook, as they say. Happen I'm off to Coombe myself, so what say we walk there together and have that chat?'

'Yes, let's,' she answered, smiling up at him. It would give them the time they needed to clear the air between them once and for all, she thought.

'Happen, I might have something to show you,' he said giving her his saucy wink and holding out his arm to her.

'Oh, and what might that be?' she asked, linking her arm through his. But, before he could answer, Mrs Bodney's strident voice sounded behind her from the doorway of Picky Pike's.

'Lily Rose, what are you doing outside at this time of the day?' Then, without waiting for her reply, she added, 'I'll see you in the parlour, directly. There's something you need to do whilst it's still light.'

Lily's heart plummeted. She wanted to go with Tom but did she dare defy her employer?

'Good afternoon, Tom. I didn't notice you there,' Mrs Bodney said, peering out of the door. Then with a brisk nod, she disappeared back inside.

'Will you wait for me?' Lily asked, looking hopefully at Tom.

'Sorry, Lily. I've arranged to meet someone before dusk and daren't keep him waiting. Give me the lamp and I'll see Beth gets it.'

Lily's heart sank to the cobbles and she could have screamed in frustration.

'Oh, well, thanks, Tom. Tell her I'll visit her as soon as I can,' she said, reluctantly passing it over. 'Will I see you again soon?' she couldn't help asking.

'Lily, just how much longer do you propose keeping me waiting?' Mrs Bodney called impatiently.

'Go on, you'd best go in before she lays an egg,' Tom said, chuckling as he went on his way.

Cursing under her breath, Lily went inside, threw her shawl over the nail beside the stairs and went through to the parlour.

'And not before time,' the other woman remarked, frowning as she looked up from her table. 'Now, we know how good your sewing is, don't we?'

'My sewing?' Lily asked, looking puzzled.

'I've not got time to listen to you parroting, Lily. I need you to sew these together,' she instructed, handing Lily six of the sprigs they'd made. 'I have things to attend to, but when I return, I'll inspect your work to see how you've got on.' With that, she swept regally out of the room, reminding Lily of the time she'd sat her ability test. The woman was still just as intimidating, she thought, threading the needle and setting about her task.

How she wished she was walking over the cliffs with Tom instead of sitting here doing this wretched sewing. He'd seemed really pleased to see her, and she hoped the bad feeling between them was completely gone. How frustrating to have had the opportunity of spending time with him snatched away from her. Perhaps she should have ignored Mrs Bodney's order and gone with him.

Luckily her mother, an accomplished seam-stress, had taught her well, for whilst her thoughts were in turmoil, she stitched automatically. It was only when Mrs Bodney reappeared carrying a lighted candle that she noticed dusk had fallen and the room was in shadow.

'Right, let's see how you've fared,' the woman said brusquely, reaching out for the completed work. 'Just as I thought,' she said, a few moments later. 'Right, Lily, go and pack your bag.'

'What?' she exclaimed. 'Oh, Mrs Bodney, I know I should have gone back–'

'What are you wittering about? I said go and get your things packed. We leave at first light,' her employer said, impatiently waving her hand around.

So she'd been right: she was to leave. Then she

realized what the other woman had actually said.

'You said "we"? Where are we going?' she asked, looking at Mrs Bodney suspiciously.

'I'll give you the details on the morrow. If it was up to me, we'd leave straight away. However, I've been advised – that travelling overnight in these parts with … well, let's just say it would be fool-hardy.'

Completely bemused now, Lily stared at her employer. 'I don't–' she began, but Mrs Bodney cut her short.

'Lily, if you want to continue working for me please take yourself upstairs and pack your things. Then I suggest you get a good night's sleep. Travelling can be tiring, not to say tiresome, and as our mission is confidential you are to tell nobody. Promise me?'

Knowing she was in no position to argue, Lily nodded and took herself up to her room to pack. Going over to the tin chest, she saw the pen and ink lying on top and wondered if she could take them with her so that she could practise her letters. Deciding she'd better not as they weren't hers to take, she placed them on the chair. Then, opening the lid, she set her few possessions on the bed, tears welling as she saw her mother's Bible and the bobbin Tom had fashioned to com-memorate her pitifully short life. The letter from Aunt Elizabeth crackled under her fingers as she stroked it. Remembering the astonishing news it contained, she had a sudden desire to go to see her. Of course she'd loved the people she'd al-ways thought were her parents, but now she yearned to find out where she'd come from.

Blinking back the tears, she noticed the rays of the moon casting a silver pathway across her floor. Crossing to the skylight, she stood looking up at the luminous sphere shining out of the inky darkness. Why, she wondered, did everyone who mattered leave her?

But we are with you still, Lily. You carry us within your heart wherever you go.

'You're back, Father,' she whispered, a sense of peace washing over her. He'd come when she needed him. Then she remembered she was leaving here. 'I've to go away tomorrow, Father, but I don't know where. How will you know where to find me for Samhain?'

Like I said, Lily, I'm with you always, watching over you, willing you to choose the right path in life.

'Oh, it's all so complicated,' she whispered.

Be true to yourself, Lily. Remember, peasants never compromise their principles.

His voice faded, and she knew he'd gone. But he'd left her with a warm feeling of optimism and she was pleased she hadn't compromised her principles. Wiping away the tears that were flowing freely down her cheeks, she finished her packing then, exhausted, collapsed into bed.

Making her way downstairs at first light, she saw the hallway was busy with activity. Despite the early hour, parcels were already loaded on a carriage that was drawn up outside.

'Ah, Lily, there you are. Hand the driver your bag, then go and sit in the carriage. We will be leaving shortly. Driver, be careful with those packages. The cost of any damage will be docked from your wage,' Mrs Bodney warned, shaking her finger at him. Seeing his indignant look, Lily hastily stepped up into the carriage. Then, as she settled back against the squabs, she noticed that same peculiar scent in the air as she'd detected in Rupert Mountsford's carriage.

'We have a long journey ahead, Lily,' Mrs Bodney said, climbing in beside her. 'Driver, where are our blankets?' she called, putting her head out of the window. 'It's perishing in here and if we expire, on your conscience be it.' Poor man, Lily thought, as he dutifully handed blankets in to them, muttering under his breath. Her employer, who could hear a pin dropping in her sleep, glared at him. 'What are you wittering about, man? Why would you need a short straw?'

Lily stifled a grin and busied herself with the rough horsehair cover, but Mrs Bodney was still fussing. 'Do get a move on, driver. I've arranged to break our fast at the coaching house on the Sidmouth Road, and at this rate it will be supper time before we get there.'

The slamming of the door was his only response. There was a thud as he climbed onto his box, then gave a shout to the horses, and the carriage began to move.

Watching the familiar rolling hills pass by the window as they climbed steadily out of the hamlet of Bransbeer, Lily wondered where they were headed. She was dying to ask Mrs Bodney, but the motion of the carriage seemed to have sent her employer to sleep. Her eyes were tightly shut and Lily couldn't help noticing that she was as white as the foam on the waves.

As she became used to the rocking motion of the carriage, Lily could feel excitement bubbling up inside her. The visit from her father had settled her and she was feeling cheerful again this morning. If Mrs Bodney was taking Lily with her, wherever that might be, it must mean she still had work to do. She couldn't help wondering about the others, though. Did they still have work? If so, who was going to supervise them? All this thinking was making her weary and before long her eyelids began to droop. She must have slept, for the next thing she knew Mrs Bodney was shaking her arm.

'Come along, Lily. What a time to go to sleep,' her employer remonstrated. Lily started to protest but Mrs Bodney was already climbing from the carriage, shouting to the driver that he wasn't to take his eyes off her packages or his life wouldn't be worth living.

'It ain't now,' he grunted, unhitching the horses and leading them towards the stables.

The coaching house was basic, but clean. Spotting the welcome glow of a fire blazing in the grate, Lily moved towards it, thinking to warm her hands. Mrs Bodney frowned, shook her head and marched over to the woman standing behind the bar.

'Room reserved in the name of Bodney and a hot meal ordered,' she announced. If the other woman was surprised by her terse address, she was too polite to show it.

'Morning, Mrs Bodney. Yer room's all ready and waiting, if yer'd like to follow me,' she said, her respectful tones seeming to mollify Mrs Bodney somewhat. The room they were shown into was smaller but comfortable, with a table set for two in the bay of the window.

'There's water in the jug for yer to refresh yerselves and I'll send Annie in with yer food shortly.'

'Thank you. We are travelling a long distance and, as time is of the essence, please be quick in serving our food.'

The woman nodded and left.

They'd barely had time to rinse their face and hands and tidy themselves up when there was a timid knock on the door. A young girl, struggling under the weight of a laden tray, appeared in the doorway. Lily got up to help but Mrs Bodney frowned, ordering her to be seated.

'We are paying guests, Lily; please remember that,' she hissed. Biting down her frustration, Lily did as she was told, watching, helplessly as the trembling girl set down plates of ham and eggs in front of them. She looked no more than eight, and seemed so ill at ease that Lily felt she could almost reach out and touch her fear. Tea cups rattled on their saucers as she placed them on the table, and her hands shook as she attempted to set down a jug that was filled to the brim.

'Mind you don't spill that,' Mrs Bodney exclaimed, making the poor girl jump so that milk slopped over onto the cloth. As she stood there staring wide-eyed, Lily's heart went out to her and, ignoring her employer's order, she jumped up to help.

'You go on now and I'll pour our tea,' she said, smiling at her. The girl didn't need telling twice and scuttled out of the room.

Mrs Bodney, eyes blazing, turned to Lily. 'How

dare you disobey me? That girl's nothing but a paid servant.'

'As am I, Mrs Bodney,' she retorted, unable to contain her fury any longer.

'I hardly think you can compare yourself to a wench who serves at tables,' the other woman said.

Furious at her high-handed attitude, Lily replied heatedly, 'I used to serve at the squire's table and Lady Clinsden never once spoke to me in such a condescending manner. But then I guess she has breeding,' she added for good measure.

Mrs Bodney's cheeks flushed as red as the flames in the grate and the room fell silent as the two women glared at each other across the table.

Chapter 39

'If you've quite finished, Lily, I suggest we break our fast,' Mrs Bodney finally said, picking up her knife and fork. 'I've no intention of wasting good food, or my hard-earned money,' she added.

Lily watched as the other woman began tucking into her meal, then shrugged and did likewise. They ate in silence, but the thickly cut ham was so delicious Lily hardly noticed the awkwardness. When they'd finished their meal, Mrs Bodney sat stirring her tea thoughtfully.

Finally, she looked up, asking, 'Feeling better now, Lily?'

'I enjoyed my meal, thank you,' she answered carefully.

'Your diplomacy does you credit, Lily,' said her employer, smiling briefly. 'Before we continue our journey, I want you to understand something. When you run a business, it becomes second nature to ensure everyone works efficiently. The old adage of time being money is still true today. When you have your own enterprise you will understand what I mean.'

'That's hardly likely to happen,' spluttered Lily, looking incredulously at her employer.

'Well, I understand from Lady Clinsden that you suggested it might be a good idea for her to have some lace collars and cuffs made so that she can attach them to her dresses and change their appearance without upsetting her husband.'

'I offered to make her some, yes.'

'And, she liked your suggestion and is commissioning you to make them when you have completed the lace for the Queen. Lily, you spotted a business opportunity that I did not, and believe you me, it's rare for me to miss one. With initiative like that, you could become a successful business trader yourself.'

'Well, even if I did, I would never be offensive to people who were trying to do their job,' Lily retorted.

'If I was a bit abrupt with that young girl it was because she was being sloppy, a trait I cannot abide,' Mrs Bodney added, as if that explained everything.

'What about the poor coach driver?' Lily couldn't help asking. 'You were rude to him.'

The other woman sighed. 'If you realized what a responsibility it is ensuring the Queen's lace is

371

safely transported, then you might understand my anxiety. Now come along, we've still a fair journey ahead of us.' Rising to her feet, she hurried from the room, leaving Lily no choice but to follow. However, she couldn't help smiling when, after settling the bill, her employer tossed a coin onto the bar.

'A tip for the young waitress girl; please see that she gets it,' she ordered, before sweeping outside.

The sun was peeping above Peak Hill, tinging its slopes with an orange hue. The air felt raw and a strong wind was blowing russet leaves from the trees in swathes. Shivering, Lily pulled her shawl tighter round her as they hastened back to the carriage. The driver was standing joking with the ostlers, but his laughter quickly changed to a grimace when he saw them approaching. Raising his eyebrows at the others, he sauntered over to the carriage and dutifully held the door open for them.

'Thank you, my good man,' Mrs Bodney said, stepping inside. His jaw dropped in surprise, and Lily had to turn her head to hide another grin. But then her employer, reverting to type, snapped, 'I trust you've looked after my precious parcels, driver?'

'Wouldn't dare do anything else,' he muttered before jumping onto his box and snatching up the reins. Lily groaned inwardly then settled back on the squabs, wrinkling her nose at the unfamiliar smell that still pervaded the interior. She was about to ask Mrs Bodney what it was when the other woman spoke.

'You know, Lily, you remind me of myself a few

years ago.'

'Oh?' Lily said in surprise, undecided if this was a good thing or not.

'I wasn't afraid to tell people what I thought either. Not that you would have dared to do so when you first started working for me. Quite the shy little thing, you were then. You've come a long way in, what is it, five months or so?'

'Thank you, Mrs Bodney,' she answered, not sure she liked being compared to her employer.

'Mind you, I wouldn't have sat there half the morning without demanding to know where I was going or why,' she continued, giving Lily a conspiratorial grin.

Lily was relaxing back in her seat, thinking that perhaps her employer wasn't so bad after all, when the carriage hit a rut. It jolted her forward so forcefully, her cap slipped down over her forehead.

'For heaven's sake do something with your appearance,' Mrs Bodney snapped, opening her bag and handing Lily a hat pin. 'Here, use this until your hair grows. I don't want the others thinking I've brought a scarecrow from the country fields with me.'

'The others?' she asked, carefully fixing the pin through her cap and into her hair, so that it didn't prick her scalp.

'Yes, the women you will be working with. All those sprigs you've made need to be sewn together to form the flounce around Her Majesty's dress. It's to measure four yards in circumference. Can you imagine?' she asked, shaking her head.

'Oh,' was all Lily could say, as she sat there trying to envisage such a thing.

'Then there's the veil, the collar, cuff edgings and all manner of adornments to be stitched and attached to the backing. I feel faint just thinking about it,' Mrs Bodney said, shaking her head.

'Where are we going to do all that?' Lily couldn't resist asking.

'Ah, curiosity at last.' Mrs Bodney raised her eyebrow. 'I have secured premises in Honiton.'

'Honiton? But that's miles away. Why can't we do this sewing up in the workroom?'

Mrs Bodney sighed. 'Because it wouldn't be big enough to accommodate the lace as it's joined together. It's delicate work, which requires the skills of sewers and finishers. Naturally, I have managed to secure the services of the finest in Devonshire. Besides, Honiton is on the staging route to London. The Queen has instructed I take the finished lace to the palace myself,' she added, as if that explained everything.

'How long will I be away from Bransbeer?' Lily asked, an image of Tom flitting into her mind.

'Three weeks; maybe nearer a month,' her employer answered. 'As I've said before, the Queen expects her commission to be fulfilled by St Catherine's Day, which is the 25th of November, as you know.'

'But if I'm in Honiton, who will oversee the ladies back at the workroom?' Finally, she was able to ask the question that had been worrying her since they'd left Bransbeer.

'As I said yesterday, the actual lace making is all but finished. When I decided I'd be travelling to Honiton today, I paid them their money and sent them home,' Mrs Bodney replied.

374

'What? Even Mary?' Lily asked with a pang.

'Mary is staying to look after things at my cottage in my absence,' Mrs Bodney said, smiling. 'That's enough talking for now. We need to get as much rest as we can manage in this rattling contraption, for we shall be exceedingly busy over the next few weeks.' And with that, her employer settled back on the squabs, pulled her cover over her, and closed her eyes.

As the carriage trundled its way through the Devonshire lanes, Lily pondered on all Mrs Bodney had told her. Mary still had a job and she herself had work for a few more weeks yet. Although her employer hadn't said, this job in Honiton must surely include board and lodging for they couldn't possibly travel all this way each day. She looked at Mrs Bodney, who was now dead to the world, and smiled. Not only was this carriage quite comfortable, it afforded them cover. She bet Mrs Bodney had never travelled in a donkey-cart, open to the elements. Of course, Rupert Mountsford's carriage had been plusher than this one, although in some ways it did appear curiously similar. And it had that same Christmassy smell. She really must remember to ask Mrs Bodney about it when she woke.

How much further was this Honiton, she wondered, shading her eyes from the midday sun as she peered out of the window. The passing countryside had the mellow air of autumn, despite the breeze blowing the coppery leaves from the trees. She sighed, remembering how she and Tom had always caught one to wish upon. Last year, when she'd failed to catch a leaf of her own, he'd pretended to pluck one from her hair, insisting she'd caught it fair and square. She saw that the hedgerows were still groaning under the weight of luscious purple berries. Back in Coombe, they'd all have been picked and turned into pies and jellies by now. She wondered if Tom's mother had baked him his favourite bramble cobbler. The thought made her mouth water.

It had been wonderful seeing Tom again, especially as he'd been like the old Tom she loved. How she wished she'd had the opportunity to tell him she was going away. Round and round her thoughts spun, like the wheels on the carriage, so that by the time they stopped to change the horses, she felt quite worn out.

'Come along, Lily, time for our break,' her employer chirped, refreshed from her snooze. The driver opened the door, looking warily at Mrs Bodney. But she smiled and thanked him so profusely he stood there shaking his head, unable to comprehend the change in her demeanour. Then, shrugging, he turned away to attend to the horses.

This hostelry was situated on the outskirts of a town and looked smarter than the one they'd stopped at earlier. They were shown into another private room, where they sat in comfortable chairs by a roaring fire. As they tucked into plates of cold meats, bread and pickles, followed by cake and hot sweet tea, Lily felt quite happy.

'I could get used to living like this,' she said, sighing contentedly as she sat back feeling replete.

'Well, you had a taste of it at the Harvest Supper,' Mrs Bodney pointed out.

'Yes,' Lily said, shuddering at the thought. 'And

I'd sooner be poor and principled than rich and rootless with my affections,' she said firmly.

'Bravo; well said, young Lily. I rather think you will go far in this life. Now we'd best be on our way.'

'This Honiton is certainly some distance from Bransbeer, isn't it?' Lily moaned, for she was comfortable and would have preferred to remain by the fire.

'Regrettably, owing to the valuable merchandise we are carrying, the driver wouldn't risk travelling across open country. It's tiresome having to travel the longer route, but safety is paramount. Thank heavens Rupert honoured his promise to loan me one of his carriages or we would be travelling by stagecoach,' she said, her expression indicating she couldn't imagine anything more awful. Suddenly Lily understood why the carriage seemed familiar and why it had the same smell.

'May I ask you something, Mrs Bodney?' she asked. The woman nodded. 'I've noticed this strange smell in Mr Mountsford's carriages that I can't quite place. Do you know what it could be?'

'I think it might be the spices that Mr Mountsford transports back to London. Now come along, we must be on our way,' Mrs Bodney answered, jumping to her feet and heading for the door. Surprised at the other woman's abrupt departure, Lily followed after her.

They returned to the carriage and settled back against the squabs. With her employer soon asleep, Lily spent the rest of the journey pondering on their earlier exchange. Mrs Bodney had been distinctly uncomfortable when Lily had questioned her about the strange smell. In fact, she'd had the same look as when Lily mentioned the packets Mr Mountsford left for her on his visits. She couldn't help feeling it was somehow connected with the activities on the beach that old Joe had mentioned.

Dusk was descending by the time they arrived in Honiton, but Lily was hardly aware of her surroundings for as soon as the carriage door was opened, a strong gust of wind threatened to blow her off her feet. Revived from her rest, Mrs Bodney ushered her up the steps of a large town house, ringing the bell impatiently. The door was quickly opened by a grey-haired woman with thin lips, who stared at Lily suspiciously.

'Maria?' Mrs Bodney said, frowning. 'I'm surprised to see you answering the door.'

'I was just passing by when I heard the bell. Thought it sounded urgent, the way it kept ringing,' she said pointedly. 'You'd best come in,' she added, somewhat grudgingly, before disappearing up the stairs. As Lily stood in the hallway glancing around, a stout, homely-looking woman bustled through to greet them.

'Mrs. Bodney, welcome. I trust your journey was not too arduous.'

'Good evening, Mrs Staple,' her employer replied. 'It has been a most taxing time but we must bear these inconveniences for our Queen, mustn't we?'

Lily stared at Mrs Bodney in amazement. Taxing time? Why, they'd stopped at two coaching houses, been well looked after and eaten two splendid meals. How difficult was that? Noticing her expression, Mrs Bodney snapped her fingers.

'Don't just stand there gawping, girl. The driver will see to our things.'

Mrs Staple turned and smiled kindly at Lily, then turned back to Mrs Bodney.

'I've a nice bit of stew simmering, if you're hungry.'

'Thank you, no. We have already eaten and are ready to retire for the night,' Mrs Bodney replied briskly.

'Well, your rooms are ready so I'll show you where to go,' Mrs Staple said affably, and before Lily could blink, she was being led up a narrow staircase and shown into a bedroom. Glancing around, she saw it was smaller than the one she'd had at Picky Pike's, but clean and tidy. To her delight, it also had a washstand in the corner.

'Right, Lily, I think this will do fine for you,' said the housekeeper. 'Once your bag has been brought up, I suggest you get some sleep. I know it's early but there's much to be done in the morning.' And with that she bustled from the room.

Thankfully, Lily sank onto the bed and closed her eyes. She wished the room would stop swaying. Why, she felt as if she'd travelled halfway round the world today. She heard footsteps coming up the stairs and the murmur of voices as they passed her room.

'It wasn't fair on Margaret, though.'

'I know, but there's little we can do. This other one's better at the job, I was told.'

'She's a right country bumpkin, by all accounts, so I'm having as little to do with her as possible.' The voices drifted off down the landing and Lily

379

couldn't help feeling sorry for this poor country bumpkin, whoever she was.

Waking the next morning in the narrow little bed, Lily took a few moments to remember where she was. Gingerly she sat up, relieved to find the room was no longer swaying. Then hearing the sound of people going about their business, she jumped out of bed and splashed her face with water from the ewer on the washstand. She'd only just finished dressing and was smoothing down her apron, when there was a brisk knock on the door. Before she could answer, Mrs Bodney entered the room.

'Come along, Lily, Mrs Staple's serving porridge. Apparently, everyone here eats together, so it will be a good opportunity to introduce you to the others.' Then before Lily could answer, she disappeared down the stairs, leaving Lily to follow her.

'Morning, Mrs Bodney,' trilled Mrs Staple. 'Did you sleep all right, dearie?' she asked turning to Lily, who nodded happily.

'Morning, Mrs Staple,' Mrs Bodney replied. Then to Lily's surprise she announced to the room in general, 'This is Lily, one of the finest lace makers in Devonshire.'

'Well done, dearie,' the housekeeper answered. 'Now you sit yourselves down and I'll get serving.'

Lily smiled as she sat down next to Maria, the sour-faced woman who had opened the door the previous evening. But her smile was met with a glacial glare. Shaken, she then noticed half a dozen other ladies eyeing her curiously.

'Morning, everybody,' she said brightly, but

their bowls suddenly seemed to be of greater interest as they busied themselves with their breakfast. Silence hung heavily in the room but Mrs Bodney wasn't having that.

'Right, let's enjoy our meal and then I'll introduce you all to Lily,' she said briskly. This was still met with silence but, to Lily's amazement, her employer winked at her. Thankfully, it seemed Mrs Bodney was in charge here as well

Lily's relief was short-lived, though, for no sooner had they finished than Mrs Staple reappeared saying, 'Mrs Bodney, there's a visitor to see you.'

'Thank you, Mrs Staple,' she answered, getting to her feet. 'Right, everyone, as I said earlier, this is Lily, my overseer from Bransbeer. Whilst I attend to my guest, I'd like you to introduce yourselves and make her feel welcome. We will begin work as soon as I return.'

As soon as the door shut behind her, Maria turned to Lily and glared.

'Boss's pet,' she snarled. 'You're naught but a lace maker. We sewers and finishers are highly skilled and we look after our own. You mark my words, we'll see you gone before the day's out.'

Murmurs of agreement rippled around the table and Lily's heart sank. Their belligerent faces said everything. Well, she hadn't asked to come here and she certainly wasn't going to stay where she wasn't wanted. She'd pack her things and return to Bransbeer on the first staging. Naught but a lace maker indeed!

Chapter 40

Peasants are plucky people. They don't run when the going gets rough. Come along, Lily; show them lace makers are made of sterner stuff.

As she heard her father's words, strength flooded through her. She was proud to be a lace maker and had never been one to walk away when the going was tough, so why should she now? Squaring her shoulders, she stared back at the sewers and finishers.

'I am not going anywhere,' she announced. Judging by their astonished reaction, they'd obviously not been expecting her to bite back. As one, they turned to Maria.

'You're not wanted here, country bumpkin. Go back to Bransbeer where you belong,' she snarled, her lips tightening into a mean slit.

'But you don't know anything about me,' Lily said, trying to reason with them.

'As if that matters. You took our Margaret's job. We'll not forgive you for that.'

'Margaret's not skilled enough to do this intricate work, as well you know, Maria,' Mrs Bodney announced from the back of the room, where she'd slipped in unnoticed. 'However, Lily is, and what's more, she's here to stay. If anyone has a problem with that, they can leave right now,' she added, looking directly at Maria, who flushed as red as a rosehip. 'Now, I want you all to welcome

Lily.' She paused, waiting until the old woman grudgingly mumbled some kind of greeting and the others, taking her lead, followed suit.

'Remember, ladies, there's never any excuse for being rude or offensive to anyone who's trying to do their job,' Mrs Bodney admonished, and Lily's eyes widened at this pronouncement. Weren't they her very words from the previous day? She had no time to dwell on the matter, though, for Mrs Bodney was clapping her hands.

'Right, we've wasted enough time. I have sorted the exact number of sprigs required for assembly of the flounce, so follow me,' she ordered, leading them into a light, airy room at the back of the house. 'The designs I'm about to show you are confidential, so once you've seen them, you will be required to remain in this building until the sewing up is finished.'

'But I've got to see to my mother,' Maria said. Lily gazed at the wizened old woman, whose face was as creased as a concertina, and couldn't help wondering how ancient her mother was.

'We've already discussed this, Maria,' Mrs Bodney snapped. 'When your cousin Margaret failed the sewing test, it was agreed she'd look after your mother whilst you stayed here.' Turning to the rest of them she continued, 'Before I show you the drawings, you must solemnly swear not to divulge to another living soul what you see in this room.'

'Well, if we ain't allowed out, we won't be seeing anyone to tell, will we?' Maria sniggered.

'Right, that's it. I've had enough of your obstreperous attitude, Maria. Pack your things and go.'

'I was only–' the other woman started to say,

but Mrs Bodney was already calling for the housekeeper.

'Mrs Staple, Maria has decided to leave, so please see that she packs her things and then escort her from the premises. Oh, and bring me a bell so I can ring for you in future. My voice is not used to all this shouting.'

If the housekeeper was surprised by these requests, she didn't show it. Nodding politely, she followed the protesting Maria from the room. The others started to voice their objections, but Mrs Bodney held up her hand.

'That's quite enough. None of you is indispensable, so if you feel unable to comply with my terms, please leave now.' She waited, studying them closely but no one moved. 'Then be seated and I'll show you what's to be done,' Mrs Bodney continued, spreading out a drawing on the table before them.

'Now, this is how the flounce is to look when it's assembled,' she said, and they all leaned forward in their seats to see where her finger was pointing. 'You are to lay out the sprigs according to the design pattern. When you've done that, call me. I will check everything's in order before you proceed further.' Then she swept from the room in a rustle of skirts.

'Cor, she's a bit of a tartar, isn't she?' whispered the plump girl who was sitting opposite Lily. Lily knew that Mrs Bodney's tongue was really no sharper than a blunt bobbin, so she merely shrugged. Her recent experience in the workroom had taught her that a little fear was no bad thing.

When all the sprigs had been set out, Mrs

Bodney was sent for. Anxiously they watched as she meticulously checked their work.

'Right, ladies,' she finally pronounced. 'You may now begin to sew. As I have to account to the Queen's Mistress of the Robes, all the materials have been weighed. There is no room for error.' She eyed them seriously, waiting whilst her words sank in. 'Work carefully and conscientiously. Remember, Her Majesty will soon be wearing what you are making here. Won't that be something for you to tell your children and grandchildren?' she smiled.

'Aren't you going to help us to sew it up, then?' asked one of the women.

'Now, why would I have a dog and bark myself?' Mrs Bodney asked, before sweeping out of the room. So now it was dogs, thought Lily, shaking her head. Cats in Bransbeer, dogs in Honiton – really, it was all quite beyond her!

Picking up her needle and thread, she started to sew. The others followed her lead, and the room fell silent as they concentrated on their work.

At noon, Mrs Bodney reappeared ringing a little bell and announcing, 'Right, ladies, Mrs Staple has broth ready for you in the kitchen. Whilst you take your break, I'll inspect the work you've been doing this morning.'

Lily stared at her employer in surprise. Not more food already? But to her amazement, when a steaming bowl was put before her she found she was hungry.

'What's Bransbeer like?' asked the plump girl, who'd finished her meal in record time.

'It's a fishing hamlet by the sea,' Lily answered.

'What's your name?'

'Rosie.'

'Yeah, dozy Rosie,' chuckled the woman who was sitting next to her. 'I'm Caroline, ducks. Sorry if we gave you a hard time earlier. Maria was that cross when Mrs Bodney told her you were to do the sewing up instead of her Margaret, she told us to ignore you.'

'Yeah,' Rosie chipped in, 'she said, ignore the country bumpkin and she'll go running home with her tail between her legs. You ain't got a tail, have you?' she asked, her eyes hopeful.

'Don't be daft, Rosie,' Caroline chided before turning back to Lily and raising her eyebrows. 'You can see how she got her name.'

'Ah, but Rosie's stitching is the finest here,' Mrs Bodney announced, coming into the room. 'Right, ladies, you've all done well this morning. Now I've some bad news, and some good news. The bad news is there is no one skilled enough to replace Maria. This means we will all have to work on later each evening to get the job finished in time.' She waited for the groans to die down. 'The good news is that you will be splitting her wage between you.' Then, as they all cheered, she clapped her hands saying, 'Right, ladies, back to work.'

All afternoon they sewed, but the ice had been broken and the atmosphere in the room was convivial. Before long Lily found herself relaxing to the rhythm of her stitching, happy to listen to the conversation going on around her. Clearly, the sewers had all known each other for some time.

As the shadows lengthened and their energy began to flag, silence descended. As Mrs Staple

386

bustled in with candles and strikes, an enticing aroma wafted through the open door behind her. They all sniffed the air appreciatively.

'I've just boiled a nice bit of bacon for your supper, dearies. Oh, and Mrs Bodney says you can finish at seven tonight, seeing as it's your first day.'

They looked at each other in amazement. Bacon for supper?

'Coo, we only gets that on high days and holidays,' Caroline exclaimed.

'I'll be as round as a barrel if we keep eating like this,' Rosie said, looking down at her ample figure and grimacing. They all giggled, and then, with the thought of a special supper to look forward to, set about their sewing with renewed vigour.

'Oh bleeding Nora.'

They all looked up in surprise.

'Whatever's the matter, Christina?' Caroline asked.

'I've only gone and sewn this spray to me apron, haven't I?' she wailed.

Caroline went over to look, then groaned. 'Cripes, you've made a right blooming mess of that. We'll have to cut it off.'

'Is there no other way?' Christina asked, looking hopefully at Lily, who walked round the table and examined the flounce.

'Take off your apron and I'll see if we can prise it apart without damaging the lace,' she said. But it was no use, the stitching was too tight. She shook her head. 'We'll need to cut it off, I'm afraid.'

'Won't that ruin the work?' Christina asked, tears rolling down her cheeks.

'It's the only way of separating your apron from the rest of the flounce. Stand up,' she said, snatching up scissors and deftly easing the stitching around the sprig.

'Is there some problem?' Mrs Bodney asked, appearing in the doorway.

Christina sank onto her stool but the others turned and looked at Lily expectantly.

'Nothing we can't sort out, Mrs Bodney,' she said, forcing her lips into a smile.

'Hmm,' the other woman said doubtfully. 'Well, when you've all finished what you are doing, make sure your work is covered. Supper is waiting for you in the kitchen.'

As Mrs Bodney disappeared, Christina stood up, turning to Lily in dismay.

'Look, it's hanging from me apron now. What shall I do?'

'There's only one thing for it. We'll have to cut the sprig off. Stand still,' she ordered, carefully cutting around the lace while leaving the apron intact. The sprig, however, was ruined.

'Let's cover up the work and go through to the kitchen,' she said as the others hovered impatiently for their supper, despite the predicament.

'Won't we be one sprig short now?' Caroline asked.

'Oh, she'll kill me when she finds out. All that work wasted,' Christina wailed.

'Look, it's only the one sprig that's actually ruined,' said Lily, inspecting their work. 'The rest of the flounce is fine.'

'But she said she'd counted the sprigs and weighed the materials,' Caroline said. 'Oh, Christina, you are a clumsy oaf.'

'Name calling's not going to change anything. Let's go and eat or Mrs Bodney will know something's up,' Lily said. But as she led the way through to the kitchen, she couldn't help wondering what they were going to do.

Despite their predicament, the hot bacon and freshly baked bread laid out on the table proved too tempting to resist. Even Christina was tucking in as though she'd never seen such food before. Maybe she hadn't, Lily thought. After all, she didn't really know anything about these women she'd found herself amongst. Except now, it seemed, they were looking to her for direction.

As Lily ate she pondered their problem. They'd need to make another sprig, that much was evident. Typically, the designs on the flounce were larger than those on the veil. She had her pillow and bobbins upstairs, of course, for no self-respecting lace maker would ever travel without those. No, the problem was lack of thread. But Mrs Bodney had slipped back into the room and was addressing them.

'Christina, please can you explain why you have threads hanging from your apron?'

'I, erm, that is...' she muttered, looking down at the table.

'For heaven's sake, answer me, girl. I am not an ogre. Has there been some mishap?' Mrs Bodney demanded.

As one the sewers all turned to Lily.

'There has been a slight one, Mrs Bodney. A sprig got joined to an extra piece of material by mistake.'

Mrs Bodney raised her eyebrows. 'That much is evident. First I noticed the sprig missing from the flounce and then I saw the extra threads hanging from Christina's apron. Well, it didn't take a genius to work out what had happened, did it? What I want to know is, why wasn't I told?'

The room fell silent as they stared down at their empty plates.

'Well, I'll tell you why,' Mrs Bodney continued. 'It was because you thought you wouldn't get the special supper I'd laid on, and believe you me, when I came into the workroom and saw the state of the flounce, I was tempted to send you all to bed without any.'

They gasped in surprise.

'Oh, yes, I could see what was wrong even then. However, I'm a fair woman and you've all put in a good day's work so I desisted. Judging from the empty plates, I take it that, despite your predicament, you all enjoyed your meal?'

A murmur of appreciation ran round the kitchen.

'Well, that's something. Now the question is, what are we going to do about the flounce?'

The room fell silent and once again the ladies turned to look at Lily.

'Surely it's not too bad, Mrs Bodney?' she ventured. 'I've got my pillow and bobbins upstairs.'

'But, no thread and, of course, the patterns for the sprigs have been destroyed,' Mrs Bodney continued. 'Now, that seems to me, to be about as bad as it can get.'

The room fell silent and once again, they turned to Lily. 'I notice you all seem to be looking to my lace maker, Lily, for leadership,' Mrs Bodney remarked. 'And amazingly, despite the poor reception you sewers gave her this morning, she appears to have accepted the role.'

The sewers squirmed in their seats, looking uncomfortable.

'Lily, from now on, you are in charge. The rest of you can retire to your beds and get a good night's sleep. Lily, come with me,' their employer ordered as, with a swish of skirts, she left the room.

'You aren't going to be in trouble, are you? Only I'll come with you if you want,' Caroline offered.

'That's kind of you but I'm sure it'll be all right,' Lily answered. Wishing she felt as confident as she sounded, she hurried after Mrs Bodney.

Chapter 41

Nervously, Lily approached the table where the flounce was laid out but, to her surprise, Mrs Bodney looked up and smiled.

'Sit down, Lily,' she said, patting the stool beside her. 'I'm afraid I need your expertise before I can allow you to go to bed.' With a smile, she held up a replacement sprig for the flounce. Lily gasped and Mrs Bodney raised her eyebrows. 'Do you honestly think I'd have travelled all this way without bringing a few spares with me?' she asked.

'But you said all the thread had been weighed,' Lily replied, shaking her head.

'And so it has, including that necessary for a few

extra sprigs in case of any accidents. You always have to think ahead in business, Lily. You'd do well to remember that.'

'So I've not got to make any more, then?' Lily said with relief, for she was feeling very tired.

'Indeed not. However, I need you to attach this tonight. With only a short time left to complete the commission, we can't afford to get behind schedule,' she said, handing Lily a needle that was already threaded.

Stifling a yawn, Lily began her task.

'Of course, we mustn't let the others know we have spare sprigs, or they could become careless,' said Mrs Bodney, pushing the flash closer to Lily, so that its bowl of water reflected added light from the candle onto her work. Not only had the room grown dark, it was cold too. Tomorrow I'll ask Mrs Staple to light us a fire,' she added as Lily shivered. 'I hadn't expected us to be working this late tonight. However, it does give me the opportunity to tell you that I'm really pleased with the way you handled the sewers today.'

Having been sure she was in for a dressing-down, Lily looked up from her stitching in surprise.

'As well as being an accomplished lace maker, we can now add sewer and finisher to your testimonials.'

'Will that make any difference?' Lily asked.

'Indeed it will. From now on you can command a higher wage,' Mrs Bodney said and, seeing Lily's look of surprise, she smiled. 'Yes, it was always my intention to pay you the same rate as the sewers and finishers, Lily. Not that you will be paid that now, of course.'

'Why not? I work just as hard as them,' she protested.

'But now you are their overseer. Expecting the same pay indeed,' Mrs Bodney said, waving her hands dismissively. 'Fiddlesticks. You will be paid a suitably enhanced rate. Really, Lily, if you are to succeed in business you will have to learn to negotiate. Still, the humble lace maker now earns more than the skilled sewers and finishers,' she said, chuckling so that Lily stared at her in amazement.

'Oh, yes, I heard what they said about you. Now what was I saying? Ah, yes, you have good leadership skills, Lily. The ladies like and respect you. That's a rare combination. Now, when you've had regular reading and writing tuition, you'll have the makings of a fine businesswoman. Wouldn't you like to run your own concern?'

'As I said before, Mrs Bodney, there's no chance of that happening.'

'Defeatist talk,' she retorted, waving her hands in the air again. 'You have a good brain and your lace making skills are second to none. Tell me, Lily, what exactly do you intend to do with your life?'

'Well, I never really thought further than this job and marrying Tom,' she answered, her brow creasing.

Mrs Bodney stared at her with owl-wise eyes. 'Well, perhaps you should. Life doesn't just happen, you know.'

'It's different for you, Mrs Bodney. I mean nothing worries you, does it?' Lily said seriously.

'Surprising as it might seem, some things do. I've had to work incredibly hard to establish my reputation, and without it, I would never have won the commission to make the lace for our Queen's wedding dress.'

'I bet you loved going to the palace, Mrs Bodney.'

'I was petrified when I heard I was to be presented to Her Majesty,' she whispered. Lily looked at her sceptically and her employer leaned closer towards her. 'If you promise not to tell anyone, I'll let you into a secret.'

'Tell a lie and hope to die,' Lily said, crossing herself.

'Yes, well, whilst I was waiting to be received by our Queen, I was so nervous that I fainted clean away,' her employer said, laughing.

'Oh, Mrs Bodney, you didn't!' Lily exclaimed, her eyes wide.

'Yes, I'm afraid I did. The staff at the palace treated me so kindly that by the time I was announced, I'd completely recovered. Do you understand what I'm saying, Lily?' Mrs Bodney asked.

'Yes, that even you are human,' she giggled.

'Indeed,' Mrs Bodney said seriously. 'However, the reason for sharing my experience is to demonstrate that we can influence the direction we wish our life to take. If I'd let my nerves get the better of me by running away, as I was sorely tempted, I wouldn't have received the commission I'd worked so hard to earn.'

'Yes, but I don't see how that affects me. I'm not going to the palace, now am I?' Lily retorted, rolling her eyes.

'Maybe not, but you could aspire to running your own concern.'

Not sure how to answer, Lily bent her head over her work and resumed stitching. To start a business you needed money, even she knew that.

'Lily, the first hurdle in the business world is making contacts. The next is winning contracts, or commissions. Now it seems to me you've already managed the first two.'

Lily stopped sewing and stared at her employer. 'I'm not sure I understand what you mean.'

'Your contact is Lady Clinsden and she is commissioning you to make lace for her,' Mrs Bodney said, shaking her head at something so obvious.

'Oh,' Lily murmured, thinking there must be more to it than that, but not wishing to appear completely stupid. She bent her head back over her work and continued sewing.

A few minutes later, she put in the last stitch and carefully finished off.

'Here, all done, Mrs Bodney,' she said, holding out the flounce.

Her employer moved closer to the light of the candle, inspecting her stitching closely.

'Well done. That's as neat as any trained sewer or finisher. You've done a good day's work, Lily, so I'll tidy up here and you can away to your bed. Good night.'

'Good night, Mrs Bodney,' she answered, stifling a yawn as she left the room. It had indeed been a long day.

Ten days later, they were sitting in the kitchen eating their midday broth and enjoying a break from their sewing, when Lily looked up to see Rosie staring at her.

'Is something wrong, Rosie?'

'I was just wondering if you was a nun, Lily,' the girl said frowning.

'Really, Rosie, that's a stupid thing to come out with, even for you,' admonished Caroline.

'Well, it's just that you always wears black, Lily, and nuns do that, don't they?'

'That's because I'm in mourning for my mother,' Lily said, noticing for the first time that the others were dressed in an array of light blues and greens. 'However, it's almost six months since she died, and when we finish our work here, I intend to visit the draper in Sidmouth and purchase some brightly coloured material.'

'Cor, you must have pots of money. Can I come with you?'

'For heaven's sake, Rosie, shut up and eat,' Caroline said, raising her eyebrows at Lily. 'Well, now the flounce is finished, what's next to stitch up?' she asked.

But just then Mrs Staple came in, wiping her hands on her overall.

'Lily, Mrs Bodney says you're to go through to the front room. You have a visitor.'

Her heart flipped. Could Tom have found out where she was working?

'See, I said she was rich. Did you see that pearl she wears in her cap?' she heard Rosie say as she hurried down the hallway. Smothering a smile, Lily's hand automatically touched the hat pin Mrs Bodney had loaned her. How Tom would laugh if he heard her being referred to as rich.

She entered the drawing room to find it was Aunt Elizabeth waiting to see her. Feeling awkward, she hesitated before crossing the room and dutifully giving her a peck on the cheek. It was no good, no matter how much she'd thought over her situation, she would always think of the woman who'd brought her up as her mother.

'Aunt Elizabeth, this is a surprise,' Lily finally managed to say. 'Is everything all right?' She noticed now that her aunt was looking nervous.

'Lily, please accept my apologies for calling unannounced, but I wanted to see you and I also have some news to share with you. I won't keep you long for I know you are busy and I am on the way to Bransbeer. When I heard the stagecoach was stopping at Honiton it seemed opportune to ask them to drop me off on the road to the coaching house.'

'How did you know I was here, Aunt Elizabeth?' Her aunt looked at Mrs Bodney.

'Lady Clinsden knew we were coming here,' her employer answered.

'Lady Clinsden? I don't understand. And why are you going to Bransbeer? Is something wrong with Beth?' Lily asked, relief rushing through her when her aunt shook her head.

Mrs Bodney rose to her feet, smiling graciously. 'If you'll excuse me, I have things I must attend to. May I offer you some refreshment, Elizabeth?'

'That's very kind, but on this occasion I must decline. I have promised to be waiting outside for the stagecoach, when the clock chimes the half-hour,' Lily's aunt said.

Smiling graciously, Mrs Bodney left the room.

'How are you, my dear?' Aunt Elizabeth asked, turning towards Lily.

'I'm fine, and you?' she said quickly.

'I was pleased to get your response to my letter, Lily. I truly wanted to speak with you when I returned to Coombe, but the opportunity never seemed right and then we had to make that sudden departure...' Aunt Elizabeth said, trailing to a halt and looking anxiously at Lily. 'I'd understand if you didn't want anything to do with me now,' she murmured, twisting her kerchief in her hands.

'Oh, Aunt Elizabeth, of course I do. I was shocked, of course, but then I realized it must have been difficult for you in the olden days,' Lily said.

'The olden days, eh?' her aunt said, chuckling. 'Well, one day this prehistoric woman will take you back to her cave and explain everything.'

'There's so much I want to ask you,' Lily said, excitement bubbling up, despite herself.

'I am grateful you wish to keep in touch with me, Lily. Regrettably, I have but a short time to spend with you today. However, I give you my solemn word that when next we meet, I will answer any question you may care to ask.'

'Oh,' Lily said frowning. 'That could be some time, with you being in Ilminster and everything. How's Robert? Is he keeping well and does he like his new trade?'

'Lily, you always were one for asking questions,' said her aunt, chuckling and relaxing back in her seat. 'Robert is very well and sends his love. He is making great progress in his apprenticeship and has the makings of a fine clock maker. It has increased his confidence enormously. And he's made you something for your betrothal,' she said, taking a parcel from her bag and handing it to

Lily. 'He sends this with his very best wishes for your future and says nothing will keep him from attending your wedding. And how is Tom? Does he mind you working in Honiton?' she asked.

Lily stopped stroking the packaging around the parcel and frowned. 'He doesn't know I'm here, Auntie. Mrs Bodney told me we were leaving Bransbeer only the night before and I had no time to get a message to him. Always supposing I knew where he was.'

'Do I sense trouble, Lily?' Aunt Elizabeth asked, leaning forward and tentatively taking her hand.

'Well, we did have words...' Lily started, but she was interrupted by the clock on the mantel chiming the half-hour. Glancing towards the window, her aunt got quickly to her feet.

'I'm so sorry, Lily, I must go. I have an appointment to see Lady Clinsden and cannot miss the stagecoach.'

'Why are you seeing Lady Clinsden?' Lily asked.

'My dear, we've had such a short time, I haven't even told you my news. Lady Clinsden wishes to open a charity school for the children of lace makers. Although I love my brother dearly, he's set in his ways and doesn't need my help at all. Anyway, Lady Clinsden sent me a communication asking if I could visit her. She seems to think I could be of assistance. It would be wonderful to be working with children again. As long as she finds me suitable, that is.'

'Of course she will, Aunt Elizabeth. Why, this means you'll be living back in Devonshire,' she cried.

'Well, let's not count our cockerels, but it would

be lovely to be near you. We have so much to catch up on,' she said, glancing at the clock and frowning. 'Lily, I must go now. The driver made it clear he wouldn't wait,' she said.

Impulsively, Lily threw her arms around her aunt.

'Good luck, Aunt Elizabeth, although I'm sure you don't need it.'

'Thank you, my dear. I will let you know how things work out. Take care of yourself and make sure you get in touch with Tom when you return to Bransbeer. He's a really nice young man,' she said, gathering up her things.

As Lily opened the front door to let her aunt out, the stagecoach drew up alongside. Her aunt gave her a quick peck on the cheek and then climbed into the carriage. Waving goodbye, Lily hoped it wouldn't be long until she saw her aunt again. They had broken the ice now and there was so much she wanted to ask her.

Making her way back to the front room, she retrieved the parcel from the chair and untied the string. Inside was a beautifully carved miniature clock and she was just admiring the workmanship when Mrs Bodney bustled back into the room.

'That's a fine clock, Lily. Would you like me to read that to you?' she said, pointing down to the note attached to the paper.

'Please, Mrs Bodney,' Lily said handing it to her.

Dear Lily,
I trust you are well. I am working very hard and am enjoying learning my new trade.

400

With much help from Uncle Vincent I have made this miniature clock as a betrothal present for you and Tom. When I receive the invitation to your wedding I will make you a full-sized model.

Please give my regards to Tom.

Your loving brother, Rob

'Well, that's a fine betrothal present, Lily,' said Mrs Bodney, handing her back the note. But Lily felt the tears welling and could only nod. Would there be a wedding, she wondered.

'You'd best return to the others, Lily, or they'll be thinking you've left them in the lurch,' said Mrs Bodney, breaking into her thoughts.

'Yes, of course,' she said, putting the note in her pocket and gathering up her parcel.

'Coo, you got a present,' Rosie said, as Lily entered the sewing room. 'Have you a got a fancy man, then?'

'Don't be nosy,' Caroline chided. 'And get back to your work. If we don't get this veil finished soon, Mrs Bodney will give us a right dressing-down.

Carefully, Lily placed the clock on the dresser then picked up a sprig with its exotic flower design and began to attach it to the others.

'So, who came to see you, then?' Rosie persisted.

'Really, nosy Rosie just about sums you up right now, young lady,' Caroline rebuked.

'Well, it's not every day you gets a present and I just wondered what it was, that's all.'

'I'll show you later,' Lily promised. 'Now, I really must concentrate. I need to make up for the time I've lost.'

They worked on until the shadows crept around the room and Mrs Staple came bustling in, bringing with her the delicious aroma of cooking stew. She lit the candles and carefully placed them where they would all benefit from the extra light reflected through the water bowls.

'Something smells nice, Mrs Staple,' Lily said, her rumbling stomach reminding her she was hungry. She couldn't believe how quickly she'd got used to eating three meals a day.

'Why, bless you, dearie, 'tis a nice bit of rabbit stewing with some vegetables. I've made dumplings for extra sustenance too, seeing as how you've all been working so hard.'

'Three cheers for Mrs Staple,' said Christina, and as they gave a rousing cheer, the woman flushed with pleasure, then hurried back to the kitchen.

'Well, we might be working longer hours, but I've never eaten so well,' Caroline said, and they all nodded in agreement.

'Wonder if she does puddings too. I likes jam roly-poly,' Rosie said, licking her lips.

'Yes, I can believe that,' laughed Lily. 'Now come along, we must get this finished before supper, otherwise Mrs Bodney won't be happy.'

They returned to their sewing and the room fell silent once more.

They had nearly finished their supper when Lily realized Mrs Bodney hadn't appeared. 'Is Mrs Bodney not joining us tonight, Mrs Staple?'

'No, dearie, she's gone out for the evening.'

'Ooh, maybe she's got a fellow,' Rosie said, her eyes widening. 'You was going to tell us if you had a beau.'

Lily opened her mouth to reply, then realized she didn't know the answer herself. She thought back to her last meeting with Tom, and again berated herself for acceding to Mrs Bodney's wishes. Why hadn't she grasped the opportunity to spend time with him? She should have stood her ground and gone with him to Coombe. But if she had disobeyed her employer, she'd have lost her job and then what would she have done? Muttering something noncommittal, she excused herself and left the table.

Lying in the little bed, she thought of Tom. Was he thinking of her too? Did he wonder where she was? With a shock, she realized he probably thought she was still working at Picky Pike's. In frustration, she thumped her pillow. It was all very well Mrs Bodney saying she could influence the direction of her life, but how could she do that when she was stuck here in Honiton?

Realizing her dreams of marriage to Tom might never come to fruition, she thumped her pillow again. How could she have been so stupid?

Chapter 42

Next morning, Lily woke early. In dire need of a hot drink, she made her way through to the kitchen where a young girl was riddling the ashes in the range.

'Oh, miss, you made me jump,' she whispered,

looking at Lily as if she'd been scalded.

'Sorry, I didn't mean to,' she said smiling at the girl. 'What's your name?'

'Sally, miss,' the girl answered timidly.

'Well, my name's Lily. Now you see to the fire and I'll go out to the pump and fill the kettle,' she said smiling.

'I knows who yous is, miss, but yous mustn't do that,' she answered, her eyes wide as pot lids, as Lily lifted the kettle. 'I'll be in trouble with Mrs Staple as it is.'

'Why?' Lily asked, frowning.

''Cos I'm meant to have all this done and be back in the scullery before anyone comes down, miss.'

'Well, it's not your fault I'm up before dawn and feeling parched. And please call me Lily,' she said, lifting the kettle from its hook over the fire.

'Oh, I couldn't do that, miss. Yous in charge of them ladies.'

'Not really, I just oversee their work. We all have our jobs to do.'

'And should know our place.' Mrs Bodney's strident voice sounded through the open door, making them both jump. 'Come along, Lily.'

Turning to Sally, Lily made a face. *'Come along, Lily,'* she mimicked, making the young girl giggle.

'There you are, Lily,' Mrs Bodney said as she entered the front room. 'I must say I'm surprised at you fraternizing with the scullery maid. Will you never learn your place?'

'Sorry, Mrs Bodney,' she said meekly. How she detested this class thing, which seemed to matter so much to her employer.

404

'Well, Lily, is this not the most glorious day?' Mrs Bodney trilled, holding out a gilt-edged card. 'And is this not the most marvellous thing you've ever seen?'

'What is it, Mrs Bodney?'

'This is an invitation from Queen Victoria herself, no less. Can you imagine it, Lily? I, Jean Bodney, am invited to be a guest at Her Majesty's wedding. Is that not the most exciting thing you've ever heard?'

Lily nodded and then smiled. Clearly, the other woman was beside herself with joy. Of course, it was hardly likely the Queen had written the card herself, but who was she to upset her employer by pointing out such a minor detail?

'Right,' Mrs Bodney said, snapping back to her brusque, businesslike self. 'How is the sewing up progressing?'

'It's coming along well. As you know, the flounce is finished and also the veil. We just have the collar and—'

'Spare me the detail,' her employer said, waving her hands at her as if swatting away a troublesome bluebottle. 'The entire commission needs to be finished and parcelled ready for collection next week. It is your job, as overseer, to ensure everything's ready and up to standard. Although I shall, of course, carry out a final inspection of all the lace before it is packaged.'

'Next week? But you said we had until the end of the month,' Lily said, staring at the other woman in dismay.

'I actually said the 25th, our patron saint's day,' the other woman corrected, as ever a stickler for detail. 'However, the Palace now requires the finished lace to be delivered by next week. Would you care to argue with our dear Queen?'

'No, of course not–' but she had no time to finish for Mrs Bodney held up her hand.

'I have a wedding to prepare for so I shall leave everything here in your capable hands, Miss Rose.'

Miss Rose? Blimey, that invitation had certainly given her airs and graces, Lily thought.

'Well, run along, or you'll be complaining you've not got enough time to finish everything,' Mrs Bodney snapped, waving her away.

Making her way down the hallway, Lily noticed the first rays of early morning sunshine filtering in through the window. Was it only just sunrise? Why, she felt as if she'd done a day's work already. Laughter emanating from the kitchen informed her that the ladies were enjoying their porridge. Not wishing to upset their first meal of the day, she decided to wait until they'd finished before telling them about the change to the schedule.

Hurrying through to the sewing room, she began assessing the amount of work they still had to do. She knew they'd already made good progress but was relieved to find that, provided they made a concerted effort, they should just make the new deadline.

Then a thought struck her. Hurrying back to the front room, she found Mrs Bodney enjoying tea and toast, whilst admiring her invitation. Clearly, their employer no longer felt she should eat with them in the kitchen.

'Well?' demanded the other woman, looking up and frowning. 'I didn't think you'd have the time to stand around with arms both the same length.'

'No, you're right, of course. However, before I inform the ladies of the change of plan, I wish to check something with you, Mrs Bodney,' Lily said, looking the other woman straight in the eye.

'Well, what is it?' her employer sighed, reluctantly putting aside her invitation.

'It's about our money...' Lily stuttered to a halt as the other woman's eyes widened.

'What about your money?' Mrs Bodney asked, slowly enunciating every syllable.

'When Maria, erm, left, you promised that as we still had the same amount of work to do her wage would be shared between us.'

The other woman's eyes narrowed. 'And I shall keep my word. I never renege on a promise,' she said, putting her nose in the air as though talking about money was now beneath her.

'Of course you wouldn't, Mrs Bodney,' Lily said quickly. 'However, you said earlier that the sewing up must now be completed by next week.'

'Yes, I did. What exactly are you getting at, Lily?' she snapped impatiently.

'As the ladies are still going to have to do the same amount of work, may I tell them they will be paid up to the end of the month, like you promised?'

Mrs Bodney stared at her, tea cup poised half-way to her lips. There was a long silence. Slowly, she returned the cup to its saucer. Then to Lily's surprise, peals of laughter echoed round the room.

'Oh, Lily, well spoken. You really are turning out to be a fine little businesswoman. Your development these past few months has been a joy to behold and, what's more, I think I may take some of the credit for that. Of course you'll all be paid the full amount, you chump. I'm nothing if not fair. Now go and tell the others. Then, for heaven's sake, get on with finishing the job.'

Lily hurried back down the hallway, her employer's tinkling laugh following after her.

'You missed your meal,' Rosie said, looking up as she entered the room. 'Mrs Staple said she would keep some back for you if you was hungry.'

'That's very kind of her, but I don't think I'll have time this morning. Now listen, everyone, I've a new instruction from Mrs Bodney.' She paused as they all stopped what they were doing and looked questioningly at her. 'The sewing up of the lace now has to be completed by next week.'

Their faces fell and her announcement was met with stunned silence.

'But that's not possible, surely?' gasped Christina, the first one to recover.

'Well, I've assessed the work and I think we can just about make the new deadline. It means we'll have to keep at it, though. Work on even longer into the evenings,' she said, anxious to reassure them.

'But why?' asked Caroline, shaking her head.

'Apparently the palace has asked for the lace to be delivered earlier than planned.'

'No. I mean why should we work on longer in the evenings? If we finish earlier, we'll not earn as much, will we?'

The others muttered in agreement and Lily held up her hand.

'Mrs Bodney has assured me we will be paid

until the end of the month as agreed.'

'You mean if we finish next week we'll still get all our money?' Rosie asked.

'Yes, that's exactly what she said,' Lily assured them, smiling at their surprised faces. 'And remember, we will all get a share of Maria's wage too.'

'Well, come on, everyone, what are we waiting for? Let's get sewing,' Caroline cried, and laughing, they picked up their needles and began sewing furiously.

'The stitching still has to be of the finest quality,' Lily reminded them, and they nodded without missing a stitch.

There was a hesitant tap on the door and she looked up to see Sally hovering with a mug in her hand. The poor girl was shaking with nerves and Lily got up quickly and went over to her.

'Mrs Staple said yous couldn't work without something in yous stomach. I said yous said yous was parched, and she said if I promised not to spill a drop, I could bring yous some tea, miss.'

'That's most kind of you, Sally, thank you. And please thank Mrs Staple,' Lily said, taking the mug from her and watching as the little maid scuttled off like a timid mouse. Gratefully, she took a sip and gave a sigh of contentment as the liquid warmed her insides.

'Do you think this piece goes here?' Rosie asked, holding up one of the smaller sprigs patterned with a scroll.

'Don't look quite right to me,' said Christina. 'Maybe it should be that one with the leaf that goes there. What do you think, Lily?'

Carefully placing her mug on the ledge behind her, Lily went over to look.

'I'm not sure. Where's the drawing?' Lily asked, frowning.

'It's here,' said Caroline, sliding it across the table. As they stood poring over the design, it took them quite some time to work out exactly which way the sprays were meant to be joined together. Then, happy they'd got it right, and conscious that every minute counted more than ever, they resumed their stitching like women possessed. Even when Mrs Staple called them for their midday broth, they ate quickly, anxious to get back to their work.

All afternoon they sewed, never moving from their seats, other than to consult the drawing, so that by the time the room was darkening and Mrs Staple appeared with the candles and flashes, they were stiff and goggle-eyed.

'My, it's perishing in here,' said Mrs Staple. 'Why don't you let me serve supper early? Then I can get a fire lit in the grate whilst you're eating. That way the room will be nice and warm when you come back again.'

They all looked hopefully at Lily.

'I think that's a marvellous idea, Mrs Staple. Are you sure it won't put you to any trouble?'

'No, of course it won't, dearie. I don't like to see all you ladies working in the cold,' she said, shaking her head. 'If I had my way, I'd light the fire earlier in the day, but I've had my instructions,' she sniffed, leaving them in no doubt as to what she thought about those. 'Anyway, come on through to the kitchen when you're ready; I've got a nice hotpot cooking.' Then, as she opened the door to go out, yet another appetizing aroma wafted in, and they all sniffed the air appreciatively. Mrs Staple's cooking was superb, and stools clattered on the flags as they hurried after her.

'We'd better cover our work in case Mrs Bodney comes in to inspect it,' Lily called after them, but they'd already disappeared into the kitchen. Carefully, she covered the work, gratified to see how much they'd achieved during the day. But there was still much to be done if they were to meet the new deadline, she thought, as she went through to join the others.

Their meal was delicious and the respite from sewing welcome. As the heat from the range warmed their chilled bodies, they relaxed back in their chairs chattering excitedly, so that it was only Lily who heard the cry of despair coming from the next room.

Chapter 43

Slipping out of the kitchen, Lily hurried through to the sewing room where she found Sally, on her knees, mopping up the brown liquid that was spreading quickly over the flags. When she saw Lily, she jumped in alarm, banging her head on the table above.

'I didn't mean to, miss. Mrs Staple will kill me,' the scullery maid sobbed, tears streaming down her cheeks.

'Now then, calm yourself and tell me what's happened,' Lily said, but looking up at the ledge with the toppled mug and dregs of tea still spilling onto the design paper, it was evident what the problem was. She snatched up the drawing, but could see it was beyond saving.

'I'm sorry, miss. Mrs Staple sent me in to lay the fire whilst yous was at supper, and me elbow knocked the mug as I was lifting the bucket of ashes. The tea spilled onto the table. I've wiped it up as best as I can, but the picture's all smudged. Is it important?' she squeaked.

Yes, Lily wanted to scream, it's the design we've been working to. But, as the girl stood trembling before her, she didn't have the heart to tell her off.

Thinking quickly, she said, 'Look, Sally, you get that fire going and I'll clear this up before anyone sees it.' The young girl stared hopefully up at her. 'Go on, quickly now,' she urged, frantically mopping up the rest of the mess. By the time everywhere was clean again, Sally had the fire burning brightly.

'Lily, where are you?' Mrs Bodney's imperious voice called, making them both jump. Lily looked at the ruined drawing, quickly screwed it up and tossed it into the flames.

'I'm in the workroom, Mrs Bodney,' she answered. Turning to Sally, she put her finger to her lips. 'Go back to the kitchen and don't say a word about this to anyone, understand?' she whispered. The little maid nodded and quickly gathered up her cloth. 'With any luck, we'll get away with it,' Lily added.

As Sally scuttled out through the side door,

Mrs Bodney swept in the front, her beady eyes as usual missing nothing.

'What's making that fire burn so brightly?' she asked, moving closer to the grate and peering into it. 'Goodness, isn't that the design sheet?'

'Yes, Mrs Bodney. As we've finished with it, I thought it wise to destroy it.' Her employer turned and stared at her for a long moment. Endeavouring to keep her composure, Lily smiled back. 'That was the correct thing to do, wasn't it?' she asked. 'I remembered that when we'd finished with the patterns in Bransbeer, you cut them up so that no one could copy them.'

'Well, I must say I'm surprised you didn't check with me first, but if you're sure it's really finished with,' Mrs Bodney said doubtfully. 'Still, you should know, you are the overseer, after all. And it must mean that you are making even better progress than I thought, so I'll leave you to it. Good night, Lily,' she said, giving her another penetrating stare, before bustling out of the room.

'Good night, Mrs Bodney,' she replied weakly.

As soon as the door had closed behind her employer, she collapsed into the nearest chair. That really was too close for comfort, she thought. Then she had a terrible thought. Supposing the ladies needed to refer to the design and she couldn't remember it? What if they couldn't finish the commission? Whatever would happen then? Would she be hanged, drawn and quartered? Shivering, she leaned closer to the fire, holding out her hands to warm them. As she sat there, pondering her fate, the others reappeared re-energized after their supper.

'We wondered where you'd gone, Lily. Mrs Staple said we should have a bit of a break whilst the fire in here was drawing,' Rosie said, feeling she should explain their prolonged absence.

'Quite right too,' Lily hastily agreed. 'But now we really need to get some more work done before bedtime. As you can see, the fire and candles are burning well, so it's bright and cosy in here.' They took their seats and began to sew, but it wasn't long before Caroline noticed the design sheet was missing.

'Where's the drawing?' she asked, and everyone peered around.

'It's not here,' Christina said. 'That must be why Mrs Bodney came rushing in here as soon as she arrived back. Funny, though, I didn't notice it in her hand when she came through to the kitchen.'

'I expect she wanted to make sure nobody else saw it,' Lily said carefully. 'Still, we all know what we are doing now, don't we?' she asked, crossing her fingers behind her back.

'Hope so, or we'll be in a right old pickle,' Caroline said.

However, the evening passed without anyone needing to refer to the design, and Lily breathed a sigh of relief.

The next few days passed in a whirl, as they worked diligently from the break of dawn until bedtime, and though they were weary, their spirits remained high. The thought of finishing their job early and still getting paid until the end of the month spurred them on. Mrs Staple ensured they were amply fed, maintaining that they needed extra nourishment to replace the energy they were expending.

Then, late on Saturday afternoon, the final sprig was stitched into place. Giving a rousing cheer, the sewers held hands and danced around the table in delight.

Their employer came rushing in to see what all the noise was about and Lily smiled widely.

'That's it, Mrs Bodney, the sewing up of the Queen's lace is complete,' she proudly announced.

'Well done, ladies,' Mrs Bodney said, clapping her hands in delight. 'Go and wait in the kitchen whilst I inspect your work. Tell Mrs Staple she may serve tea and a slice of cake each.'

'Cake, how wonderful,' cried Rosie.

'You, young lady, would do well to forgo some of these sweet treats. No man wants a barrel for a wife, you know,' Mrs Bodney said, shaking her finger.

'No, Mrs Bodney,' Rosie answered, looking down at the ground. Then, the other woman's features softened.

'Well, as you've worked so hard, you can start on the morrow,' she relented, and Rosie rushed through to the kitchen before she could change her mind.

When they were sitting at the table enjoying their refreshment, Caroline turned to Lily and asked, 'Can we go home now we've finished?'

'More to the point, can we have our money now we've finished?' Christina butted in.

'I guess it depends on whether our work passes Her Majesty's eagle eyes,' Rosie said, helping herself to another piece of seed cake.

'I'm afraid I can't speak for Her Majesty, Rosie,' Mrs Bodney said, making them jump as she appeared in the doorway. 'For myself, however, I would like to say you have all done a splendid job. Yes, Caroline, you may go home this afternoon and yes, Christina, you can have your money now. As for you, Rosie, please remember what I said about men not wishing to marry little barrels.' They all laughed as Rosie looked longingly at the cake in her hand, then reluctantly put it back on her plate.

'Right, ladies, please listen,' continued Mrs Bodney. 'Lily, as overseer, you will remain until the lace has been suitably parcelled and collected. The rest of you may go and pack your things. And, I have no doubt you will wish to come and see me before you leave,' she added, her eyes twinkling with amusement.

Lily watched as they rushed from the room, chattering like excited magpies, and sighed. What was she going to do once her job here was finished?

When the door had shut behind them, Mrs Bodney turned to her saying, 'I have something to ask you, Lily.'

'Oh?' she asked, her hopes rising.

'When I return to Bransbeer, I intend promoting Mary to housekeeper. She lives close enough to return home each evening. However, I will need a live-in maid to assist her.'

Lily's heart sank. So that was to be her fate. Well, it was better than being out of work and she did need somewhere to live...

'Lily Rose, are you listening? I asked you what

416

you thought of my idea,' Mrs Bodney said, looking at her expectantly.

'I suppose I don't really have any choice. I mean, it's very kind of you but I hadn't really thought of working as a maid–'

She was interrupted by a peal of laughter.

'Not you, you chump. You're capable of much better things. No, I was thinking of that young scullery maid,' she said, getting up from the table. 'Sally, a word, please,' she called, and the little girl came scuttling in, her lip trembling as if she was expecting a dressing-down. 'How long have you been working in that scullery, girl?'

'Since the summer hiring, ma'am,' she said, bobbing a curtsy and earning a grunt of approval from the older woman.

'Well, I'm in need of a housemaid, so what do you think? Would you like to work for me in Bransbeer?'

The little girl's eyes widened in surprise and she nodded vigorously.

'What do you think, Lily? Would Sally be up to the job?'

The girl stared at Lily in mute appeal and she smiled, giving her a surreptitious wink behind the other woman's back.

'I'm sure Sally will be more than capable, Mrs Bodney.'

'Right then, that's settled, I take it you can speak, child?' she asked as an afterthought.

'Yes, ma'am.' It came out as a whisper but Mrs Bodney, seeming satisfied, waved her away with the promise of arranging things with Mrs Staple.

The room had only just gone quiet again when

the sewers reappeared, swarming excitedly around Mrs Bodney like wasps at a picnic.

'Right, ladies, quiet please,' she said, going over to her reticule and drawing out her purse. 'Hold out your hands,' she ordered before carefully counting a generous number of coins into each palm. 'You have all done very well. When people remark on the fine workmanship of our dear Queen's wedding dress, you can be proud to know you had a hand in making it. Now I'll bid you goodbye and good luck, ladies,' she said, sweeping out of the room.

Looking down at the shiny coins in their hands, the women's eyes widened in surprise. Despite being the finest sewers and finishers in the county, they'd never earned this much before. Suddenly, eager to be on their way, they turned to Lily.

'Goodbye, Lily. Hope we'll see you again one day,' they chorused. Then gathering up their bags they headed for the door, leaving her alone in the deepening shadows.

So that was it then. Everyone had somewhere to go, apart from her. Alone as usual, Lily Rose, so you might as well get used to it, she thought.

Peasants don't pity themselves, Lily. They prepare for the next thing life has in store.

'That's all very well, Father, but I don't know what that is.'

You must have faith, Lily.

Chapter 44

As she pondered her father's words, Lily hardly registered the knock on the front door, or Mrs Staple muttering under her breath about unexpected callers as she hurried to answer it. However, it was Mrs Bodney who appeared in the doorway.

'Lily, please go through to the front room. Your presence is required immediately.'

What now? she thought, getting wearily to her feet.

'Yes, Mrs Bodney,' she answered dutifully.

'And for heaven's sake pinch some colour into your cheeks. You look as white as the chalk cliffs back home.' Not having the strength to argue, she nodded, thinking the other woman did take worrying about appearances to extremes. Making her way along the hallway, she was about to enter the room when she stopped in the doorway, her eyes widening in surprise.

The figure warming his hands in front of the fire turned to greet her, but she'd have known those broad shoulders anywhere.

'Hello, Lily,' he said, grinning.

'Tom! What are you doing here?' she gasped, her heart thumping wildly.

'Just thought I'd drop in,' he quipped, his eyes sparkling with mischief.

'But how did you know where I was?'

'I didn't for ages,' he said. 'When I got back from Coombe and found you'd left Picky Pike's, I was that sore. Thought you'd done a runner on me. Just when I thought we was getting on well again. I asked around, but no one knew where you'd gone. I was out of me mind.'

'But, Tom, I didn't know we were coming here until the last minute. I–'

'Well really, Lily, that's no way to treat a guest. 'Where are your manners?' her employer asked, bustling in. Lily's eyes widened in amazement, for Mrs Bodney herself was carrying a tray of refreshment. 'Tom, it's good to see you again. Please take a seat and make yourself comfortable.' If he was surprised at the change in Lily's employer's manner towards him, he chose to ignore it.

'Thank you, Mrs Bodney,' he answered politely. 'It's nice to see you too.'

Smiling graciously, she set down the tray. 'I'm afraid you'll have to excuse me, Tom, but I'm frightfully busy preparing for a wedding,' she announced regally, before bustling out.

'But I thought your job here was finished now?' he said, turning to Lily and frowning.

'It is, Tom, but Mrs Bodney's received an invitation to attend the royal wedding and she's in a right state deciding what she's to wear.'

'You women and weddings,' he said, grinning. Then, realizing what he'd said, he sat there looking uncomfortable.

'Tea?' Lily asked in the heavy silence that filled the room. Tom nodded. Relieved to have something to do, she busied herself with the tray. Then, as she passed him one of the fine bone-

420

china cups, he burst out laughing.

'You'll be expecting me to sip daintily and hold up me pinkie next,' he quipped, demonstrating with his little finger. He looked so funny, she burst out laughing and the awkwardness passed. 'Oh, Lily, I've really missed you,' he declared, setting down his cup so suddenly it clattered in the saucer. 'I done a lot of thinking on that walk to Coombe, and realized you and me had a good thing going before–'

'I know, Tom, and I'm sorry I didn't believe you about the ring,' she said.

'Yes, I thought about that too. I guess it must have seemed strange, me going on about not having enough money for one and then giving you that ruby. It's a beauty, even if I do say so meself. I'd been nagging Nana for ages to let me have it for you. Luckily, being her blue-eyed grandson, I finally managed to talk her round,' he said, a twinkle in his eye.

'So I understand,' she said, recalling Mrs West-lake's words.

'I had the devil's own job persuading her to let me have it the second time, though, and Mother didn't help, of course.' Bemused, Lily stared at him. The second time? But, as if he'd said too much, he abruptly changed the subject.

'The trouble I had finding you,' he told her, shaking his head. 'I looked everywhere I could think of and asked everyone I saw, but it was like you'd vanished into thin air.'

Her heart did a double flip. So he did still care for her. And he'd tried to find out where she'd gone.

'So, how did you discover I was here, in Honiton?' she asked.

'Your Aunt Elizabeth told my mother that she had something important to tell me and that she'd be at Mrs Goode's if I wanted to find out what it was.'

'Aunt Elizabeth! Of course she had an appointment with Lady Clinsden. I wonder how she got on.'

'Well, gal, you can ask her yourself later, 'cos we travelled here together.'

'Aunt Elizabeth is here as well?' Lily asked, shaking her head in surprise.

'Yes, she's taking tea with Mrs Bodney. They are being discreet,' he said, moving towards her.

She moved to meet him and as his arms closed around her she knew without a shadow of doubt that this was where she belonged. Then, as his lips came down on hers, setting her pulses racing, she could think no more.

'I stand by what I said about the ruby matching that fiery spirit of yours,' he gasped, when they finally pulled away from each other. Then, to her astonishment, he dropped to one knee, holding out the betrothal ring before her.

'Lily Rose, will you please put me out of my misery and say you'll marry me?'

'Oh, yes, Tom,' she whispered, her heart singing like a thousand choirs. Grinning, he got to his feet and gently placed the ruby ring back on her finger, where it belonged. Then, he let out a whoop of delight, lifted her off the floor and swung her round and round until she was helpless with laughter. Suddenly her cap went flying across the

422

room. Tom set her back on her feet and stood there staring at her. Her hand flew to her shorn locks and, for a long moment, the only sound in the room was the crackling of the logs on the fire.

'I'm sorry Tom, I was in a temper and chopped off my hair, but it will grow back eventually. Then we can be wed, can't we?' she asked, her words coming out in a tumble.

He looked at her aghast. 'Oh, no, Lily,' he said, shaking his head.

Her heart flopped. So Mrs Bodney had been right about appearances all along...

'Don't worry, Tom. I understand you won't want to marry me now,' she mumbled, biting her tongue to hold back the tears.

'But that's just it, Lily. I do want to marry you now. Well, as soon as it can be arranged. I'm certainly not waiting until your hair grows back. Besides,' he said, his lips curling into a smile, 'I rather like your new hairdo. It makes you look sort of impish. Come here, you dollop. Hair or no, you'll always look good to me,' he declared, kissing her cheek. Then he bent and retrieved her cap. 'Here, best put this back on before the old dragon reappears,' and he placed it gently back on her head.

'You're sure you don't mind?' Lily asked.

'I don't, but you'd best not let my mother see you looking like that,' he said, wagging his finger at her. 'She's been on at me to get a decent hair-cut for years.' He grimaced, tugging at the fair hair curling around the nape of his neck. 'Now me wife's going to have shorter hair than me,' he exclaimed, looking so indignant that Lily burst

423

out laughing. Then Tom joined in and the room rang with the sound of their merriment.

'Well, if I'd known we were celebrating I wouldn't have bothered with that tea,' Mrs Bodney said, smiling at them from the doorway. They stared at their untouched cups on the table as if wondering how they'd got there. Then Aunt Elizabeth appeared behind her.

'Look, Auntie,' Lily cried in delight, holding out her hand, and the ruby winked up at them in the firelight.

'Congratulations, both of you,' Aunt Elizabeth said, giving Lily a hug and then shaking Tom's hand.

'And I too wish you every happiness,' said Mrs Bodney. Then, practical as ever, she asked, 'Do I take it this means you won't be coming back to Bransbeer with me, Lily?'

'Oh, I don't know,' Lily said looking askance at Tom, who was standing there beaming like a beacon.

'Indeed, she won't, Mrs Bodney, for you are now looking at the new blacksmith of Coombe,' he announced proudly. 'And when my betrothed and I are wed, we shall be living in the cottage right opposite the forge there.'

'Why, Tom, that's marvellous,' Lily cried, clapping her hands excitedly. 'But how can that be?'

'Well, it's like this—'

'Yes, well done, Tom,' cut in Mrs Bodney, flushing with excitement. 'That will afford you a much better standing in the community, Lily. Now, shall we make ourselves comfortable while Tom tells us all about it?' she asked, signalling to Aunt

Elizabeth to take a seat before neatly perching on the chair nearest the fire.

Lily looked at Tom and grimaced. True to form, her employer had no intention of missing anything. Only Mrs Bodney would have the audacity to think she had the right to share their private moment.

'Do hurry up, Tom. I'm waiting,' she demanded impatiently.

'Well, I had an inkling the sea weren't the life for me a while back, and began looking around to see what else I could do. Remember you asking me why I was always at Coombe, Lily?'

'Oh, yes. It crossed my mind you might have been seeing someone else,' she said, her eyes clouding as she remembered the hours she'd spent fretting.

'You are a dollop, Lily Rose. As if I'd ever look at anyone else,' he said. 'I'd heard old Benjamin was looking to retire, but wouldn't till he found someone to take over. He could never let the horses suffer for want of shoes, he said. Anyhow, he saw I had the nice calm sort of nature that was needed...'

'Tom Westlake, that's a fib if ever I heard one. You, nice and calm?' spluttered Lily.

'Well, as it happens, I do seem to have a way with the horses. I was troubled about giving up the lugger, being as how it was Father's. Then, when we got caught in that blow, it kind of decided things for me. Anyway, with the money I got for selling it, I was able to buy Benjamin's tools and pay the rent till the next quarter-day. I've been dying to tell you, but–'

'Oh, so that was the surprise you had to show me,' Lily cut in, remembering their last meeting.

Tom nodded, sighing. 'Yes, old Benjamin's been teaching me the trade. I thought, I'd show you the forge, and see if you liked it.'

'That's all very well and fine,' interrupted Mrs Bodney, 'but I take it you won't be moving in until you are wed, young lady?' She looked sternly at Lily then exchanged glances with Aunt Elizabeth.

'Goodness me, no,' Tom exclaimed. 'Perish the thought. I mean, I've got Lily's reputation to think of, Mrs Bodney,' he added, pretending to look affronted, then winking at Lily behind her back.

'Quite right, Tom,' Mrs Bodney agreed. 'Thank heavens someone understands the importance of keeping up appearances.'

'Indeed, Mrs Bodney,' Tom said gravely. 'I took the liberty of speaking with Mrs Goode whilst I was there. She agreed that Lily can stay with her until we're man and wife. It wouldn't do to set tongues wagging, now would it, Mrs Bodney?' he asked, sounding so earnest that Lily had to bite down on her lip again.

'Indeed, it would not,' Mrs Bodney agreed, turning to Lily. 'I always said Tom was a fine, upstanding young man, didn't I?'

And Lily, not trusting herself to speak, could only nod in agreement.

'Well, it seems this is an evening for good news, for I too have something to tell you,' said Aunt Elizabeth, smiling. 'Lady Clinsden is opening a charity school in Coombe and has engaged me to help with its running. It will be for the children of lace makers, so young Beth will be able to

426

attend and learn her letters.'

Mrs Bodney gave Lily one of her meaningful looks, and she smiled back knowingly.

'Aunt Elizabeth, that's wonderful news,' said Lily, going over and giving her a hug.

'Yes, isn't it? And as part of my working agreement, Lady Clinsden will provide me with a cottage next to the school,' she said, her eyes shining.

'And talking of Lady Clinsden, I expect you will be taking on her commission when you return, Lily?' Mrs Bodney asked.

'Yes, of course. Though I don't know where I shall work,' Lily said, frowning.

'Well, my love, I have news for you. For hasn't your wonderful betrothed just limewashed the cottage opposite the forge for you to use. You'll be able to make your lace without fear of getting smuts on it,' Tom announced, beaming with pride.

'Oh, Tom, that's perfect. Though I don't suppose it will take long to make the collars and cuffs for Lady Clinsden so I shall have to see what other work I can find.'

'Lily, if all goes to plan, a royal christening gown will be required and I'm hopeful of being granted the commission for that. I will certainly require your help then,' said Mrs Bodney.

Lily and Tom looked at each other in delight. 'Oh, this is so exciting,' exclaimed Mrs Bodney, her dark eyes shining like ebony. 'Now I have two weddings to prepare for.'

'Yes, and I have lace to make for my own wedding gown,' Lily said, smiling up at Tom. He pulled her closer and she let out a sigh of contentment.

So peasants can be picky people, Lily; and you picked well, my girl.

Her father's voice sounded in her ear, and knowing he had bestowed his blessing made her happiness complete.

Acknowledgements

My warm thanks to Teresa Chris for her inimitable wisdom, guidance and encouragement Jane Bidder for pointing me in the right direction. Diana and her lovely ladies in Springfields, Colyford for teaching me to make lace. Allhallows Museum, Honiton, for their kind help in providing details of the lace Queen Victoria wore. And last but not least, Maxine and Leon for their special gift that began the writing process.

The publishers hope that this book has given you enjoyable reading. Large Print Books are especially designed to be as easy to see and hold as possible. If you wish a complete list of our books please ask at your local library or write directly to:

Magna Large Print Books
Magna House, Long Preston,
Skipton, North Yorkshire.
BD23 4ND

This Large Print Book for the partially sighted, who cannot read normal print, is published under the auspices of

THE ULVERSCROFT FOUNDATION

THE ULVERSCROFT FOUNDATION

... we hope that you have enjoyed this Large Print Book. Please think for a moment about those people who have worse eyesight problems than you ... and are unable to even read or enjoy Large Print, without great difficulty.

You can help them by sending a donation, large or small to:

**The Ulverscroft Foundation,
1, The Green, Bradgate Road,
Anstey, Leicestershire, LE7 7FU,
England.**
or request a copy of our brochure for more details.

The Foundation will use all your help to assist those people who are handicapped by various sight problems and need special attention.

Thank you very much for your help.